No Child of Mine

Gwen Madoc lives in Swansea with her husband,
Harry. She worked as a medical secretary and
managed a medical clinic before joining the Civil
Service. She studied for five years with the Open
University. She loves Swansea and its people, and
has a keen interest in local history.

GWEN MADOC

No Child of Mine

CORONET BOOKS

Hodder & Stoughton

First published in Great Britain in 2004 by Hodder and Stoughton
A division of Hodder Headline
First published in paperback in 2004 by Hodder and Stoughton

A Coronet Paperback

4

A CIP catalogue record for this title is available from the British
Library

ISBN 978 0 340 82351 4

Typeset in Plantin Light by
Phoenix Typesetting, Auldgirth, Dumfriesshire

Printed and bound in Great Britain by
Mackays of Chatham plc, Chatham, Kent

Hodder Headline's policy is to use papers that are natural, renewable
and recyclable products and made from wood grown in sustainable
forests. The logging and manufacturing processes are expected to
conform to the environmental regulations of the country of origin.

Hodder and Stoughton
A division of Hodder Headline
338 Euston Road
London NW1 3BH

For all my friends and fellow writers at the
Manselton Writers' Workshop. Our
get-togethers are a tonic.

I

Swansea, February 1920

The air was icy cold and Bethan Pryce shivered as a stiff breeze, rushing inland from Swansea Bay, cut through the thin material of her coat. Longing to warm herself before the kitchen fire at her parents' home near Cwmbwrla Square, she hurried up Carmarthen Road.

She had been rash in promising her young brother to take him for a walk across Gors Downs later. She had something better to do on her half-day off than watch Freddie throw pebbles in the Burlais Stream. They would perish in this cold and probably get their feet wet into the bargain.

She thought about the remnant of Jap silk she'd bought in Swansea Market the other week. It would make a lovely blouse. But a fond image of Freddie's eager little face and imploring eyes came into her mind then, and she knew she could refuse him nothing.

As she passed beneath the railway bridge at Cwmbwrla, a train rattled across overhead on its way to Swansea station from West Wales. Rather them than me, Bethan thought smugly. She'd soon be huddling before the range in her mother's kitchen, sipping hot tea and tasting one of Mam's Welsh cakes, hot off the griddle. Suddenly twice as eager for the warm hearth, she quickened her step towards home, and then came to a stumbling halt.

Little Freddie Pryce had suddenly appeared around the corner of the towering edifice of Libanus Chapel. Without a coat or hat, he raced down the pavement towards her, his thin legs pumping like pistons. He shouted something as he ran pell-mell but Bethan couldn't understand his words although she could see he was very upset. From nowhere the hand of fear gripped her heart. With a sharp cry she ran to meet him.

'He's dead, Beth!' Freddie shouted. 'Our dad is dead.'

He flung himself at her, his arms grasping her tightly around the waist, his face upturned to hers.

Bethan still could not take in the sense of his words.

'Freddie! Why're you out in this weather without a hat or coat?' she asked. 'Mam will give you what for when I tell her. You'll catch your death of cold, boy.'

'Dad is dead, Beth,' he repeated loudly. 'Didn't you hear me? He's dead.' His voice rose in a wail. 'I want my dad.'

He buried his face in her coat and Bethan could only stand rigid, holding him close, trying to take it in. Their father was dead? It could not be true. It wasn't true! Freddie was always playing tricks on her. This one wasn't funny.

'If this is a joke on me, Freddie Pryce, I'll tan your backside with the broom handle.'

He looked up at her, eyes glistening, choking back sobs.

'He died at the colliery, Beth,' he spluttered. 'They said it was an accident.'

Bethan felt numbed and befuddled. Garngoch Colliery was an open-cast mine. How could an accident happen there? Suddenly she was filled with horror. Although a pit disaster seemed hardly possible, fires were always breaking out at Garngoch. Had Dad died in a fire? Oh, God, no! Not that!

She became aware that Freddie was shivering violently.

'Come on, Freddie *bach*,' she said anxiously. 'We must get you home.'

Taking off her coat, she put it round his narrow shoulders and, shivering herself, hurried him along the pavement while he sniffled and moaned piteously.

As they rounded the corner of the chapel into Libanus Street, Bethan's steps faltered. A small gathering of neighbours stood around the open door of her home. Mrs Pickering from next door detached herself from the group and hesitantly came towards her.

'Oh, Beth *bach*, there's glad I am you're home! Your poor mother is beside herself. Wanted to send for the panel doctor, I did, but she won't have it.'

Bethan stared at the woman.

'Is it true, Mrs Pickering?' she whispered in dread. 'Is my father really dead?'

Mrs Pickering nodded. 'He didn't suffer, *cariad*. That's what they said, anyway. Struck by the locomotive, he was, as it was hauling out the coal trucks. Killed instantly, see.'

Terrible images filled her mind and Bethan clapped both hands over her mouth to stifle a scream. A great pain welled up inside her, saturating every nerve and fibre of her body. Instinctively, she recognised it as grief, and knew it would be with her for a long time to come.

Freddie was pulling at her skirt.

'I want my dad, Beth. When's he coming home?'

'*Duw! Duw!*' Mrs Pickering muttered, shaking her head. 'There's heartbreaking, isn't it? The whole street is sorry, *bach*.'

Beth managed to mumble her thanks and, stumbling through the front door, hurried down the passage to the kitchen. Her mother Esme was sitting hunched on the wooden chair beside the range, head sunk on to her chest, hands lying loosely on her lap.

'Mam?' Beth quivered, shocked to see that Esme seemed somehow shrunken since Beth had left the house at breakfast time. She dashed forward and, kneeling down by the side of the chair, put both arms around her mother, holding her tightly.

'Mam, are you all right?'

There was no answer, and her mother's cheek felt cold against Beth's own. Crying, Freddie struggled to get on to his mother's lap. Beth included him in her fierce embrace, feeling hot tears course down her cheeks. This was a nightmare. It could not be happening.

'I made tea but she won't look at it,' someone said, and Beth looked up to see Mrs Gibbs, another neighbour, come out of the scullery, brown earthen teapot in one hand and a cup and saucer in the other. 'Hot sweet tea would do her the world of good.'

'It won't bring my Percy back from the dead, will it?' Esme wailed suddenly. She lifted her face, swollen with crying. 'It's the end, Beth,' she muttered. 'The end of us all.'

'No, no, Mam!' she cried, her own heart breaking at the misery in her mother's voice. 'Dad wouldn't want that.' She kissed Esme's damp cheek. 'He'd want us to go on. And we will, somehow.'

Her mother shook her head. 'I can't do it without him.'

'Get this hot tea down her gullet, Beth *cariad*,' Mrs Gibbs said firmly. 'We can't let good stuff go to waste.'

Beth took the cup and saucer with trembling fingers.

'Come on, Mam,' she urged. 'Drink this now.'

She held the cup to her mother's slack mouth, and Esme took a half-hearted sip before letting out another wail.

'Percy's gone, Beth, and I want to go as well.'

'Oh, Mam! Don't say that!' Beth was shaken at the

words. 'You've still got little Freddie and me. Don't go leaving us all by ourselves. We love you.'

Beth stared at her mother pleadingly. It was dreadful that a woman of only thirty-six wished to die.

'She don't know what she's saying,' Mrs Pickering said from the doorway. 'Grief can send you potty, mind. My Auntie Ceinwen was the same.'

Beth glimpsed the curious faces of other neighbours standing in the passage peering over Mrs Pickering's shoulder. Their family tragedy was turning into a peepshow and suddenly she was impatient with the onlookers, well-meaning or not.

She jumped to her feet and took the teapot from Mrs Gibbs's hand, putting it on the hob.

'Thank you all for your kindness,' she said firmly, 'but I think my mam needs rest and quiet. She's had a terrible shock.'

'You ought to get the panel doctor to her, you know,' Mrs Pickering muttered over her shoulder as Beth resolutely herded the women and stray children down the passage to the front door. 'And watch her. She might do something silly.'

When the front door was closed on them, Beth leaned against it for a moment, her mind in a haze. She didn't have the faintest idea what to do next. Obviously Mam was in no fit state to see to anything, so it must rest on her shoulders, at least until her stepbrothers, Gwyn and Haydn, came home from the tinplate works. As the eldest, Gwyn would surely take charge now and be the head of the house. Surely her mother's fears were unfounded?

But Beth was uneasy. She'd always been aware of Gwyn's simmering resentment against Esme, his bitterness at his own mother dying so young and Esme's taking her place. And he seemed to resent Beth, too, for some reason. But Percy Pryce's name was on the rent book for the house in Libanus Street. Gwyn couldn't take that from them, could he?

Beth went back to the kitchen to find Esme sitting with her head in her hands, sobbing her heart out, and Freddie doing his best to comfort her. Beth hurried to enclose them both in another hug, feeling the weight of responsibility bow her down. Even if Gwyn was inclined to take over the tenancy, the job of keeping the family together was hers until Esme recovered from the agony of loss.

Her mother stirred and tried to stand. 'The boys' meal isn't ready,' she murmured thickly. 'I'd better start it.'

Beth pressed her back on to the chair. 'I'll see to it, Mam. You look done up as it is,' she said. 'Go rest on the bed, why don't you?'

It was nearly half-six when Gwyn swaggered in through the back door, hanging up his coat, cap and rucksack. He went to wash his hands at the stone sink, glancing at Beth.

'What's the matter with you then?' he asked pithily. 'Looks like you been sucking lemons.'

Beth winced at his flippancy, but forgave it. He must have come home along the back lane, met no one and hadn't heard the terrible news yet. She hesitated, reluctant to speak the words, uncertain how to tell him. She wished his brother were there, too, so she could tell them together.

'Where's Haydn?' she asked, bringing the cast-iron pot of mutton stew to the table.

Gwyn grinned. 'Stopped to talk to young Maudie Pickering,' he said, wiping his hands on the kitchen towel. 'Fancies his chances there.'

Then Haydn would already know, Maudie would see

to that. The whole district must have heard about their loss by now. She'd better tell Gwyn before the callers started.

'Gwyn, I've got something to tell you. An awful thing has happened . . .'

He pulled out a chair at the table and sat down, glancing around. 'Where's Esme got to?' he asked. 'And where's old Percy? Have they gone gallivanting?'

'No, I'm still here,' Esme said quietly from the doorway, red-rimmed eyes startling in her pale face. 'But Percy's gone.'

'Gone?' Gwyn stood up, scowling. 'Do you mean he's buggered off and left us to it?'

'I mean he's dead!' screeched Esme, and Beth ran to her, putting an arm around her shaking shoulders.

'What?'

'Dad was killed at the colliery earlier today,' said Beth, struggling to hold back tears. 'Struck down by a loco-motive.'

Gwyn stared at them silently, his expression inscrutable. Beth swallowed hard. She'd known him all her life, but never understood what went on inside his head. It was as though he didn't want anyone to get close to him. He was very different from his younger brother. Haydn was so easy to know, easy to love, and she wished with all her heart he would come home from work now and help them through this.

'Percy Pryce is dead?' Gwyn asked in a low voice.

'You're head of the house now, Gwyn,' Beth said tentatively.

He snapped a glance at her. She saw surprise in his eyes and something else. Was it triumph? It looked remarkably like it and she was shocked to the core.

'Where have they put him?' he asked. 'In the parlour?'

Beth gulped at the lack of emotion in his voice.

'No,' she whispered, holding her mother tightly. 'He was taken to the town mortuary straight away. One of his workmates identified him.'

At that moment Haydn burst in, his smooth young face white with shock.

'*Duw annwyl*, Mam!' he exclaimed. 'Is it really true what Maudie tells me? Percy was killed today?'

Esme gave a little cry of desolation and Haydn came straight to her. Putting a hand on her arm, he drew her to a chair at the table where she slumped down.

'Are you all right?'

Esme nodded miserably, her lips clamped together as though willing herself not to start crying again.

'Oh, Mam, there's sorry I am,' Haydn said. 'Knocked down by a loco. How could a thing like that happen? Percy's worked at Garngoch since he was a boy. Knows the place like the back of his hand.'

'He must've been drunk,' Gwyn said nastily.

With a sharp cry Esme jumped to her feet and smacked him across the face. He stepped back startled, lifting a hand to his reddening cheek, staring at her.

'Your father was never drunk in his life!' Esme shrieked. 'How dare you say such a thing?'

'Percy Pryce was *not* my father,' Gwyn shouted. 'He was nothing to me, nor Haydn neither.'

'Steady on, mun, Gwyn,' Haydn said in a shocked tone. 'Let's have a bit of respect for the dead.'

'Respect!' he bellowed. 'What did he ever do for us?'

'You ungrateful wretch!' Esme cried. 'He worked his fingers to the bone for you and Haydn.'

A sound of derision came from Gwyn's throat.

'Percy was mother and father to you both,' Esme went on loudly. 'No, he wasn't your real father. When your mother died after less than a year of marriage to him he could've dumped you both in the orphanage, but he didn't, although no one would've blamed him for it.'

'I wish he had,' Gwyn muttered. 'Maybe then I'd have found parents who'd have helped me get on in life.'

'Percy loved you like his own,' Esme said in a low voice. 'And now he's dead, you deny him? You're a disgrace, Gwyn Howells.'

'Loved me, did he?' Gwyn rasped. 'But not enough to pay for an apprenticeship for me.' He pointed a finger at Beth. 'Somehow he found money for *her* apprenticeship though, didn't he? And there's no difference between us.'

'Shut your mouth, Gwyn!' Esme said tremulously. 'Percy had no right . . .' she glanced apprehensively at Beth, who stared back bewildered.

'*Duw, Duw,* mun, Gwyn,' Haydn interposed quickly. 'This isn't the time or place for blaming or digging up the past.'

A heavy silence followed, and Beth was puzzled by the glances that flashed between the brothers. She had the strangest feeling that there was something here she was excluded from, that they shared a secret, but quickly dismissed it as her overactive imagination. She was still in shock over her father's sudden and terrible death.

Gwyn's face was dark with anger. 'Well, I'm not soft like you, Haydn,' he muttered. 'I resent sweating my guts out in the tinplate works. If Percy had treated me right I'd have learned my trade as a motor mechanic by now. Motorcars are getting more numerous. Mark my words, in years to come every man will own one and then there'll be damned good money to earn for indentured mechanics.' His mouth tightened. 'Percy robbed me of that chance.'

'That's all you think about, isn't it?' Esme snapped. 'Money. Never mind about family, never mind about a

good husband and father lying dead on some cold
mortuary slab, just as long as *you're* all right for money.'

Gwyn's lips tightened in fury. 'I've got nothing to thank
Percy Pryce for, and I don't give a bugger that he's gone
either.'

Beth clapped a hand over her mouth in shock that such
cruel words could be spoken at this time. There was a
sharp cry of distress from Esme, and Haydn turned
quickly to her.

'Gwyn didn't mean it, Mam,' he said. 'Did you, Gwyn,
mun?'

'Yes, I bloody well did,' he stormed. 'And why the hell
do you call her Mam? She's no mother to us.'

It was too much for Beth.

'You cold-hearted hypocrite, Gwyn Howells!' she
shouted. 'She's looked after you both since you were tots
– treated you no different from Freddie or me. She
nursed you when you were sick, fed you . . . and now you
turn on her like a savage wolf.'

He scowled at her but made no reply.

'What's the matter, Gwyn?' she went on mockingly.
'Afraid Mam's going to ask you for more money now
Dad's gone, is it?'

Gwyn still didn't speak but he looked furious.

'I'll help all I can,' Haydn offered. 'I'll see if there's
some overtime going.'

'You're a fool, Haydn,' Gwyn grated. 'I'm buggering
off from by here. None of them is any kin of ours, and I
won't stand still for them to put a yoke around my neck.'

'I knew it!' Beth cried. 'Well, I say we'll be better off
without you, Gwyn. So good riddance to bad rubbish!'

'Beth, please!' Haydn said. 'Don't be like that, mun.'

'Oh, you'll side with him all right,' she snapped. 'He's
your brother after all.'

Esme's face was very white, but she looked up at Gwyn defiantly.

'You'll at least have the decency to wait until after Percy's funeral, I suppose?' she asked in a strained voice. 'Or are you ready to shame us, and make us the talk of the neighbourhood?'

'What do I care about that?' Gwyn said with a sneer. 'We'll do as we like, Haydn and me, and to hell with the rest of you.'

Esme looked at the other young man. 'Does that go for you, too?' she asked quietly.

He looked from her to Gwyn, his expression dismayed.

'Must we quarrel like this?' he asked. 'Percy's hardly cold.'

Esme's face crumpled and Beth put comforting arms around her mother.

'And must you be so callous?' she snapped at him.

Haydn's face fell. 'I didn't mean anything by it, Mam,' he said shakily. 'I liked Percy. He was a good man, and I'm grateful to him.'

'Oh, bugger this!' Gwyn snarled. 'I'm going down the Commercial for a pint.'

'What about your meal?' Beth asked. 'I've made mutton stew for you.'

'Do as you like with it,' he snapped. 'Chuck it down the drain for all I care.' He glanced at his brother. 'Are you coming for a pint or not, Haydn?'

He shuffled his feet uncomfortably. 'I dunno, Gwyn,' he said. 'Don't seem right, like.'

'Suit your bloody self,' his brother sneered. 'Stay by here then and wallow in grief with the rest of them. But don't expect me to join in.' He snapped his fingers. 'I'll not mourn Percy Pryce, not for one minute.'

With that he grabbed his coat and cap and slammed out of the back door.

*

Despite the row they'd had the night before, Esme had her stepsons' meal ready the following day when they came home from work. Still angry, Beth was ready to let Gwyn go hungry, and chaffed her mother for bothering, but Esme was insistent.

'Looked after them all these years, I have,' she said. 'I'm still responsible for their needs.'

'Haydn's all right,' Beth conceded. 'But Gwyn won't thank you for it.' Even as she spoke she knew it was useless to argue when her mother's mind was made up.

The young men sat at the table, obviously expecting everything to be as normal, and Beth's lips thinned as she noted Gwyn's determined silence and dark expression. Haydn's forced chatter was jarring in contrast as he tried to bridge the silence at the table. Beth was glad Freddie was already in bed. The child was too sensitive to bad atmospheres and would've been very disturbed by this.

She felt a sense of intense relief when a knock came at the front door, and hurried to answer it, glad to get away from the table for even a few moments. She was surprised to see a workmate of her father's, Dai Spooner from Cwmavon Terrace, standing on the doorstep.

'Hello, Beth *cariad*,' he began solemnly, removing his cloth cap and holding it against his chest. 'There's sorry I am about your dad.'

She gulped, feeling tears well up again.

'Thanks, Mr Spooner. It was good of you to call. Come in.'

'It's your mam I want to speak to, like,' he said as he followed her down the passage to the kitchen. 'I've got something for her.'

He stood awkwardly in the doorway on seeing everyone sitting around the table.

'Oh, I don't mean to interrupt when you're having your grub. I'm on my way home from work, like, and thought I'd call and give you this, Mrs Pryce.'

He held out a large brown envelope to Esme, who rose looking bewildered.

'What is it, Mr Spooner?'

'It's Percy's bank money,' Dai Spooner said, handing it to her.

'Bank money?'

'Oh, aye.' He nodded. 'One or other of the old timers at the colliery has had a bank running at Garngoch for years. The mine owners thought it was a good way to curb men squandering all their money in the pubs on payday. Percy and me have been in it since we were youngsters, although he very rarely dipped into his savings.'

Dai chuckled, and then stopped abruptly, looking confused as though guilty of a faux-pas.

'I don't understand,' Esme said in a quiet tone.

'Percy's been saving regularly, Mam,' Haydn explained. 'Dai's brought it for you. It's yours now. There's a godsend for you, isn't it?'

Gwyn pushed back his chair and stood up.

'How much is there?'

'Seventy pounds, exactly,' Dai said.

'Seventy pounds!' Esme flopped on to a chair looking astounded. 'I never knew Percy had so much money. I can hardly believe it,' she said in wonder. 'He never told me about any bank.'

'There's a kind of statement in the envelope, too,' Dai said. 'It's a record of everything Percy put in and drew out over the years.'

'Huh!' Gwyn's lip curled derisively as he looked at Dai. 'How do we know someone else hasn't been dipping into it since Percy died?' he asked harshly. 'There might've been much more than seventy quid over the years.'

Dai Spooner looked shocked at the question, his face turning white.

'Gwyn!' Esme spoke sharply. 'How dare you suggest such a thing? Apologise to Mr Spooner this minute.'

Gwyn looked scornful and didn't speak.

'I don't know what kind of workmates you've got in the tinplate works, Gwyn Howells,' Dai said tightly, 'but we all respected Percy up at Garngoch. We're not thieves or liars.'

'There's sorry I am Mr Spooner, for Gwyn's bad manners,' Esme murmured, looking crestfallen and shamed. Beth's heart went out to her. 'But we're all upset, you understand,' she went on.

'That's all right, Mrs Pryce *bach*,' Dai said, shooting Gwyn an angry look. 'I don't blame you.'

'Don't you go bloody apologising for me,' Gwyn rasped. 'I don't take back one word, see.'

'I'm sorry for your troubles, Mrs Pryce,' Dai went on, ignoring the interruption. 'How will you manage now?'

'That's none of your business,' Gwyn burst out. 'We don't want any Tom, Dick or Harry poking their nose in. Why don't all you so-called do-gooders bugger off and leave us alone?'

Everyone was silent and all stared at him in consternation. Even his own brother looked shaken, but Gwyn's expression was unrepentant.

'I'd better go,' Dai said quietly. 'Before I do something I'll regret.'

'Talk!' Gwyn sneered as Dai turned his back. 'All bloody talk, he is.'

Esme showed Dai out, and Beth could hear her mother's stuttered apologies and Dai's rumbling assurances. She grasped the back of a kitchen chair to steady her shaking hands and glared at her older stepbrother.

'What kind of a devil has got into you, Gwyn Howells?' she blurted. 'Insulting Dad's friends and workmates, and humiliating Mam like that? You should be ashamed of yourself.'

'You keep out of this, Beth.' He pointed his finger at her. 'It's nothing to do with you.'

'Oh, is that right!' she snapped. 'Well, I've got news for you, Gwyn Howells – I'm *making* it my business. I won't stand by and see you treat Mam like this. And what're you trying to prove anyway?'

'Percy kept bloody quiet about that bank money, didn't he?' he snarled. 'I don't believe your mother knew nothing about it, either. She wants to keep it all for herself.'

'And why shouldn't she?' Beth retorted. 'Dad left it to her, and she's going to need every penny she can get in the future. There's no real breadwinner in this house now he's gone.'

'Half that money should be mine . . .' Gwyn paused, glancing at his brother. 'Mine and Haydn's, I mean. It's only right.'

'Well, you can forget that!' Esme exclaimed from the doorway. 'You've no right to any of it. You're only twenty-three, single with no responsibilities. You can earn all the money you need. I can't.'

'Mam's right,' Haydn said, getting to his feet. 'I don't want a penny of it. You're going too far, Gwyn.'

The brown envelope was lying on the table and Gwyn snatched it up.

'Give that to me!' Esme shouted, rushing forward, but he turned away, holding it out of her reach, and putting a thumb under the flap, tore it open. Some white notes fluttered down as he took a folded sheet of paper from the envelope. Esme scooped up the loose notes and put them in her apron pocket. Beth could see more notes in the envelope.

'Stop it, Gwyn!' she cried, rushing forward to help her mother. But he put the envelope out of sight in his pocket, and then studied the paper.

'There you are!' he shouted angrily, striking the sheet with the back of his hand. 'All the proof you need. Percy said there was no money for *my* apprenticeship, but look at this.' He jabbed an index finger at an entry on the paper. 'A large sum withdrawn two years ago, round about the time Beth started her apprenticeship as seam-stress with Lewis Lewis.' He glared at Esme. 'Why the favouritism?' he asked belligerently. 'She's no more to him than I am.'

'Gwyn!' A cry came from Esme and she lunged for the envelope sticking out of his pocket. 'Not another word! I'm warning you, mind.'

Gwyn pushed her away. 'I want what's mine,' he snarled. 'And no one's going to stop me getting it.'

'Favouritism?' Beth burst out. 'What are you talking about? He was my father, after all. It's only natural.'

'Your father!' Gwyn's lips twisted with scorn. 'It's time you knew what's what . . .'

Before he could go on, Esme's hand caught him across the cheek in a stinging slap. Furious, he rounded on her, his arm raised threateningly.

'Damn you, Esme,' he shouted. 'You've done that once too often.'

Beth screamed and tried to intervene as Gwyn's fist swung at Esme's face, but Haydn was quicker. He caught at his brother's wrist forcefully, wrenching it back.

'Good God, mun, Gwyn!' he bellowed into his

brother's twisted face. 'Have you gone mad or what? Hitting Mam! What the hell are you thinking of?'

'Get off me!' Gwyn snarled, shrugging him away. 'I'm doing this for you too.'

'Well, you can bloody well pack it in then,' Haydn said angrily. He took the envelope from Gwyn's pocket, knocking his brother's hand away as he tried to prevent it.

'Here you are, Mam,' he said gently, handing it to her. 'It's all yours, and you're welcome to it as far as I'm concerned.'

'You're a bloody fool!' Gwyn said furiously.

'I don't need any of Mam's money, and neither do you,' Haydn insisted. 'For pity's sake, mun, Gwyn! How can you behave like this? Money's going to be tight around here from now on. Mam will need all she can get.'

'Well, let her ask her fancy man for money, then.' Gwyn spat out the words.

Beth stared. 'What does he mean, Mam?'

'Spite! That's what it is,' Esme said loudly. 'Plain spite. But I'm taking no notice. Some of this money will go towards your father's funeral. He'll have a good send-off, I'll see to that.'

'Bloody waste!' Gwyn snarled.

'Oh! Had enough of you, I have,' Esme snapped. 'Percy's name is on the rent book of this house, and soon it'll be mine. There's no room here for you any more, Gwyn Howells.' She tossed her head angrily. 'Pack your bags tonight and get out in the morning.'

'Mam!' Haydn exclaimed in dismay. 'You can't kick him out like that. Let him find other lodgings first. Some time next week, like, after the funeral.'

'No!' Esme said firmly. 'This is the last night Gwyn sleeps under Percy's roof, ungrateful beggar that he is.'

'If I go, Haydn goes too,' Gwyn said. 'You'll be on the bone of your arses in no time without our keep money.'

'I'd rather starve than have you in this house any longer,' Esme blurted. 'If Haydn wants to go with you, so be it. That's his lookout.'

'Mam, wait a minute,' Beth said. 'Haydn hasn't done anything wrong. Don't pick on him, mun. Ask him to stay with us.'

She felt a hollowness in her heart at the thought of Haydn leaving them. She might never see him again, and she would miss him too much.

'No, no, that's all right, Beth,' Haydn said, his face white. 'If Mam wants me out too, then I'll go. I don't want any trouble, and besides . . .' he glanced at Gwyn. '. . . he is my brother. Family should stick together.'

Esme turned her back on them and was silent. Beth stared from one to the other. What was happening? Their whole household was breaking up just when they needed each other the most, needed each other to get through this grievous time. It was madness.

Without a word Gwyn turned towards the stairs in the corner of the room, and she heard his feet thump angrily up them.

Haydn stared at Esme's backview for a moment, and then at Beth. 'I'd better go up too,' he said quietly. 'There's a lot to do before I sleep tonight. If I can sleep, that is.'

He hesitated again, looking wistfully at Esme's back, and then turned and followed his brother upstairs.

Beth flopped on to a kitchen chair, feeling exhausted.

'I can't believe what's just happened, Mam,' she said. 'I know you're angry with Gwyn and I don't blame you. He was like a brute. I don't know what's got into him. If Dad was here . . .'

Beth caught her bottom lip between her teeth, shocked that for a split second she'd forgotten her father was gone.

'I'm sorry, Mam.'

Esme turned to her, her expression weary.

'It's all right, *cariad*,' she said in a tired voice. 'Don't fuss yourself. It hasn't sunk in yet for me either. All that is yet to come.'

'Oh, Mam! How will we get through it?'

Esme squared her shoulders.

'There are going to be changes around here, Bethan love, big changes. Like Haydn said, money will be short. I'll have to find some cleaning work or something. But even with what I can earn and the little bit you bring in, I won't be able to afford to keep both you and Freddie.'

Beth jumped to her feet, shocked at her mother's words. Esme wanted *her* to leave home too? 'Mam! What are you talking about?'

Esme came and put her hand on Beth's arm, squeezing it tightly. 'There's no other way,' she said quietly. 'You'll have to go and live with your Auntie Mae and Uncle Dan in Brynmill.'

'What?' Beth grasped frantically at her mother's hand. 'But I don't know my Auntie Mae and Uncle Dan. They're strangers to me.'

'They are still your kin,' Esme said firmly.

'But you've had nothing to do with your sister for years,' Beth persisted desperately. 'I've often wondered why. And if there has been a quarrel between you, Auntie Mae won't want me in her home.'

'She'll have no choice, I think,' Esme said. 'Your Uncle Dan will agree to it.'

'Why, Mam?' asked Beth miserably. 'Why are you sending me away from home? *I* haven't done anything wrong. I don't understand.' She was stunned by the grim expression on Esme's face. 'Don't you love me any more, Mam?'

Esme pulled her hand from Beth's desperate grasp. 'It can't be helped,' she said. 'And anyway, it's only right.'

Esme's heart ached at the look of abject misery on her daughter's face. It was true that money would be too scarce now for the three of them to live comfortably, but that was not the only reason why she must part with her beloved daughter. With Percy gone the truth would come out and should come out, but she could not look Beth straight in the eye and explain her own past shame, not yet.

Esme thought of her sister. Mae had done her an injustice all those years ago, and done her down, too. Perhaps having Beth near her would prick her conscience. While Esme knew Mae's heart would never soften towards her, Beth might win her aunt over. Perhaps the inheritance denied to Esme would go to Beth eventually. And Dan, too, must face his responsibility at last. It was only right.

2

Twenty-one Years Earlier – Hafod, Swansea, Summer 1899

'But why can't I have some of Da's money?' Esme Parkyn demanded, tossing her head petulantly, her long plait swinging like a pendulum. 'That money is as much mine as yours.'

Mae Parkyn looked at her younger sister through the dressing-table mirror and felt irritation rise in her chest. Esme had become even more difficult to handle since Da had died.

'Da left everything to me because he knew I'd be sensible, as well you know,' she answered brusquely, resentful of her sister's ingratitude. 'Besides, you were under age at the time and you still are. Sometimes you even act like a baby.' She flicked an impatient glance at Esme. 'Look at you now. Late for chapel, as usual.'

She peered at her own reflection in the mirror again and adjusted the angle of her best Sunday hat. The responsibility for both their lives rested on her shoulders, and Esme's lack of appreciation rankled.

'Huh! You think you've got all the brains and I'm stupid,' she cried shrilly. 'All I want is enough money to put me through typing school. They're advertising courses at that new commercial college in Mount

Pleasant. I don't want to be skivvying by here all my life. I want an office job.'

'Skivvying!' Mae was affronted. 'I don't ask you to do any more work than I do myself,' she said sharply. 'We've a good business going here, Esme, thanks to me. You should be grateful I've got the savvy to get us started and keep us going, and nicely, too.'

'Boarding-house keeper!' Esme said with disgust. 'It's the lowest of the low. Everyone at the chapel looks down on us.'

Mae stood up to adjust the waistband of her black alpaca skirt, neat across her slim hips, the hem brushing her instep just above her patent leather shoes. She twisted, inspecting her appearance in the mirror, and felt satisfied.

'Well, they shouldn't then,' she said dismissively. She picked up a small prayer book from the dressing table. 'We've got more money in the bank than the rest of them put together.'

Mae couldn't help the touch of pride in her voice. And she had every reason to feel proud, she told herself. At barely twenty years of age, she'd had the gumption to sell Da's ironmongery business after his death for a very respectable sum, transform the home he'd left them into a boarding house so as to make a decent living, and had turned a nice little profit as well. Da would be pleased with the way she'd managed everything. But Esme would never be satisfied.

'You don't know you're born, my girl,' Mae remarked, as she turned to leave her bedroom. 'You could be in service, emptying chamber pots and scrubbing floors.'

'I feel like I *am* in service,' Esme said plaintively as she scuttled in her sister's wake. 'It's polish this and mop that all day long, and I'm sick of it, Mae. I want to make something of myself.'

'Oh, for goodness' sake!' her sister snapped as she went into the sitting room of their basement flat to fetch her purse. 'You won't be fifteen until November. Besides, office work is for men. What's the point of spending good money training a girl? You'll only get married and then it'll all be wasted.'

'I won't marry.'

Mae gave her sister an amused glance. Esme would marry all right. Slender and small-boned like their mother, she was far too pretty not to catch the eye of more than one boy. Mae had already noticed how they clustered around her young sister after chapel, like bees to a honey pot.

Mae was the one who worried she might not find the right man. He would have to be tall, of course. She could never marry a man shorter than herself. She wouldn't be made to look ridiculous.

'I'm not standing here arguing with you, Esme,' she said sharply, pulling on her kid gloves. 'The service starts in fifteen minutes. I don't want to rush and get there all flustered. Go and fetch your hat and gloves and let's be off.'

'I'm not going to chapel this morning,' the girl said defiantly. 'And you're only going so's you can prance about in front of Davies the Chemist, hoping he'll ask you out.'

Mae felt her face heat up. It was nearer the truth than she liked to admit even to herself. 'Now you're going too far, my girl,' she retorted, really annoyed. 'I won't put up with your obstreperous behaviour any longer.'

'I don't know how you can even look at him,' Esme went on, wrinkling her nose. 'He's old.'

'Idris Davies is not old,' Mae exclaimed huffily. 'He's thirty. That's not old, not really. He's had a lot of worry in his life with his wife dying young and all.'

He was the only tall man of her acquaintance who wasn't already married, but that wasn't the most important consideration. His chemist's shop was a well-established business. It wouldn't do to marry a man who wasn't her equal financially.

Mae glanced at her sister and didn't like the smirk on Esme's face. 'Well, I'm going to chapel, and I'll hold my head up high, too,' she said boldly. 'Da's family has lived in the Hafod for years, and despite what you may think, Esme, the Parkyns are well respected hereabouts.'

Pretending not to remember there was just the two of them now, she stalked down the passage, opened the front door, and stepped into the small flagstoned front courtyard from where steps led up to pavement level. Esme followed her and stood on the doorstep.

'And I hate living in this basement, too,' she grumbled peevishly. 'It's damp. We ought to rent this out and live upstairs.'

'You've had life too easy, Esme,' Mae retorted as she started to climb the steps. 'That's the trouble with you, my girl.'

'Easy!' Esme shrieked. 'I'm treated no better than a servant. I hate you, Mae Parkyn!'

'Er . . . excuse me, ladies.'

The man's deep voice startled Mae and she almost missed her footing on the next step. Gasping, she looked up. A tall man wearing a brown suit and brown bowler stood on the step before the main front door, peering down at them over the iron railing.

Flustered and embarrassed, Mae's voice took on a strident tone. 'Yes, what do you want?'

'Good morning,' he said cheerfully, lifting the bowler hat. 'I'm looking for a room to rent. I'm told there's a vacancy here with the Parkyn family.'

'It's Sunday,' she said stiffly. 'We don't do business on the Sabbath.'

'Of course not. I beg your pardon,' he said, holding the hat respectfully against his chest. 'But I'm a bit desperate for good respectable lodgings, and didn't stop to think.'

Mae sniffed, annoyed despite his deferential manner and still embarrassed that he had overheard her spat with Esme. Quarrelling in public was very lowering. Esme might still be young but she ought to know better.

Reluctantly, Mae continued up the steps, wanting to get rid of him as soon as possible.

'There is a room to let, as it happens, but you and your wife must come back tomorrow,' she said firmly.

'I'm not married,' he replied quickly, and then gave a wide smile. 'Or spoken for.'

'Oh!' Mae hesitated, looking at him with more interest. He was tall, several inches taller than she was, broad-shouldered and very good-looking. Mae blinked. No, he was more than that. He was really handsome. His eyes were startlingly blue, his mouth generous and nose straight. She eyed his firm cleft chin. Here was a man with a will of iron, a man who'd get on in life and make no compromises.

Mae felt a little quiver in the pit of her stomach.

'You're desperate for lodgings, then?' she asked cautiously.

He gave a deep sigh, still clutching his hat.

'Yes, Mrs . . . er?'

'Miss Parkyn – Mae Parkyn.'

'Henshaw is my name,' he said. 'Dan Henshaw.' He hesitated. 'I can see you're in a hurry, Miss Parkyn,' he went on. 'Look, I won't keep you any longer. I'll come back tomorrow, if I don't find anything in the meantime.'

'No, it's all right,' she said hastily. 'I'm too late for chapel now.' She wetted her lips nervously. 'Perhaps you'd like to see the room first? It's a front room over-looking the street.'

He smiled again. 'Well, it's very kind of you to take the trouble on a Sunday morning.'

Mae opened her purse and rummaged for the front-door key, intrigued by his accent.

'You're not from around here then, Mr Henshaw?'

'No, I'm from Bolton,' he said. 'Not much doing there now for a man of my abilities. Swansea's a boomtown. I think I might make my fortune here.'

Mae gave a little breathless laugh as she put the kcy in the lock. She liked his attitude, the strength of his voice, and his smile so full of confidence. New to Swansea, he wouldn't have met many peoplc yet, formed no relationships.

'This way,' she said, feeling suddenly self-conscious. 'The room is first-floor front, quite spacious really compared to some on offer around here, and fully furnished of course.'

She stepped inside. She was very proud of their hallway, which was wide enough to accommodate a full-sized polished table beneath a gilded mirror. She glanced with satisfaction at the linoleum shining like glass, and the rather splendid red Wilton runner she had found in a second-hand shop, and hoped Mr Henshaw appreciated the quality of it.

Unsure of the proper etiquette, she went before him up the stairs, feeling discomfited, and opened the door on the left at the top.

Dan Henshaw followed her into the room and looked around.

'Compact, but very neat and comfortable, Miss

Parkyn,' he said. 'Just what I'm looking for. Perhaps I should speak with your father first?'

She bridled. 'My father is deceased,' she said tightly. 'I run this house – with my younger sister. I assure you, I'm more than capable.'

He blinked at her sharp tone, and then smiled apologetically.

'I'm sure you are, Miss Parkyn. No offence meant, I assure you. How much is the rent?'

Mae clasped her hands before her nervously, feeling her mouth go a little dry. He wasn't upper-class, she judged, not by the way he spoke anyway, yet the cut and quality of his three-piece suit suggested he could afford the best. Her business instinct warred with her desire not to drive him away.

'Thirty shillings a week,' she said, business instinct winning. 'In advance.'

His eyebrows lifted and he looked very surprised but said nothing, although his gaze was keen.

'That may sound steep, Mr Henshaw,' she went on defensively. 'But when you consider you have food provided and cooked, fuel, laundry and cleaning included, I think you'll find it fair.'

'Looking at it that way, you're right,' he said pleasantly. His gaze was keen again. 'You're an astute business-woman, Miss Parkyn.'

Mae flushed, pleased.

'My father owned an ironmonger's shop in town, a long-standing family business,' she explained. 'I kept the accounts for him once I left school, so I know what I'm doing.'

'I don't doubt it.'

'No cooking of any description to be done in the room, Mr Henshaw,' she said, feeling surer of herself. 'And no one uses the kitchen except me, although tenants may make the odd cup of tea, of course.'

'How many tenants are there?' He smiled. 'I like to know who my neighbours are.'

'All very respectable people,' she assured him quickly. 'Four ladies and one married couple.' She hesitated. 'I don't normally let to single gentlemen, you understand, Mr Henshaw, but I can see you're a decent man.'

And he did have a way about him that was out of the ordinary, definitely a cut above the average working man. Dan Henshaw would be somebody in time, Mae was certain of that. She felt that little quiver of excitement again, and cleared her throat nervously.

'When would you want to move in, Mr Henshaw?'

He paused to consider and Mae held her breath, wondering if she had been too pushy with the rent. But it was a reasonable sum, under the circumstances. After all, a single man would cause a lot more work. At least the ladies kept their rooms tidy and would even consider a little light dusting, except that good-for-nothing Mrs Nolan.

'Would tomorrow be too soon?' Dan Henshaw asked.

'Not at all,' Mae fluttered. 'I'll see the bed is aired and everything prepared for you, and get a key cut.' She hesitated, wondering how he'd take her next words. 'The front door is bolted after half-nine at night, Mr Henshaw. Our tenants keep early hours. I hope that won't inconven- ience you?'

'I'm a man of regular hours and habits, Miss Parkyn,' he said. 'A man of very few vices.'

'Vices?'

He smiled reassuringly. 'I don't smoke or drink, and I'm certainly not a gambler. I am a prudent man but a determined one.'

His gaze held hers for a moment during which Mae felt a tingle run up and down her spine, and wanted to gasp in air, but controlled herself.

'Well, I hope you'll be happy here, Mr Henshaw,' she said breathlessly. 'If you have any complaints or need anything extra, like boot cleaning, please leave a note in the box on the hall table.'

'Thank you, Miss Parkyn.'

Mae waited, looking up at him expectantly, and after a moment, his eyes widened in embarrassment.

'I'm sorry,' he said quickly. 'Of course, a week's rent in advance.'

He took a pound and a ten-shilling note from his wallet and handed them to her.

'Thank you,' she murmured. 'I'll see you get a rent book tomorrow, duly made up.'

With a shy dip of her head, she went before him from the room and down the stairs. In the hall he offered his hand, and she took it hesitantly. His palm was rough and calloused, the hand of a man used to hard work, and she felt reassured.

'Until tomorrow then, Mr Henshaw.'

'Tomorrow, Miss Parkyn.'

Then he was gone. Afterwards Mae lingered in the hall, looking at her reflection in the hall mirror. Her new Sunday hat, sitting very easily on her thick dark hair, made her look quite fashionable, she thought. She'd noticed Dan Henshaw's gaze taking in every detail of her appearance. She hoped he'd liked what he saw.

Dan Henshaw stopped on the corner of Picton Place, turned and stared back at number fourteen, the only double-fronted house on the street. A smile widened his mouth. A little goldmine that, although he had no interest in becoming a boarding-house keeper. No, his sights were set much higher.

The rent was more than he had planned to pay, but he'd manage, and with his connections would soon find work. Yes, this situation had definite prospects. A comfortable billet and a nice little chicken to be plucked. Not bad-looking, either. Good figure, fine eyes. And while Mae Parkyn had a mind as sharp as a tack, he could tell she was inexperienced where men were concerned.

He chuckled to himself. A man of few vices. Well, it was true. His only vices were ruthless ambition and a weakness for shapely women. He wasn't ashamed of either of them. He jingled the change in his pocket, telling himself: Henshaw, you've fallen on your feet!

Mae was still looking in the mirror when Esme came up into the hall from the back stairs.

'What did that man want?'

'A room.'

'You were a long time.'

'He's taken it. Thirty shillings a week, all found.'

Esme looked doubtful.

'The room's too small for two people. His wife will be complaining in no time.'

'He's not married.'

Esme stared.

'You've let to a single man? Mae, what're you thinking of? You swore you'd never do that. More trouble than they're worth, single men are, so you said.'

'Dan . . . er . . . Mr Henshaw is different,' Mae insisted.

'You mean, he has references?'

'Umm, no, not quite,' her sister answered defensively. 'But he struck me as a very upright man.'

'You know absolutely nothing about him,' Esme persisted. 'He isn't coming just to paint the outside lavatory, mind, Mae,' she went on forcefully. 'He's going to live in our house. For all you know he could be a robber, or worse.'

'Oh, don't be so childish!' Mae exclaimed, snatching off her hat. 'I'm a good judge of character, and Dan Henshaw is trustworthy.'

'So you hope!'

'I'm not standing by here arguing with you, Esme. Into the kitchen and start peeling potatoes. We have the lunches to get.'

On Monday morning a week later they were in the washhouse just off the kitchen, tackling the household laundry. Mrs Kittle, employed to do the rough work in the house, was turning the handle of the mangle vigorously, her florid face turning redder with every gyration.

'This new bloke,' she panted, 'I hope he hasn't got a dirty job. Them dungarees is buggers to get clean.'

Mae drew the back of her hand across her sweating brow as she bent over the washtub. She hated washdays which started before six in the morning. By bedtime she felt she'd been through the mangle herself. She couldn't wait for the time when she could afford to pay someone to sweat in her place.

'No, he hasn't,' she assured Mrs Kittle wearily. 'He's just got the job of rent collector for the Beaufort Estates.'

'Oh, rent collector, is it?' Mrs Kittle sniffed, her tone disparaging. 'Hoping to collect more than rents, half of 'em. I know the sort.'

'Mr Henshaw isn't like that,' Mae said shortly. 'And don't go spreading any more rumours about our tenants, Mrs Kittle.'

She straightened her aching back and gave the older woman a stern stare. She'd dearly like to sack Mrs Kittle, but she was too good a worker. They wouldn't be able to manage without her now.

'It was as much as I could do to stop Mrs Nolan seeing her solicitor,' Mae went on severely. 'After you spread it about that she's a shoplifter.'

'Her solicitor, my backside!' Mrs Kittle sniffed again. 'Her father was an idle bugger and her mother used to work down the fish market, same as mine did. Family never had a penny to scratch their arses with. Now look at her, with her airs and bloody graces.'

'That doesn't make her a shoplifter.'

Mrs Kittle refolded the bed sheet she was mangling, her mouth twisted in derision.

'Well!' she said stubbornly. 'It stands to reason. She's in and out of them shops in town all week. And the stuff she comes back here with is nobody's business! Where does the money come from? Answer me that.' Mrs Kittle nodded sagely. 'No, you can't, can you? Her old man's only a railway porter. How can she afford silk stockings, never mind a solicitor, on the pittance he earns?' She gave Mae a scornful look. 'Flannelling you, she is, mun.'

Privately Mae agreed, but would not give Mrs Kittle the satisfaction. Mrs Nolan's threat about a solicitor was obviously an empty one, but Mae felt she could not be too careful.

'It's none of our business,' she retorted sharply. As long as the tenants paid their rent on time she didn't care what they got up to outside the house.

'Perhaps Mrs Nolan has a private income,' Esme suggested innocently as she emptied a bucket-load of sudsy white cotton into the stone sink, and turned on the cold water tap to rinse it through.

Mrs Kittle gave a throaty laugh.

'You could be right, *bach*,' she said. 'Because if she isn't doing a bit of shoplifting then she's getting money from someone else.' She winked and tapped the side of her bulbous nose. 'Know what I mean?'

'Mrs Kittle!' Mae was shocked, and glanced apprehensively at her young sister, but Esme's glance at the older woman was puzzled.

'What, like a rich uncle or something?'

Mrs Kittle hooted, and slapped her fat thigh.

'Rich uncle! Hey! That's a good one, that is.'

'That's enough, Mrs Kittle,' Mae exclaimed loudly. 'Esme, leave that rinsing and get in the kitchen. There's plenty of work to do there before dinner-time.'

Esme went eagerly. Anything to get away from the steamy atmosphere of the washhouse. Mae looked daggers at Mrs Kittle, furious that she now had to do Esme's share of the laundry, too.

'No more gossip,' she warned fiercely. 'If I lose a tenant because of your wagging tongue, especially a respectable good-paying one like Mr Henshaw, you'll lose your job. Understand?'

Mrs Kittle looked sullen, sucked on her teeth noisily, but said nothing, and returned to mangling with a vengeance.

Carrying two buckets of coal, Dan Henshaw climbed the stairs to his room on the first floor. Four weeks at Picton Place had flown by, yet he was no closer to winning over Mae Parkyn than on the day he'd moved in.

She was attracted to him; he could tell by the way she always coloured up when he came to pay his rent. And at meal times, served in the communal dining room, his plate was always put before him first, even before Ernest

Nolan, a tenant of long-standing. Yet otherwise Mae remained elusive, as though still uncertain of him – or perhaps uncertain of herself.

He had wracked his brains to think of ways to prove himself worthy, to gain her confidence. Befriending Mrs Arnold, the old lady who rented the room next to his, looked to be a good start. To save Mae, he carried meals up to the old lady on those days when Mrs Arnold's arthritis was too painful for her to come down to the dining room, and every morning and evening he fetched her a bucket of coal. This benevolence must surely impress Mae eventually.

Leaving one bucket outside his room, Dan tapped on Mrs Arnold's door and opened it.

'It's Dan, Mrs Arnold, bringing the coal.'

The door was jerked wider suddenly, and the pert young face of Daphne, Mrs Arnold's granddaughter, appeared. Dan was immediately wary. She was too bold for fifteen years, with knowing eyes that sized him up and made him uncomfortable. Sometimes he suspected she saw right through him.

'Hello, Dan.'

She smiled coyly and thrust her underdeveloped chest at him.

'Mr Henshaw to you, Daphne,' he said severely, although she was too pretty to cause real annoyance, and far too young for his attentions. In ten years' time maybe . . .

'Daphne, stop that!' Mrs Arnold hobbled to the door with the aid of two sticks, and smiled up at him. 'There's good of you, Mr Henshaw. Come in, come in, that bucket looks heavy.'

'Dan's got muscles. He's strong, aren't you?' Daphne said, giggling, and sashayed into the room ahead of him.

'I bet he could lift me up and twirl me above his head with one hand, couldn't you, Dan? Want to try it?'

He had difficulty in hiding a smile, amused despite her impudence.

'Tsk! Tsk! There's a way to talk, isn't it?' Mrs Arnold said, scandalised. 'I blame that mother of hers.'

The teasing look left Daphne's face. 'Now, Gran,' she scolded. 'I won't visit you any more if you say nasty things about my mam.'

Dan emptied the coal into the scuttle and quickly retreated, anxious not to be involved.

'Good night, both,' he said from the safety of the doorway. But the two of them were scowling at each other, and he quietly closed the door.

Phew! That Daphne was a handful, young as she was. Pity the man who ended up with her as a wife.

'There's a little madam for you, isn't it?'

The throaty voice made Dan spin on his heel. His opposite neighbour, Mrs Nolan, was leaning against the doorpost of the room she shared with her husband. She was wearing a silky kimono-like wrap, patterned with roses in full bloom. Her hair was loose about her shoulders, and she was smiling at him. 'She'll end up bad, mark my words.'

'She's only a child,' he said cautiously. He'd been aware of Nora Nolan's interest in him for weeks.

'Huh! But for how long, the way she's behaving?' Mrs Nolan said with a sniff. 'Flaunting herself, ogling anything in trousers, and at her young age – it's disgusting! She could accuse a man of anything. You want to be careful . . . Dan.'

'I'm always careful, Mrs Nolan,' he replied quickly, picking up his bucket of coal, ready to open the door. 'Good night to you.'

To his astonishment, she darted forward and grasped his arm.

'I've told you, call me Nora,' she said breathily, looking up eagerly into his face. 'Why don't you come in my room for a chat? I've got a bottle of port. Ernie's on two 'til ten shift. He won't be home for a couple of hours. We've got plenty of time.'

He was practised in fielding unwanted propositions, mindful after painful experience that hell had no fury equal to that of a slighted woman.

'Very tempting, Nora,' he said softly, smiling down at her. 'And I'd love to, but I'll have to go without on this occasion. I've a stack of paperwork to get through by morning. My boss expects me to do it on my own time, and I don't want to lose my new job.'

She pouted. 'Oh, all right, then. If you're sure.' She smiled. 'Maybe some other evening soon?'

'Oh, definitely.' He chucked her under the chin. 'I look forward to it.'

Nora Nolan chuckled. 'That kid's only got youth,' she said, nodding towards Mrs Arnold's door. 'I've got experience. Know what I mean, Dan?'

'I certainly do, Nora.'

She was pressing closer, her face lifting purposefully towards his, and he felt nonplussed at her rapaciousness. Then a footfall on the staircase behind them gave him the opportunity to step away, and next moment Mae Parkyn appeared, carrying a stack of clean towels. As she joined them on the landing, her expression of shock and fury revealed her thoughts clearly.

'Excuse me!' she said as she pushed past them on her way to the bathroom at the end of the passage. Dan was dismayed as he stared after her. Damn Nora Nolan! She might have ruined his chances.

'Po-faced little bitch,' Nora hissed under her breath.

Mae, disappearing into the bathroom, must have heard, for she closed the door with a resounding bang.

'Excuse me, Nora,' Dan said hastily, and retreated into his room.

'But, Dan . . .' Nora's cry was plaintive.

He paused a moment behind the door until he heard her go into her own room, and then, cautiously, came out again. The bathroom door was still closed and he waited anxiously at the head of the stairs for Mae. She appeared eventually, pausing uncertainly when she saw him still standing there, then she stalked forward, her nose in the air, obviously intent on ignoring him. His mind raced to think up a story she would believe, and then for some reason he recalled their first meeting and knew he'd hit on the perfect solution.

'Miss Parkyn,' he began when she drew level. 'Can I ask your valued advice?'

She paused in her stride, obviously surprised at the question, but her expression was still huffy.

'I was just asking Mrs Nolan which chapel she went to,' he went on quickly, and was pleased to see Mae's eyes widen.

'You wasted your time, then,' she said sharply. 'That woman doesn't worship anywhere. She's a real back-slider.'

'So I found out,' he said, feigning chagrin.

Mae sniffed and gave him a sideways glance. 'I'm beginning to suspect her morals, even. I only put up with her because Mr Nolan is such a nice man, but I won't have any improper behaviour under my roof.'

'Quite right, Miss Parkyn,' Dan said emphatically. 'I couldn't agree more.'

She stared up at him, searching his face almost

suspiciously, but he kept his expression serious and as sincere as he could. She turned to leave, but he took a quick step forward.

'The thing is, Miss Parkyn,' he went on hastily, 'I'm a staunch chapelgoer myself. At least, I was when I lived in Bolton, and I want to find a friendly chapel here. Perhaps you can help me?'

Her attitude thawing a little, Mae touched her hair self-consciously.

'Well,' she said, 'we attend Mount Calvary in Pedrog Street, and have done since we were young children. In fact, Esme teaches in the Sunday School there.'

'That's recommendation enough,' Dan said, smiling. 'Would it be too much to ask if I can accompany you both next Sunday morning? Just as an introduction, you understand. I don't want to intrude on your privacy every week.'

She flushed.

'Of course you can come along with us, Mr Henshaw. Do you sing? Mr Silwyn, the minister, is always looking for choristers.'

Dan adjusted his tie. 'As a matter of fact, I've a good baritone voice, or so I've been told.'

Mae's smile was bright.

'You'd be welcomed with open arms then,' she said, and flushed again. 'Everyone's so companionable at Mount Calvary, Mr Henshaw. You'll soon find your bearings and make friends.'

'I wish you'd change your mind about coming to the wedding tomorrow,' Esme said later that evening. 'I think it was good of Gladys and Percy to ask you, seeing as how you mostly ignore them in chapel.'

'We can't both be off gallivanting at the same time,' Mae reminded her. 'And besides, I don't approve.

Gladys's husband has been dead less than a year. She's years older than Percy Pryce, and she's got those two young boys as well. There's talk in the chapel over it.'

'Gladys is only five years older than him,' Esme corrected her. 'And I can't see that it matters how long she's been a widow. People should mind their own business.'

'Persons in our position can't be too careful who we associate with,' Mae sniffed. 'We're in business and have our standing to maintain locally.' Irritated, she glanced sharply at her younger sister. 'It beats me why you're so friendly with them,' she went on haughtily. 'Both of them old enough to be your parents. It isn't natural, a girl of your age.'

'It was Percy who persuaded me to be a Sunday School teacher, as you know full well, and I'm glad he did. I enjoy it very much,' Esme said archly. 'I got to know Gladys because her oldest boy, Gwyn, is in my class. He's only two, mind, and can say the Lord's Prayer right through without a fault.'

Mae said nothing but continued darning the hole in the toe of her stocking. She had nothing against Percy Pryce, who was a nice enough man, but didn't envy Gladys marrying a collier. There'd never be enough money in that family, and he'd never amount to anything. She saw no reason to encourage them as friends.

'Gladys's youngest is ten months,' Esme went on. 'And there's a happy little chap Haydn is, too. It's awful to think his father died before he was born.' She shook her head. 'Tragic, mind.'

Mae bit off the thread with a snap.

'Oh, by the way,' she said casually, 'Mr Henshaw will be coming to chapel with us next Sunday morning, and possibly in the evening as well.'

Esme sat up straight, frowning.

'What for?'

'He was a big chapel man in Bolton, apparently, and wants to find a good one here,' May said. 'I told him he couldn't do better than Mount Calvary.'

'He doesn't strike me as a chapel man,' Esme said doubtfully. 'He's too . . . handsome.'

'You do talk daft on times, our Esme,' Mae laughed. 'I think Mr Henshaw will be an asset to the congregation. He's going to make something of himself, that man is. He told me the other day he's got plans to open a coal merchant's business.'

'Oh, aye! I wonder what other plans he's got,' Esme said slyly.

'What do you mean?' Mae glanced at her sister sharply, wondering what lay behind that remark. Did Esme know something she didn't? Mae recalled that moment on the upper landing earlier, when she'd thought she had caught the couple kissing or about to. Now she knew she was completely mistaken. Dan Henshaw thought far too much of himself to bother with a woman like Nora Nolan.

3

Early May 1901

Esme made sure she was in the hall early when Dan came downstairs on his way to work. He always stopped to inspect his appearance in the hall mirror before going out into the street, adjusting the angle of his bowler, tightening the knot in his tie.

Esme watched him from the top of the basement stairs, her heart swelling with love for him. He was achingly handsome, so dashing; no other man she knew could equal him, and she bit her lip, stifling a little groan of longing. She must speak to him immediately, let him know how she felt before it was too late, before he agreed to something they would both regret.

Mae had gone to Swansea Market first thing that morning on a quest to buy a fresh Gower goose. It was her twenty-second birthday, and she'd told Esme they would celebrate in style that evening with a slap-up dinner to which Dan was invited.

But Esme was convinced that there was more to this celebration than a mere birthday, much more, and it involved Dan Henshaw. Mae had been walking on air lately: preening in the mirror when she thought no one was watching; singing and smiling to herself; being so pleasant with everyone, even Mrs Nolan. It wasn't natural.

Mae was planning something with Dan, and Esme felt sick at the thought that there might be an understanding between them. She must tell him what was in her heart. Once he knew she loved him things would change. Mae would be forgotten and he'd love Esme only, deeply, as she loved him.

It looked as though he was on the point of leaving the house and she walked quickly along the passage, paused, and leaned against the newel post at the bottom of the stairs.

'Dan, wait a minute!'

He turned to smile at her.

'Good morning, Esme.' He looked her up and down. 'You're all dressed up, I see. Going somewhere nice? Don't tell me you've got a young man already. You're far too young.'

She had dressed up for him and was hurt. 'I'm not a child, Dan,' she cried. 'I'll be seventeen in November. Old enough to get married. In fact, I'm old enough now.'

He chuckled. 'Sweet sixteen and never been kissed. Well, hardly ever!'

'Don't laugh at me!'

'Esme, I wouldn't do that,' he said seriously. 'I'm too fond of you. You're like a little sister to me.'

'You didn't say that when you kissed me in the kitchen the other night,' she answered tartly. 'You showed me exactly how you felt then.'

He looked uncomfortable. 'You're mistaken, Esme, that was purely a brotherly kiss.'

'Oh, no! You held me tight, very tight,' she protested earnestly. 'I could feel you were trembling. I could feel everything,' she went on meaningfully. 'Why are you denying it, Dan?'

He reddened, and his tone was sharp. 'I see you as a sister, nothing more.'

'I'm *not* your sister,' Esme blurted in distress.

His answering smile was tight and controlled. 'You may be before long.'

'I knew it!' She grasped his arm. 'Dan, you can't do it! You can't marry my sister, not when you love me. You know you do. Admit it! And I love you so much.'

He drew back. 'Esme, please! Be careful what you say.' He glanced up the stairs, as though fearful someone would overhear.

She didn't care if they did. She had spoken her feelings at last; feelings that had made her heart swell with love for him for over a year. She could deny it no longer, wouldn't deny it. She was younger and prettier than Mae. He did love her best. His kiss had told her everything.

'You don't know what you're saying,' Dan protested in a strained tone. 'You're just a child.'

'I'm not, I tell you!' she blurted, and immediately burst into tears.

'Please don't cry, Esme.'

He opened the door of the tenants' communal sitting room and, after a quick glance around, pushed her inside. Desperate, Esme turned to him and tried to embrace him, but he held her at arm's length.

'Esme, listen to me,' he said tensely. 'I'm more than ten years older than you and at sixteen you're far too young for marriage or commitment. What would people think?'

'But I love you,' she sobbed. 'You must've known it when you kissed me.' He didn't answer and she rushed on, her voice rising, 'You don't love Mae, I know you don't!'

'But I do,' he said, and she was shocked to hear a new

harsh tone in his voice. 'I've asked her to marry me. We'll make the engagement official tonight and announce it tomorrow.'

'Dan, you don't realise what you're doing,' Esme said desperately. 'You and Mae don't belong together, but we do. I can feel it in my soul, and if you're honest so do you. You'll never be happy if you marry my sister.'

'I don't know what you think you're doing, Esme,' he said irritably. 'One little kiss, that's all it was, and you get everything out of proportion.'

'How can you be so cruel?'

He was silent for a moment while she stood with her head in her hands.

'Esme, this is just a passing fancy,' he said in a placatory tone. 'There's time enough for you to meet many young men your own age. Mae and I plan to marry in two years' time. You'll have forgotten this by then.'

'I'll never forget,' Esme sobbed. 'I'll never love anyone but you.'

'Then I'm sorry for you,' he said firmly. 'But nothing will stop me marrying Mae. We have big plans, Mae and me.'

'Plans? What kind of plans?' She stared, bewildered. 'Mae has said nothing to me.'

'Why should she?' Dan frowned down at her. 'They concern our marriage and our future together, and are no one else's business.'

'You're shutting me out!' Esme cried in dismay. 'What is to become of me when these plans come about?'

He took his watch out of his waistcoat pocket.

'You've made me late,' he said impatiently and turned towards the door, then paused. 'I won't say anything about this to Mae, and neither will you, I'm sure. Today was meant to be a happy day for both of us. Don't spoil it, Esme, just for a passing fancy.'

'Why are you marrying my sister, Dan?' she asked in a strident tone. 'Is it for money?'

He looked exasperated. 'You insult me now when a minute ago you were saying how much you loved me,' he said bitterly. 'Esme, do me a favour, go away and grow up!'

'Half that money is mine, you know, by rights,' she exclaimed loudly. 'It's not a fortune either, even though Mae likes everyone to think so. She can't do anything with it unless I give my permission.'

'Everything is in Mae's name, as you know well enough,' he said. 'And your sister's no fool. I've no intention of robbing her, as you seem to imagine. In fact, I'll make more money for her than she ever dreamed of.'

'You'll never be happy together,' Esme sobbed. 'It's *me* you should marry.'

Dan's face darkened. 'If you ruin this chance for me, Esme, for the sake of one kiss and your childish puppy-love, I'll never forgive you.'

He swung on his heel and left her standing there, miserable and humiliated. She had offered him all she had and he had thrown it back in her face.

Sweating, his chest tight with tension, Dan left the house almost at a run, desperate to get away from Esme's imploring eyes. What a fool he had been to let his desire for her lovely young body get the better of him the other night! He should never have kissed her, never have let her enticing vulnerability get under his skin. He had come close to ruining everything.

His jaws clamped together at the realisation. It must never happen again; he would not risk putting his bright future in jeopardy a second time. He wished he could bring his wedding to Mae forward. Once married he would feel safer, but any undue haste on his part might make her suspicious of his motives. She was too canny by half.

He reached the stop just as the tram arrived and handed the conductor the fare with shaking fingers. Two years was a long time to have to resist continual temptation.

Esme had composed herself by the time Mae came back from town later. She rushed into the basement kitchen, her face flushed.

'Esme, I've just had the most awful shock,' she exclaimed, putting the laden wicker shopping-basket on the table before taking off her hat and gloves. 'I met Mrs Tucker from Carrog Street in the market, and she had the most terrible news. Idris Davies has been killed by the Boers in South Africa!'

'Has he?' Esme murmured glumly before turning away. Her heart was heavy with Dan's rejection and she was numbed of all feeling.

'Is that all you can say?' Mae asked, sitting down heavily on a nearby chair, her face white. 'To think I might've married him. If I had, I'd be a widow now.'

'He wouldn't have gone to the war if he'd had a wife,' Esme said flatly. 'But he had no one who cared, so probably he didn't care either.'

Mae frowned. 'That's an awfully bleak and unfeeling thing to say, Esme,' she said. 'I'm really cut up about it. He was a nice man.' She paused. 'I wonder what will happen to the business?'

After a moment she jumped up.

'I've got a lovely plump goose for tonight's dinner,' she said more cheerfully. 'And all the trimmings. I'll invite Miss Gates and Miss Mower.' She sighed. 'I wish old Mrs Arnold was still alive. She'd have enjoyed it.' She frowned. 'I'm not asking Miss Dodd, though. She's always so frosty with men.'

'Is it wise to start having tenants to dinner?' Esme asked.

Mae was usually rather standoffish with their tenants, as though she were a cut above them. No doubt she saw this as another opportunity to show them how much better off she was, Esme decided, and was disgusted.

Mae looked coy. 'Tonight is a very special occasion.'

'I won't be here for dinner, by the way,' Esme said quickly. She didn't want to hear her sister say the words, and knew she would not be able to bear watching them together, knowing it ought to be herself and Dan celebrating.

Mae looked aghast. 'You *must* be here, Esme. Dan and I have an important announcement to make. You can't miss it.'

'I know already,' she said, forcing herself not to snap. It wouldn't do for Mae to know of her feelings for Dan. She could be vindictive when she wanted. 'He told me this morning. I've already promised Percy Pryce to mind the children tonight while he goes for a drink with his workmates.'

'But this is an important family celebration, Esme,' Mae objected. 'I think you should make the effort. Besides, it'll look strange if my own sister isn't there.'

'I promised Percy, and I never break a promise.' Esme was adamant.

Mae's lips thinned in anger. 'Drinking with his workmates, indeed,' she said, tossing her head with annoyance. 'He should stay home and face his responsibilities.'

'He's been doing that since poor Gladys died last year,' Esme retorted hotly. 'Percy's been father and mother to those children since she was taken. You're so concerned about Davies the Chemist, who you hardly knew, by the way, but what about Percy? A working man left alone with two small children, and you don't give a fig for the plight he's in. Well, I do! And I'm going to help him all I can.'

'I see!' Mae stood up. 'Of course, I know what this is all about. You're envious.'

'What?'

'You're jealous that I've found a bit of happiness with Dan.'

'He doesn't love you!' Esme cried out. 'He's only after Da's money.'

'Why, you spiteful little cat!' Mae was furious. 'I'm glad you're not joining us for dinner. You'd spoil everything.'

With that she marched out of the kitchen.

Mae took every opportunity over the next few days of showing off the engagement ring Dan had given her: making a melodrama of taking it off before washing up, pretending it was lost and getting in a tizzy. Everyone said the ring was lovely, but Esme couldn't bear to look at it. An engagement ring didn't mean anything, really, she told herself. Engagements could be broken, and it would be two years before they married – plenty of time to make him change his mind. But her heart was heavy, and people were noticing.

'Are you all right, kid?' Percy Pryce asked her on Saturday when she came to the rooms he rented on Neath Road to mind the children while he went to a rugby match in Cardiff. 'You look down in the dumps.'

Esme glanced up at him from stooping to help little Haydn into his coat, planning on taking the boys to the park for the afternoon. Scrubbed and polished for his trip, Percy seemed uneasy in his bowler hat and blue serge suit. Wide of shoulder and of medium stature, he was no oil painting, but he had kindly eyes and she was glad he was her friend even though he was twice her age. He and Gladys had been happy together before she was so suddenly taken, and Esme felt pity for his loneliness.

'Do you think I'm pretty, Percy?' she asked before thinking how it would sound.

His expression changed and she couldn't read it. 'What's this all about, Esme?'

'Oh, it's nothing,' she said, brushing it aside, wishing she hadn't spoken.

'You're unhappy, kid, I can see. Now tell Uncle Percy all about it?'

She had to smile. 'You'll miss your train in a minute,' she chided. 'You don't want to miss the kick-off too, or whatever it is they do in rugby.'

'Never mind about the match,' he said seriously. 'We're not friends for nothing. I want to help you, like you've helped me with the children since my Gladys went.'

'You can't help me, Percy,' she said forlornly.

'Is it Dan Henshaw?'

She stared at him in surprise. Were her feelings so obvious? 'What makes you ask that?'

'He hasn't been trying to . . . take advantage of you, has he?'

'No! Of course not.' She would not mention the kiss. In those moments in Dan's arms she had glimpsed how wonderful and powerful his lovemaking would be, and she yearned with all her being to experience it.

'Then what is it?'

'I'm in love with him,' she said simply. 'And I told him so.'

'Esme!'

'Yes, he was shocked, too, and quite cruel.' She paused, remembering, and stifled a sob. 'It won't last, you know, Percy, this engagement. Mae isn't right for him. I must find a way to make him change his mind about me.'

'Esme, you're being foolish.'

She stared at him in dismay. She had thought he would understand and not treat her like some imbecile child. 'Not you too, Percy.'

He took off his hat and shook his head.

'I remember what it was like being in love for the first time,' he said gently. 'It's painful, and no one else seems to understand what you're going through, least of all the one you love.'

'He speaks to me as though I'm a child, but I'll prove to him that I'm not. I'll show him I'm a woman!'

'Be careful, Esme,' Percy warned. 'I've watched Dan Henshaw this last year. He's become very active in chapel life, mixing with some of the more prominent members of the congregation, but I can see his heart isn't really in it. It's a means to an end with him. One more ladder to climb.'

Esme was thoughtful. 'He told me he and Mae have big plans.'

'I'd bet my last penny that he has, and he's not the kind of man to be swayed by sentiment,' Percy went on. 'But he's only human, and could be tempted to do something . . . foolhardy, if you push him.'

She frowned. 'What do you mean?'

Percy paused, looking embarrassed.

'Don't throw yourself at him,' he said frankly at last.

'He might take advantage in a weak moment, but he'll never give up Mae and his ambitions.'

Esme was silent and thoughtful. Percy was wrong about Dan. Yes, he was ambitious, but she was sure he was honourable, in his way, and wondered if she was strong enough to put him to the test.

4

Early June 1902

Elated, tingling with excitement and anticipation, Mae took Dan's arm as he escorted her from the solicitor's offices in Walter Road. Everything was coming right and their future looked rosy. Her father would be so proud of her.

'We really did it!' she said breathlessly. 'I can hardly believe it. Me, Mae Parkyn, a fully-fledged partner in a thriving coal merchant's business. Oh, if only Da could see me now!'

Dan laughed, squeezing her arm against his side as they strolled down the tree-lined road towards the centre of town.

'It's all thanks to you, Mae,' he said. 'Believing in my judgement and having the gumption to grab an opportunity.' He turned and looked at her. 'You know, not many women your age would have the courage.'

Mae flushed at his praise. She trusted him and his strength of purpose. They'd go far, the pair of them. It was a good match, and she congratulated herself for the umpteenth time.

'You'll never regret it, Mae, I promise you,' Dan said seriously.

'I'll make sure of that,' she answered.

She'd never had a moment's doubt since he'd come to

her with the proposition, but sensibly had inspected the books and the business premises in Victoria Avenue on the west side of town before telling him she recognised a good thing when she saw it. But she had another reason for going ahead with the deal. With Dan as her business partner as well as her husband next year their relationship would be well and truly cemented, and she would feel much more secure and sure of him.

'There's just one thing, Mae,' he said hesitantly, interrupting her thoughts. 'I wonder at the wisdom of your retaining the majority share.'

She had sensed something was bothering him. 'It's only two per cent, Dan.'

'Yes, but with only forty-nine per cent it means I'm not in complete control, and after all, I'll be running the business. You're my silent partner, Mae.'

She nudged him with her elbow. 'It's only for the time being, my dear,' she said lightly. 'After all, I'm putting up all the money and Mr Carradog-Jones thinks it's important.'

'Don't you trust me, Mae?'

'Of course I do, my dear. I'm marrying you, aren't I? When I see a good return on my money, I'll make the two per cent over to you.' His arm seemed to tense and she knew he was not completely satisfied. 'There will be profits, Dan, won't there?'

'Of course! I'll double them within a few years,' he asserted. 'Brynmill is a fashionable area, and still under development. New housing will mean new customers.'

Mae was thoughtful. She was tired of the drabness of the Hafod, blackened by decades of heavy industry, and aspired to something better. The leafy roads and smart villas of west Swansea impressed her. This was where she wanted to be, deserved to be.

'We'll buy a good house in Brynmill, near the park perhaps,' she said. 'A house to fit our new status.' It certainly wasn't fitting she should continue as a boarding-house keeper now.

'Hold your horses, dear,' Dan warned. 'Let's not gallop before we learn to canter. Building up a business takes years and a great deal of patience. You're doing very nicely in Picton Place. Make up your mind to stay put for a while yet.'

For a moment she was inclined to argue with him, and then thought better of it. She wouldn't spoil the day, and there'd be plenty of time to get her own way after they were married.

Esme took the news with a tightening of her lips, her eyes flashing angrily.

'Why wasn't I told?' she cried. 'It's my money, too. You're throwing it away on a pig in a poke!'

'It's a very sound business deal, Esme.' Mae looked disdainful. 'But you wouldn't know that because you have no head for business, like I have. Besides, I didn't think it necessary to consult you. You're still a minor.'

'Well, you can just go and tell the solicitor you've changed your mind, Mae,' Esme insisted. 'Before it's too late and we lose everything Da left us.'

'It's all signed and sealed so there's no undoing it even if I wanted to, which I don't,' Mae snapped, and then went on more persuasively. 'Look, Esme, I'm investing your money for you, in a way. Your share will be much increased by the time you come of age.'

'I'd rather have my share now,' Esme retorted contrarily. 'I've a right to lead my own life.'

'Oh, don't be such a stupid, wilful girl when I'm trying to do my best for you!'

'You're not thinking of me at all,' she countered obstinately. 'All you think of is yourself and Dan. But you'll be sorry, though, because he'll let you down in the end.'

'The green-eyed monster is perched on your shoulder again, Esme,' Mae said cuttingly. 'Very unattractive! Now do something useful for your keep – like, slope off down Morris the Baker's and order tomorrow's loaves.'

The uncovered boards of the basement stairs felt rough and cold under Esme's bare feet as she crept up them in the darkness, afraid to light a candle for fear of being discovered.

She shivered under her cotton wrap, but it wasn't from cold. She was terrified by what she was about to do yet determined to go through with it.

She had thought about it all day, weighing Percy's advice to stay clear of Dan against her own love for him. Dan could protest indifference all he wanted, but his kiss had told her all she needed to know. He wanted her as much as she wanted him. They were destined for each other, and she would not let his plans with Mae spoil that. Besides, Mae had Da's money; why should she have Dan too?

Perhaps Percy was right, though. Perhaps she was being foolish in what she intended to do tonight. Dan might reject her again . . . Well, she had to take that risk. It was the only way to prove to him that she wasn't a silly child indulging in daydreams. At seventeen she was an adult with all the feelings and longings of womanhood. He would realise this at last when she came to him, offering herself, all she had.

It was even darker in the passage leading to the stairs which climbed to the first floor and Dan's room. Miss Dodd's door was right at the foot of the stairs and Esme hesitated guiltily, seeing a sliver of light under it. Why was Miss Dodd up at this unearthly hour? Surely she wasn't marking schoolbooks in the small hours?

Esme crept past, afraid she'd bump into a table or chair in the darkness. If Mae ever discovered what she intended to do, Esme wouldn't dare imagine what her sister's revenge would be like.

Breathless from tension, she was at last at the top of the stairs, right outside Dan's door. She held her breath, listening. Everything was quiet. She'd got away with it so far.

Hand trembling, Esme grasped the doorknob and eased the door open. She knew it wouldn't be locked because Mae wouldn't supply tenants with keys, asserting that locked doors were not necessary as long as the front door was secure.

The curtains were closed, and in the darkness she could hear Dan's regular breathing. She didn't need a light but walked confidently towards the bed, knowing her way, having cleaned this room innumerable times. At the bedside she hesitated, her heart in her mouth. If he woke with a start he might cry or even lash out.

Moving to a side table, she felt for the candle and match. By the candle's glow she looked down on his sleeping form. Bare-chested, he was lying on his back, the thin cotton sheet half-covering him; one knee was flexed, sole against the other calf. The outline of his muscular thighs beneath the sheet made her catch her breath. On the pillow his face was turned towards her, his features relaxed in sleep, and he looked so young in the flickering light. She wanted to bend and kiss him there and then, but stifled the desire. Instead she sat down on the chair near the bed and gazed at him. What would he do when he saw her? What would he say?

As she watched he moved restlessly, perhaps disturbed by the light. Still she waited, not able to move a muscle now the time had come. Her heart skipped a beat as his eyes opened, but although his gaze was fixed directly on her he appeared not to see her for a moment. Then, with a whispered oath, he sat bolt upright and stared disbelievingly.

'Esme! Good God! What are you doing here?'

'Don't be cross.'

'Cross! I'm flabbergasted,' he said in a low voice. 'You shouldn't be here. If Mae finds out . . .'

'I belong here with you, Dan,' she said stubbornly, standing up and taking a step towards the bed. 'I belong in your arms. In your bed.'

He stared aghast. 'You don't know what you're saying, child.'

'Don't call me that! And don't be a hypocrite, Dan. Not after the way you kissed me. No man kisses a child that way.'

Impulsively, she sat down on the bed beside him. He flinched away as though touched by a flame.

'This isn't wise, Esme. I want you to go.'

'No, you don't mean that. I won't be sent away,' she answered breathlessly, leaning towards him. 'You want me, Dan, I know you do, and I want you.'

'This is madness!'

She got to her feet again, loosening the tie of her wrap, and let the garment slip from her shoulders to fall around her feet. He took in a huge gulp of air as she stood before him, naked and unashamed.

'Mae would never come to you like this, would she?' Esme asked softly.

He shook his head dumbly. She watched as his gaze played over her pert breasts, sliding to her firm belly and pubic hair. In the candlelight she saw sweat appear on his upper lip and was elated at the raw animal hunger that flickered in his eyes. He *did* want her.

'You asked her, I'll bet, but she refused,' Esme said, guessing. 'She doesn't love you as I do. She has no fire in her. She's only interested in getting on in life. But I think only of you, Dan.'

'Stop talking like this, Esme, for God's sake!' He was about to get out of bed then appeared to change his mind. 'You could destroy everything for me. I should send you packing, you little tease,' he muttered, but there was a rasp of longing in his voice.

'I'm not teasing, Dan,' she said earnestly. 'I've come to you tonight because I want to. I want you to love me. I know what I'm doing.'

He turned his gaze away, and she saw he was trembling.

'Put your wrap on, for pity's sake,' he pleaded in a whisper.

Instead she grasped the edge of the bed sheet, flung it aside, and kneeling on the bed, thrust her body towards his.

'Touch me,' she whispered urgently.

'Esme, for God's sake! It's more than any man can stand,' he murmured in a strangled tone. 'You're playing with fire . . . we both are.'

'This is meant to be, Dan. You're the only man I'll ever love.' She reached out and put her hand on his chest. 'Love me, now. I want you to.'

'Think of Mae . . .' he said weakly.

'Forget my sister. She'll never surrender herself to you as I will,' Esme urged, moving closer to him and stretching out on the bed. She raised her arms beseech-ingly. 'Kiss me, hold me. I'm yours tonight, Dan.'

With a groan he clasped her, lifting her up in his arms to hold her tightly against his chest. The heat of his skin seemed to burn hers, and Esme was filled with sensations she'd never known before.

'God forgive me for this folly,' he whispered. 'I'm risking my whole future for you Esme, all my carefully laid plans. I must be crazy!'

'This isn't folly,' she said. 'This is fate, Dan, our destiny. Now, kiss me.'

'Esme, fetch the other tureen of potatoes from the kitchen, please,' Mae instructed as the tenants were seated at the refectory table for dinner.

Esme rose quickly and did as she was asked without murmur. She'd not seen Dan since she'd left his room at four o'clock that morning, and longed to talk to him. Sitting opposite him at the table in the company of others was unbearable. He hadn't acknowledged her or even looked in her direction. She was still in thrall at the things they had done together in the candlelight, her body quivering anew with desire at the thought. Yet he seemed so cool and calm, she was amazed by his composure.

'Were you moving furniture in the early hours, Mr Henshaw?' Miss Dodd was asking in a chilly voice as Esme returned with the tureen. It almost slipped from her fingers. 'I heard the most peculiar noises overhead in the night.'

The school teacher turned a suspicious glance towards Mae as though expecting a guilty reaction to her words, but Mae in her innocence was unperturbed and looked with amusement at Dan, brows raised.

'I heard nothing,' he answered in an off-hand tone, lifting a forkful of cabbage to his mouth. 'But then, I sleep like a log.'

Esme set the tureen down in front of Dan, the only man at the table that evening, letting her arm brush against his shoulder as she did so. She felt suddenly feverish with excitement at their secret knowledge. If the others only knew, they'd be shocked beyond belief!

'Probably those gypsies from next-door,' Miss Mower opined. 'Always banging about. They're a rum lot.'

Mae bridled. 'There are no gypsies in Picton Place!' she said sharply. 'This is a very respectable neighbourhood.'

'It could've been a burglar,' Miss Gates said nervously. 'They climb on to the roof, you know, and get in through the skylight. I'm all alone in the attic . . .'

'We don't have a skylight,' Mae said impatiently. 'Miss Dodd is just imagining things.'

'Well, I don't worry,' Nora Nolan said, flashing a smile at Dan. 'Even when Ernie's on nights. Not with a big strong man like Mr Henshaw in the house.'

Mae looked furious at the pleasantry and, standing up abruptly, began clearing the plates away.

'Esme! Help me bring in the puddings.'

After the meal was finished Dan was the first to leave the dining room. Excusing herself to Mae by saying she was off to the lavatory in the yard, Esme followed him up the stairs to the landing above, catching up with him as he opened his door.

'Dan, I've got to talk to you!'

He whirled towards her, his expression startled.

'Not now, Esme. You heard what that busybody said. It's too risky.'

She giggled. 'I nearly had a fit when Miss Dodd spoke up, didn't you? Were we that noisy? I don't remember. I was having such a heavenly time.'

The tension in his face relaxed for a moment. 'So was I.'

Delighted, she stepped closer to him, aching to be in his arms. 'Oh, Dan, I never knew loving between a man and a woman could be so wonderful.'

He stepped back, suddenly nervous again, and glanced over her shoulder down the stairs. 'We mustn't be seen talking like this,' he said. 'Mae might put two and two together.'

'I'll come to you again tonight,' Esme said breathlessly.

'No,' he retorted hastily. 'It mustn't happen again, Esme, never. I've been a fool. You caught me at a weak moment.'

'I'll be with you just after midnight,' she said, ignoring his rebuff. He didn't mean it. He had shown her what he really felt for her in the early hours. That was all she needed to know. She knew what was best for both of them. 'I can hardly wait, darling.'

'Esme, have a bit of sense.' His voice was sharp. 'You – we – could ruin everything I've built up.'

There was chatter in the passage below as Miss Mower and Miss Gates came out of the dining room, and Dan flung open the door of his room and dodged inside before the two women appeared at the bottom of the stairs.

Abandoned, Esme hurried along the passage to the bathroom to hide there until the women had gone. She would go to his room tonight, she resolved, and every night – well, as often as she could manage without arousing Mae's suspicions. Soon he wouldn't be able to live without her. He loved her as much as she loved him, and she'd make him admit it. And then they'd tell Mae the truth. Esme was looking forward to that as much as anything else.

5

September 1902

Esme stood at the sitting-room window overlooking the road. The house across the street had a single tree growing in the front garden. Its leaves were turning red. A few had already fallen and were fluttering around on the pavement. Autumn was almost here. When spring came again her baby would be born. Dan's baby. A satisfied smile curved her mouth at this secret knowledge, and she felt triumphant. He couldn't marry Mae now, and there was nothing her sister could do about it. In fact, she'd be positively livid when they told her they were to wed.

Friends and acquaintances, especially those from the chapel, would be surprised at the hasty wedding, Esme reflected, and there would probably be gossip, but they'd get over it. Mae was always going on about getting away from Picton Place, buying a house in Brynmill. Now it would be Esme and Dan doing that. Soon the gossips would forget them. Out of sight, out of mind.

She must tell him the news as soon as possible. As though on cue, the sitting-room door opened and he strolled in, newspaper in hand. He looked surprised to see her.

'You're not at Sunday School this afternoon then?' he said.

'No,' she said. 'I stayed home because I want to talk to you in private. We won't be disturbed by here for the moment.'

He looked wary. 'Where's Mae?'

'Gone over to Brynmill to call on Elias Morgan and his wife. She'll be ages yet, unless she comes back in a hackney.' Esme grimaced. 'Tsk! She's acting like the lady of the manor just because Elias Morgan works for you.'

Dan frowned. 'I wish she wouldn't interfere with employees.'

Esme sat on the sofa and spread her skirt carefully over her knees. She patted the seat beside her, but Dan took an armchair instead. Esme couldn't prevent a smile at his nervousness. Soon everyone would know they were to marry.

'What does she want with the Morgans anyway?' he asked gruffly.

'Mae is dying to get rid of Mrs Kittle,' Esme said, 'and she's hoping Elias Morgan's daughter will take her place doing the rough work about here.'

'What? Cissie Morgan? The poor girl's only thirteen and simple-minded. What does Mae want with the likes of her?'

'Mrs Kittle is getting out of hand, according to Mae,' said Esme. 'She needs a drudge, someone she can bully. Cissie is too dim-witted to answer back.' She paused, looking at him keenly. 'Mae will soon need another pair of hands anyway because I won't be around Picton Place much longer.'

He looked startled. 'What's that?'

Esme wetted her lips. 'I'm in the family way, Dan, my dear,' she said softly. 'We'll have to marry soon and move to Brynmill.'

He leaped out of his chair. 'What?'

'I knew you'd be surprised,' she said. 'It was a bit of a shock to me too, at first, but now I see it as a blessing in disguise.'

He stared at her open-mouthed, his face turning red. 'What are you talking about?'

'I'm having your baby, Dan.' Esme smiled at him. 'Isn't it wonderful? We'll have to tell Mae, of course, the sooner the better.' She couldn't help tittering. 'There'll be ructions! She thinks she's so superior to me . . . to everybody. She does, you know!'

'You're *pregnant*?'

Esme winced. 'Don't use that word, Dan. It sounds so horrible and sordid.'

He stood there, staring, the newspaper quivering in his shaking fingers. 'Why are you telling *me* this?' he croaked.

Esme raised her brows. 'Well, the father should always be the first to know, don't you think?' she joked. 'It won't be until next March, but we'll need to make plans now.'

'Oh, no!' He flung the newspaper on to his chair. 'Oh, no, you don't. You're not lumbering me with your bastard!'

'Dan!' Esme gaped, lifting her hand to cover her mouth in shock. She couldn't believe what she was hearing.

'Don't Dan me!' he exclaimed wrathfully. 'You're a fast little baggage. I realised that the first night you came to my room, offering yourself like a street-girl.'

Esme jumped to her feet. 'Dan, don't! How could you? I love you, that's why I came to you. It's *your* baby.'

He pointed a trembling finger at her abdomen. 'That's no child of mine.'

'Of course it is!' Esme screeched. 'You're the only man I've ever lain with.'

'I don't believe you,' he thundered. 'No innocent,

inexperienced girl behaves as you do. You're no better than Nora Nolan.'

'I'm not like her at all. How could you say such a thing to me?' Esme whimpered. 'I love you, I tell you, and you love me.'

'Love! Don't make me laugh,' he rasped. 'You did it to spite your sister as much as anything, and to trap me.'

Esme shook her head dumbly, too overwhelmed by his terrible words to defend herself.

'I was shocked, I'll tell you,' Dan went on relentlessly. 'But what red-blooded man refuses something offered on a plate?' He shook his head emphatically. 'No, I'm not the first. You were no innocent when you came to me, and I'm not paying the price for some other man's bit of fun.'

'You don't mean this,' Esme whispered at last. 'You love me. You *must* do.'

His lips twisted. 'Now you're being as stupid as Cissie Morgan. Love didn't come into it with you.' He gulped, and Esme thought he looked sick as he said it. 'I love Mae, I tell you,' he went on, his voice rasping. 'And we'll be married next year.'

'But what about me?' Esme cried in distress.

'You got yourself into this mess,' Dan answered. He looked as though he was fast recovering from the shock. 'And you can get yourself out of it.' There was a sneer on his face. 'Get one of your other fancy men to make an honest woman of you.'

'Oh! You're a swine, Dan Henshaw!'

'Maybe, but I'm no fool, Esme. You picked me for the father because you think I've got a bit of money. Well, it won't work.'

'But it's your baby!' she cried in anguish. 'I'll tell Mae!'

'I'll deny everything,' he snapped. 'And what do you think she'll do when she knows you're pregnant?'

Unable to answer, Esme opened her mouth and took in a great gasp of air, suddenly fearful.

'She'll kick you out, that's what,' he grated. 'You're a fallen woman, a disgrace, and you know how proud she is, especially now, with the new business. She'll wash her hands of you. You won't see a penny piece of your father's money.'

Esme clapped a hand over her mouth again. What was she to do?

Dan nodded as though he'd heard her unspoken question.

'You'd better look for another mug to marry, before your mistake starts showing itself.'

With that he turned on his heel and slammed out of the room.

Esme cried until she couldn't cry any more. She stayed in her bedroom. When Mae came to her later to demand why she wasn't ready for evening worship at the chapel, Esme muttered through the locked door that she had a fierce cold with a temperature and was going to bed. She couldn't sleep for brooding over Dan's betrayal and wondering what she should do next. The answer seemed to be that she must run away, disappear until after her baby was born. But how would she live? She had nothing. Should she confess all to Mae and throw herself on her sister's mercy? Esme dismissed that thought immediately. Dan was right. Mae would disown her.

It would be weeks yet before she began to show. She decided she mustn't be hasty but think things out carefully. Who knows? Dan might change his mind after he'd got over the shock. Meanwhile, she must get on with life, she reflected when she rose from bed the following morning. If she could only get some money out of Mae, she might be able to disappear. And pigs might fly!

She couldn't look in Dan's direction when serving his breakfast, and he studiously avoided her eye.

'Cissie Morgan is starting work here tomorrow,' Mae told her sister later. 'She's a lump of a girl, but willing. And she'll do it for next to nothing.' Mae sounded smug.

'*Duw! Duw!* There's clever of you,' Esme sneered.

Mae paused and stared at her. 'What's the matter with you, then? You've got a face like the back of a hackney. Take an aspirin if your cold's bothering you. There's too much work for moping.'

She marched out of the kitchen with a tray of teacups, leaving Esme washing up the breakfast dishes. Mrs Kittle came in from getting on with the laundry.

'Could do with a hand out there, I could. I'll be glad when the new girl starts,' she muttered. 'Bloody fed up with that mangle, I am. She can do it from now on.' She stared at Esme. 'You haven't been sick this morning, have you?'

Esme almost dropped a plate. 'What do you mean?'

'You look real peaky.' Mrs Kittle stuck her tongue in her cheek, a knowing smirk on her lips. 'I've seen that look too often. Been doing something you shouldn't, have you?'

'That's enough!' Esme blurted. 'You'd better know your place. Mae's planning to get rid of you. *That's* why she's taken Cissie on.'

'Well, I'm buggered!'

Longing to get out of the house the next day, unable to maintain her brave front much longer before Mae's sharp eyes, Esme begged to do some shopping in the market, pleading that the fresh air would help her cold. She was passing the patent medicine stall when she saw Percy Pryce and stopped immediately.

'Percy, why aren't you at the colliery today?'

He turned to her. 'Haydn's poorly,' he said, a worried look on his homely face. 'Something on his chest. Getting some cough medicine, I am.'

'Oh, poor little mite!' Esme exclaimed, for the moment forgetting her own troubles. 'Have you called the panel doctor?'

'I will if he gets worse,' Percy promised, as he handed over money to the stallholder and pocketed the bottle. 'Losing a lot of time, I am, at the colliery of late,' he went on. 'Lose my job, I will, if I'm not careful.'

'Tsk!' Esme made a sympathetic murmur. It was hard for him, a man on his own with two young boys. He ought to marry again, but she wouldn't dare suggest it to him. He was still grieving over Gladys. He stood for a moment awkwardly, and she sensed he wanted to be off home, worried about the child.

'Listen,' she said, 'I'll call in some time this evening, see how he is.'

'Oh, I don't want to trouble you, *bach*,' Percy said, although he looked hopeful. 'A young girl like you must have plenty to amuse her without bothering with us.'

'It's no trouble,' Esme said quickly. Anything was better than being stuck indoors with Mae, keeping up the pretence that everything was normal. Life would never be normal for her again.

Good as her word, Esme arrived at Percy's home in time to give the boys their tea. They were both in the kitchen, a roaring fire in the grate even in September. There'd never be a shortage of coal in this house.

Gwyn, the eldest boy, squatted on the mat before the fire, playing with a red wooden fire engine. He looked up at her, a sullen expression on his face. Still missing his mother, Esme thought, her heart going out to him.

Haydn was on the couch alongside the range, bundled up in a wool blanket. His little face looked pinched, and he had a dry cough. Esme eyed him thoughtfully.

'Have you tried goose grease?' she asked. 'If we could get a spoonful down him it might ease his chest.'

Percy made a face and shuddered. 'Goose grease! *Duw!* I'd rather have the cough.'

'My mother used to swear by it,' Esme assured him.

'I'll nip next door and see if old Ma Griffiths has any,' said Percy.

He was back within a short while, carrying a small pudding basin. Esme fetched a teaspoon, and scooping out a dollop of the soft white fat, held it towards the child. Haydn immediately pulled back his head. 'Ugh!'

'Hold his nose,' Esme instructed Percy, and then pushed the spoon between Haydn's open rosebud lips. She gently stroked the child's throat until he swallowed involuntarily, whereupon Haydn burst into tears, howling in rage. Which wasn't surprising, Esme thought, knowing how disgusting the grease tasted. Never mind. It would do him good.

'You've got a way with children. You'll make a wonderful mother,' Percy said in admiration, and Esme stared at him in dismay, the spoon slipping from her fingers. Before she could stop herself, she burst into tears.

Percy was dismayed. 'Esme, whatever is the matter?'

She flopped on to the couch beside Haydn, shaking as though with ague while tears poured down her cheeks. She just couldn't control them.

Percy laid a hand gently on her shoulder. 'What is it, *cariad*?'

'Oh, Percy, I've been very, very stupid.' Esme hung her head with shame, and pulling a handkerchief from her sleeve, wiped viciously at her nose. She felt a wave of relief that she was about to tell someone she trusted. Percy wouldn't talk.

'And now I'm in the most terrible trouble – desperate trouble,' she finished.

There was a heavy silence, and after a moment Esme ventured to glance up at him. He was looking at her with a disappointed expression on his face.

'So, you're expecting,' he said dully. 'Esme, I'm sorry.'

She managed a weak smile. Trust Percy not to blame or condemn. He had a very generous nature, and she knew she could confide all to him.

'I love him, Percy, honestly I do, even now; otherwise I would never have done it.'

'Are we talking about Dan Henshaw?' Percy asked in a tense voice. A vein was throbbing in the side of his throat.

Esme nodded, dabbing at her damp cheeks. 'I believed he loved me, too,' she said miserably. 'I really thought he'd marry me.' She gave a sob. 'But he was so cruel and hateful when I told him about the baby. Denied it was his. He said the most awful things. He cut me to the heart.'

'What will you do?'

Esme bit her lip, and shook her head. 'I don't know.' She glanced up at him. 'Throw myself in the River Tawe perhaps.'

'Don't be silly, Esme.'

She gulped. They both knew she didn't mean it for one minute. She had more courage than that. 'If I had money I'd get away from the Hafod,' she said forlornly. 'Have my baby where no one knows me. But I'm afraid to tell Mae, under the circumstances. She'll turn against me, I know she will.'

Percy was silent, staring down into the burning coals of the fire. He looked as though he were turning something over in his mind. 'If I had money I'd give it to you gladly, Esme,' he said quietly after a moment.

'I know you would,' she said. He would, too. Percy was a true friend, the only one she had, really. 'Anyway, you've got as much as you can do, providing for the boys.'

'I want to help you, though,' he said. 'You've been very kind to the boys and me, giving your time and all to look after them so I could go off. Not everyone would bother.'

'Percy, it was nothing,' she assured him, and glanced at the two children. 'I'm fond of them, poor little motherless kids.'

'Esme, I haven't got any money . . . well, not enough for your purposes,' he said. 'But there is one thing I can give your child, and that's my name.'

She shook her head. 'I don't understand.'

Percy squatted down at the side of the couch, looking at her eagerly. 'You could marry me, Esme *cariad*, before the baby is born,' he said. 'Register me as the father, don't you see?'

She jumped to her feet, astonished. 'Percy!'

He rose too. 'I'll get a special licence,' he rushed on. 'We can be wed as soon as you like. I'll rent a house away from the Hafod. I want to get away from by here anyway. The house reminds us all too much of Gladys. The boys will never settle down here.'

'Percy, I don't know what to say.' Esme bit her lip. 'It's such a big step you're suggesting.' An irrevocable step, which once taken could never be retraced. If she married him she could say goodbye to any hope of ever being Dan's wife. But he had already made it painfully clear that that was out of the question. She had to think of herself and her baby now.

'No one could point the finger at you with a wedding ring on your hand,' Percy said. 'Oh, there'd be gossip around here at first, but we'd get over that. We can start afresh elsewhere.'

Esme still hesitated. She liked Percy, liked him a lot, but had never thought of him in husbandly terms.

'I'd be good to you, Esme, I swear,' he said quietly, not moving any closer. 'I'd take care of you, and do my best to provide for you and your little one.'

'You're a good man, Percy,' she said, smiling softly. 'But I don't know whether it's the right thing to do.'

He looked a little embarrassed. 'I wouldn't make demands – you know what I mean,' he said hesitantly. 'I wouldn't ask anything of you. You wouldn't have to do anything you didn't want to do, I swear it. I'm not like Dan Henshaw. I respect you, Esme, and – and I'm very fond of you.'

Overwhelmed at his generosity and sincerity, she stepped forward and took his hands in hers.

'You're very kind and thoughtful, Percy,' she said. 'And I cherish your offer.' He'd offered all he had of value: his name. 'But I must think carefully about it. We're talking about the rest of our lives.'

'I know,' he said quietly. 'And I'd spend it very happily with you, Esme.' He squeezed her hands. 'We could be happy, I know it.'

'I need time.'

'Of course you do.' He released her hands and stepped away. 'I'm always here for you, Esme.'

She smiled at him and then reached for her hat and coat. 'I won't keep you waiting long for an answer, Percy,' she promised. 'I'll call back teatime tomorrow. By then I'll know what I intend to do.'

Two weeks passed before Esme found the courage to tell Mae of her forthcoming marriage. Percy had arranged a special licence for the second week in November, and had even secured the tenancy of a terraced house in Cwmbwrla, where they would move immediately after the wedding. Esme was determined to make the best of it, and that meant a new dress for the occasion, but she had no money. Mae must be persuaded to help her, although she dreaded revealing news of the baby, not knowing how her sister would take it.

When the Saturday evening meal was cleared, and the tenants had returned to their rooms, Mae went to her bedroom in the basement to change, telling Esme that she and Dan would be spending the rest of the evening together in their sitting room.

'Could you make yourself scarce tonight?' Mae asked her. 'Dan and me have a lot to talk about, and we want some privacy – you know. We don't often get a chance to be alone together.'

Esme felt pain shoot through her heart. It should be her and Dan sharing intimate moments. After all, she was carrying his child.

'I don't see why I should be kicked out,' she said sharply. 'Why don't you go to his room?'

Mae looked offended. 'Don't be stupid! That would look nice, wouldn't it? You can imagine the tongues wagging.' She glanced at Esme's sullen expression. 'Why don't you go around to Percy Pryce's? You're back and forth there often enough.'

Esme bit her lip, words crowding into her mouth. She wanted to spit them out, but they seemed to be stuck in her throat.

'Well, what are you hanging about for?'

Esme gulped. 'I'm getting married, Mae.'

'What?' Her sister stared at her blankly. 'What did you say?'

'I'm getting married on my birthday in November by special licence. I need money for a dress and other things,' Esme rushed on. 'So I'll have my share of Da's inheritance straight away, if you please.'

Blinking as though someone had smacked her in the face, Mae flopped down on the bed.

'You're getting married!' she said after a moment. 'To whom, for heaven's sake?'

'Percy Pryce.'

'Good God!' Mae jumped up from the bed. 'I've never heard anything so absurd in my life. Have you gone raving mad, girl?'

'Percy has asked me to marry him and I've accepted.'

Mae exploded. 'You little fool! What were you thinking of, accepting the first man who asks you?' she exclaimed angrily. 'He's after money, of course.' Her lips thinned. 'Big in the chapel he's supposed to be, and a Sunday School Superintendent as well, but I knew he was too good to be true. He's out for what he can get. Huh! Well, if he thinks he'll get his hands on my money through you, he's mistaken.'

'It has nothing to do with money,' Esme said. She hesitated, unable to say the next words.

'Then what has it to do with?' Mae scoffed. 'Not love, I'll be bound.' She looked determined. 'You leave this to me, Esme,' she said firmly. 'I'll have a word with Percy Pryce; give him a piece of my mind, I will. He won't get away with trapping you, the conniving hypocrite!'

'You'll do no such thing,' Esme snapped. 'You leave Percy alone. It's nothing to do with you. I *want* to marry him.'

Mae looked nonplussed. 'But he's nearly twice your age, girl, and he's got those children hanging around his neck.' She shook her head. 'You don't know what you're doing.'

'Percy's a good man,' Esme exclaimed hotly. 'As good as Dan Henshaw any day – probably better.'

'Oh, don't talk so ridiculous, will you?' Mae snapped. 'And don't mention them in the same breath either. There's no comparison. Dan's the best man I know, and he's honourable.'

'Perhaps you don't know him as well as you think you do,' Esme said bitterly.

Mae looked at her sharply and then her eyes narrowed. 'Now, what's behind all this nonsense, Esme? Is it jealousy again?'

She swallowed hard, feeling her body quiver with tension and fright. 'I *have* to marry, Mae. I – I'm in the family way.'

Her sister stared at her, mouth gaping and face turning pale.

'What's that?' She swayed. 'What did you say?'

'I'm expecting a baby in March. So, you see, I must marry Percy.'

'Oh, my God! Oh, the filthy swine!' Mae flopped on to the bed again, looking as though she would faint. 'Thank God Da isn't alive to witness this. As it is, he must be turning in his grave.'

'That's a horrible thing to say,' Esme exclaimed. 'How could you?'

'Well, what do you expect?' Mae snapped, rallying. 'You're still only seventeen, and you've thrown away your reputation, your life even, for what? For nothing. The whole of the Hafod will be talking about us. Oh, the shame of it! How will I ever lift my head in the chapel again?'

'Is that all you've got to say?' Esme yelled. 'You're selfish to the core, Mae. Always thinking about yourself. Never mind me, what I'm going through.'

'You brought it on yourself,' her sister fumed, and sniffed, shaking her head. 'I don't know what Dan will say when he hears about your disgrace. Business people in our position can't have scandals in the family.'

'Dan? Shocked?' Esme gave a snigger that was near hysterical.

Mae glared at her. 'There's nothing remotely funny about the mess you've got yourself into,' she said angrily, and then gave Esme a long bewildered stare. 'I don't know how you could've gone with Percy Pryce, of all men,' she said, grimacing. 'He's no oil painting, is he?'

'Oh, and Dan is, of course,' Esme cried. 'He's good-looking so therefore he can do no wrong.'

'Don't you get uppity with me,' Mae flared quickly. 'After what you've done.' She threw up her hands. 'The disgrace! The gossip! You'll put me in an early grave, you will.'

'What's all the shouting about?' Dan asked, standing in the passage outside the door. 'We can hear you quarrelling upstairs.'

'Oh, no!' Mae scrambled off the bed and drew him into the room, closing the door. 'Dan, something terrible has happened. Esme has got herself in the family way.'

He started visibly, and swung round to look at Esme. She avoided his gaze and stared at the floor.

'Yes, you're shocked too, Dan love, and I'm not surprised,' Mae said. 'I can hardly look you in the eye. What must you think of her?'

'Who – who does she say the father is?'

'That scoundrel Percy Pryce,' Mae rushed on. 'Twice her age he is, the rotter!'

'He's only five years older than Dan,' Esme exclaimed, glaring at him.

He looked away quickly, and she had the urge to blurt out the truth, but Mae would never believe it, not now Esme had told her about marrying Percy.

'Led her astray, he did, the snake,' Mae went on. 'The man should be horsewhipped. I've a good mind to report him to the minister. Corrupting young girls! The likes of him should be driven out of the chapel, yes, out of Swansea, too.'

'Would you do that to every man who gets a girl into trouble or just to Percy?' Esme asked pithily, catching Dan's gaze. He cleared his throat loudly and stepped closer to Mae, putting an arm around her shoulders.

'Don't take on so, Mae love. It's not your fault.' He looked at Esme. It was a cold, merciless glance. 'Is Pryce prepared to make an honest woman of her?'

Esme gasped at his audacity, and hated him at that moment.

'Yes, thank heavens.' Mae looked suddenly sullen and vengeful. 'I wash my hands of it all,' she said. 'I won't be at the so-called wedding. In fact, as far as I'm concerned, I don't have a sister any more. Pack your things and get out, you little hussy!'

'Mae!' Esme was horrified at the sudden change in her sister's attitude. 'You can't throw me out of my own home!'

'If Da were here that's what he'd do,' Mae muttered with a toss of her head. 'He was right not to trust you with his money. And don't think you'll see a penny piece of it, because you won't!'

'You can't keep it from me, and besides, I – we – need the money even more now with a baby on the way.'

'I won't have a slut under my roof,' Mae shouted. 'Nor will I finance immoral behaviour.'

'Oh, if only you knew . . .' Esme began angrily.

'Your sister's right,' Dan exclaimed loudly, cutting across her words. 'It's best you leave straight away. This is a respectable boarding house. Mae's got her tenants to think of. Pryce got you into trouble, let him take responsibility for you now.'

'It's nothing to do with you,' Esme retorted angrily, and then was struck by the irony of her words. It had *everything* to do with him.

Mae pointed to the door. 'I want you out.' Her mouth was a hard line, her eyes cold. 'You won't sleep under this roof tonight or any other night.'

'I've fixed it,' Percy said later. 'Ma Griffiths next door has a spare room now her daughter is married. She'll put you up until the wedding, then we'll have our own place, away from here.' He touched Esme's wet cheek. 'Cheer up, girl,' he went on gently. 'Everything's going to be all right. You'll see.'

6

Eighteen Years Later – February 1920

Esme stood on the pavement looking up at the sign hanging high above the tall wrought-iron double gates to the yard in Brynmill: *Dan Henshaw, Coal Merchant.*

The main gates were padlocked, but a small side gate was standing ajar. Clutching her handbag tightly under her arm, she walked through into the yard. It was sizeable, with stables large enough for four horses or more to one side, and on the other sheds to house coal drays. Dan had done well for himself, but she wasn't surprised. She'd always known he was a go-getter, and at anyone else's expense but his own.

At the back of the yard was a two-storey brick building that obviously served as the business's offices. After a moment's hesitation, Esme pushed open the glass door and went in. A small thin man in a rumpled blue serge suit and wearing rimless spectacles on the end of his nose looked up.

'Yes,' he said enquiringly. 'Can I help you?'

'I want to speak to Mr Henshaw.'

The man sniffed as though annoyed. 'If it's about deliveries,' he said, 'I deal with them.'

'No,' Esme replied stiffly. 'It's a private matter.'

'Eh?' He squinted at her.

'I'm Mrs Pryce, Mr Henshaw's sister-in-law. Will you tell him I want to see him?'

He blinked then sniffed again. 'Yes, all right. Wait here.'

He disappeared through a door and silence reigned for a good ten minutes. It was probably a shock for Dan, her turning up like this after all these years. She wouldn't be surprised if he refused to see her.

Esme sat down to wait on a small bentwood chair, determined she wouldn't budge until she'd had her say. Meetings between Mae and her had been acrimonious and purely accidental over the last eighteen years. No, Dan would avoid seeing his sister-in-law if he could. The Henshaws had moved from the Hafod to Brynmill within a year or two of marriage. Esme had walked past the new house out of curiosity once, and been astonished at the swankiness of it. But then, that was Mae all over.

The thin man came back. 'Er, Mr Henshaw is busy just now . . .'

'You tell him I won't leave until he sees me,' Esme said loudly.

She wasn't surprised to see Dan appear from behind the door, as though he'd been standing there listening.

'Esme!' he said with forced joviality. 'Of course I'll see you. What a nice surprise. Come through to my office.'

Head held high, Esme preceded him through the door and down a passage to a room at the end. She went in and he closed the door behind them.

'What the hell are you doing here?' he snarled. 'What's your bloody game?'

Esme wasn't intimidated or impressed. She'd been expecting such an attitude. Without a word, she put her handbag on the desk nearby and took off her gloves. She was conscious of Dan's towering presence standing over her. With deliberate coolness she sat down on a chair in front of the desk and looked up at him.

'Why are you so hostile, Dan? Anyone would think you were afraid of me. Or perhaps it's your guilty conscience.'

'Don't beat about the bush,' he snapped. 'You want something. What is it?'

Taking her time, she looked him over. He was every inch the successful businessman, well dressed and well fed. And his looks had hardly changed in eighteen years. He was just as handsome as ever; just as attractive as when they had been lovers.

Esme felt an old desire stir and snake through her body. She was taken completely by surprise at the power of it. She'd thought she hated him for betraying her all those years ago, but she didn't, not really, not deep in her heart. Even though he'd hurt her as badly as a man can hurt a woman, she'd loved him. She loved him still.

Her heart whispered, Please forgive me, Percy.

Esme swallowed down her emotion. 'You know my husband was killed at the colliery?'

Dan nodded. 'Yes, we heard.'

There were no condolences, she noticed.

'Things will be tight from now on,' she said meaningfully.

'You haven't come here for a handout, have you?' he rasped. 'You're not still on about getting some of your father's money?'

'I've got more sense than to expect that,' Esme answered quickly. 'And I haven't come to quarrel either. But I do need help in another way.'

'You've got some neck, after what you did.'

Esme sprang to her feet. 'Don't you take that tone with me, Dan Henshaw! We're alone. You don't have to pretend. I only did what you wanted.'

'I didn't start it,' he snapped. 'You made all the running, as I remember.'

Esme resumed her seat again, smiling thinly. 'So, you do still remember?'

With an oath he walked around to his chair behind the desk, and sat down. 'What the hell do you want, Esme? I'm a busy man.'

'I've come about Beth. She's seventeen next month, if you recall.'

He frowned. 'Beth?'

'Your daughter,' Esme snapped. 'Don't pretend you've forgotten.'

He jumped to his feet.' Now, look here . . .'

'Beth *is* your daughter,' Esme said harshly. 'I know it, you know it, and it's about time Mae knew it.'

He stared at her for a moment, his gaze resting on her face, and Esme felt self-conscious. Time had left him mostly untouched, but what had it done to her? She was no longer the tender seventeen-year-old he'd held in his arms night after night. She had had a good husband in Percy, but life had not been easy for her. There had been no spare money for pampering herself. What did he see when he looked at her now? She had taken care of her figure, but were her eyes a little duller? Did her skin have a little less bloom?

'Mae wouldn't believe you,' he said tightly.

'I think she might – after your fling with Daphne Arnold as was.'

Dan's face paled.

'Oh, yes, I heard about it,' Esme went on briskly. 'I also heard Mae still hasn't forgiven you for that escapade. Separate rooms now, isn't it?'

'Damn you, Esme!'

Her face was grim. 'You did that eighteen years ago

when you ruined me, Dan Henshaw.' She stared at him reproachfully. 'You hurt me then, through and through.'

'You got over it,' he sneered. 'You married Pryce quick enough.'

'I had no choice,' she retorted bitterly. 'You seem to have a thing for young girls, Dan. Daphne was only a few months older than me, wasn't she?'

'She was twenty-four when I met her again, totally by accident,' he snapped. 'Hardly a young girl. And besides, she was married by then.'

Esme raised her brows. 'How convenient for you.' She gave a bitter little laugh. 'You make her marriage sound like an excuse.' She paused, studying him, wondering how far she could push him. 'Another little bird told me her husband was heartbroken when Daphne died in childbirth,' she went on. 'He blames you, Dan. It was your child, he says. You've made a powerful enemy in Jarvis Prosser-Evans. They say he's a man who holds a grudge for years.'

'I deny everything! I warn you, Esme, don't spread these malicious lies.'

'Yes, it must've been a double blow for Mae,' she persisted. 'What with your unfaithfulness *and* discovering the other woman was having your baby, while Mae's still childless after all these years. Imagine what she'd do if she knew about Beth?'

He glared at her for a long moment, but Esme held his gaze fearlessly.

'God, you've turned sour, Esme,' he said at last. 'You're positively gloating.'

Her mouth twisted. 'I've nothing much to gloat about, have I? I've lost a good husband in Percy. Worth twenty of you, he was.'

Yet even knowing Dan was untrustworthy, knowing

she'd married the better man, she still yearned for what they'd had together those long nights long ago.

'Who's been feeding you all this information about me?' he asked tetchily.

'I often bump into Mrs Kittle in Swansea Market, and Cissie Morgan's not as stupid as people suppose.'

'The Kittle woman hasn't worked for us in years,' he said. 'And thanks for warning me about Cissie. She'll get the push as soon as I see her.'

'I'm not concerned about them,' Esme said quickly, sitting on the edge of her chair. 'I'm only concerned about our daughter. You've got to take her in, Dan. It's only right that you be responsible for her. I can't afford to look after her now. It's your turn!'

'What are you talking about? I denied she was mine then and I deny it now.'

Esme ignored his words. They'd hurt her badly once, but not anymore. Percy was gone and she didn't care what happened now. In fact, truth to tell, she was ashamed that Dan could still start that tingle deep inside her. It felt like she was betraying Percy even having such thoughts.

'With Percy gone, there won't be enough coming in for the three of us to live on,' she said glumly. 'Gladys's boys have left home, so there'll be no money coming in from them. Beth's wage as an apprentice is a pittance. You have to take her, Dan. She's your daughter.'

'Don't be so bloody stupid,' he burst out. 'How can I do that?'

'I don't care whether Mae learns the truth or not,' Esme said angrily. 'I've looked after our daughter for seventeen years. Now it's your turn. Tell Mae it's an act of charity on your part, taking in her niece, if you like.'

'She won't wear it,' he said firmly. 'Your name is never spoken. She meant it when she said she had no sister.'

'Well, Dan, you'd better start using that legendary charm of yours and get her to change her mind,' Esme said pithily. 'It's that or else I tell her the truth. She's vengeful, is our Mae. After Daphne, Beth might be the last straw as far as her marriage is concerned. And didn't I also hear you've applied to be a magistrate?'

'You can't blackmail me like this . . .'

Esme stood, gathering her bag and gloves. 'You've got until a week on Friday,' she said. 'Beth will be packed and ready for you then. You can fetch her. I'm sure you know where I live. I expect to see you then.'

Dan sat staring at the closed door for a few minutes after Esme had gone. He had been angry and suspicious when she was announced, and rightly so. She was obviously determined to foist her daughter off on him.

His daughter too, though he would never admit it. Never.

Mae had finished their marriage, if it could be called a marriage, because of his fling with Daphne. If she discovered he had fathered a child with her sister, she would oust him from the business without a second thought. She might even sell him out to Jarvis Prosser-Evans. Esme was right, her sister was vengeful enough. And now Esme had him over a barrel, too.

With an oath he jumped up and went to the filing cabinet. From the top drawer he took a bottle of whisky and a tumbler. Taking them back to the desk, he poured himself two fingers of the liquid and slumped back on to his chair. How was he to square both women and get out of this unscathed?

He thought about his wife, and then started comparing the sisters. Despite his exercising all his charm, Mae had stubbornly refused to relinquish her controlling shares, even though the business was more than successful. Now she never would put him in control. He suspected she had never really loved him, not the way Esme had.

And there lay his way out perhaps. Esme was still susceptible to him, he would stake his life on it. He knew women, knew the look in their eyes when they loved or desired. He had been astonished to see that look in Esme's eyes a few minutes ago, even though she had tried to hide it.

He had felt a shock like a punch to the stomach finding himself face to face with her again. She was older, of course, but still lovely, still Esme, the woman he might have loved all those years ago had he allowed himself to succumb. But love had had no place in his plans. It only got in the way. That had been his philosophy, and it always would be.

But Esme still cared after all these years, after all that had happened, and he could use that to his advantage.

He threw the whisky into the back of his throat, the sting of it reviving him. He would see her again, work on her, win her over and prevent her from betraying him.

He stirred restlessly. In the meantime he had no choice but to take in Esme's daughter. He would play on Mae's pride; persuade her it was her Christian duty to help her destitute sister's child. Otherwise what would people think if she refused to help a grieving widow? Dan laughed quietly to himself at the irony of it all. Stake his life on Esme's love? He was staking his whole future.

Beth had cried all day at her mother's unfairness, feeling she was being cruelly punished for something she hadn't done. After dinner, her last in this house until she didn't know when, she sat on a low stool near the kitchen range, knees hunched up, head in hands. This was the second worst day of her life. First the shock of her father's death, and now her mother had turned against her for some reason Beth didn't understand. She glanced up and saw the battered suitcase Esme had placed at the side of Da's chair, and tears flooded again.

'Now stop that, Beth,' her mother said severely. 'Your nose will go all red and then your Aunt Mae will think you're ugly.'

'Mam, why must I go and live with strangers?' she whimpered miserably. 'I don't want to go. I don't want to leave you and Freddie.'

'They're not strangers,' Esme insisted, her lips thinning. 'They're your kith and kin, same as we are.'

'But they don't need me,' Beth said in a strangled voice, doing her utmost to stop the tears. 'You do. I'll work hard, Mam, harder than I've ever worked before, I'll get two jobs, a day and a night job. I don't need much sleep. You won't be sorry, Mam, I promise you.'

'Now don't start that again,' Esme snapped. 'You're going to Brynmill, and that's that.'

'You don't love me any more!' Beth cried out in a piercing wail. 'What did I do wrong?'

'Love?' Esme retorted. 'There's more to living than love, my girl. As I found out to my cost.'

'What do you mean?'

'Never you mind! I'm doing this for your own good, even if you don't realise it.'

'But, Mam . . .'

A brisk knock at the front door interrupted Beth's plea, and her heart stood still as she realised the caller must be her Uncle Dan, come to fetch her.

'That'll be your uncle now,' Esme said briskly, confirming her thoughts, and hurried down the passage to answer the door.

Beth's whole body stiffened as she waited for him to speak. She'd only seen her Uncle Dan once in her life before when her mother had pointed him out in the street in town. She'd wondered at the time why they hadn't gone over to speak to him. Years had passed before she'd understood a family rift prevented such contact, but nothing was ever explained. Why then was she now to live with her aunt and uncle? Had there been a reconciliation?

'Yes?' Beth heard her mother say in a sharp tone.

'Come for the girl, I have,' a man's gravelly voice answered. 'Is she ready? Haven't got all day, I haven't.'

'Who are you?' Esme asked testily. 'Where's Dan Henshaw?'

'Elias Morgan, I am. Drayman for Mr Henshaw,' the man said grumpily. 'And the boss don't waste his time fetching scullery maids, I can tell you. Now, is she ready?'

'I beg your pardon!' Esme sounded ready to explode.

'A scullery maid being fetched!' the man growled bad-temperedly. 'Never heard the like before.'

'I'll have you know my daughter's no scullery maid,' Esme thundered. 'Beth is Dan Henshaw's . . . niece.'

'Don't know nothing about that,' Elias Morgan rasped. 'All I know is my Cissie's been given the push up at the house so as your girl here can take her place.' He muttered something under his breath which sounded suspiciously like an oath. 'And I has to fetch her into the bargain. Makes the blood boil, it does.'

'I won't take any old buck from the likes of you,' Esme said in a dangerous voice. 'I'll complain to Mr Henshaw.'

Beth jumped up and hurried into the passage. A short stockily built man stood on the doorstep. He wore rough leather chaps tied with string at the knees over his trousers, and a loose leather tabard over a flannel shirt.

His strange flat hat was leather, too, with a flap at the back which covered his neck and reached his shoulders.

'Mam, what's going on? Where's Uncle Dan?'

'You may well ask,' Esme said pithily.

'Is this her?' Elias Morgan asked grouchily. 'Get a move on, gal. Where's your bits and pieces?'

Looking past him, Beth could see a horse and cart waiting by the pavement. There was a red-painted sign on it: *Dan Henshaw, Coal Merchant*.

'He's sent a coal dray to fetch me, Mam,' Beth said in dismay. 'I'll get my clothes all dirty with coal dust. I'm not going.'

'Go and get your case,' Esme commanded in a hard voice. 'And put your coat and hat on. There's a misunderstanding, that's all. Your Aunt Mae will sort it out.'

'But, Mam . . .' One look at Esme's face told Beth there was no point in arguing any longer. She was cast out, and there was no changing her mother's mind.

With drooping shoulders, Beth brought the case from the kitchen, and took down her coat and hat from the peg in the passage. Elias Morgan grabbed the case from her hand and scuttled off to the dray. Beth stood on the doorstep looking at her mother wistfully.

'When will I see you again, Mam?'

'Give yourself a few weeks to settle in,' Esme said. 'Then come round to tea one Saturday afternoon.' She took Beth's hand and squeezed it tight. 'I do love you, Beth, and I'm not throwing you off. This move is for your own good. It's been long overdue.'

'I don't understand?'

'You will in time. Now cut along. The drayman's on his seat already.'

Sitting high on the cart beside the drayman, Beth felt

the curious eyes of the whole neighbourhood were on her as the dray rumbled along Libanus Street towards the Carmarthen Road. She thought she might die of shame or grief. No matter what her mother said, she was being thrown off, and thrown amongst strangers, too.

Elias Morgan was giving her penetrating glances as he chivvied the horse along, and she turned her head to stare at him defiantly.

'What's so special about you as a scullery maid then?' he asked gruffly, looking her up and down. 'You don't look as though you're used to getting your hands dirty.'

'I'm *not* a scullery maid,' Beth snapped. 'I'm an apprentice seamstress with Lewis Lewis. I'll take up a position in their alteration department in time.' She lifted her chin proudly. 'My father paid for my apprenticeship.'

'Ummph!' Elias Morgan didn't seem impressed. 'Then why was my Cissie given the sack?' he asked querulously. 'Good girl, she is. Hard worker, too. Worked for the Henshaws best part of eighteen years, isn't it? And then they chucks her out.'

He turned an accusing glance on Beth.

'I'm sorry for that,' she said archly. 'But it's nothing to do with me.'

For a while she watched the rhythmic sway of the horse's rump as it clipped down Carmarthen Road towards the town's High Street. She didn't understand what was happening to her life, and wasn't used to encountering such hostility.

'I don't want to go to Brynmill to live, you know,' she said. 'I want to stay with my mother and little brother.' She put her gloved hand to her mouth to stifle a sob. 'We lost Dad recently, and now I've lost the rest of my family as well.'

'Here now! Don't be blubbering,' Elias said quickly,

and sniffed loudly. 'I suppose you can't be blamed for my Cissie losing her job.'

'And I don't understand why it's happened,' Beth said. '*I* won't be taking her place, I'm not going there to work. Mrs Henshaw is my auntie.'

'And all I know is, the boss told me to go up to Cwmbwrla and fetch their new scullery maid, that being you,' Elias said firmly.

Beth shook her head stubbornly. Like her mother had remarked, it was all a misunderstanding. Her Aunt Mae would sort it out.

'Look here, gal,' Elias said more kindly, 'here's a warning. Watch out for Whining Wilky. A dragon, she is, a proper Tartar. Made our Cissie cry more than once.'

Beth didn't like the sound of that. 'Who's she?'

'The Henshaws' cook and housekeeper,' he said shortly. 'Acts like Lady Muck in the kitchen, and narrow-minded as well. Always on the lookout for sin, she is. Even accused my poor Cissie, who's as pure as the driven snow.'

Beth was pensive. What kind of a household was she moving into, and what kind of a life could she expect? Well, if life proved unhappy at Brynmill, she'd run off home, back to her mother. Surely Esme wouldn't want to see her daughter unfairly treated?

Trotting along High Street, they passed the double-fronted expanse of the elegant department store of Lewis Lewis. Beth wished fervently she was in there now at her sewing machine, instead of on her way to strangers.

Where the High Street ran into Castle Street, Elias turned the horse's head right, down Goat Street, rumbling along narrow twisting streets, through the very heart of the bustling town, teeming with shoppers and traders, and then headed westwards towards St Helen's Road and on to Brynmill. It would be a long way to walk to her home in Cwmbwrla, but walk it she would if life at her aunt's didn't suit her.

They reached Brecon Parade at last, which proved to be a leafy suburban street of fairly new houses. The dray pulled up in front of tall double gates, painted bottle green. The roof and chimneys of a large detached house could be seen behind them.

Elias jumped down from his seat and helped Beth on to the pavement, handing her the suitcase.

'If I was you, gal,' he said, 'I'd go round to the back door.'

Beth compressed her lips. She'd do no such thing. She wouldn't be treated like a servant when she was one of the family.

'Thank you, Mr Morgan,' she said stiffly. 'I know my own business best.'

He shrugged and climbed back on to the dray, touching his strange leather cap. Then he flicked the reins and the dray horse reluctantly lifted its feathered feet and walked on.

Beth stood on the pavement watching the cart roll down the street for a moment, feeling suddenly very lonely and even afraid. Her mother should have come with her. Mae Henshaw was her sister, after all. Proper introductions should have been made. Then there would be no misunderstandings.

After a moment she plucked up courage and pushed open the gates so as to march resolutely to the front door. Lifting the highly polished brass doorknocker, she gave a sharp rat-tat-tat and then waited anxiously. Presently the door was opened and Beth stared into the pale-skinned face of a woman wearing a high-necked black dress with skirts that reached her instep. Was this her Aunt Mae? But she could see no family resemblance.

'Yes? What do you want?' the woman asked in a voice as dry as winter-wizened leaves. 'If you're selling pegs, you can go away.'

'I'm Beth Pryce,' she said, livid to be taken for a gypsy. 'My Aunt Mae's expecting me.'

The woman's nostrils flared. 'Pryce? The new scullery maid? Get around to the back immediately, my girl,' she said harshly. 'How dare you come to the front door?'

Before Beth could protest, the door was slammed in her face. She lifted a hand to pound the knocker again, but thought better of it. Judging by the woman's expression the door would not be opened a second time. Around the back the door was closed too and Beth knocked again, still seething at being treated in such a shabby way. The woman in black answered her knock eventually, after an unnecessary wait.

'I should think so too!' she snapped, and held the door wider. 'Well, come in then! Don't stand there gawping.'

Beth stepped past her into a big bright kitchen where everything looked new and shiny. There was no sign of anyone else and she wondered where her aunt might be. Surely she'd be ready to welcome her own niece?

Beth turned to the woman in black. 'Are you Wilky?'

The woman gave an astonished gasp, and then her lips thinned angrily. 'How dare you call me that? My name is Wilks – Mrs Wilks to you, and don't you forget it, you chit of a girl!'

'And I'm Mrs Henshaw's niece,' Beth retorted, trying to put a haughty ring in her voice though it didn't sound convincing. 'Where is my Aunt Mae? I expected her to welcome me.'

'Hoity-toity!' Mrs Wilks tossed her head. 'Madam doesn't wish to see you,' she said pithily. 'She's given me firm instructions about you. You take your orders from me, and you're to begin your duties immediately. Now get out of that coat and hat and put on an apron. There's work to do.'

'I will not!' Beth exclaimed, furious.

'You've got no choice if you want to eat,' Mrs Wilks snapped. 'And by the way, are you clean? I'll not have an unclean girl in my kitchen. Take off your gloves. Let me see your hands.'

Defiantly, Beth put both hands behind her back. 'Certainly not! This is my aunt's kitchen, not yours, and I'm family.'

Mrs Wilks's lips thinned. 'Oh, I see we have a right uppity one here.' She stared hard at Beth for a moment, as though weighing her up. 'I'll say this for Cissie Morgan,' she said at last, 'she's as thick as two short planks, but at least she knew her place and was spotless with it. You, my girl, need to be taught a lesson in humility.' Her eyes narrowed. 'I can see sin in your face. It's in the blood, I expect.'

Beth stared, gaping in outrage. 'How dare you speak to me like that?' she cried loudly. 'I'm from a respectable family.'

'Don't answer back!'

'I'll answer any way I like, you horrid creature!' Beth bellowed. This was worse than she'd expected. She glared at the older woman. 'You won't browbeat me like you did Cissie Morgan. I won't stand for it. I'll complain to my aunt.'

'What's all this disturbance?' a new voice asked.

Beth whirled round to look at the newcomer and gasped. Although taller in stature, the woman standing in the doorway was so like Esme to look at that Beth felt momentarily confused.

'It's this new scullery maid,' Mrs Wilks said quickly

before Beth could answer. 'Insolent and wilful she is. Totally unsuitable.'

'I'm Esme's girl,' Beth said haltingly, staring at her aunt's grim face.

'I can see that!' Mae Henshaw said sharply. 'Why are you making this vulgar rumpus in my kitchen?'

Beth flashed a glance at Mrs Wilks. 'This woman is very insulting and there's no cause for it. She's treating me like a servant, Aunt Mae.'

'Well, that's what you are in this house.'

'What?' Beth was flabbergasted.

Mae came further into the room. She wore a long hobble skirt in fine alpaca and a cream silk blouse. A string of pearls adorned her throat.

'And don't presume to call me Aunt Mae either,' she went on haughtily. 'I'm Mrs Henshaw to you, or Madam, although I hardly expect to have much contact with you. Mrs Wilks is in charge of servants.'

'My mother won't like me being treated so shabbily,' Beth protested. The wind had been taken completely out of her sails.

'What Esme likes or dislikes is neither here nor there,' Mae snapped. 'Beggars can't be choosers.' She threw up her hands suddenly. 'Destitution! I always knew it would come to this.'

'My mother's *not* destitute!' Beth exclaimed. 'With my father dying so suddenly she's just fallen on hard times, that's all. She thought you'd welcome your own niece, one of your family.'

'You're no family of mine. I disowned Esme years ago along with all her brood,' Mae snapped. 'So why would I welcome you? Why should I think you're any better, with Percy Pryce for a father?'

'Disowned?' Beth's head was spinning at her aunt's

words. And she didn't understand the implied insult to her father.

'Huh! So she hasn't told you,' Mae sneered. 'Ashamed, of course. So she should be. Pity she didn't feel shame before she got mixed up with that scoundrel Pryce.'

'How dare you speak of my late father like that?' Beth exploded. 'You didn't even know him.'

'Oh, yes, I did,' Mae contradicted. 'Big in the chapel he was, the hypocrite! Lured our Esme into loose ways.'

'You're mad, saying such things!' Beth cried, aware of Mrs Wilks standing by listening with a mocking smile on her thin lips.

'Your mother disgraced herself,' Mae said tightly. 'Percy Pryce was to blame. He put her in the family way, and had to marry her. I washed my hands of such immorality.'

Beth looked around to see where she had dropped her suitcase.

'I'm not staying here to listen to this,' she said, holding back tears of humiliation and anger. 'You're a wicked, lying woman!' she burst out. 'It's a wonder God doesn't strike you dead.'

'Oh!' Mae took a step back, shocked, and then recovered. 'Yes, go!' she retorted. 'I didn't want you here in the first place, not even as a scullery maid. It was my husband who persuaded me. He thought we should give my sister a helping hand. I knew it was a mistake.' She paused, tightly clasping her hands together. 'Dan's too kind-hearted for his own good.'

Beth caught a look of utter surprise on Mrs Wilks's face as she glanced at Mae Henshaw, and wondered at it, but she was too keen to get out of the house to care.

'Then I pity him, married to you,' Beth cried furiously.

Enraged, Mae lifted a shaking finger and pointed at the back door. 'There's the door. Get out!'

'Oh, I'm going, don't worry,' Beth yelled in fury. 'But not by the back way. I won't be treated like rubbish. I'll leave through the front door.'

With that she darted towards the open kitchen door, which she hoped led to the main part of the house. Mae threw her arms up, trying to prevent her from passing, but Beth was too nimble for her.

She rushed through the doorway and into a short passage, her aunt and Mrs Wilks hot on her heels, both screaming at the tops of their voices for her to stop, but Beth was determined no one would thwart her from making this gesture. She flung open the door at the end of the passage and found herself in the hall.

'Stop!' Mae shouted. 'Stop at once.'

The heels of her shoes clipping loudly on the parquet flooring, Beth didn't hesitate but rushed towards the front entrance. Suddenly a dark shape appeared on the other side of the leaded glass of the door. The next moment it swung open and a tall dark-haired man strode in, an astonished expression on his face.

'What the hell is going on, Mae?' he asked irritably. 'What's all this shouting? It sounds like a lot of fishwives.'

Panting with exertion, Beth came to a skidding halt before him. 'Are you my Uncle Dan?' she asked breathlessly.

Dan Henshaw stared at her, his face suddenly turning pale. Beth was puzzled at his reaction, but had no time to ponder as both her aunt and the housekeeper gabbled at him.

'She's a wilful little hussy,' Mrs Wilks was saying loudly. 'Disruptive, that's what she is, sir. I won't have her in my kitchen.'

'I knew it wouldn't work, Dan,' Mae said, twisting her hands. 'Like father, like daughter. She's a bad lot, young as she is. You should've heard the things she said to me. Disgraceful!'

'I will not be made a servant,' Beth exclaimed heatedly. 'My mother expected you take me in as one of the family. I'd have paid towards my keep, of course. I'm an apprentice seamstress in Lewis Lewis.'

Dan Henshaw lifted a hand. 'One at a time! One at a time!'

'I'm going home,' Beth said emphatically. 'When my mother hears about this she won't be pleased, I can tell you.'

'Now just a minute,' Dan said hastily. 'No one's going anywhere until I've sorted this out. And the hall isn't the place for loud discussion. Come into the sitting room, and talk like civilised people.'

Mae looked rebelliously at her husband, though Mrs Wilks's eyes were bright with interest. Beth hung back, too. It was a long walk home and she wanted to start. This had been a complete waste of time, and she'd already lost a half-day's pay.

Dan gestured towards the door, his expression determined. 'If you please!'

Head high Mae stalked forward, and reluctantly Beth followed her. Mrs Wilks also moved forward but a glance from Dan stopped her in her tracks.

'That will be all, Mrs Wilks, thank you,' he said firmly.

The housekeeper's face was a picture of frustration, lips pinched in fury as she turned on her heel to go back to the kitchen.

The sitting room was over-furnished with chintz-covered sofas and walnut china cabinets crammed with ornaments. There was even a grand piano standing before a large bay window, its top covered by a green chenille cloth. Beth stared at it, fascinated, for a moment.

No one she knew had a piano, and the one in the chapel hall tinkled as though it had never been tuned.

'Let's all sit down,' Dan suggested in a tone that brooked no argument.

Beth waited uncertainly until Mae was seated, then perched herself on the nearest chair. Dan stood with his back to the fireplace. Now she was calmer, Beth could take a longer look at him. Dan Henshaw was quite handsome, tall, well-built and distinguished-looking, with that touch of silver at his temples.

'Now,' he said, 'what's the problem?'

Beth and her aunt both spoke at once. He held up a hand again, irritation in his expression, and nodded at his wife.

Mae's lips were a tight line. 'I never wanted her here, Dan, as well you know. She's not deserving of our help. She's impertinent and quite unruly. I did warn you, didn't I? A family like that!'

'You leave my family alone,' Beth stormed, rising to her feet. 'I don't know who you think you are, but my mother's worth twenty of you, for all your swank.'

'Oh! The cheek of her!'

'Now that's enough . . . er . . . Beth,' Dan said. 'Your Aunt Mae doesn't deserve to be spoken to like that.'

'Oh, and I suppose *I* deserve to be treated like a servant, do I?' Beth yelled.

'Don't raise your voice to me, my girl,' he said curtly. 'Remember who and where you are.'

'What does that mean?'

'It means, you'll behave yourself while under my roof.'

'I'm not staying here,' she said emphatically, and reached down for her suitcase again. 'I'm off!'

'Now wait a minute, Beth,' Dan said quickly. 'We're doing this for your mother's sake.'

Beth paused in her flight, her attention arrested by his tone.

'You can't expect to live here scot-free,' he went on in a more reasonable tone. 'Any housework you did would be in lieu of your keep.'

She lifted her chin. 'I'm not afraid of work,' she said proudly. 'And I was willing to do my share and pitch in with part of my wages, but I won't be labelled a scullery maid. I'm a seamstress. That's my trade, and I intend to carry on with my apprenticeship.'

'That's out of the question!' Mae exclaimed loudly. 'There's too much daily work to do, dusting and polishing, and Mrs Wilks needs help in the kitchen.'

'Then you shouldn't have sacked Cissie Morgan, should you?' Beth snapped. 'Trying to do things on the cheap for all your money.'

'Be quiet, both of you,' Dan thundered. 'We must come to some arrangement, for Esme's sake. After all, Mae, your sister has lost her breadwinner. We have to be charitable, and leave the past buried.'

'Yes, you'd like that, Dan, wouldn't you?' she said pithily.

For some reason his face turned dark red and he looked furious for a moment. Beth stared from one to the other, completely at a loss. Something told her things were not completely right between them.

'We're not talking about me,' he retorted stiffly. 'This is about your own sister. After all, she is your flesh and blood, Mae. Isn't it your Christian duty to help those less fortunate?' His mouth twisted mockingly. 'After all, you're always throwing it in my face how pure and blameless you are.'

Mae lifted her chin but remained silent, her expression closed.

Dan turned to Beth and spoke in an almost pleading tone, she thought. 'I think you should stay, for your mother's sake.'

'I'll not give up my apprenticeship, no matter what *she* says,' Beth insisted, indicating her aunt, sitting bolt upright, her back rigid as a martyr's. 'My father worked hard to find the money for my training. It would be wrong and stupid to throw that away. Besides, I love my work.'

'Very well.' Dan nodded. 'You may continue your training.'

'But, Dan . . .' Mae started. He cut her short.

'But you must do your share of housework or whatever is needed,' he went on. 'Your wage isn't enough to cover the expense of your keep. I'm sure your Aunt Mae can assign you some tasks.'

'I certainly can!' Mae exclaimed, glaring at Beth resentfully. 'Before you leave for work each day you'll spend an hour cleaning, and that's final. Sunday mornings you'll attend church with the rest of the household.'

'I'm chapel!'

'Business people and their servants go to church, so you're church from now on,' Mae said firmly. 'And you'll help Mrs Wilks in the kitchen every evening. I won't have you idling away your time. There'll be no opportunity for mischief. I'll see to that.'

'What about time off?' Beth asked stubbornly. 'Even convicts get shortened sentences for good behaviour.'

'Be quiet! Keep a civil tongue in your head, my girl,' Mae stormed.

'I think Cissie Morgan should get her job back,' Beth said, ignoring her aunt's outburst. She'd already made her mind up that if she did stay she wouldn't hesitate to speak her mind whenever it was necessary. 'Her father told me she was unfairly dismissed.'

'Cissie was sacked because she was disloyal and spread malicious gossip about her employers,' Dan retorted heavily. 'She had her chance.'

Beth stood up. 'Very well, Uncle Dan, I'll stay on those terms, for my mother's sake only. If it weren't for her I wouldn't stay another minute under the same roof as my aunt.'

Mae made a sound of derision, and Beth's hackles rose again.

'My family and I have nothing to be ashamed of,' she said forcefully. 'Percy Pryce was a wonderful father, the salt of the earth. I won't have a word said against him, do you hear me?'

Mae muttered something under her breath, which made Beth even more furious. 'If there's any malicious gossip about, it's your doing, Aunt Mae,' she exclaimed hotly, lifting her chin. 'And another thing – neither you nor Mrs Wilks had better try bullying me because I won't put up with it!'

Mae stood up suddenly. 'This is going to end badly,' she said loudly. 'Mark my words, Dan, we'll come to regret the day this girl ever entered our house.'

'Why are you so jealous of my mother?' Beth snapped. 'Is it because she has children and you haven't?'

Mae stared at her, stricken, and Beth was immediately sorry for her words.

'Aunt Mae, I'm sorry!' She put out a hand towards her aunt but Mae recoiled from the touch.

'Keep away from me! You're your mother's child, all right,' she hissed. 'And with a poisoned tongue, too. But you'll pay the price, just like your mother did. A fallen woman!'

7

It was almost a month before Beth was allowed a Saturday afternoon off to visit her mother, which happened to be her seventeenth birthday. Esme had written to her over the weeks, and with each one she received, Beth hoped her mother would beg her to return, but her expectations were always dashed. However, she had high hopes of this visit.

She was quite prepared to walk to Cwmbwrla and back, but Uncle Dan insisted that Elias Morgan should take and fetch her on the cart. Pride and common sense warred in Beth over this. To arrive in Libanus Street on a coal cart was the worst indignity, but time free to see her mother was too precious to spend tramping the streets.

'Stop by here,' Beth commanded Elias as they neared the turning into Libanus Street. 'I'll walk the rest of the way. And you can pick me up at this spot at five o'clock.'

As she opened the door of her old home and walked down the passage Beth was filled with an emotion so strong she wanted to burst into tears. Oh, it was so good to be home again. She wished fervently that she need never leave.

Esme and Freddie were in the kitchen when she arrived. He sprang up and threw himself at her, chattering excitedly. Beth gave him the penny bag of sweets she'd brought him, then hugged him tightly, struggling not to start blubbering.

Esme came forward and kissed and embraced her warmly. 'Happy Birthday, love. And how are you, Beth, my dear girl?'

'I'm well, Mam, but how are you?' Beth looked anxiously into her mother's face. She was thinner, and there was a strained look around her eyes. 'How have you been coping without – without Dad?'

'It's been hard, love,' Esme said sadly. 'Percy was my friend as well as my husband, and I can't tell you how much I miss him.'

She drew Beth towards the range. 'Take your coat and hat off. There's a pot of tea just brewing and a fresh batch of Welsh cakes.'

Beth sat on her favourite stool and drank the hot tea, with Esme in the wooden chair opposite and Freddie squatting on the mat at her feet, never taking his large soulful eyes from her face. She'd always enjoyed family natters around the fire when she'd come home from work in the old days, and now these moments were precious indeed.

'How is Mae?' Esme asked. 'Does she ever mention me?' There was a wistfulness in her mother's tone which made Beth's heart ache with pity, so how could she tell her the truth?

'There's lovely these Welsh cakes are, Mam,' she said evasively. 'I've missed your cooking.'

Esme raised her brows. 'Mae was always a better cook than I was.'

Beth was scornful. 'My aunt doesn't cook any more or lift a duster. Far too posh for that. She has Mrs Wilks to cook for her. A proper sourpuss she is, too. Her cooking isn't a patch on yours, Mam.'

'Lovely house, is it, inside?' Esme asked, her eyes full of curiosity. 'Looks proper swish from the road.'

'Oh, yes, it's swish all right!' Beth said. She almost remarked that it was she who kept it shining, too, but decided it was too risky admitting how disdainfully she was treated in the house on Brecon Parade. 'She's even got a grand piano,' Beth went on hurriedly, wanting to gloss over her new life.

'Tsk!' Esme tipped her chin in contempt. 'Mae was always one for putting on the style, and now she's got all the money in the world to do it.'

Beth was thoughtful. 'I don't think she's happy, though, Mam,' she said. 'There's something not quite right between her and Uncle Dan.'

'Another cup of tea, Beth love?' her mother asked quickly, jumping up to lift the teapot from the hob.

'Have you found work, Mam?' she asked when her cup was filled.

'Yes, I'm cleaning and cooking daily for a lady in Sketty.'

'That's an awful long way to go,' Beth said. 'How do you get there?'

'Shanks's pony, love,' Esme said. 'She pays very well, see, and they're nice people, not stuck up, like.'

'What about Freddie?' Beth asked, filled with doubt. 'You must be on the road half the day. Who takes care of him?'

'Mrs Pickering has been very kind,' Esme said. 'She gives him his tea, and he stays next door until I come home.'

'Mam,' Beth began hesitantly, 'I ought to be here with you to look after him. We'd manage all right, I know we would.'

'No!' her mother said emphatically. 'Your place is in Brynmill.'

'My place?' Beth was suddenly angry. 'I'm no more

than a servant to my Aunt Mae,' she blurted. 'She despises me. She despises us all, Mam, and I don't understand it.'

Esme glanced away.

'Mam?'

'One day you'll understand,' Esme said quietly.

'I want to understand now.' She still could not bring herself to repeat the disgraceful things Mae had said about her sister. Beth was all too afraid they might be true and she couldn't face that, yet she resented being kept in the dark. 'Don't treat me like a child, Mam.'

'Well, for one thing,' Esme blurted, 'Mae deliberately kept my share of our father's inheritance from me. She's swanking it on *my* money – well, half of it's mine anyway. I'll never benefit now, but you might.'

'Grandad Parkyn has been gone well over twenty years,' Beth said, astounded. 'It's a bit late to be squabbling over his will.'

'Money isn't the only reason why you belong at Brecon Parade . . .' Esme hesitated, looking uncomfortable for a moment, and then she frowned in annoyance. 'I'm your mother and I don't have to explain myself to you, Beth,' she said tersely. 'You'll do as you're told, understand me?'

Not wanting to quarrel with her mother, especially on her birthday, Beth quickly changed the subject and all too soon it was nearing five o'clock. She kissed Freddie, promising him more sweets next time she came, although she didn't know when that would be.

'I don't know when I'll see you again, Mam,' she said, forcing down her emotion. 'Aunt Mae is very demanding, and very mean about giving me time off.'

'Come when you can, Beth.' Esme grasped her hand. 'I'm sorry I was harsh with you, love, and on your birthday, too, but I want justice for you.'

'Justice, Mam? What a funny thing to say.'

★

April was almost over before Beth was able to get time off again. She didn't wait to be taken to Cwmbwrla but set off walking before her Uncle Dan could suggest the cart, even though she knew there'd be less time to spend with her family this way.

She was walking up the Carmarthen Road, just half a mile from Cwmbwrla, when she spotted a familiar horse and gig trotting in the direction of town, Uncle Dan at the reins. She was about to raise her arm to wave as he passed, but a sudden thought prevented her from showing herself. It seemed unlikely her uncle was on business on a Saturday afternoon, so what was he doing in this neighbourhood?

Reaching her mother's house on Libanus Street, Beth pushed open the door and hurried down the passage to the kitchen. Esme was alone, looking in the mirror over the range, and was just twisting her long hair into a bun at the nape of her neck, fixing it with hairpins.

'Hello, Mam.'

Esme spun around, startled, her eyes wide, and for a moment Beth thought she looked frightened of something. 'Where did you spring from?' she asked abruptly. 'How long have you been tiptoeing around?'

Beth was taken aback, feeling her mother was almost accusing her of underhanded behaviour. It wasn't much of a greeting after they'd not seen each other for weeks.

'Walked I have from Brynmill,' she said, feeling sharp disappointment. 'Are you going out somewhere?'

'What makes you ask that?' Her mother's tone was still prickly.

'You don't usually redo your hair at this time of day.'

For some reason Esme looked flustered. 'It was untidy, that's all,' she said somewhat defensively.

'Where's Freddie?'

'With Mrs Pickering,' her mother said, reaching for the kettle and taking it to the tap to fill with water. 'She looked after him while I had an afternoon nap.'

So that's why her hair was untidy, Beth thought. Why didn't she say so? Her mother wasn't normally one for afternoon naps, though she did look tired and strained. Beth suspected her job was too much for her.

'I'll slip next door for Freddie,' Beth said. 'I'm longing to see him. How is he, Mam? He must get lonely for you, poor little chap.'

'Don't say that!' Esme exclaimed sharply. 'It's not my fault things are the way they are. We have to live, Beth, and I have to take whatever work I can find, no matter how inconvenient it is.'

She shook her head, frowning. 'I wasn't blaming you, Mam. I only wish there was some way I could make things easier for you.'

'I'll manage. You stay here,' Esme went on. 'I'll go next door and fetch Freddie myself.'

When he came dashing in Beth handed him the bag of sweets she had promised him and a toffee apple which she had bought in the market as she passed through the town. He beamed at her, his little face lighting up. At least her young brother was happy to see her.

'There's lovely to see you, Beth,' he chortled as he squatted at her feet near the fire. 'I've grown a whole inch since last time you was here. My pal Willy Williams is shorter than me now. He had a football for his birthday, and he lets me have a turn with it.'

He looked happy enough, Beth thought, but her heart ached because he was growing up and she was missing it all.

'So you had to walk here, did you?' Esme asked as she

handed her daughter tea and a slab of rich fruitcake.

'I don't mind,' Beth said, taking a fair-sized bite from the cake and munching happily. Swallowing, she went on, 'Funny thing, though, I saw my Uncle Dan on Carmarthen Road just now, no more than five minutes away from by here. I wonder what he was doing around these parts? I wish I'd known he was coming this way, I wouldn't say no to a ride in that new gig of his.'

Esme was silent and Beth looked up at her mother quizzically. 'Uncle Dan didn't call on you, Mam, did he?'

'Heavens above!' Esme snapped, and looked exasperated. 'Why are you questioning me like this? How should I know the comings and goings of Dan Henshaw?'

Beth bit her lip in chagrin. It seemed she couldn't visit her mother these days without falling out with her. They'd been so easy in each other's company before she left home; now she felt a strange tension between them. She almost suspected she wasn't welcome any longer. But why?

Beth played with Freddie for a while until her mother's mood finally mellowed, and then she was glad to talk about ordinary things and hear the local gossip.

'Maudie Pickering engaged to be married?' Beth exclaimed, when her mother gave her the news. 'Well, well. Haydn would be disappointed to hear that. Have the boys written?'

'I did have a letter from him a couple of weeks ago,' Esme admitted. 'They're doing all right apparently, although they've parted company. Gwyn's working in London now. I knew they'd fall on their feet. Haydn hinted he'd like to come home, but I won't be made into a doormat again.'

'Haydn wasn't like that, Mam,' Beth said. 'I'd like to see him again. He's not like Gwyn, I'm very fond of Haydn.'

She pictured his face for a moment and felt a warm glow. She wished he was here now. If he were, she knew that everything would be all right again.

Esme glanced at the clock on the mantelpiece. 'You'd better be starting back,' she said. 'You've got a long walk ahead of you, and it still gets dark early these April nights.'

Reluctantly Beth put on her coat and hat. She hugged Freddie and then embraced her mother warmly, kissing her cheek.

'I'll try and squeeze another half-day out of Aunt Mae soon,' she promised. 'Although I can't say when it will be.'

'No,' her mother said quickly. 'I'd rather you didn't visit on spec. I might be at work, and you'd have a wasted journey. I'll write and let you know when you can come again, give you a specific day, then Mae can't quibble about it.'

Beth stared at her mother, not understanding the expression on her face. 'Don't keep me at arm's length, Mam. I don't deserve it. Don't shut me out of my own home.'

'You don't live here any longer, Beth,' her mother said firmly. 'We each have our own lives to lead now. You're very welcome here, of course you are, but I will have things my way from now on. For too long I've given in to the needs of others. Now it's my turn.'

Beth left Libanus Street to start on her long walk, feeling very miserable. There was no comfort or happiness in her life at all, and from where she stood the future seemed very bleak indeed.

Beth was glossing a dry mop over the parquet flooring in the hall early one morning in June when the postman arrived. She eagerly watched his shadow through the leaded glass as he shoved some envelopes in, and dashed forward to inspect them. Shuffling them quickly, she saw there was nothing for her. This was the fourth week without a letter from her mother and her spirits fell. Today was her afternoon off and she'd hoped to spend it in her own home.

Suddenly she felt rebellious. It was too bad that she had to wait for an invitation to visit the house where she was born. Mam was taking things too far. And how could she forget to write to her only daughter?

She would go, she decided, despite her mother's instructions. In fact, she'd go straight from leaving the sewing rooms at Lewis Lewis at midday. Surely Mam would give her a little bit of dinner.

'What are you sauntering about by here for?' Mrs Wilks asked sharply as she came through the door from the kitchen. 'The table hasn't been laid for breakfast yet. Mr Henshaw will be down in a minute. Come on! Get a move on, my girl. I'd have jumped over your head at your age.'

'I'm going as fast as I can,' Beth retorted, furious.

'No backchat! And what are you doing with those letters? Give them here, you nosy little madam!'

The bundle of letters was snatched from her fingers.

'There might've been one for me,' Beth said in self-defence.

'Letters? Huh! You get too much leniency, you do, my girl,' Mrs Wilks opined, with a shake of her head. 'Given an inch, you take a yard.'

With breakfast over, at least for Uncle Dan who had already gone off to business, Beth washed up quickly. It was getting close to half-past eight and Elias Morgan would be waiting on the road outside to give her a lift into town. She was just about to get her coat and hat when there was a knock at the back door. She opened it, half expecting to see Elias. Instead a woman stood on the step, and for a moment Beth didn't recognise her.

'Oh, Beth *cariad*, there's glad I am to catch you,' the woman said breathlessly.

Beth blinked, bewildered. 'Mrs Pickering! What on earth are you doing here?'

'I've come with bad news, *bach*. Can I come in?'

Her heart jumping into her mouth with fright, Beth stood aside hastily as Mrs Pickering stepped over the threshold.

'Oh, can I sit down, Beth?' her old neighbour panted. 'I've walked all the way from Cwmbwrla and I'm done in, kid.'

Beth pulled out a kitchen chair for her, her heart racing.

'What is it, Mrs Pickering?' she asked, a tremor in her voice. 'Is it my mam? Has something happened to her?'

'Yes and no, like,' Mrs Pickering said, catching her breath. 'I don't know how to tell you, *bach*. It's little Freddie . . .'

'What?'

'He was taken bad a couple of nights ago. Your mother was working down at Sketty, cooking for a dinner party.' Mrs Pickering shook her head as though someone was blaming her. 'I didn't know what to do. When your mother came home he was right poorly. The panel doctor wanted him to go into hospital, but your mother wouldn't have it.' Mrs Pickering paused, putting a gloved hand to her mouth, and a sob escaped her. 'Oh, Beth *cariad*, Freddie died in the early hours of this morning. Brain fever. Your mother's beside herself.'

Beth stood as if turned to stone, locked in silence, unable to move a muscle. She stared at Mrs Pickering, watched her lips move, but could hear nothing. A vivid image of little Freddie's face, his eyes pleading with her to play with him, filled her mind. Her brother dead? It wasn't possible. First her father and now this, how would she bear it? And her mother – she must be out of her mind with grief and perhaps guilt.

Beth snapped out of her trance. She must go home at once.

'Mrs Gibbs is with her,' Mrs Pickering was saying. ' "Watch her like a hawk," I told her. "She's upset enough to do anything." '

Beth snatched off her apron and dashed for her coat and hat, struggling into them.

'What's going on here?' Mrs Wilks demanded as she came into the kitchen. She took one look at Mrs Pickering and the corners of her mouth turned down with anger. 'Who gave you permission to have callers? How dare you take liberties!'

'There's a family bereavement!' Mrs Pickering exclaimed, offended, and stood up. 'Have a bit of respect, whoever you are.'

'I'm going home,' Beth said, her voice quavering. 'Tell Aunt Mae my little brother Freddie has died suddenly. I must be with my mother.'

Mrs Wilks's cheeks puffed out in indignation. 'You can't just walk out like that, my girl. You've got work to do here.'

Beth's grief flared into anger. 'And who's going to stop me?' she yelled. 'Not you, you dried up scraggy cat! My brother's dead! Have you no feelings?'

With that she grabbed Mrs Pickering's arm and bustled her through the back door. They hurried around to the front. Beth prayed Elias Morgan was still waiting for her. She needed to get to her mother as quickly as possible.

Bursting through the green double gates, she was relieved to see the coal dray still there and Elias waving irritably.

'Come on, mun,' he shouted. 'Get a move on, will you?'

'I'm not going to work,' Beth panted as both she and Mrs Pickering clambered on to the seat while Elias stared. 'Take us to Libanus Street.'

'Well now, I dunno about that . . .' he began uncertainly, but Beth interrupted quickly.

'There's been a death at home, Mr Morgan,' she said, her lips trembling as she fought not to break down. She had to stay strong for her mother's sake.

'Oh!' he said, shaking his head. 'Oh! There's sorry I am.'

The dray made good time, Elias pushing the horse harder than usual. As they neared her home, Beth began to tremble uncontrollably, dreading what lay ahead of her. Death seemed to be stalking the house in Libanus Street and she feared for her mother, too.

'Thank you, Mr Morgan,' Beth said simply as she helped Mrs Pickering from the dray. 'I'm very grateful for your kindness and understanding.'

'If there's anything I can do . . .' he began.

'There's kind of you, but we'll manage somehow.'

The kitchen was ominously empty when Beth ran in. 'Mam!' she screeched, suddenly terrified not to see her mother there.

'Hush, mun!' Mrs Gibbs came out of the scullery, tea towel in hand. 'Upstairs she is, *bach*. Just dozed off,' she continued in a hoarse whisper. 'Put a drop of gin in her tea, I did. So out of her mind she was, she didn't notice the taste.'

'How is she?' Beth snatched off her hat and shrugged out of her coat.

Mrs Gibbs shook her head, looking gloomy. 'In a rare old state, weeping and talking wild, she was. Poor dab! It makes your heart bleed, mind. Losing her husband and now her son. I'd be up the loony asylum if it was me, I can tell you.'

'Go up and see her, I will,' Beth said, swallowing hard.

'Don't wake her, *cariad*,' Mrs Pickering put in quickly. 'She can't feel the pain when she's asleep.'

On the small square of landing at the top of the stairs, Beth looked sadly at the closed back bedroom door, the room she'd shared with Freddie for most of his life. What she wouldn't give to see his little face peeping at her from around the door, and hear his piping laugh. She couldn't believe she'd never see him again.

In the front bedroom Esme was prone on the bed, her wool dressing gown thrown over her. Beth brought the dressing-table stool nearer the bed and sat, gazing wistfully at her mother. Her face was so white and drawn even in sleep, Beth shivered involuntarily, feeling she was looking at a dead woman. She reached out a hand to wake Esme, needing the reassurance of seeing her eyes open, hearing her voice, but stayed her impulse. Esme had already suffered so much, and there'd be more to come. It would take her a long time to get over losing Freddie, if she ever did.

Beth stayed at the bedside unaware of time passing, feeling her own pain at the loss of her brother. Her world was disintegrating around her and she could do nothing to prevent it.

After about an hour Esme stirred and opened her eyes. She stared blankly for a moment, and then her gaze fell on Beth's face.

'Oh, Beth love!' It was a cry of sheer pain, and Esme tried to rise from the bed. 'I haven't been asleep, have I?

Oh, God! How could I sleep with my poor baby lying dead somewhere? Oh, Beth, I'm a wicked woman . . .'

'Hush, Mam. Stay where you are,' Beth said gently, pushing her back on to the pillows. 'You needed that sleep. Exhausted, you were. Now I'm here to look after you.'

'Freddie's gone, Beth,' Esme whispered hoarsely. 'First my husband and now my son. It's God's punishment for my wickedness. I've brought it on myself.'

'Mam!' Beth was distressed. 'What are you talking about? You're not wicked, don't say such things. Of course it's not your fault.'

Esme grasped her hand. 'I *am* a wicked woman. You don't know, you're so innocent, Beth. If you did know . . . Oh, God! What am I to do?'

'Mam, I *do* know,' Beth said quickly, then swallowed hard. She hadn't meant ever to speak of the things her aunt had said, but seeing her mother's obvious distress now she wondered if there was some truth in them. If so Esme needed reassurance that her human weakness in the past had nothing to do with her present misery.

'Aunt Mae told me you had to get married when you were expecting me.' She shook her head. 'It's not so terrible, Mam. Dad married you because he loved you. You weren't the first to make a mistake, and you wouldn't be the last. Besides, it was years ago. Put it out of your head now, and rest.'

Esme's grasp on her hand tightened. 'There's something else, *cariad*,' she whispered. 'I must tell you. I need to tell you before it's too late. It's about your father . . .'

There was a tap at the door and before Beth could move, Mrs Pickering put her head around it.

'There's a man downstairs,' she said. 'Says he's a relative. Mr Henshaw.'

'Uncle Dan!' Beth was astounded, wondering if her aunt was there too.

Esme gave a loud moan. 'I don't want to see him,' she whimpered. 'Tell him to go away. Tell him I never want to see him again.'

'We can't do that, Mam,' Beth said. 'It was good of him to call.' She turned to Mrs Pickering. 'I'll come down. Could you stay by here while I speak to my uncle?'

'I'll watch her, love.' She looked down at Esme pityingly. 'Poor dab!'

Beth hurried downstairs. Dan Henshaw stood in the living room, hat in hand. Somehow he looked out of place in his expensive three-piece suit amid their clean but well-worn furnishings.

'Thank you for coming, Uncle Dan,' Beth began. She looked around. 'Aunt Mae isn't with you?'

'No, she couldn't come.'

'Wouldn't come, you mean,' Beth said sharply. 'How hard she is. Her own sister is in bad trouble, and she's too mean to offer her condolences.'

He frowned. 'That's no concern of yours or mine, Beth,' he said. 'Their differences go back years, and I haven't come here today to discuss them.'

'I'm sorry,' Beth said, relenting. She had no right to blame him for her aunt's callousness.

'I have come to offer any help I can,' he went on. 'I know your mother is in straitened circumstances, and I understand she's distraught. Let me assume the burden of making all the arrangements for the funeral.'

'That's good of you, Uncle Dan.' Beth was more than grateful. His unexpected kindness brought tears to her eyes, but she wiped them away with cold fingertips.

Dan shifted uncomfortably on his feet, obviously embarrassed by her open grief.

'I . . . er . . . I'll pay all expenses, too,' he said. 'It's the least I can do.'

'We don't need your money, Dan Henshaw,' Esme cried loudly from the doorway, with Mrs Pickering peering in over her shoulder at them.

'Mam!' Beth was stunned at the outburst and ran to her mother's side, putting an arm around her shoulders. 'You're not well.' She turned back to their visitor. 'Forgive her, Uncle Dan. She doesn't know what she's saying.'

'Oh, yes, I do.' Esme shrugged Beth's arm away. 'Why have you really come, Dan? You shouldn't be here . . . I don't want you here!'

'Esme, please!' he said. He looked genuinely distressed. 'I'm family. I want to help you.'

'No one can help me now. My son is dead!' Esme tottered and Beth caught at her again, holding her firm. 'God has taken my son in retribution for my sinfulness,' she whispered hoarsely. 'Oh, why have I been so weak and foolish?'

Mrs Pickering gave a shocked gasp. Beth had forgotten she was there.

'Thanks, Mrs Pickering,' she said pointedly. 'I can manage my mother now. You ought to be getting off home.'

Mrs Pickering gave a faint smile, then after giving Esme a pitying stare, shook her head and stalked off towards the front door.

'What are you waiting for?' Esme asked, staring at Dan. 'Go now.'

'Mam!'

'It's all right,' he said calmly. 'I'll go, but what I said stands. Leave the funeral to me.'

'I'm staying with my mother from now on,' Beth told

him. 'She needs me. I'll collect my bits and pieces from Brynmill some other time.'

He nodded, and with one last strange lingering glance at Esme, turned on his heel and left. Beth felt mortified. The only explanation she could think of for her mother's bizarre behaviour was that she was out of her mind with grief. She prayed it wouldn't be permanent.

Esme's anguished self-reproach lasted for several days, during which she wouldn't eat and had little sleep. Beth spent her nights in a chair at her mother's bedside, half dozing, afraid to leave her alone. But on the morning of Freddie's funeral, Esme rose purposefully and Beth saw that a cold calm had settled on her. Now she seemed dead herself and just going through the motions of living. This new attitude frightened Beth even more.

Mrs Pickering and Mrs Gibbs had offered to help Esme with the ham spread at the house afterwards, which was good of them. However, Beth was shocked to learn that her mother actually intended to attend the funeral herself. They were invariably the men's prerogative, and few women would dare intrude.

'He's my son!' she cried when Beth questioned the wisdom of this, feeling other people would see it as strange and mawkish. 'I don't care what the custom is. I want to be with him until the last, until he is put into the ground.'

'Then I'll come with you, Mam,' Beth offered, resigned, although she dreaded the ordeal.

And it was an ordeal she'd never forget. She was glad of Dan Henshaw's close attendance of them throughout, and couldn't understand Esme's occasional vitriolic glance at him, laced with hatred. Beth felt her mother was carrying her feud with Aunt Mae too far.

★

Two days after the funeral Esme asked a question which shook Beth to the core.

'When are you returning to Brynmill? You'll lose your place at Lewis Lewis if you stay away from work much longer.'

'I've got compassionate leave, Mam, as you know,' she said quickly. 'Back to work I'll be next Monday morning, but I'm never going back to Aunt Mae's. I never want to see her again after the way she's treated you.'

'What goes on between me and my sister is none of your business,' Esme said, a sharp edge to her voice. 'You're not staying here, Beth. I'll not repeat what I've said before, but I tell you now – this house is no longer your home.'

'Mam! You can't mean that?'

'I want you to leave in the morning,' Esme went on relentlessly. 'I don't want to see you in this house again. You're no longer welcome.'

As soon as the front door closed behind Beth's drooping shoulders, Esme burst into uncontrollable weeping, collapsing on to a chair near the range. She had just lost her beloved son because of her own wickedness, and now she must lose her daughter, her firstborn. She had been so cruel to Beth a few minutes ago, yet her own heart had been torn apart in her breast doing it. But it had to be done. She must sever all links lest Beth be tainted with her own mother's shame.

Oh, God! Esme thought. What had she done to her family?

Her family, past and future. She put a hand to her abdomen, thinking of the new life being created there. It was early days, yet she knew the signs and was certain she had fallen for another child. A child without a name. He would deny this one as he had denied Beth.

Oh, why had she let Dan charm her again? Why had she been weak-willed enough to allow him to come near her? She was gutless as well as wicked. But no more! She would never see him again. And he would never learn of this child.

Neither must Beth ever learn of it. She must not come to this house in future; she must never discover her mother's disgrace. Esme knew she would not be able to face her daughter; could not bear to see the condemnation in Beth's eyes as her condition became apparent. Best for everyone if they never met again.

Esme pushed herself up from the chair and walked slowly into the scullery to wash up the breakfast things. She must be alone from now on, she told herself, and she deserved to be. But, oh, what was she to do?

8

Christmas 1920

'Mr and Mrs Henshaw are going to Bolton to spend Christmas with relatives,' Mrs Wilks told Beth arrogantly only the week before. 'I shan't be here either. My sister has invited me to her place.'

Beth flopped down on to a kitchen chair. 'What about me?'

'Mr Henshaw has given permission for you to stay here.' The housekeeper gave a loud sniff. 'Big mistake, I think. You could be up to all kinds of mischief behind our backs.'

Beth was appalled. 'You mean, I'll be here all by myself?' She'd never in her life spent Christmas alone.

'Yes, and you'll have to make your own arrangements as regards food. Any breakages and you'll pay, let me tell you.'

'I'll go to my mother's,' Beth said belligerently. 'She'll write soon and ask me, you'll see.'

But she wasn't at all sure about it. Although she wrote to her mother at least once a week, letters from Esme had been infrequent over the last seven months, and never once had there been an invitation to call at Libanus Street. Hurt at her mother's neglect and seeming coldness was still acute. But surely, at Christmas time, when families were traditionally together, her mother wouldn't continue to hold her at arm's length. Didn't they need each other all the more at this time?

'It's no concern of mine where you go or what you do outside this house,' Mrs Wilks snapped, and stalked off.

But there was a letter from Esme the next day, and Beth's fingers quivered with suppressed excitement as she tore open the envelope and quickly read it through. Her mother was now working as cook-housekeeper for a lady in the Uplands who wanted her to live in. Esme was thinking seriously about it. Too many painful memories hung around the house in Libanus Street, and Beth was disturbed to read that her mother might give up the tenancy. No invitation for Christmas was given, and Beth's heart sank in misery.

Waking up in her small room at the top of the house all alone on Christmas Day, she couldn't help weeping at what had befallen her family during the year. She made some porridge, drank a cup of tea and then set off on foot for Cwmbwrla. Invitation or no invitation, she'd see her mother this special day no matter what the welcome.

When she turned the corner into Libanus Street she saw Maudie Pickering, as was, on the doorstep of her mother's house. Maudie was big with child, and her pretty face glowed with happiness.

'Hello, Beth kid. Merry Christmas!' Maudie called out gaily.

'Merry Christmas to you as well,' she answered jovially, although her heart ached.

'Hey! Haven't seen you for ages,' Maudie went on. 'How are you keeping then, kid?'

Beth smiled faintly, reluctant to answer. 'You look well, Maudie,' she commented, feeling a twinge of envy. To be married and starting a family seemed wonderful to her.

To be loved and to belong. Would she ever know that happiness again?

Maudie stroked her bulge, sighed contentedly, and then looked at Beth with a frown. 'Have you come to see your mam?'

'Yes,' she said. 'And I'd better be going in. She'll be wondering where I am.'

Maudie's face fell. 'Your mother's not at home, Beth. Hasn't been back for a couple of days now. Working up the Uplands she is, mind. Didn't you know?'

'Oh, yes!' the girl said quickly. 'I know about that, but I thought . . .'

'Hey, look!' Maudie exclaimed energetically. 'Come in and have a bit of dinner with us. Mam would be tickled. There's loads of grub, mun.'

'Oh, no, I couldn't.' Beth stepped back, embarrassed. 'Thank you all the same though, Maudie.'

Why had she come here? It was turning into a complete disaster.

'Hey now, come on!' Maudie went on persuasively. 'You can't walk all the way back to Brynmill without some Christmas dinner inside you, especially in this cold weather.' She grasped Beth's arm, pulling her forward, smiling into her face. 'We're old friends, remember, and I want you to meet my hubby, Teifi. But no flirting with him, right!'

It was springtime and she ought to be feeling on top of the world, Beth thought gloomily. Her apprenticeship was finally finished and she'd been promised a permanent position in the alteration department of Lewis Lewis. Life should be rosy, but it wasn't. It was her eighteenth birthday today, but there was no letter from her mother.

After bumping into Maudie again in Swansea Market

at the end of January, Beth learned that Esme had lost her job in the Uplands, so was still at Libanus Street. Despite many pleas in her letters, though, Beth hadn't set eyes on her mother for a year. It felt as though Esme was avoiding her, though it just didn't make sense. But today Beth was determined to get to the bottom of it. It was half-day at the shop and she intended to walk to Cwmbwrla as soon as she'd finished her chores here.

Mrs Wilks marched into the kitchen just as she was finishing washing up the lunchtime crockery. 'Get a move on with that,' the older woman said. 'Spring-cleaning begins today. For a start, I want you to go over the master bedroom with a fine-tooth comb this afternoon. I don't want a speck of dust left anywhere.'

Beth was dismayed. 'But it's my birthday,' she said. 'I'm going to see my mother.'

'No time for birthdays,' Mrs Wilks snapped. 'You should be glad you've a roof over your head, my girl. You owe Mrs Henshaw a lot, but are you grateful? Not you. Huh! You're a selfish little madam, you are.'

'I pay my way!' Beth exploded. 'I'm not a charity case.'

'Keep a civil tongue in your head,' Mrs Wilks thundered, her mouth pinched in fury. 'If you don't work, I don't see why you should eat. If I had my way . . .'

The front door bell rang.

'Well! Don't stand there idling,' Mrs Wilks barked. 'Go and answer it.'

Seething, Beth stalked down the passage and into the hall. Nothing would stop her going to Cwmbwrla today. Nothing! What could Mrs Wilks do to her anyway, except complain to Aunt Mae? Well, let her! Beth jerked the front door open and glared at the caller.

'Yes?'

'Beth kid . . .'

She stared. 'Maudie! What are you doing here?'

The girl's face looked pale as she stood hesitantly on the front step, her baby's pram nearby.

'I've come with some awful bad news, Beth love.'

She reeled as a feeling of déjà vu stole over her. It was as though she was about to experience a familiar nightmare, and some instinct told her she'd left everything too late.

'What's going on?' Mrs Wilks pulled the door open wide and stared haughtily at Maudie. 'There's no time for chattering on the doorstep. What does this person want?'

'It's nothing to do with you, you bad-tempered old crab!' Beth hurled the insult at her furiously. 'Wait there, Maudie,' she said hurriedly to her friend. 'I'll get my hat and coat. We can talk on the way home.'

'Don't you dare walk out,' Mrs Wilks shouted after Beth as she ran back to the kitchen to tear off her apron and grab at her hat and coat. 'Come back at once, do you hear me?'

But Beth didn't come back until she was ready, struggling into her coat as she hurried.

'Mrs Henshaw will hear about this,' Mrs Wilks spluttered helplessly as Beth rushed past her. 'She won't be pleased, I can tell you.'

'Yes, go and tell her,' Beth shouted over her shoulder, almost hysterical with dread. Something in Maudie's eyes told her the news she brought was the worst anyone could hear. 'Tell my Aunt Mae something bad has happened to her sister, something very bad, then maybe she'll be sorry for the way she's treated her in the past.'

With one last glare at her tormentor, Beth grabbed Maudie's arm. 'Come on, Maudie,' she said. 'Let's get home.'

Home! She had no home anymore.

When they were clear of the green double gates, Maudie trundling the pram in front of her, Beth found the courage to ask.

'It's my mam, isn't it?' She gulped, suddenly terrified of hearing the truth. 'Is she dead, Maudie?'

Her friend stopped and turned to Beth. Tears rolled down her cheeks. 'Oh, it's terrible, and there's sorry I am, Beth *cariad*.'

Beth swallowed again, willing herself not to break down. There'd be time for grief and weeping in the lonely months and years ahead of her. 'When did it happen?'

Maudie sniffed. 'Last night, at the hospital.'

'What was it?' She whispered the dreaded word. 'Cancer?'

Maudie shook her head.

Perhaps it was a heart attack, Beth thought. She wouldn't be surprised if her mother had died from a broken heart after losing both her husband and darling son.

Maudie grasped impulsively at Beth's hand. 'Beth kid, prepare yourself for another shock.' She paused a moment as though reluctant to speak the words. 'The thing is, Beth, your mother died in childbirth.'

'*What?*' Beth was so stunned she took a step back. 'What are you talking about? That's impossible. My mother's been a widow for over a year.'

'Listen, kid,' Maudie said, pushing the pram forward again, 'this is awful for you, I know, but you've got to hear the whole truth of it. Your mam lost her job after Christmas because that lady in the Uplands twigged she was in the family way.'

'Mam, expecting? I can't believe it's true.' A thought struck Beth. 'Why wasn't I told?' She turned her head to stare accusingly at Maudie. 'You must've known at

Christmas time, but you never breathed a word. Maudie, you said you were my friend. How could you keep it from me?'

'I was all for telling you, honest I was,' the girl said hastily, shaking her head. 'But your mother made my mam promise on the Bible to say nothing. Well, she was ashamed, wasn't she?'

Beth was silent, unable to speak. Ashamed? In the family way, and with no husband of her own, any woman would be ashamed. She couldn't believe it of her own mother, and with her father so recently dead, too. It was unbelievable.

They paused at the kerb, waiting to cross the road as a tram rattled by. Beth stared at the ground, feeling some of the shame herself. Her own mother! She was conscious of Maudie's sidelong glance as they finally reached the safety of the pavement on the other side.

'There's something else, Beth,' she said, then paused, looking uncertain, and began fussing with the coverings in the pram.

'What?' Beth urged. 'What is it?'

'Your mother's baby,' Maudie said, looking up at her guardedly. 'A baby boy she had, see. He's at my mam's. The St John Ambulance men wouldn't let him go to the hospital with your mother, wouldn't be responsible for him on the journey, they said.'

Beth stared. The baby still lived! She was dumbfounded and speechless.

'She wouldn't have the doctor or midwife for the birth, see,' Maudie went on. 'She was afraid people would find out and talk. The midwife from Gurnos Street was sent for at the last minute when Mam realised something was wrong, and when your mother got awful bad Mam called our panel doctor. Rushed in, she was, but it was too late.'

Beth put up a hand to cover her mouth, suddenly over-come with grief and deep pity for her mother. It was unfair how wretchedly life had treated her.

'The poor little thing *will* have to go into an orphanage now, won't he?' Maudie said sorrowfully. 'Like your mother planned.'

'Orphanage?' Beth's wandering attention snapped back to what Maudie was saying.

Her friend nodded. 'That's what she was going to do, Beth. Didn't want another baby, she said. It breaks my heart to think of him in an orphanage. He's a lovely little scrap.'

Her baby brother! Well, half-brother. With Mam and Dad gone, and little Freddie, the new baby was all the family Beth had left. The responsibility was hers now; all her mother had left her.

'He's *not* going to an orphanage,' she declared resolutely. 'His place is with me. I'm eighteen now, and I'm his half-sister, his kith and kin.'

'Don't be too hasty, Beth love.' Looking worried, Maudie stopped the pram again. 'He'll need continual feeding and tending, and you've got no idea about looking after a baby. How life changes when there's one depending on you.' She glanced at her own child asleep in his pram. 'And how will you manage on your own? How will you live, and where?'

Beth stepped forward decisively. 'I'll manage somehow. Perhaps my Aunt Mae will help.' But she thought that highly unlikely.

Mrs Pickering was in the kitchen sitting on a stool near the range, a shawl-wrapped bundle in her arms. She was crooning to it softly.

'Here's Beth, Mam,' Maudie said as they came in.

Mrs Pickering rose and looked at her mournfully. 'There's sorry I am for your loss, *bach*. She was a good woman, your mother, despite everything,' she said awkwardly. 'Loneliness, that's what did it, loneliness and grief.'

With a nod, Beth reached for the precious bundle, and holding it against her breast, gazed at the wizen little face amongst the folds. Her mother died for this scrap of humanity, but he wasn't to blame. As she gazed at his face, frowning in sleep, her heart was suddenly filled up with tenderness and a desperate love for him.

'What is his name? she whispered.

Mrs Pickering looked perplexed. 'He hasn't got one, *bach*. Your mother never had time . . .' She bit her lip. 'Of course, we'll have to find one for the birth certificate when he's registered. He'll need a birth certificate when he goes to the orphanage.'

'That's not going to happen,' Beth said firmly. She was even more determined since seeing and holding him. It would be impossible to part from him, loving him as she did already. And she must have someone to love, now that her whole family was gone. 'He's my brother. I'll fend for him.'

'Oh, no, *cariad*, that's silly,' Mrs Pickering exclaimed, trying to take the baby from her. 'It's best to let the authorities have him. They'll find a wet nurse for him until he's weaned.'

But Beth held firm. 'I'll never let strangers have him,' she said doggedly. 'Take him back to Brynmill, I will.'

Mrs Pickering looked aghast. 'But think of the disgrace for your aunt,' she said. 'She might cut up rough at having her widowed sister's illegitimate child in the house.'

'What can she do to me?' Beth asked tartly. 'Chuck me

out?' Even as she said it, a chill ran up her spine, knowing it was a real possibility now that Esme was dead. Mae had never wanted Beth in the house from the beginning.

'You can't go back there anyway,' Mrs Pickering said hastily. 'Well, not until after the funeral at least. Arrangements will have to be made tomorrow, mind. Best have the Co-op.' She nodded sagely. 'They do a nice funeral. You'll have to provide a bit of food for the mourners afterwards. I'll help you prepare it, *bach*.'

Beth felt stunned. 'Funeral? Food?' How would she pay for it all?

'Would you like me to look after the baby until the funeral is over?' Maudie offered. 'Might as well look after two as one.'

Beth shook her head. 'Thanks, Maudie, but no. He's my responsibility, and I mean to start as I intend to go on.' She smiled faintly at the other girl. 'I'll have to learn the hard way, as you did.'

'I had my mam to guide me,' Maudie said sadly, and shook her head. 'You're on your own, Beth love.'

'I can do it.' She nodded. 'I *will* do it.'

'You're as proud and stubborn as your mother was,' Mrs Pickering said, with a touch of approval in her voice. 'All right, we'll have a cup of tea and then I'll show you how to change a nappy and prepare the baby food. Let's hope he survives without mother's milk.'

'Here's the key of next door,' Mrs Pickering said later. 'The rent's been paid for the week.' She hesitated before offering kindly, 'But you can stay with us tonight, like, if you don't want to be on your own with the baby?'

It was a relief to realise that she and the baby had somewhere safe to stay for the time being, and perhaps she need never go back to Brynmill at all.

'I'll be all right, thanks,' Beth said gratefully.

'Well, knock on the wall any time if you need help.'

'Do you think the landlord would let me have the tenancy instead of my mam?' Beth asked hopefully. 'I'm eighteen now, mind.'

Mrs Pickering pursed her lips, shaking her head dubiously. 'I doubt it, *cariad*, not a single girl like you.'

Beth said nothing. She would have a word with the landlord herself. If she could stay at Libanus Street among friends, she might just manage.

'Oh, by the way,' Mrs Pickering said. 'You'll find everything you need for the baby next door. Nappies, clothes . . . Your mother was collecting things for months, enough for an army of babies.' Tears glistened in her eyes. 'Poor dab! Dying so young. It doesn't seem fair, does it?'

Mrs Pickering and Maudie insisted on coming next door to settle her in, and roped in Teifi to light a fire in the kitchen grate. Beth was overwhelmed by their kindness yet glad when she was finally alone.

She sat on her mother's chair near the range, holding the baby, and at last gave vent to the pain and grief that she had held at bay for hours. It broke her heart to remember Esme's coldness towards her this last year. Now she would never be able to mend things between them or understand why her mother had turned against her. Never again would she see her mother's warm smile or feel the tenderness of her touch as she had as a child, and it broke Beth's heart.

But there was no point in dwelling on the past, she decided, choking back another sob. She was alive and so was the baby, and somehow they had to find a way of going on. She looked down at the infant in her arms.

'You must have a name,' she whispered to him. 'I know! You'll be Thomas, after my Grandpa Parkyn. Little Tommy Pryce.' She looked around the kitchen. 'If only we could stay here, Tommy.'

Tommy wailed for food again at the crack of dawn, and Beth dragged herself out of bed, feeling exhausted. After she'd fed and changed him there seemed no point in going back to bed. She wouldn't sleep, and there was too much to do today. The Co-op Funeral Parlour was in High Street. She would call there first to make arrangements, she decided, then go into Lewis Lewis to explain her situation and pick up whatever pay she had coming. She hoped the management would be sympathetic. Losing her job on top of everything else would be a disaster.

After breakfast she was about to take Tommy next door to be minded by Mrs Pickering when there was a knock on the front door. That was probably Mrs P, Beth thought, and answered the knock with a grateful smile, but it was wiped from her face when she saw Aunt Mae standing on the doorstep. Elias Morgan sat in the seat of a trap parked at the kerb, and stared at them with open curiosity.

'What's happened?' Mae demanded loudly. 'Why didn't you come back to Brynmill last night? What have you been up to, my girl?'

Beth swallowed, stung by her aunt's sharp and suspicious tone. 'You'd better come in.'

Mae hesitated, looking uncertain and uneasy, too.

'Oh, it's all right!' Beth snapped. 'There's nothing contagious in this house.'

Mae's mouth was pinched with anger but she turned and nodded at Elias before stepping forward to follow

Beth into the kitchen. Her own anger mounted on seeing Mae glance contemptuously about her.

'No, we're not posh like Brecon Parade,' Beth said bitingly. 'But we're clean.'

'You're too lippy for your own good, you are, my girl,' Mae said. 'Now, where's my sister? What's happened?'

'Don't you know?'

Mae gave an impatient sigh and drew back her chin. 'All I know is, Mrs Wilks told me this morning that you didn't come back last night. Esme being taken ill is the only proper reason I can think of for you to be out all night.'

'Don't pretend you really care about Mam,' Beth blazed. 'Concerned about losing a skivvy, more like.'

Mae's lips thinned. 'I've had enough of this. Now where's Esme? Upstairs, is she?'

She moved towards them, but Beth's next words stopped her.

'No, she's in the hospital morgue,' she answered brutally, wanting to hurt. 'She's dead, Aunt Mae, dead and gone, and you can't hurt her any more.'

Mae stared, her face turning deathly pale. 'Dead? Esme dead?' She swayed and then dropped on to a nearby chair. 'My sister! Why? How?'

At that moment, upstairs, Tommy let out a wail of hunger.

Mae jumped to her feet. 'What's that?' She frowned. 'Is there a baby in the house?'

Beth's shoulders drooped, and she nodded. She was reluctant to tell Mae the truth, feeling shame for her mother. But of course it would have to come out, though she dreaded the questions for which she had no answers.

'Whose baby is it?' her aunt asked in a hard voice. 'The truth now!'

'His name is Tommy,' Beth said dispiritedly. 'He was born to my mother on Thursday. She died giving him life.'

Mae's jaw dropped and she sat down heavily on the chair again. She stared at Beth for a long moment before speaking.

'I can't take this in,' she said weakly. 'My sister, widowed for over a year, has given birth to a . . . to a . . .'

'Don't you dare say it!' Beth shouted, wagging a finger in Mae's face. 'You turned your back on her years ago, so you have no right to judge.'

'I have every right,' her aunt shouted back. 'Esme disgraced herself once before, years ago, and now she's done it again. But it won't be she who suffers humiliation this time, it'll be me.' She lifted a gloved hand to her mouth. 'Oh, the scandal! How will I face people?' She shook her head. 'I don't know what Dan will say.'

'It's no one's business but mine,' Beth blurted angrily. 'I'll take care of Tommy and bring him up. I'll be a mother to him.'

'And who is the father?' Mae asked in a brittle voice. 'Huh! A married man, I'll be bound.'

'I don't know who the father is,' Beth said stubbornly. 'And what's more, I don't care. He has no rights to the boy, whoever he is.'

Mae stood up and pulled in her chin, giving Beth a haughty stare. 'I don't know how you can look me in the eye,' she said. 'You stand there, as brazen as you like, as if Esme has done no wrong.'

'You'd better not say a word against her,' Beth warned, a tremor in her voice. There would be plenty of condemnation to face in the future, but she would not take it from her mother's sister.

'Huh! One illegitimate child is bad enough, but two is utterly disgraceful.' She sniffed. 'I was right to disown her.'

'You had better go,' Beth flared.

'A word of common sense before I do,' Mae snapped. 'Send him to an orphanage immediately. You're merely a child yourself, not fit to mother anyone let alone a newborn. And don't think you can bring him back to Brecon Parade with you, either. I won't have that disgrace under my roof.'

'Tommy is not a disgrace,' Beth shouted. 'And I wouldn't have him stay in that rotten little box-room at the top of your house either. Your next skivvy can have it and welcome.'

'Big words for someone who'll be homeless soon enough,' Mae sneered. 'You'll be in the workhouse yet, and that brat of Esme's with you.'

'I'll get the tenancy of this house,' Beth answered quickly. 'I've got plenty of friends in Cwmbwrla, mind, people who really care.'

'You're going to need them, my girl,' Mae snapped, standing. 'I wash my hands of you.'

'Well, that's all right with me,' she shouted. 'I never wanted to come to Brynmill anyway, and I hated every minute of it. Now, get out, Aunt Mae. You have no place in my mother's home.'

Beth was still shaking later when she took Tommy next door. Mrs Pickering's expression was full of curiosity, having spotted the trap and the fashionably dressed woman who had knocked on the door, but Beth was in no mood to divulge family secrets. She went back home and fetched the rent book, which was kept behind the clock on the mantelpiece.

Arranging the funeral was less of an ordeal than she'd imagined, although she had a moment of panic when the price was mentioned, but she steeled herself, realising

Esme probably had some sort of insurance. She'd find the money somehow. Meanwhile her mother must have a decent send-off.

Dealing with her employers was less easy. They were sympathetic at her loss, handed over her wages promptly, but asked pointedly when she would return to work. Beth was evasive, not daring to mention her new responsibility, but she could sense Mrs Brewer, head of the alteration department, was not satisfied.

'You've only just been made up to permanent, Miss Pryce,' the woman said warningly. 'You can't play fast and loose with your job, mind. We've got important clients to consider. They won't wait for their alterations. If you stay away too long we'll have to replace you.'

Meekly, Beth took her leave and went straight to the offices of the landlord's agent, also in the High Street, where she made her request for the tenancy of the house in Libanus Street. The agent, a Mr Samuel, pursed his lips doubtfully and shook his head when she told him her age and how much she earned per week.

'Can't be done, miss.'

'But why not?' Beth asked hotly. 'I'm old enough surely, and in regular employment.'

'But you're unmarried. Besides, by the time you pay the rent you'll have barely five shillings a week to live on.' He shook his head again. 'In no time you'd be in arrears. I've seen it happen before. A tenancy is out of the question on your wage, a girl alone.'

'But what am I do to?' Beth wailed, suddenly frightened. She had been so sure she would get it.

'Look, your best bet is to rent a room somewhere.'

Beth scowled at him. 'It's difficult to find lodgings with a baby.'

'A baby!' He gave her a strange look. 'You never

mentioned one. That puts the tin hat on it, my girl.'

'He's my brother!' she said angrily, interpreting his look of disapproval. 'My mother died giving birth.'

'I'm sorry, but there's nothing I can do.' He snatched the rent book from her fingers, and glanced at it. 'The rent is paid up until tomorrow,' he said brusquely. 'You must vacate by midday at the latest.'

'But the funeral!' Beth exclaimed in dismay. 'It's arranged for next Wednesday from the house. You can't kick me out before then, surely? You'll have to give me a week's notice, at least.'

'I would if you were the tenant,' he said. 'But Mrs Pryce is deceased, so notice doesn't apply. Besides, we have a list of people waiting to rent, working men with families.'

'It's disrespectful,' Beth cried passionately. 'Even the workhouse has more sympathy than that.'

'Now look here, my girl . . .'

She held out her pay packet. 'Please! Give me until Saturday week. What can it hurt?' She gazed at him pleadingly. 'Let me bury my mother with some dignity at least.'

He scratched his head as though bewildered by his own weakness. 'All right, but I need my head read for agreeing.'

Beth handed over the eleven shillings for next week's rent, and he marked up the book. Now she had only five shillings left.

He handed it back to her. 'Surrender this next Saturday,' he told her gruffly. 'You'll have to move out every stick of furniture by then, mind. We want vacant possession.'

Beth made her way home with a heavy heart. What would she and Tommy do after Saturday week? Where could they go for shelter over their heads? The future seemed very frightening at that moment, and she prayed for the strength to go on.

*

It rained on Wednesday, and the gloom of the day matched Beth's despairing mood. Despite the disgrace of Esme's passing, the neighbours rallied round, and Beth was grateful. Mrs Pickering and Mrs Gibbs saw to the ham spread, such as it was, while someone donated a slab of fruitcake and someone else a bottle of cheap port.

As was the custom, Beth remained at home with the womenfolk while their husbands and sons attended the burial at Calfaria chapel a couple of miles up the Carmarthen Road at Fforestfach.

'What can I do about Mam's furniture?' Beth asked sadly of Mrs Pickering as they sat with the other women drinking tea, awaiting the return of the mourners. 'The house must be cleared by Saturday.'

'I could do with another double bed for our Edna now she's getting married,' Mrs Gibbs said. 'How much do you want for the one in the front bedroom, love?'

'Two pounds,' Mrs Pickering said quickly. 'It's a good bed.'

Mrs Gibbs frowned at her interference, but nodded in agreement. 'Pay you Friday,' she said. 'When my old man gets his wages.'

'I like this sideboard,' Mrs Lumley from number twelve remarked, smoothing her fingers along the polished surface. 'What's it worth?'

Beth glanced helplessly at Mrs Pickering, who rose swiftly, obviously delighted to take charge of the sale.

'Give me a piece of paper and a pencil, *cariad*,' she said to Beth. 'I'll make a proper list of who wants what and how much they owe you.'

By the time the men had returned most of Beth's home was sold up, to be collected during the next couple of days. All except for the large wardrobe in the front bedroom and some other bits and pieces.

'My chap says he might be interested in taking the rest,' Mrs Cooper from number sixteen told Beth later. 'His mate deals in second-hand furniture. Might even give you a good price, but I'm not promising, mind.'

'Thank you,' Beth said miserably. 'I'll be grateful for anything.'

Thursday and Friday, people came and went through Beth's front door, removing their purchases, while she nursed Tommy in the kitchen, disturbed to see her mother's home dismantled piece by piece, although she was grateful for the few pounds Mrs Pickering had squeezed out of their neighbours.

Having spent Friday night at the Pickerings', Beth was having breakfast with the family when Mr Cooper came with his mate and a large handcart for the wardrobe. Calling for the key to her former home, he handed her the sum they had agreed on for the wardrobe.

She was surprised later when he knocked on the Pickerings' door again and came into their kitchen carrying a large tin box. Beth stared. She had completely forgotten the existence of that old box. It was where her mam kept important papers, like birth certificates and such.

'Where did you find that, Mr Cooper?'

'Hidden on top of the wardrobe it was, *bach*,' he said. 'Thought it might be important, like.'

Beth took the box from him, filled with new hope. Perhaps there was an insurance policy with enough to cover the funeral expenses, for she was expecting that bill any time now.

'I haven't seen this in years,' she said. 'Thanks, Mr Cooper.'

'Take it in the parlour, *cariad*,' Mrs Pickering said

kindly. 'I'll see you have a bit of privacy. Don't worry about Tommy.'

Alone in the parlour, Beth lifted the box's lid and began taking out the contents. Freddie's birth certificate and her own were on top, and her parents' marriage lines. There wasn't anything that looked like an insurance policy, and Beth felt acute disappointment.

The next thing she took out was a large brown envelope. It looked bulky and familiar. She glanced inside and then gasped in astonishment to see a bundle of five-pound notes held together by a piece of string. Dad's bank money from Garngoch was still intact. It looked as though Mam hadn't touched a penny of it.

Overwhelmed, Beth put both hands to her cheeks. All this money was now hers – hers and Tommy's. But instinctively she knew it shouldn't be spent unless there was no other way. It would pay for the funeral and perhaps provide a roof over their heads, but the bulk of it must be put away for Tommy. That's what Mam would have wanted.

A white envelope lying at the bottom of the tin caught her eye and she lifted it out, not surprised to see her own name written on it in her mother's large handwriting. Beth felt tears well in her eyes as she took out the sheets of folded paper, laid them on the table and read her mother's final words to her.

January 1921

Dearest daughter, Beth,

When you read this, I will have gone to glory be with Percy and Freddie. It is time you learned the truth about your real father, the man who denied you all those years ago.

Flummoxed, Beth sat down heavily, staring at the paper in front of her. Her real father? What did it mean? Snatching up the sheet, she read on.

> *You see, Beth, my dear girl, Percy Pryce was not your real father, although he gave you his name and loved you like his own.*

Still bewildered, she read the words again, even running the tip of her finger across the page in an effort to understand, but it still didn't make sense. Of course Percy was her father; she knew no other. He'd been there for as far back as she could recall.

> *Try not to think badly of me for what you already know and for what I am about to tell you. Always remember that you are very dear to me. I may have seemed uncaring towards you over this last year, but after you have read this letter you will understand that sending you away to live with Dan Henshaw was for your own good.*

Frowning, Beth sat back in the chair utterly confused, and then felt a spurt of resentment. How could she believe Esme had really cared after the way she had kept them apart? Sending Beth to Brynmill was the worse thing her mother could have done. She felt anger swell at the injustice of it, remembering all the hard work imposed on her and the humiliation she had suffered being at Aunt Mae's beck and call. What excuse could her mother have for such an action?

> *I have kept the secret for many years, but I fear I will not survive this baby. It will be a shock to you to learn that Dan Henshaw, my sister Mae's husband, is your real father, although he will deny it as he did all those years ago.*

Dan Henshaw, her father? Beth was astounded. It couldn't possibly be true. She had a sudden image of him in her mind, tall and rather forbidding whenever he looked her way, as though he resented her. She stared again at the letter, and the words seemed to dance on the page. The implication was appalling. She was illegitimate!

I was seventeen and really thought Dan would marry me. Instead he denied you.

Beth's fingers shook as she held the letter, her anger growing moment by moment. So, Dan Henshaw was her father, and knew it, yet he had allowed her to be treated like a servant by Aunt Mae and that battle-axe Mrs Wilks.

Meeting him again after all those years my deep feelings for him were rekindled, and he took advantage of it. The baby I carry is Dan's child. Your Aunt Mae knows nothing of this. You are Dan Henshaw's daughter, and he must now make recompense for his years of neglect and denial of you. Perhaps I am a coward but I leave it to you to decide how he should pay.
Your loving mother, Esme

With a cry of anguish, Beth snatched up the pages and, crumpling them into a ball, threw it on the floor. Not only did she bear the stigma of illegitimacy, so did Tommy. Dan Henshaw had a lot to answer for. Beth rose shakily to her feet. By heaven, he would pay for what he had done! She would not rest until he had.

9

'I can't see for the life of me why you want to go back to Brynmill,' Mrs Pickering said anxiously as Beth got Tommy ready later. 'You won't get a welcome, mind, not with the baby.'

'It's something I have to do,' Beth said tensely. She could barely contain the deep feelings of hurt she'd nursed since learning the truth about her parentage, and Dan Henshaw was going to know about it too. She would confront him; force him to help her. Now she understood her mother's remark that it was only right. 'It's important for our future.'

Mrs Pickering looked at her expectantly, but Beth wouldn't say more. She could not reveal her own shame and add to the local gossip, for she had no doubt that Esme's name was already being bandied about the neighbourhood on account of Tommy's birth by those less than charitable.

'Well, leave the baby here for the time being, until you can come back for him,' her neighbour said kindly.

Beth shook her head. 'Tommy is part of the reason I'm going.'

'You will come back here, won't you, Beth *bach*? You'll have to come back.' Mrs Pickering hesitated and then rushed on, 'I could sleep in the box room while you and Tommy have the back bedroom.'

With a smile of gratitude, Beth turned to the older woman.

'You've been very good to us, but we can't impose on you any longer, Mrs Pickering,' she said. But a sob almost choked her, for here she felt safe among friends. But the house was overcrowded what with her and Maudie's new family. 'We're under each other's feet as it is, and no one would get any sleep with two squawling babies in the house.'

'Oh, never mind that,' Mrs Pickering exclaimed impatiently. 'You can't go off on your own, girl, with nowhere to lay your head. And what about Tommy? You can't lug a young baby from place to place.'

'I'm going to find his father,' Beth blurted. 'He'll have to help.'

Mrs Pickering stared. 'You know who he is, then?' she said, unable to hide her curiosity.

Beth nodded. 'I can't tell you more than that.'

'He's not a local man, I take it?'

'No.'

Mrs Pickering's eyes narrowed. 'I see.' She put a hand on Beth's arm. 'Do you know what you're doing, *cariad* ?'

Beth nodded emphatically. 'Oh, yes.' She swallowed hard, suddenly fearful. 'I'm going to face him and make him pay.'

'Be careful, my girl. He could turn nasty if there's a wife in the picture, too.' Mrs Pickering sighed and shook her head. '*Duw! Duw!* I wish you wouldn't take Tommy with you. It doesn't seem right, somehow.'

'Tommy belongs with me,' she said. No matter what the outcome with Dan Henshaw, she and Tommy would never be parted.

Soon Beth was ready to go. Apart from her handbag, which contained her mother's letter and the envelope of money, she also had a small suitcase and a canvas bag containing Tommy's food, bottle and nappies. She wondered how she'd carry the baby as well.

'Wait a minute,' Mrs Pickering said. 'I've got a big woollen shawl in the cupboard upstairs. You can use that, Welsh fashion. It'll be easier to carry the baby and keep him warm as well.'

The fringed shawl of soft Welsh wool was brought down. Folding it cornerwise, Mrs Pickering wrapped it around Beth and the baby, who lay tucked snugly in the crook of her arm, the loose corner pushed securely under him. It formed a warm cocoon for both of them.

Mrs Pickering, Maudie and Teifi stood on the doorstep to see her off, watching as she walked to the corner with the main road. She turned for a moment to look back at them.

'Good luck, love,' Maudie called, waving.

'Don't hesitate to come back, mind,' Mrs Pickering said. 'We'd manage somehow.'

Beth felt her throat close in an effort to hold back tears. She had a long way to walk and didn't know what to expect at the other end, though she was certain Dan Henshaw wouldn't be pleased to see her.

It was well after midday when Beth reached Brecon Parade. Although only a few days old, Tommy seemed to grow heavier with every mile she tramped and by then the pain in her arm was like toothache. She was also hungry and tired and knew Tommy was, too, for he did not stop grizzling. She passed through the green gates and went around to the back door. Mrs Wilks always took her half-day on Saturday afternoon, so there was no fear of running into her. Dan Henshaw had Saturday afternoons off, too, so unless he'd gone to play golf he was in the house somewhere.

The back door was unlocked, as usual, and Beth let herself quietly into the kitchen. Tommy's feed must be her first priority. She made a comfy nest for him in a shallow laundry basket, then put a match to the stove and set about making his bottle of baby milk. After feeding him, she ate some bread and cheese to satisfy her own hunger, then knew the moment had come for the show-down.

Wrapping Tommy in the shawl again, she carried him from the kitchen and into the hall. The house was very quiet but now she was ready, she felt less nervous. It wasn't going to be easy, she knew, but she was determined to get justice for Tommy, if not for herself. No, it was too late for her, but Dan Henshaw must acknowledge his son.

The sitting-room door was open and Beth glanced in, but there was no sign of Dan. She stood for a moment, wondering if she had the house to herself. If so, she'd had a wasted journey because she didn't know how long she could hang around waiting.

But suddenly the muted sound of a match being struck came from behind the closed door of the room Dan Henshaw called his study, and Beth hurried towards it. The baby clutched in one arm, she didn't bother to knock but flung the door open and marched in.

Dan was seated at his desk, puffing his pipe, the house-hold accounts book open in front of him. He looked up as she came in and his mouth dropped open in astonishment, the pipe falling with a clatter on to the desk to spill smouldering tobacco over the accounts. He jumped to his feet, staring, and Beth stared, too, trying to take in the fact that this tall, handsome man was her father.

It was a moment before he found his tongue. 'Beth, what are you doing here?'

'I live here, remember?' she exclaimed heatedly, angered by his distant tone of voice. He must know the truth of their kinship; he must always have known. 'Or at least, I used to.' She couldn't keep the fury from her eyes and he recognised it, and hurriedly moved out from behind the desk.

'I was sorry to hear about your mother . . .'

'Liar!' she screeched, infuriated even more by his hypocrisy. 'You treacherous liar!'

'Damn it!' he shouted back. 'I won't have you speak to me like that in my own house. You'd better mind your tongue, my girl.'

'Your girl? How very apt.' She tossed back her head angrily. 'How should I speak to a man who would deny his own daughter? Shall I call you Father?'

His jaw worked for a moment before he spoke, his tone tight. 'I don't know what you mean by that.'

'Yes, you do.' Beth spat out the words. 'And you know why I've come back.'

His eyes narrowed. 'Now look here, don't make trouble in this house, I warn you, or you'll be in very hot water. You'd better go, and take . . .'

'Your son, Dan Henshaw!' Beth shouted. 'This child I'm holding is your son. Do you dare deny him, too?'

Dan's eyes opened wider. 'Esme gave birth to a boy? I didn't know.'

'And didn't care, did you?' Beth snapped. 'But your son lives and is in need, so what are you going to do about it . . . Father?'

'Don't call me that, damn it! I'm not your father. Percy Pryce was your father, Esme admitted it.'

Beth took her mother's crumpled letter out of her pocket and held it out to him.

'This says different,' she contradicted harshly.

He stared at the letter, his face paling.

'My mother's last words to me, and she wouldn't lie,' Beth said triumphantly, then paused, staring at him narrowly, trying better to understand the person she was dealing with here. 'What kind of a man are you anyway? You caused my mother's downfall when she was a young and innocent girl, split her from her only sister, and now you've wronged her again, for your own selfish ends. You knew she loved you and you used her, like . . . like . . .'

His lips drew back in a furious snarl. 'Like a woman off the streets? Your mother was no better. She tried to trick me into marriage when she was carrying Pryce's bastard brat . . . you!'

Beth's jaw dropped at the awful insult. 'You lying swine! You don't really believe that. You're blackening her name just to save yourself. Aunt Mae knows nothing of this, does she? No, but she will, I promise you.'

'Don't threaten me, you little hussy,' he growled. 'Mae won't believe the likes of you, her own scullery maid, Percy Pryce's illegitimate leavings. She despises you for that.'

'I wish to God Percy was my father,' Beth cried passionately. 'He was a man to be proud of, a better man than you. He was poor but honourable. You can never claim that, for all your money.'

'Oh, so this *is* about money, is it?' Dan said with a sneer. 'Trying a little blackmail? Well, it won't wash, miss, because there's no proof.'

'You think you're so clever, don't you, Dan Henshaw?' She stared at him, hating him with all her strength. 'But you can't lie about Tommy. My mother names you as his father, in ink on paper, her dying words, more or less. Aunt Mae will believe *that*.'

'Then she was lying again,' Dan thundered. 'Trying to

take revenge because I wouldn't throw Mae over all those years ago. God knows who the father is,' he went on mockingly. 'Any number of men, I shouldn't wonder.'

'God will strike you dead for your own wicked lies!' Beth screeched. 'And I will never forgive you. A man who denies his son should . . . hang.'

Dan Henshaw pointed a shaking finger at Tommy, whimpering in her arms.

'That is no child of mine,' he thundered. 'And neither are you. Now get out of this house, the pair of you.'

'I'm not going anywhere until I see Aunt Mae,' Beth shouted back. 'I'm going to show you up for the woman-ising blackguard you really are.'

Dan cursed violently, his face reddening. 'You'll leave now, even if I have to manhandle you,' he snarled. 'I'll take no more of this.'

'Take your hands off me!' Beth shrieked loudly as he took her by the shoulders to propel her into the hall. They were struggling in the study doorway when the front door opened and Aunt Mae came in. Dan let go of Beth immediately, taking a step back. Mae stared in astonishment.

'Dan! What's going on?' Then she recognised Beth and her mouth tightened. 'I told you never to come here again, didn't I?' she said angrily. 'And you've brought that disgrace into my house as well. How dare you?'

'The only disgrace here is him!' Beth shouted, pointing at Dan. 'Tommy has every right to be here. He's Dan's son.'

There was a sharp intake of breath from Mae. She didn't speak but turned a hard stare on her husband.

'It's a lie, of course, Mae,' he said carelessly, putting both hands in his pockets and taking a step into the hall.

'An attempt to prise money out of us.' He grimaced. 'You know yourself what the Pryces are like. Always on the breadline, forever on the scrounge.'

'Will you believe him or the dying words of your own sister?' Beth cried. 'Here!' She held out Esme's letter. 'Read them for yourself.'

Mae hesitated and then came forward to take the letter from Beth's trembling fingers.

'It's a trick, I tell you, Mae love,' Dan said, though his voice was not too steady now. 'You can't believe the words of a spiteful, jealous woman. You disowned Esme, remember, and you did right, too.'

'I don't need your approval, Dan,' she snapped, surprising both Beth and her husband, who looked suddenly very nervous. 'And even though I did wash my hands of her,' she went on, 'Esme was kin and now she's dead.'

There was a silence as Mae read through the pages, her fingers quivering before she'd finished.

'Mae!' Dan's voice was harsh. 'You can't believe that woman's lies.' He cursed aggressively. 'I won't have you doubt me like this, your own husband. I'm insulted you'd consider for one minute that I'm capable of such treachery.'

Mae's stare back at him was harsh. 'We both know what you're capable of, Dan.'

'Mae, listen!' He sounded chastened for a moment. 'That was years ago. I regretted it and you made me pay for it.'

Beth didn't understand what they were talking about, but she sensed Dan was on the defensive, and was quick to take advantage.

'His treachery doesn't start with Tommy,' she interjected fiercely. 'As you can see, he's been deceiving you for years. Percy Pryce wasn't my real father. Dan Henshaw is.'

'Be quiet!' Mae shouted. Her features suddenly contorted with fury, she flung the letter back in Beth's face. Her wrath was directed at her niece now not Dan. 'I warned you not to come here. You're not wanted, and neither is that brat.'

Beth stared at her, wide-eyed. 'But you've read the letter. You *know* it's true, I can see it in your face, Aunt Mae. What are you going to do about it?'

'There is nothing to do.' She took a deep breath as though to compose herself, and lifting her head, looked down her nose at Beth. 'I want you to leave immediately.'

'But the letter . . .'

'That means nothing to me,' Mae snapped. 'I have no sister. Now clear out this instant and take that child with you.'

Beth was flabbergasted. 'But we have nowhere to go, Aunt Mae. They wouldn't give me the tenancy of the house in Libanus Street.'

'That's not my concern,' she said, turning away. 'If you're homeless, blame your own mother. Her wilful, loose ways have brought you to this.'

'I can't believe you mean it or that you could be so hard,' Beth gasped. 'Please let us stay, if only for a few nights until I find rooms. Tommy won't be any bother, and I'll rub and scrub for you.'

'You must think me a fool,' her aunt grated. 'Letting you stay would be an admission that we owe you something. There's nothing for you here, nothing. Go on! Go now!'

Numbed with shock, Beth fled, running back to the kitchen to get her case and other belongings. Aunt Mae did not or would not believe her. Dan Henshaw had won.

*

Mae watched the girl rush towards the kitchen, frantically clutching the baby to her breast. When she had disappeared through the door, Mae turned and started for the staircase.

'Mae?' Dan's voice made her pause. 'Thank you for believing me. Listen, my dear, I'm tired of sleeping in the other bedroom. Shall I move my things back to our room tonight?'

She turned to him slowly. 'You're wrong, Dan. I believe every word of that letter.' She studied his tall broad-shouldered figure. 'First Daphne Prosser-Evans and now my own sister.' She paused. 'But, of course, it was the other way about, wasn't it? Esme first, Daphne second,' she went on, a raw edge to her voice. 'I suppose I came a very poor third.' She shook her head. 'I should've realised from the start you were just too good to be true. You betrayed me under my own roof. If it wasn't for the business I'd leave you. You'll never have control of it now, Dan.'

'Mae! For God's sake,' he interrupted, starting forward. 'That's not fair. I've worked hard all these years, and I deserve to own that business. You promised as much when we married.' He uttered an oath. 'I can't face ruin now!'

'Oh don't worry,' she assured him with a sneer. 'I'm not prepared to throw away everything just because you can't keep your flies buttoned.'

He looked shocked at her frank words.

'You can't believe Esme over me,' he said forcefully. 'I'm your husband. Esme always resented not getting her share of your father's money, and she held me responsible.'

Mae tilted her head questioningly. 'What is it about

you, Dan? It seems almost every woman you bed perishes.'

His face paled with shock. 'That's a terrible thing to say to me, Mae.'

'Maybe.' She gave a high laugh. 'It's ironic though, isn't it?' she said. 'You've always wanted a son to carry on your name and business. Well, now you have one, but you can't acknowledge him publicly without making a scandal for yourself.'

Dan swallowed, and looked pale. 'We . . . we could adopt him,' he said hesitantly. 'It wouldn't look odd taking in your dead sister's boy. Christian charity, people would say. Think of it Mae. My son – our son.'

A spasm of pain contorted her face for a moment. 'You inconsiderate beast! You don't give a damn about my feelings, do you?' She paused, determined to pull herself together, and threw back her shoulders, holding her head high. She still had the upper hand because she was still in control of the business. 'You won't foist another woman's child on me, even if she was my own sister.'

'It's not too late for us,' he said rather desperately. 'Let me come back to your bed.'

'Oh no! I was right to lock my door against you, and it's staying locked.' She smiled coldly. 'You were always a charmer, Dan. Luckily I wasn't *too* overwhelmed all those years ago.'

'I could have had any woman,' he said. 'I chose you, Mae.'

She shook her head, bitterly amused that he thought he could still turn her head. 'We both know why, don't we? But thank God I had enough sense to keep the major shareholding.'

'You talk as though I did you down,' he rasped. 'I've made money hand over fist for you; raised you up from keeping a squalid boarding house. You've come a long way from Picton Place. You are somebody in this town now, and *I* did that for you.'

Mae's nostrils flared, but she kept her temper. His words might have hurt her once but not now, not since his betrayal of her with Daphne. Now she understood him too well and consequently felt nothing for him.

'Be careful, Dan,' she said evenly. 'You've made a bitter enemy of Daphne's husband. Don't make an enemy of me as well because when Jarvis Prosser-Evans decides it's time you should pay the price . . . and he will, mark my words . . . you'll need all the friends you can get.'

10

Beth's mind was in a whirl as she trudged across the junction from Brecon Parade into Parc Beck Terrace, unsure where she was heading. She couldn't believe Aunt Mae's obstinate refusal to doubt her husband's loyalty.

But she wasn't clear about her own expectations either. What had she hoped for anyway? Dan would never admit he'd wronged her mother, so she couldn't expect any help from him or from Aunt Mae. She and Tommy were on their own from now on.

The first thing was to find a place to live. But where? For a moment she was tempted to start the walk back to Cwmbwrla, to throw herself on Mrs Pickering's mercy again, but she hesitated. As friendly and helpful as Mrs Pickering and Maudie had been since Esme's death, Beth sensed they were relieved at her going even though they'd tried to hide it. She couldn't impose on them and perhaps strain their friendship. She really was on her own now, and must learn to be independent. At least money wasn't a problem at the moment, and she was thankful for that.

Tommy was grizzling bitterly, needing a feed and a change. With a growing sense of desperation, she took note of the houses she passed, keeping a watch out for signs about rooms to rent. Eventually she saw a sign in the bay window of the last house in the terrace. Beth climbed the steps to the front door and pounded on the knocker. A thin woman, spectacles balanced on the end of her nose, answered and stared at her in a very unfriendly way.

'I've come about the room for rent,' Beth began.

The woman looked her up and down with cold eyes. 'No babies!' she snapped, and slammed the door in her face.

Beth stood for a moment, mouth agape, For two pins she would ring the bell again and give the woman a piece of her mind, but she'd had enough confrontation for one day. All she wanted now was to rest.

There was another house with a vacancy on Victoria Street, not far from Dan's yard. Beth took a firm hold on her nerves as she knocked, not knowing what to expect. The woman who answered seemed no friendlier. She stared at the baby and then scrutinised Beth with a suspicious frown on her face.

'I need a room urgently,' Beth began, straining to quell a pleading tone. 'The baby needs feeding and changing.'

'Where's your luggage, then?'

Beth indicated the small case at her feet, and the woman lifted her brows scornfully.

'I'm not destitute, mind,' Beth said hastily. 'I'm willing to pay the rent whatever it is.'

'I'll bet you are!' the woman retorted. Her suspicious look deepened. 'A bit young to have a baby, aren't you? Don't see a ring on your finger, either.'

'He's my brother,' Beth said defensively.

'Huh! A likely story!' The woman tossed her head. 'Go on, push off! This is a respectable house, this is.'

Beth hurried away from the door, feeling the woman's gimlet eyes on her back. It was mid-afternoon already, and she had nowhere to go. There was nothing for it but to go back to Libanus Street.

'Hello, Beth gal, what are you doing down this way then?'

She was walking with her head down in dejection, but looked up startled to see Elias Morgan on the pavement in front of her. He was obviously just going home from the yard, for his face was smudged with coal, the dust glistening in the folds of his clothing.

'Thought you was back in Cwmbwrla,' he went on then hesitated, his manner suddenly awkward. 'Sorry to hear about your mam, like.'

'Thank you,' Beth murmured. He was eyeing the baby uncertainly. 'This is my brother,' she explained quickly. 'He's got no one but me now.'

'*Duw! Duw!* There's hard on you, *bach*, isn't it? And you're just a babe yourself, mind.'

Beth bridled. 'I'm eighteen!'

He nodded. 'Yes, just a babe.'

Tommy let out a wail of misery.

'Tsk! Tsk!' Elias shook his head. 'You wants to get home and see to the poor little mite's needs,' he said severely. 'Instead of traipsing about the streets with him.'

Beth bit her lip. 'We haven't got a home,' she admitted impulsively, feeling ashamed although she didn't know why.

'No home?' Elias looked puzzled. 'What are you talking about, gal?'

Beth reluctantly explained her failure to get the tenancy of the house in Cwmbwrla. 'And my Aunt Mae has kicked us out of Brecon Parade as well.'

'Kicked you out?' Elias looked astounded. 'For why?'

Beth looked down at her feet, unwilling to reveal their family scandal. 'We quarrelled,' she said evasively. 'And there's no going back.' She paused. 'I'm looking for a room to rent, but no one is willing to take a baby in. Do you know of a place, Elias?'

She watched him hopefully as he lifted his leather cap and scratched his head. 'Well now, that's a tall order, that is.'

Beth's shoulders drooped. 'Never mind.' She picked up her case again. 'I'd better be going,' she said dejectedly, dreading to part from the only friendly face she had seen in Brynmill. 'I'll keep looking, I suppose.'

'Hold on!' he said, shuffling his feet, his expression indecisive. 'It's Saturday night, gal. A kid like you can't be still walking the streets when the drunks are slung out of the pubs. It isn't safe.'

'I'll surely find something before then,' Beth said, although it was a forlorn hope.

'No, wait a minute.' He took the case from her hand. 'You'd best come along with me. You can stay at our house for the night, or maybe two. You can look for lodgings on Monday first thing.'

Beth was astonished, and grateful too at the unexpected suggestion. 'Your house?' She knew he rented a two-up-two-down terraced house on nearby Caemawr Street. 'Are you sure? Will there be room for me and the baby?'

'We'll find you a corner, gal. Come on, it's not far.' He took her by the elbow. 'Mind you, it's no palace, not like you're used to at Brecon Parade, but the missus and me does the best we can, see.'

Beth almost laughed as she trotted along beside him. She had had no comfort at her aunt's home, stuck in a tiny room at the top of the house.

'One thing, though, gal,' he said cautiously. 'My missus . . .' He sounded worried. 'You must take her as you finds her. She is one to fly off the handle in a minute, is my Peggy, but deep down she's got a good heart.'

Beth faltered in her step. 'Then she won't like it, you bringing me home without asking her first. I don't want to cause trouble, Elias.'

'Her bark is worse than her bite,' he said, but he sounded nervous.

Within a five-minute walk they'd reached Caemawr Street, and Elias pushed open the door of number six. Beth followed him down a short narrow passage to the back room which smelled of fried onions with a hint of boiled cabbage.

'It's me, Peg,' Elias called.

There was a great clatter of pots from the scullery, and a woman's raucous voice shouted: 'Cissie! Fetch the tin bath. Your father's home.'

Elias gave Beth an apologetic smile. 'It's the coal dust, see. Got to bath every night, like a miner. But don't worry, I'll do it after supper.'

A short stocky woman with frizzy red hair, whose florid face was somehow familiar, marched out of the scullery, wiping her hands on a towel. 'Eli!' she bellowed again. 'You're late!' She stopped and stared when she saw Beth. 'Who the heck is she?'

'It's like this, see, Peg . . .' Elias began.

'Out she goes!' Peggy Morgan yelled an interruption. 'I'm not having your bits of fluff in my house.' She paused. 'And with a babby, too.'

'Don't be *twp*, Peg, will you?' Elias exclaimed, casting an embarrassed glance at Beth. 'It's nothing like that, mun. This here is Beth, Dan Henshaw's niece. You remember.'

'What?' she howled, glaring at Beth. 'Not her what stole our Cissie's job?'

'I didn't steal anybody's job,' Beth retorted. She was

wondering if accepting Elias's offer was such a good idea after all. 'I've got my own. I'm a qualified seamstress.'

'Huh! Our girl got the push though, didn't she, on account of you?'

Beth turned to Elias. 'I'd better go. I'm not welcome.'

'Now hold on a minute, mun,' Elias said. 'Peg love, give us a chance to explain, will you? The Henshaws have kicked her out. She's on the street with nowhere to go.'

Peggy Morgan gave a loud sniff of disdain. 'I'm not surprised, bringing trouble to the house with a baby. It's a disgrace.' She tossed her head. 'Our Cissie might be a bean short of an ounce, but she's a good clean-living girl.'

'So am I,' Beth hooted in anger. 'This baby is my brother.' She was tired of telling people that. Why were they so suspicious and quick to think the worst of her? 'My mother died last week, giving birth.'

Peggy's rugged face fell. 'Oh! *Duw! Duw!*'

She glanced at Elias for confirmation and he nodded. 'It's true, Peg,' he said. The Henshaws have turned on Beth for some reason. But we won't turn our backs, will we?'

'Of course we won't, you silly beggar,' she exclaimed loudly as though he had suggested they might, and bustled forward. 'Here! Give the babby to me. He wants changing by the smell of him.'

The shawl was quickly unwrapped, and Tommy was lifted from Beth's arms. She was astonished by the sudden change in Peggy Morgan's mood, and glanced at Elias for guidance to find he was grinning broadly.

'She's a wonder is my Peggy. Heart as big as a kingdom, she has.'

'Take your coat off,' Peggy instructed Beth. 'You looks

done in, girl.' She sat on a chair with Tommy on her broad lap and proceeded to undo his nappy. 'Where's the doings?'

Beth indicated the canvas bag, but couldn't rest herself until Tommy had been fed. 'I need to mix some feed as well,' she said tiredly. 'The poor little mite is starving.'

'*Cissie!*' Peggy Morgan shrieked at the top of her voice, making Beth nearly jump out of her skin. 'Put the kettle on, there's a good girl. We're sinking in by here for the want of a cup of tea.'

'You'll have to share Cissie's bed,' Peggy told Beth later when she had eaten her portion of potatoes, liver, onions and cabbage. 'We'll find something for the baby to sleep in.'

'He's got to be with me,' Beth said hastily. 'I'll need to see to him in the night.'

'Of course, of course,' Peggy said impatiently.

'I'll see to him, if you like?' Cissie Morgan offered quickly. 'I've got no job to get up early for.'

She was a big awkward girl, dwarfing her parents, and had a round, ingenuous face and a good-natured manner. Beth liked her immediately and felt sorry the girl had lost her job at Brecon Parade through Beth's arrival.

'Oh, there's kind of you,' she said gently, not wanting to hurt the other girl's feelings. 'But I'll manage.'

'I'll mind him for you any time,' Cissie offered. She'd eagerly fussed over Tommy all evening, and Beth saw she was itching to nurse him.

Beth turned to Peggy who she sensed was the real head of the household. 'Can you put up with us until Monday, please, Mrs Morgan?'

'Peggy my name is,' the older woman said quickly. 'And you can stay until you find a place of your own,' she went on generously.

'I'll pay my way,' Beth said hastily. She didn't want charity. 'You tell me how much you need for our keep?'

Peggy looked confused, obviously a new experience for her.

'We'll talk about that later,' she said brusquely. 'Now I'm off to bed. I'm up at four in the morning, on my rounds.'

Beth suddenly knew why her face was familiar. Peggy drove a pony and trap for Edwards the Milk, and had called most mornings at Brecon Parade to dole out jugs of milk from the churns she hauled in the trap.

'Thank you, Mrs Morg— er . . . Peggy,' Beth stammered. 'You know I'm very grateful.'

Beth was glad of Cissie's offer to mind Tommy on Monday morning. Looking for lodgings might take most of the day, and she also had to call in at Lewis Lewis to explain why she couldn't resume work just yet. She hoped they would understand, but began to tremble as she walked into the shop's workroom just after nine o'clock, and saw Mrs Brewer's lips tighten at the sight of her.

'What time do you call this, Miss Pryce?' the supervisor asked pithily.

'I haven't come back to work, Mrs Brewer,' Beth said hastily. 'I can't just yet.'

Mrs Brewer frowned. 'Can't? Why not, then?'

'I have to find lodgings today. It's not easy with a baby.'

'Baby? What baby?'

Beth ignored the question. She wouldn't explain it again.

'It'll take me a day or two to find somewhere. I hope I can start back Thursday.' She wondered vaguely where on earth she could leave Tommy. She couldn't imagine bringing him to the workroom.

Mrs Brewer's mouth was prune-shaped with disapproval.

'Thursday is not good enough, Miss Pryce. I don't know what Mr Wallace will say about this. You wait here while I speak to him.' She shook her head. 'He won't be pleased, I can tell you.'

'But I can't help it,' Beth exclaimed anxiously. She couldn't lose her job on top of everything else. 'Surely he'll make allowances for a death in the family?'

Mrs Brewer sniffed and left the room. Beth waited in high anxiety. She had completed her apprenticeship without losing one day's work. That must count for something. It would be so unfair if she were to lose her job just when she might earn some money.

Mrs Brewer came back and Beth could tell from the stern look on her face that Mr Wallace's decision was harsh.

'You've already taken off ten working days,' Mrs Brewer said severely. 'Mr Wallace says death in the family or no, it's too much. I did warn you the other week, didn't I? He says you're finished, Miss Pryce, as from last Friday, so you can't expect any outstanding pay.'

'Finished?' Beth was stunned. 'Just like that?'

'Yes. Now, if you'll excuse me, I've work to do.'

'But what about a reference?' she cried desperately. 'Surely he can do that? I'll need a reference to get another job as seamstress.'

Mrs Brewer raised her brows as though surprised at Beth's denseness. 'References have to be earned,' she said loftily. 'You've only just finished your apprenticeship.' She shook her head. 'You have had no experience, none at all. You haven't actually worked for us as a seamstress so you can hardly expect a reference, Miss Pryce. Now, good day!'

Beth came out of the shop in a daze and stood for a moment outside the King's Head public house in the High Street, not knowing what to do next.

Nowhere to live, no job, no wage coming in, and with a young baby to care for – how would they survive? The money her mother had left wouldn't last long. She was destitute! What on earth could she do?

Too depressed and worried to search for lodgings after getting the sack, Beth returned to Caemawr Street, to brood and think.

Peggy Morgan had returned from her milk delivery round and was busy in the lean-to out in the backyard, doing the weekly wash. She already had some nappies flapping away on the clothesline and looked surprised to see Beth.

'You're back soon. Found something?'

Beth bit her lip. 'No, the opposite,' she said miserably. 'Oh, Peggy, they've given me the sack from my job! They wouldn't even give me a reference. Can anything worse happen to me?'

She shook her head. 'It's bad luck, girl, but there's always something worse around the corner, so don't go looking for it.'

'But how can I search for lodgings when there's no money to pay the rent?' She wouldn't mention the money Esme had left her. It was no one else's business. 'Now I must find work instead.'

'Then you'd best stay here with us,' Peggy said, hands on hips.

'What?'

'I've been thinking,' she went on. 'How would you manage to work with a babby on your hands anyway? Now I've got an idea . . .'

She marched into the scullery, lit the gas ring and

dumped the iron kettle on to it. Beth followed her in, wondering what she meant.

'Stop looking so gloomy and make yourself useful,' Peggy snapped bossily. 'Get the cups and saucers. We'll have a cuppa while I tell you what to do.

'Now then,' she began. 'For starters, you've got a place to live.' She tapped the table with the top of her index finger. 'Right here with us, if you don't mind sharing a bed with Cissie?'

Beth nodded with the eagerness of one who has no bed at all. 'I don't mind that.'

'Good.' Peggy nodded satisfied. 'Right, now we'll come to some arrangement about rent and your keep, and you can pull your weight around the house when you have some time off.'

'Huh! I've nothing but time off now,' Beth said dejectedly.

'I'm coming to that,' Peggy snapped. 'For seconds, you'll have to give up your highfaluting ideas about finding a job like you had before.'

'But it's my trade!'

'You need to get a job,' Peggy insisted firmly, her finger pounding the table. 'And get one quick. Beggars can't pick and choose, girl. They take what they can get.'

'I'm *not* a beggar,' Beth said indignantly.

'Next step up from one,' Peggy contradicted her sharply. 'Wake up, girl! This is real life. Now, as for the babby, Cissie can look after him during the day, and you can pay her something for her trouble.'

Beth blinked at the common sense of it, though she didn't like the idea of giving up her trade. Her father had worked hard for the money he had paid for her apprenticeship. She still thought of Percy Pryce as her father, and she always would.

'Thank you, Peggy, for your generosity,' Beth said with sincerity. 'And Tommy and I are thankful for your hospitality, too.' It was more than she had received from her own kin. 'But I'm not ready to give up on my trade just yet.'

'Tsk! Stubborn, you are. You won't take telling, will you?' Peggy scowled. 'All right, girl, we'll see how you feel in a couple of weeks when you've been turned down umpteen times, and the only thing in your purse is fluff.'

'But I don't know anything else,' Beth argued dispiritedly.

'You know how to clean, don't you?' Peggy said sharply. 'You know how to get down on your knees and rub and scrub? And don't tell me you're better than that, because we are all better than that, but needs must when the devil drives.'

Beth felt chastened. She was clinging to the remnants of her old life and perhaps she could no longer afford to.

Three weeks later found her no nearer gaining a position as a seamstress in any of the first-class shops in town, or even the second-class ones, yet she was reluctant to give up altogether, despite Peggy's sniffs and snorts of impatience.

When her benefactress came home from her milk round one morning, Beth was upstairs cleaning the bedrooms and was startled to hear her name screeched at full volume up the narrow stairs.

'*Bethan!*' Peggy's hollering could have woken the dead. 'Beth! Come down here. Found you a job, I have.'

Beth scuttled downstairs. 'Not driving the milk trap, is it?' she exclaimed in horror. 'I could never manage the pony.'

'Of course not!' Peggy snapped, fists on her broad hips.

'Credit me with a bit of common sense, girl. You've got to have a talent for that job. No, Beth, this work is right up your alley.'

Her heart lifted. 'Sewing, is it? Where?'

'Put the kettle on,' Peggy said evasively, turning away. 'My mouth is parched.'

They sipped the hot liquid, the colour of dark brown leather, while Beth waited for Peggy's explanation with a queasy feeling in her stomach.

'I was on my round along the Oystermouth Road,' Peggy began. 'Delivery to them boarding houses, you know, just past the Bay View Hotel, when I seen this sign in a window – help wanted.'

Beth frowned. 'What kind of help?'

'Well, I goes in to ask, don't I?' Peggy said aggressively. 'A young woman of good character they want for general help.'

'I don't like the sound of it,' Beth said decisively. 'Skivvying is what it is, and I had enough of that with my aunt.'

Peggy's lips tightened. 'Now look here, my girl,' she said, her voice rising an octave. 'I don't know where you found the money to pay our Cissie and the rent these last weeks, but wherever it comes from it won't last for ever.'

'That's no one's business but mine, Peggy,' Beth said sharply.

'Maybe, but the Smarts are paying good money.' Peggy tapped the side of her nose. 'I saw to that. I told them I knew of a girl of the highest integrity, suit them down to the ground, for the right money.'

Beth blinked. 'Smarts?'

'That's the name of the family what runs the place,' Peggy explained. 'I've known Ada Smart for years. Runs a tidy house, mind, I'll say that for her. Commercial travellers, mostly.'

'It's still skivvying,' Beth said stubbornly.

'Tsk!' Peggy was impatient. 'Are you going to wait until you're on the bone of your arse, or what?' Her expression softened. 'Look, Beth *cariad*,' she went on, 'trying to help you, I am. You're heading for trouble, clinging to what used to be. Skivvying is the way of life for the likes of you and me, and always will be.'

Beth thought of Dan Henshaw, their father, living in comparative luxury, turning his back on his own children because of pride, or was it stubbornness? One day she'd make him pay. One day he would come begging, and she would treat him as he was treating Tommy and her.

'You're not work-shy, Beth, so what is it?' Peggy went on. 'Pride?'

'No,' she answered quickly. 'All right, Peggy. I'll go and see this Mrs Smart.'

'They wanted you to live in . . .'

'Oh, that's it!' Beth exclaimed, throwing up her hands. 'That's the finish!'

'Wait a minute, will you?' Peggy said irritably. 'I've told Ada it's out of the question because of family commitments. But don't mention Tommy whatever you do. Children are the reason why many married women can't find jobs. Employers think they'll lose too much time.'

'I'll go and see her in the morning,' Beth said resignedly.

'You'll go this afternoon,' Peggy said firmly. 'Before someone else snaps it up.'

Beth rounded the side of the Bay View Hotel and came on to the Oystermouth Road, the smell of the sea in her nostrils from the wide sweep of Swansea Bay. The houses along here were three storeys tall and well built, with imposing bay windows which overlooked the beach.

On the sea side of the road ran a high poll-stone wall, and behind this a locomotive was puffing past just out of Rutland Street station on its way to Hereford. Beyond the railway line, Beth could hear the excited cries of children playing with their buckets and spades on the sands.

Most of the boarding houses along Oystermouth Road sported unlikely names, but the Smarts had chosen perhaps the most pretentious: Windsor Lodge. The front door stood open and gave into a short but wide hall where a push bell stood on a small table near the inside glass door.

'Hello!' Beth called out nervously, but there was no answer.

Hesitantly she brought her palm down on the push bell, and nearly jumped in fright at the loud ping. After a moment the sound of shoes clipping smartly towards her came from the other side of the glass door. When it opened, a small, painfully thin woman with mousy-coloured hair peered at her questioningly.

'Yes, what you want?'

'Are you Mrs Smart?'

The thin woman's mouth drew back in a wide toothy grin. 'No, love. She'd make two of me, she would. What you want her for?'

'I've come about the job,' Beth said hesitantly. 'Peggy Morgan sent me.'

'Oh, right!' The thin woman glanced her up and down with open curiosity. 'Hold on a minute. I'll call Ada.'

When footsteps sounded again they were heavy and lumbering, and this time a tall, weighty, big-boned woman appeared. Her shrewd glance seemed to size up Beth immediately.

'So you're the girl Peggy the Milk recommends, are you?' Ada Smart asked in posh tones, although straining not to drop any aitches. 'You don't look very strong. Weaklings are no good to me.'

'I am strong,' Beth assured her. 'But I won't hump furniture about,' she went on hastily. 'That's men's work.'

Ada Smart raised her eyebrows, looking down her nose as though there was a nasty smell under it. 'Oh! Won't you, then?' She nodded. 'We've got a fit one by here, all right. If I take you on, my girl, you'll do as you're told or get the push.'

'What is the work anyway?' Beth retorted. 'Perhaps I'm not interested.'

'You'd better come in. We can talk in the kitchen.'

Beth followed the big woman through the glass door, along a passage and then down a steep flight of stone steps. The kitchen was big and surprisingly airy, giving on to a small courtyard at the back. Ada Smart indicated a chair and Beth sat.

'Now then,' Ada began, standing over her with arms folded across her ample bosom. 'I don't suppose you've got references, have you?'

Beth shook her head, and Ada looked smug. 'Your sort never do,' she said.

'My sort?' Beth was nettled. 'What do you mean, Mrs Smart?'

Ada sniffed. 'Where did you work before?'

'Lewis Lewis.'

Ada looked surprised. 'What? Cleaning?'

'No. I'm a trained seamstress.'

'Why did you get the push then?' Ada's eyes narrowed. 'It wasn't for thieving, was it?'

Beth jumped to her feet. 'Certainly not! And I resent the question.'

Ada sniffed. 'Resent all you want, my girl. I'm not taking on any jenny highjinks off the cuff. I want to be certain you're honest. I've got some very important people living here mind.'

'Who?' Beth scoffed. 'Commercial travellers?'

'No, not *them*,' Ada said disparagingly, and stuck her nose in the air. 'I'm talking about people with class. Like Mrs Russell for one. Her late husband was a town councillor.' Ada nodded sagely and rubbed her thumb and index finger together. 'Plenty of money, see. And then there's Major Boyd.' She smiled smugly. 'Oh, a proper gentleman is the Major. Raises the tone nicely, he does.'

'You haven't told me what the job is yet.'

'Helping me prepare and serve food mealtimes, and cleaning and tidying rooms. That's why I need an honest girl. Mrs Russell and the Major have some very valuable stuff, very valuable.'

'You can rely on my honesty,' Beth said seriously. The job didn't sound so bad after all. She would enjoy helping in the kitchen.

'You'll get here by half-six, for a start.'

Beth's mouth dropped open. 'So early?'

'Oh, well,' Ada said offhandedly. 'If you're work-shy, I don't want you here.'

'I'm a hard worker,' Beth retorted. 'You ask Peggy Morgan.'

Ada sniffed. 'All right then, you can start tomorrow morning,' she said. 'A guinea a week I agreed on with Peggy the Milk, and you can keep all the tips you get.'

Beth brightened. A guinea! 'I'll be here,' she hurriedly assured her new employer.

'Yes, and not a minute late, mind,' Ada warned with a superior look. 'I can't abide slackers.'

Pleased, Beth nodded and turned to leave.

'Oh, there's one other thing,' Ada said sternly. 'Watch yourself with them commercial travellers. I'll have no hanky-panky under this roof.'

11

As Beth came down to the kitchen at Windsor Lodge the following morning she saw Ada Smart glance at the clock on the wall and nod with satisfaction.

'Five minutes early, I see. Good! Off with your coat and hat as quick as you like,' Ada said brusquely. 'Get stirring this pot of porridge, and stop yawning.'

'Yes, Mrs Smart,' Beth answered dutifully, though she wondered how she would keep her eyes open for the next several hours. Tommy had kept her busy in the night with feeding and changing so sleep had been scarce. She could hardly explain that to Ada Smart.

The thin woman who she had seen the previous day came in from the backyard, two scuttles of coal in each hand, the weight making the sinews in her scrawny arms stand out.

'This is Flossie,' Ada said casually. 'She does all the heavy work.'

Flossie winked at Beth and went briskly up the stone steps as though carrying feather dusters.

While Beth diligently stirred the porridge, making sure no lumps survived, Ada was busy at the Raeburn cooker where several pans of bacon, fried bread, sausages and eggs sizzled deliciously.

'Get them dishes of porridge up to the dining room,' Ada instructed curtly. 'Them travellers will be down by now. They like to start early on their rounds.' Beth noticed her posh tones of the day before had been abandoned.

She carried the tray gingerly into the dining room where four men sat around one table, two already smoking cigarettes. Three wore crumpled three-piece suits, while the fourth was dressed like a tailor's dummy. All of them looked up as she came in, and one gave a low whistle. Beth felt her face flame up.

'What have we got here?' the well-dressed man said with a twang that sounded strange to her ears. He sported a trimmed moustache, while his hair was slicked close to his head with too much brilliantine. 'A new little dolly, by gum. Nice, too.'

'I saw her first,' a red-faced man said.

'Bugger off, Pearce,' the dandy retorted harshly. 'You had the last one.'

Beth stood still, holding the tray, petrified.

'Well, come on,' another man urged her. 'Serve it up. Our bloody breakfast is getting cold.'

Nerving herself to move closer, Beth quickly dumped the dishes of porridge on the table, conscious of four leering faces, and beat a hasty retreat, accompanied by cat-calls.

Outside in the passage she leaned against the wall for a moment, shaking with embarrassment, hand over her mouth. She had never experienced anything like that before, and was distressed to realise it somehow made her feel unclean.

'You'd better get used to it,' a sharp voice said nearby, and Beth looked up, startled, to see a girl about her own age standing on the last step of the main staircase, leaning nonchalantly against the newel post. She was smartly dressed, slim and shapely, with long blonde shoulder-length hair, but her prettiness was marred by a painted mouth and rouged cheeks.

Beth swallowed. 'I don't think I will,' she said faintly, wondering who this might be.

'It's second nature to them,' the girl said. 'It's only a bit of fun. Where's your sense of humour?'

Beth bridled. 'I don't like it,' she rejoined. 'And I won't put up with it, either. I'll complain to Mrs Smart.'

The girl gave a scornful laugh. 'Then you won't last long here. Mam don't like skivvies what causes trouble with the guests, even salesmen.'

With that she marched past Beth and went downstairs to the kitchen, Beth following.

Ada Smart was all smiles to see the girl, and Beth was astonished at the tender light in the woman's normally hard eyes.

'Gloria love, there's nice you look in your new frock.'

Gloria made a moue and pulled at the neckline. 'It's all right, Mam, but I don't know what Syd will think when he sees it. It's last year's fashion, and Syd likes to see me in the latest thing.'

Ada's lips tightened. 'And I don't know what *you* see in that Syd,' she said. 'He'll never amount to anything.'

'Well, Dad likes him.' Gloria pouted. 'Always ready to buy him a pint at the Bay View, Syd is.'

Ada rounded on Beth. 'Come on, girl!' she said harshly. 'Don't stand by there doing nothing. Fetch my daughter her breakfast.' She turned to Gloria, her tone softening. 'You sit down, love, and eat.'

Gloria flashed Beth a sly look. 'The new girl has a complaint, Mam,' she said spitefully. 'Hasn't been here five minutes and she's already on the moan.'

Ada stared at Beth questioningly. 'What's that?'

Beth swallowed. 'It's the men in the dining room,' she explained hesitantly. 'They insulted me. I don't like it.'

'Thin-skinned, are you?' Ada said brusquely. 'Too bad

if you are. If you want to work here, my girl, you'll put up with more than that. Words and leers won't hurt you, just keep out of the way of their hands.'

'It's disrepsectful, the way they behave,' Beth objected heatedly. 'They talked to me as if I were – cheap.'

Gloria gave a hoot of laughter, while Ada pointed to four plates of food on a large tray. 'Are you going to take those up now?' she asked nastily. 'Or do I look for someone who will?'

Knowing she was beaten Beth carried the tray up to the dining room, bracing herself to meet the onslaught of their jeering voices and lascivious glances, but now the men ignored her, having had their fun, and were talking shop with serious expressions. Beth dumped the plates before them and scampered out.

'Mrs Russell and Major Boyd will be down to breakfast about nine,' Ada told Beth later, after she had worked her way through the washing up. 'I'll see to them while you clean and tidy their rooms. You've got an hour so don't dawdle. And don't go breaking anything,' she added, 'because it will come out of your wages.'

'What about those men's rooms?' Beth asked with dread. She hadn't liked the suggestive way the dandy had smirked at her, and didn't want to run into him by accident upstairs. 'Must I do their rooms, too?'

'Once a week is good enough for them,' Ada said with a dismissive sniff. 'The commercials, as I call them, usually don't stay longer than that. Anyway they're out most of the day.'

When Beth came down to the kitchen later she found another pile of dirty crockery waiting for her, but she got on with it without a word, eager to show she was a willing worker.

'Right! Now you've finished that lot,' Ada said later, 'there's the laundry to see to.'

'I don't do washing,' Beth exclaimed indignantly.

'No one is asking you to,' Ada snapped impatiently. 'We use the Chinese laundry on St Helen's Road, You'll find the bundles of dirty linen out in the backyard. Fetch the handcart from the back of the pub, bring it around the front and Flossie will help you load up. Fetch the clean linen back with you.'

Beth stared, dismayed. 'You expect me to push a handcart through the streets?' This was worse than anything Aunt Mae had demanded of her. 'The laundry collects and delivers,' she went on. 'I've seen their carts about the streets.'

Ada looked annoyed. 'Yes, and they charge for that, too. What do you think I'm paying *you* for, miss?' Her lips tightened. 'If you won't do it there's plenty about as will.' She wagged a finger in Beth's face. 'Now look here, my girl, if you don't want this job just say so. You can push off home, but don't expect to get any money. You've earned nothing yet.'

Beth thought of the guinea a week Ada had promised. Tommy needed so much, and they had to live somehow. Her pride would take a knock, but she knew she would make any sacrifice for him. Her shoulders dropped. She knew she had no choice. 'All right, Mrs Smart. I'll get my hat.'

'I should think so, too!' Ada said with triumph. 'And be quick about it.'

The bundles of dirty linen, piled high, were heavy and made the cart difficult to manoeuvre; try as she might Beth could not prevent it swinging into the path of other vehicles from time to time. Her arms began to ache as she tried desperately to keep one wheel in the gutter to avoid the horses and carts that rattled past, and shut her ears to the angry curses and shouts of the drivers.

Almost in tears with the shame of it, Beth thought of Dan Henshaw. His treachery and selfishness had brought her to this. She was destitute and desperate because of him, and her shame turned to anger against him. She would pay him back one day.

Anger lent more power to her arms, and eventually she reached the laundry and was thankful for their help with unloading. She was on her way back with the cart laden with pristine linen when a loud toot from a passing motorcar startled her, making her lose her grip on the shafts. The cart tipped forward and Beth screamed, seeing the precious load about to slide off. She grabbed the rising shafts and using all her strength managed to right it, but not before several bundles of linen fell on to the road.

'Oh, no!' Mrs Smart would be furious.

There was a screech of female laughter from the open motorcar that had pulled up a few yards on, and looking up Beth saw the grinning face of Gloria Smart in the front seat. Beside her was a young man, also grinning. He reminded Beth of the dandy salesman, with the same slicked-back hair and air of self-assurance.

Turning her back on them, Beth secured the front of the cart, pulling down the wooden stand that kept it stable for loading, and began to lift the heavy bundles back into place, biting her lip to see how dusty they were from contact with the road. Mrs Smart would dock her wages for this, and it wasn't even her fault.

The next moment the young man was standing at her side, lifting up one of the bundles.

'I'll give you a hand, love,' he said. 'Sorry about this.'

'Leave her, Syd!' Gloria called angrily from the motorcar. 'She deserves it. She's a halfwit anyway.'

Syd took no notice of her. 'You're the Smarts' new girl, then?' he said unnecessarily. 'I'm Syd Woods. Pleased to meet you. What's your name, kid?'

Beth wasn't so pleased to meet him. He was a sharp-featured young man, with knowing eyes that wouldn't quite meet her own. The word 'sly' came into her mind, and she judged that summed him up completely.

'You ought to be more careful,' she said crossly, evading having to answer his question. She jerked her thumb towards the car. 'If you can't control that contraption, you shouldn't be on the road with it.'

He grinned. 'Do you mean the motor or Gloria?'

Despite her caution, Beth had to smile, 'Both,' she said. The last bundle was lifted and put back on the cart and, stealing a glance behind her at Gloria's furious face, she went on, 'You'd better get back to her. I think she's about to throw a fit.'

'Never mind Gloria,' he said offhandedly. 'Tell me, do you live in with the Smarts?'

'No,' Beth answered quickly. She released the stand, and got between the shafts again. 'I must be going. Mrs Smart is watching me like a hawk. You've already made me late and I don't want to get the sack.'

'Syd!' There was a high-pitched cry from Gloria. 'Come here this minute!'

'Listen, kid,' he said persuasively to Beth, 'I like the looks of you. You're pretty. Would you like to come for a spin in the motor some time?'

'No, thank you,' Beth said quickly. 'Now please go away!' She flicked a glance at the furious Gloria. 'You're making trouble for me.'

He stepped away. 'Okay, but you'll be seeing me again,

kid,' he said with a cheeky grin. 'I'm round at Windsor Lodge all the time.'

Beth trundled on with the cart and didn't look back. Gloria Smart already had it in for her for some reason, now Syd Woods had made things worse.

She was exhausted by the time she reached the Smarts' boarding house, and was thankful when Flossie came out immediately to help hump the bundles into the house.

A small, thin man with shirt cuffs hanging loose stood in the doorway, hands in pockets, watching them. He made no attempt to help.

'Who is that?' Beth whispered to Flossie as they struggled with the linen. 'Does he work for Mrs Smart?'

'Not if he can help it. That's Bert Smart, Ada's hubby,' Flossie answered quietly. 'Lazy beggar he is, too. Never done a day's work in his life.'

Beth looked him over covertly. Ada was so big and he was so small, they made an odd couple, she thought. Bert was badly in need of a shave, and his scruffy appearance seemed at odds with Ada's obvious snobbishness. His crumpled trousers were too short, the turn-ups barely touching his anklebones. Beth spied bare feet in tatty slippers. His waistcoat, unbuttoned over a flannel shirt, was stained with egg and what looked like tomato sauce. A cigarette dangled from the corner of his mouth.

'The missus dotes on him,' Flossie said with disgust. 'I'd be kicking his arse down the street if he were mine. Shifty bugger!'

As Beth came in with the last of the bundles, Bert Smart grinned at her. The cigarette bobbed and appeared to be permanently stuck to his yellowed lip.

'You done a good job there, girl,' he said in a tone which suggested he knew what he was talking about.

Beth smiled faintly, not knowing what to make of him.

He grinned back, showing a mouthful of stained teeth.

'Bert Smart's the name,' he told her, and winked. 'Smart by name and smart by nature, that's me.'

Beth decided to tell Ada straight away about the accident with the cart before Gloria had a chance and made it sound worse than it was.

Ada's expression was stony. 'If there's any damage I'll dock it out of your pay,' she said sharply.

'That's not fair!' Beth exclaimed hotly, trying to hold on to her temper. 'It wasn't my fault.'

'You were in charge of the cart,' Ada snapped back. 'So who else's was it?' She looked Beth up and down. 'Tsk! I'm beginning to regret listening to Peggy the Milk. You're a dead loss.'

'I'll do better next time,' Beth said quickly, fearing she was heading for the sack.

'There won't be a next time,' Ada said ominously. 'From now on Flossie will take the cart to the laundry twice a week. You can do one or two of her jobs instead. Riddle and blacklead all the grates throughout the house daily, set all the fires, including the kitchen range, and hump in all the coal.' She nodded with satisfaction. '*That* should put some muscle on you, my girl.'

As she had suspected Gloria tried to make trouble for her over the incident with the laundry, but Beth's prompt confession had diffused Ada's wrath, which appeared to make Gloria boil with fury. Passing Beth on the stairs the following morning, she gave her a venomous look.

'You're wasting your time trying to get off with Syd. He's *my* boyfriend,' she said sourly. 'You're too dowdy for him. He says you're plain anyway.' She flicked back her hair, stuck her pert nose in the air, and stepped past down the stairs. 'You've got no style, you haven't,' she called over her shoulder. 'No man could fancy you.'

It didn't get any easier over the following weeks, but Beth found the strength to cope, even though she went home each night to her shared room at the Morgans' household feeling tired out. She would not give in, though, because of Tommy. Each night she cuddled him until he fell asleep, then watched him in his makeshift cot, aching with love for him, promising herself he would never want for anything while she was alive to fend for him.

She was sparing with the guinea she received each week from Ada, and spent nothing on herself. Instead she saved up and managed to afford a second-hand pram, looking forward to the coming summer when she could take Tommy for walks along the prom on weekend afternoons.

She was planning such an outing on the first Saturday in May, and was hurrying to finish all her chores at Windsor Lodge that morning before taking her Saturday half-day.

It was already half-past twelve. The commercial travellers had vacated their rooms and she was cleaning them ready for the new intake on Monday. She was dusting and humming a tune she had heard Gloria play over and over on her gramophone, realising she hadn't felt so happy in a long time, despite the hard work.

Flossie came up to the room as Beth was on hands and knees, cleaning the linoleum under the bed with the brush and dustpan.

'Beth, you've got a visitor.'

She was startled and jerked up, bumping her head on the iron strut of the bedstead. 'What?' For some reason her mind immediately jumped to Dan Henshaw.

'It's Peggy the Milk's barmy daughter,' Flossie told her. 'And she's in a right old state. You'd better come down. Ada's spitting tintacks.'

Cissie was sitting hunched up in the kitchen, her face blotchy with crying, while an exasperated Ada stood over her. When Beth came in, Cissie sprang to her feet with an anguished howl.

'Beth, Tommy's gone! They took him.'

'Took him? Who took him?' Beth exclaimed, frightened and confused. 'What's happened? What are you talking about?'

Cissie gulped deeply, wiping her dripping nose on the sleeve of her cardigan. 'Nursing Tommy, I was, out by our front gate, see,' she gabbled. 'A horse and trap stopped and two men got out. They said they had come for the baby . . .'

'Baby?' Ada interposed sharply. 'What baby?' She glared at Beth. 'You never let on you had a baby.' Her mouth tightened. 'You're not married, are you?'

'Tommy is my brother,' Beth snapped impatiently. 'Cissie! For God's sake, tell me what happened? Who were these men?'

'I dunno!' she exclaimed miserably. 'Two working men they were.' Her face crumpled. 'Tommy is kidnapped!' She began to howl like a she-wolf.

'Cissie!' Beth grabbed both her arms and shook her. 'Stop it!'

'Smack her face,' Flossie suggested. 'She's hysterical.'

'Now look here,' Ada boomed at Beth, 'I'm not paying you to idle about by here. There's work to do. See to your domestic problems in your own time, if you please.'

Beth rounded on her. 'You stupid woman!' she burst

out angrily, making Ada stare. 'Don't you understand, my baby brother is missing?' She turned to the sobbing girl. 'Did you just hand him over?'

'Of course not!' Cissie said indignantly. 'I ran in the house with him, didn't I, and tried to shut the door, but they followed. They snatched him from me, and took the shawl as well.' She lifted her head and began to wail again. 'Oh, my little Tommy! They'll cut off his ears, I know they will. We'll have to pay the ransom, Beth.'

'Ransom?' Ada frowned. 'What the hell is she talking about?'

Beth put both hands to her head to think. This had nothing to do with money. She was willing to bet her very life that Dan Henshaw lay behind it. Tommy was his flesh and blood, and although he wouldn't acknowledge him honestly, Dan wanted his own son.

'Here! I've had enough of this,' Ada exclaimed when Beth remained silent. 'Flossie! Go and fetch a bobby.'

'No!' Beth shouted. 'There's no need for that. I know who has taken him and why. Its nothing to do with ransoms.'

'Who is it then?' Ada demanded.

Beth swallowed hard, embarrassed. 'A relative,' she said simply.

'Oh, well!' Ada said. 'There's nothing to worry about then. The kid isn't in any danger.'

'If you think I'm going to leave it like that,' Beth said forcefully, 'you can think again, Mrs Smart. I'm going to get my brother back right now.'

Her coat and hat were hanging on a hook behind the back door. She snatched them and put them on. Ada went red in the face.

'You can't just walk out like that, my girl,' she exclaimed angrily. 'I won't have it.'

'This is a family emergency,' Beth said. 'I'm going, so there! Come on, Cissie.'

'I'll dock your wages!' Ada yelled in fury as they raced up the steps from the kitchen. 'You won't have a job to come back to. You can be replaced, Beth Pryce, and more cheaply too.'

12

Outside Windsor Lodge Beth stood panting with anxiety.

'You go home now, Cissie,' she said breathlessly as the other girl fell into step beside her.

Cissie grabbed her arm. 'But I want to come with you, Beth, to find Tommy. I'm awful worried.' Her plain face crumpled. 'It wasn't my fault, honest.'

Beth patted her hand distractedly. 'No one is blaming you, Cissie,' she reassured her. 'I'll get him back, don't worry.'

'They're big men, mind,' she warned, her voice trembling. 'Let's get my dad to go with us.'

'There's nothing to worry about,' Beth said emphatically. 'I know who has him all right, and I know how to deal with it.' She only hoped that were true, yet had no idea how she could compel Dan to give the child back.

'But who is it? It's an awful cruel thing to do, mun, stealing a baby. Maybe we *should* tell the bobbies?'

'Cissie, please! Go home.'

Beth strode away at a fast pace towards Brynmill, leaving the other girl standing reluctantly on the pavement outside the boarding house.

Reaching Dan's house in Brecon Parade, Beth didn't waste time going around to the back door but pounded on the front, and kept pounding until the door was opened. Mrs Wilks's face was a picture of guilt when she saw Beth standing there.

'What do you want?'

'You know well enough,' she exclaimed loudly. 'There's nothing goes on under this roof that you haven't got your nose into.'

'Well, really! The insolence!'

'Where's Dan Henshaw? I demand to see him now.'

'He's not here.'

'You liar!' Beth put a hand against Mrs Wilks's shoulder and pushed her out of the way. 'Where's Tommy?' she said, forcing her way into the hall. 'I want my brother back *now*. Go and fetch him, wherever he is.'

'You're mad,' Mrs Wilks spluttered as she staggered to one side. 'I don't know what you're talking about . . .'

'Dan Henshaw!' Beth hollered. 'Come out and face me like – like a father.'

'If you don't get out,' Mrs Wilks was still spluttering, 'I'll call a constable.'

'Your employer wouldn't like that,' Beth flashed back. 'Too many skeletons in his cupboard.'

'What's the meaning of this disturbance?' Dan came out of the sitting room, a stern expression on his handsome face. 'Beth!' He pretended surprise. 'What are you doing here?'

Beth marched up to him. 'Where's Tommy? I demand to see him,' she cried loudly. She was shaking with anger and apprehension and couldn't control either. 'I'm taking him home now, where he belongs.'

'You're not making sense,' Dan said casually. 'You're hysterical. Calm down.'

'Why did you take him in such an underhand way?' Beth asked raggedly. 'You could've seen him at any time. You only had to ask.'

Dan glanced at Mrs Wilks and nodded, and the housekeeper walked away.

'Has she gone to fetch him?' Beth asked hopefully.

'No!' He turned abruptly and walked back into the sitting room as though dismissing her, but Beth quickly followed in his steps.

'Don't you ignore me,' she said, furious he had turned his back on her.

'Get off your high horse,' Dan retorted. 'You burst into my house uninvited. I could have you arrested.'

'Well, have me arrested then,' Beth flared. 'And I'll tell the authorities you have abducted my brother. See what they think of that!'

'I did not abduct him,' he denied vehemently. 'I rescued him. Look, Beth, be reasonable. The boy is no longer your concern.'

'You can't do this,' she cried passionately. 'You can't take him from me – you can't separate us. It's callous and you've got no right.'

'I can do as I like. Tommy is my son.'

Beth gaped, staring at him. 'You finally admit it then?' she said in hushed tones.

'There are no witnesses to what I say in this room,' he said brusquely. 'I'll deny it anywhere else. I've taken the child in because you are unfit to care for him. As far as the world is concerned he is my orphaned nephew.'

'I've taken very good care of him,' Beth burst out. 'He hasn't wanted for anything. And he's loved, which is perhaps more important.' She gave him a scathing look. 'You don't love him so don't pretend you're concerned for his welfare. All you're interested in is an heir.'

'My motives are none of your business,' Dan retorted harshly. 'But as it so happens I do intend to take him into the business with me in time, and he'll inherit it all when I'm gone.'

'How cold and empty that sounds,' Beth said. 'He'll grow

up a lonely little boy separated from those who love him.'

'The boy is better off with me than living in that hovel with a half-witted woman taking care of him,' Dan said angrily. 'You left him all day with strangers.'

'I have to work,' Beth said angrily. 'Cissie is devoted to him. But I don't think much of his chances if he's left to the mercies of that horrible Mrs Wilks.'

'I'll get a proper nursemaid,' Dan conceded. 'There's nothing more to say, Beth.' He gave here a crooked smile. 'You ought to be relieved to be rid of the responsibility. Now you can get on with your own life, find yourself a husband, get some babies of your own.'

She shook her head. 'It's not ending here, Dan. You've got no legal right to him. You're his real father, but not legitimately, whereas I'm his flesh and blood kin.' She lifted her chin, trying to look surer of herself than she was. 'I'll go to the authorities,' she said. 'They'll decide. You could find yourself in serious trouble.'

Dan's face reddened in fury. 'Now look here, you stubborn little minx!' he hissed, a malevolent look in his eyes. 'You'd better forget Tommy and any claim you think you have, because if you make trouble for me, I'll make plenty for you. Starting with your pal Elias Morgan.'

'What do you mean?' Beth stared at him, feeling frightened suddenly.

'Either you agree that Tommy stays with me, while you stay out of my life altogether,' Dan said ominously, 'or Morgan gets the sack, and I'll see that he doesn't find another job in this town or in this county even.'

Beth was appalled. 'You wouldn't do that to an honest man who has been a faithful employee for so long?'

His stare was filled with arrogance. 'If you knew me better you wouldn't even ask that. No one stands in my way, Beth.'

She swallowed hard, feeling her throat tighten. Could this man with his distinguished looks and air of authority really be her father? For all his handsomeness, Beth detected a deep lack in him. There was no warmth in the fine eyes, no hint of tenderness in the well-defined lips. Here was a hard man who went his own way, driven by his own needs. Could such a man ever find love in his heart for his unwanted child? She doubted it, and the knowledge brought sorrow to her own heart and a deep sense of loneliness.

'How can you treat me like this?' she asked raggedly, the pain deep in her chest. 'I'm your child too.'

His expression was stony. 'You are no child of mine.'

The words were all too familiar, and they cut deep, but the pain brought renewed resentment to Beth's heart.

'You're right,' she said vehemently. 'You are the last man I want for a father. You don't know the meaning of the word. I doubt you even know what love is.' She shook her head. 'No, Dan, I want nothing to do with you, and I certainly want nothing *from* you.'

'Then we are of the same mind,' he said harshly. 'Now, leave this house.'

'Not yet!' Beth shouted. 'There's something you've forgotten. Aunt Mae. She won't want Tommy here. Does she know you've taken him?'

'This has nothing to do with Mae,' he thundered.

'If I can't see Tommy then I'll see my aunt. Where is she?'

'I told you to get out!'

Beth turned and ran into the hall, not caring whether he followed or not. There was no sign of Mrs Wilks, and Beth made for the staircase and began to race up the stairs.

'Come back!' Dan roared the command. 'You're to leave Mae alone. She's not well.'

Guessing Aunt Mae was in her bedroom getting ready to go out as she usually did on a Saturday afternoon, Beth headed straight there. She could hear Dan's feet pounding on the stairs behind her, but didn't hesitate for a second. She had every right to speak with her aunt, even if she got a cold reception.

Beth burst into Mae's bedroom without even stopping to knock.

'Aunt Mae, I must see you!' she began breathlessly. 'Dan has abducted my brother . . .' The remainder of her words died on her lips as she stared at her aunt with shock.

Mae was sitting in a basket chair near the window, a rug over her knees and a shawl around her shoulders. She turned her head as the door opened and Beth was stunned by her changed looks. She had lost weight and there was a deathly pallor to her skin. Her eyes, which were normally bright and fierce, had a sunken look.

Mrs Wilks, who was mixing some dark liquid in a glass at the washstand, darted forward. 'Get out! Can't you see madam is not well?'

Ignoring her, Beth came forward to her aunt's chair, suddenly very concerned. 'Aunt Mae, what is it? What's wrong?'

Mrs Wilks was trying to bustle between them. 'It's none of your business,' she said.

'It's all right, Mrs Wilks,' Mae said in a weakened voice Beth hardly recognised. 'My niece won't be staying long.'

'You're ill,' Beth said helplessly. 'I didn't know.'

'No reason why you should be told,' Mae said. 'We are no longer connected.'

Beth shook her head. 'This is no time to continue the ill-feeling between us,' she said gently. 'I'd have come to see you sooner had I known you were ill.'

'Who said you would have been welcome?' Some of Mae's old fire flashed through her briefly, but very briefly. When she spoke again the embers were extinguished. 'And I know why you've come today. It's because of Esme's child, isn't it?'

'You know what he's done?' Beth said in astonishment. 'And you approve?'

'No, I certainly don't,' Mae said. 'But as you can see I'm in no fit state to challenge him. Dan will do as he pleases from now on,' she went on in a resigned voice.

'Well, if you won't interfere, I will,' Beth said adamantly. 'He's acting as though he is beyond the law.'

'It's none of your business, Beth.'

'Huh! That's what everyone keeps telling me,' she said bitterly. 'And I'm sick of hearing it. Dan had Tommy taken from me by force. That's against the law unless I'm very much mistaken. He has threatened me too, and my friends.'

'There is nothing either of us can do about it,' Mae said wearily. 'And if you know what's good for you and your friends, you'll stay out of Dan Henshaw's way. He means every threat he utters.' She passed the back of her hand across her forehead as though she were bone weary. 'Now, please leave me alone. I'm exhausted as it is with the pain . . .'

Mrs Wilks rushed forward with the glass of milky-brown liquid, and Mae seized it eagerly and drank.

'Oh, I'm so sorry,' Beth said and impulsively reached forward to kiss Mae's cheek, but her aunt recoiled from the touch.

'That's enough!' Dan was in the doorway. It was obvious to Beth that he had been there listening for some time. 'You heard what Mae said. Leave her alone. Get out of this house and don't come back. You're not welcome.'

Beth looked at her. 'Do you really want me to go, Aunt Mae?'

'There's nothing to keep you here,' she answered grimly.

Beth turned to her father. 'I'll make you pay one day, Dan Henshaw,' she hissed fiercely into his face. 'You'll be sorry you did any of this.'

He stared at her stonily, lips clamped together. Beth brushed past him into the passage outside. As she walked quickly to the head of the stairs she heard Aunt Mae speak.

'I suggest you take Beth's threat seriously, Dan,' she said, and then gave a low bitter laugh. 'She has inherited a ruthless streak. Like father, like daughter.'

On her way back to Oystermouth Road, Beth had plenty of time to review her future. Her heart ached for Tommy, but she knew there was nothing she could do. For the moment Dan Henshaw was the victor. She had to look to her own life now, and the most urgent matter was saving her job at Windsor Lodge, if she could. She would have to grovel to Ada. Well! So be it.

When she went down the steps to the basement kitchen at the boarding house, Ada Smart was poised over the big table making pastry, rolling pin in hand. She stared in astonishment when Beth appeared.

'Well,' she said. 'You've got some brass neck, you have, coming back here.'

'I'm sorry, Mrs Smart, really I am,' Beth began humbly. 'I don't want to lose my job here. Such a thing won't happen again, I promise you.'

Ada stiffened her neck and hunched her shoulders. 'I'm not sure I want you back,' she said coldly. 'I can't run a business with people darting in and out when they feel like it.'

'It was a family matter, and I had to see to it.'

'A stolen baby doesn't sound like a family matter to me,' Ada retorted sharply. 'More like police business.'

Beth shook her head. 'It was all a misunderstanding,' she assured the older woman hurriedly. 'My aunt and uncle have taken my brother in. They'll bring him up.' She wondered if she would ever see Tommy again.

'Just as well.' Ada sniffed. 'You've got a living to earn, and that's hard enough without a baby hanging around your neck.'

'Does that mean you'll keep me on?' Beth asked hopefully.

'I don't know yet,' Ada answered evasively.

'Do you still want me to live in?' Beth asked. 'I can now.'

'Yes, I do,' Ada said abruptly, obviously making up her mind. 'Boarders are always wanting something, even in the middle of the night, especially Mrs Russell.'

Beth's shoulders drooped. It looked as though she would be on call twenty-four hours a day from now on.

'Where would I sleep?' She hoped it wouldn't be up under the eaves again.

Ada pointed to a door in the far corner of the kitchen. 'Down that passage there's a room next to the storeroom,' she said. 'Overlooks the backyard. Plenty of room for one.'

'I'll look at it,' Beth said.

Ada tossed her head. 'I don't think you're in any position to be fussy, miss. It's that or nothing.'

Beth hung her head in defeat. She needed this job and a place to live. Peggy and Elias Morgan had been good to her, but now it was wisest to separate herself from them. Dan Henshaw might still take out his spite on them if they continued to befriend her.

'Yes, Mrs Smart,' Beth said meekly. 'I'll move my stuff in later tonight if that's all right with you.'

Ada nodded obviously satisfied. 'All right. Now you're here, make yourself useful,' she said. 'There's still plenty to do getting supper ready. Get a move on! Let's see how willing you really are.'

Beth dreaded telling Peggy and Elias that she was leaving later that night, but decided to be honest about Dan's threat. It was just as well that Elias knew the kind of man he worked for.

The Morgans were silent as she explained what had happened and what she intended to do.

'It's for the best,' she told them, and impulsively kissed Peggy's weathered cheek and gave Elias a quick hug. 'Thank you for everything.'

'I've a good mind to give notice,' Elias said wrathfully. 'Dan Henshaw don't deserve my loyalty.'

'Don't be *twp*,' Peggy scoffed. 'What good would quitting do? It won't get the babby back.' She looked mournfully at Beth. 'What about Tommy's things?'

'Give them to a needy mother hereabouts,' she said. 'Where's Cissie? I want to thank her, too.'

'Up in the bedroom. She's been crying her eyes out all day. My poor girl loves Tommy like her own, you know.'

'I know she does,' Beth said gently. 'Cissie is one of the best.' She shook her head sadly. 'I doubt I'll find a friend like her again.'

Upstairs, Cissie was sitting hunched over on the bed, her face blotched with crying. Beth sat down beside her and gave her a warm hug, feeling like bursting into tears herself.

'Have a cup of tea before you go,' Peggy said later. 'I hate to see you leaving us.' Her mouth tightened. 'Damn Dan Henshaw!' she exclaimed. 'He's got a lot to answer for.'

Never a truer word spoken, Beth thought, but shook her head. 'I'd better get back to Windsor Lodge,' she said sadly. 'Ada Smart will be watching my every move from now on.'

'Well, remember this,' Elias said kindly. 'If ever you need us, Beth, day or night, you know where we are.'

She left them feeling more grateful than ever that her friends were true and generous. It was more than she could say of her own flesh and blood.

Beth's room at Windsor Lodge, next door to the kitchen, was reached via a short passage. The room was narrow, with a small window that faced the backyard, and just big enough to take a single bed, a tall chest of drawers and a small chair. But it was surprisingly cosy. Beth put her hand against one wall, feeling warmth. She knew that on the other side was the big kitchen range where the fire was never allowed to go out. Meagre as it was, Beth decided she liked it. It was out of the way of the rest of the house-hold and therefore private. As she put her head on the pillow much later than usual that night, she knew this room was to be very much part of her life from now on, perhaps for a long time to come.

Beth settled in, working hard, knowing Ada Smart was watching and could change her mind about employing her at any time. Mrs Russell, Ada's star boarder, proved a tyrant at night. The old-fashioned bell system for summoning servants was still working in the kitchen, much to Beth's dismay, and Mrs Russell, who occupied two rooms on the first floor, had access to a bell-pull which she used at the most inconvenient times, usually after midnight, to demand hot milk to help her insomnia.

Beth ventured to complain to Ada about her disturbed

rest, but her employer was unsympathetic. 'We must make allowances,' she said sternly. 'Mrs Russell has been used to better things. We're lucky to have her as a boarder.'

Beth yawned widely, and Ada tutted.

'Tsk! Oh, all right!' she exclaimed. 'I'll pay you an extra shilling a week for the inconvenience.'

And Beth had to be content with that.

While Mrs Russell and her demands were a nuisance at least she wasn't a hazard, but other boarders could be. It was at the beginning of August that the dandy salesman, one Ralph Dawson from Stepney, returned to Swansea to peddle his goods in shops around the town, and as usual he found accommodation at Windsor Lodge.

Beth ignored his leers as she served him breakfast with the other salesmen in the dining room and kept her distance as much as possible. She made very certain that all of them had left on their rounds before she ventured to enter their rooms to clean or change sheets or towels.

She was polishing the oak washstand in his room mid-morning one day when the door opened and in stepped Ralph Dawson. Beth whirled round, staring in consternation at the wide grin on his face.

'Well! What have we here?' he began. 'The pretty little sweetie who serves me breakfast every day. Lucky I had to come back for my order book. I've been wanting to get you alone for a long time.'

'I've just finished, Mr Dawson,' Beth said hastily, gathering up her cleaning cloths and edging towards the door. 'If you'll excuse me, I'll go now.'

'Don't be in such a hurry,' he said, pushing the door shut with his foot. 'Let's get to know each other. A man gets lonely on the road, you know.'

Beth's heart hammered in her chest as she stared at

him, trembling at the determined expression on his face. 'Mrs Smart is waiting for me,' she said loudly. 'Please open the door, Mr Dawson. I want to leave.'

'Not yet,' he said huskily. 'How about a little kiss, eh? I bet you let your boyfriend have plenty of kisses . . . and what else do you let him do? Come on, sweetie. He won't miss one little kiss.'

'Get out of my way, Mr Dawson, or I'll – I'll scream.'

He laughed. 'Don't be a silly girl. I'm only after a kiss. You might like it. I've never had any complaints.'

Beth's hips were pressed against the washstand and suddenly the room felt very small as he took a step closer.

'I'm warning you, Mr Dawson,' she quavered. 'Come any closer and you'll feel my fingernails across your cheek. How will you face your customers with scratch marks on you?'

He stopped, putting his fingers to his chin thoughtfully, and grinned.

'Not such a country bumpkin as I thought, are you?' he said. 'You've got brains, you have. You're right. Nail marks would cramp my style no end.' He grinned again. 'Pity. You are a nice bit of stuff all right. Your boyfriend is a lucky young devil.'

He stepped aside and Beth darted to the door, waves of relief washing over her. 'Don't ever come near me again,' she said breathlessly.

Her heart was thumping and she was still shaking with fright as she hurried downstairs. She wanted nothing more than to escape to her room for a few moments and pull herself together, but the kitchen seemed to be full of people. Ada and Flossie were there, and so were Gloria and Syd Woods. Beth came in as quietly as she could, hoping not to be noticed in the general chatter, but sharp-eyed Ada spotted her immediately.

'You've been a hell of a time upstairs,' she said irritably. 'Those spuds want peeling. Get on with it. What am I paying you for?'

'I'm sorry, Mrs Smart.' The words came out in a quivering voice, and her hand trembled as she reached for a saucepan.

Flossie noticed it. 'What's happened, kid?' she asked. 'You're as pale as a sheet.'

They were all staring at her, and Beth could hold back no longer. 'It's that salesman, Mr Dawson,' she blurted. 'Caught me while I was cleaning his room, didn't he? He wouldn't let me out, and made suggestions . . .' She swallowed. 'I was frightened.'

'It's your own fault, you stupid little fool,' Ada stormed. 'I've warned you often enough, haven't I? Keep clear of the commercials.' She shook her head, looking obstinate. 'Don't expect me to tell him off over it. He's a regular, and a generous tipper, as well. I won't lose a good customer over you, my girl.'

'I thought he'd gone,' Beth said sharply. Ada's animosity and lack of sympathy somehow revived her spirit. 'I did nothing to encourage him, Mrs Smart. He caught me unaware.'

'Sez you!' Gloria chimed in, her tone scathing. She looked down her nose at Beth. 'She probably asked for it, Mam,' she went on spitefully, flashing a glance at Syd. 'She's always flaunting herself about in front of the men.'

Beth was angry. 'I do no such thing!'

'Did he touch you, Beth?' Syd started towards her, a hard look on his face. 'Did he lay a finger on you? I'll go up and punch his lights out if he did.'

'Syd! What are you doing?' Gloria shrilled. 'You don't need to stand up for the likes of her.'

Syd ignored her, but looked at Beth keenly as she shook

her head. 'I'll give him a good hiding anyway,' he went on. 'Just say the word, Beth, and he'll be missing his front teeth.'

Gloria was fuming. 'Syd! Come away from her.' She dashed forward to grab his arm, her glance spitting fire at Beth.

'I don't want you to do anything, Mr Woods,' Beth said haughtily, backing away. 'Like Mrs Smart says, it was my own fault for being careless. He won't catch me again.'

She turned and walked over to the sink, ready to start peeling potatoes. To her consternation Syd followed.

'Just the same, I could have a word with him. Warn him off, like,' he said persistently. 'In case he tries it on again.'

'Ooh!' There was a cry of rage from Gloria and then Beth heard her high heels clipping up the steps.

'Push off, Syd,' Ada commanded sternly. 'You're getting in the way down by here. Beth! Stop wasting my time and money. You're here to work, not gas.'

Syd Woods was at Windsor Lodge most days after that, hanging around the kitchen despite Ada's caustic hints for him to take himself off. Beth was astonished to realise that somehow she had become the object of his unwanted attentions.

'I've got a new motor,' he told her one day when Ada was out of the kitchen, having a lie-down because of a headache. Syd leaned an elbow on the draining board, watching as she washed the luncheon dishes. 'Like to come for a spin with me on your day off?'

'No, thank you, Mr Woods.' Beth tried to sound as distant as possible, hoping Gloria would not put in an appearance at that moment.

'You used to call me Syd.' He grinned. 'I liked that better.'

'Gloria doesn't like it,' Beth said dryly. Her employer's daughter would make trouble for her if she could, out of pure spite and jealousy, and Beth felt her very job might be at risk.

'How about the Empire then?' he continued. 'Hey! I've heard there's a good comic appearing this week, and a tenor from Italy. I'll get us some tickets.'

'Take Gloria,' Beth suggested, wishing he would leave her alone. She didn't like him much; something about him she couldn't take to. Although he never made any offensive remarks, or seemed threatening in any way, his relentless persistence worried her.

'All right,' he said. 'I'll tell you what I'll do, Beth. If you come to the Empire with me next Saturday, I'll cough up for supper for us afterwards at the Baltic Lounge in High Street. How about it?'

She couldn't help laughing. Only people with pots of money could afford to dine there. 'Robbed a bank, have you?' she asked sarcastically.

He didn't answer, but put his hand in his inside jacket pocket and brought out a wallet. He flipped it open for her to see the thick wad of bank notes inside. Beth stared in astonishment. She had never seen so much money. Syd Woods didn't appear to have a job, and it was on the tip of her tongue to ask where he had got it, but caution made her hold back, all at once afraid of knowing too much.

'It's very kind of you to ask me, Mr Woods, but . . .'

'Kindness has nothing to do with it,' he said, still grinning. 'I like you, Beth, like you a lot.'

'You're Gloria's boyfriend,' she reminded him.

'She might think so,' he said. 'But I'm a free man. Come out with me, Beth, and I'll show you a really good time.'

'You here again?' Ada bellowed as she came down into the kitchen. 'Push off, Syd. I won't tell you again.'

To Beth's relief he went, giving her a meaningful glance as he did so, and she knew he had no intention of taking no for an answer.

'Do your courting elsewhere, Beth,' Ada said sharply. 'You're here to work, remember.'

'I can't help it if he talks to me, Mrs Smart, Beth said defensively. 'I don't ask him to.'

'Tsk! Young fly-by-night he is!' Ada remarked. 'I wish he'd leave our Gloria alone, too.'

Over the next few days Beth avoided being alone in the kitchen when Syd Woods was about, and kept out of Gloria's way as much as possible, fearing the other girl would do her some damage if she could.

She came back a little earlier from her half-day the following Saturday, and as she opened the door to the passage that led to her room behind the kitchen she bumped into Gloria. The other girl looked startled when she saw Beth, who was immediately suspicious.

'What are you doing here?' she asked sharply. There was only the storeroom and her bedroom along this passage, and Gloria had no reason to visit either.

'None of your business.'

'You've been in my room!' Beth accused hotly. 'How dare you!' The other girl's right hand was held behind her back guiltily. 'What have you got there?' Beth demanded sharply. 'You've stolen something. Give it back!'

Gloria tossed her head indignantly. 'Don't you speak to me like that, you . . . you bastard!'

Beth blinked and her jaw dropped, and she stepped back, stunned. 'What did you say?'

'You heard me,' Gloria said waspishly. 'That's what they call people whose mother and father weren't legally married.'

Beth could only stare, speechless, and Gloria smiled triumphantly. 'I've got written proof here,' she said. 'And I'm going to tell everyone, including my mother. Wait until I tell Syd that you were born on the wrong side of the blanket. He'll be disgusted. He won't touch you with a barge pole.'

'You've been through my things!' Beth was appalled. 'You've stolen my mother's letter!' She held out her palm. 'Hand it over, Gloria, this minute.'

'Or what?' she asked defiantly, tossing back her blonde hair. 'When Mam hears about this you'll get the sack. We're respectable, we are.'

'I'll smack your spiteful face if you don't give up that letter this minute!' Beth shouted wrathfully. 'You're a vicious little cat, Gloria Smart.'

'And you're an alley cat,' Gloria shouted back. 'Chasing after Syd. He's mine! You can't have him.'

'I don't want him, you can keep him,' Beth stormed, feeling her neck and face heat up with a boiling rage. 'Now, give me that letter. You've got five seconds, Gloria, or you'll get the back of my hand across your chops.'

'What in heaven's name is going on here?' Ada thundered. Beth whirled round to see her employer standing in the doorway. She was glaring at each of them, fists on hips. 'I thought it was a couple of fishwives rowing.'

Gloria immediately rushed towards her mother. ' It's her, Mam. Look what I found.' She waved the letter in plain sight. 'It tells the truth about her.' Gloria pointed a finger at Beth. 'She's a bastard.'

'*Gloria!*' Ada screeched in shock. 'Go and wash your mouth out with soap this minute.'

'But she *is*, Mam,' Gloria insisted defiantly. 'Her mother and father weren't married. She is a dirty bas—'

'Gloria,' Ada warned in an ominous tone, 'if you say

that word again I'll tan your backside black and blue, big as you are.'

'But, Mam!' Gloria looked crestfallen. 'Aren't you going to sack her? We don't want *her* kind under our roof.'

'Shut your trap, Gloria,' Ada snapped. She held out a hand. 'Give it here.'

Gloria looked rebellious, putting the letter behind her back again. 'She's tainted, she is.' She glowered sulkily. 'Wait until I tell Dad. He'll have something to say, all right.'

'I'll box your ears in a minute, you stubborn little madam!' Ada bellowed. 'Now give it!'

Gloria reluctantly handed the letter to her mother, giving Beth a killing look.

'Now get upstairs, Gloria,' Ada ordered. 'Go on! Before I do give you a clip.'

Gloria flounced away, muttering under her breath, while Beth waited tensely for Ada's pronouncement. It looked like it was about to happen again – no job and no home, no safe place to lay her head – all because of Gloria's jealousy.

'You've got no right to read that,' Beth couldn't stop herself exclaiming loudly when the older woman looked at the front of the envelope. 'It's mine and it's private.'

An expression of hurt passed across Ada's face for a brief moment. 'I've got no intention of reading it,' she said, and to Beth's astonishment handed the letter to her. Beth grabbed it eagerly and pushed it into her pocket.

'Hide it more carefully next time,' Ada went on.

'It wasn't hidden,' Beth said defiantly. 'I have nothing to be ashamed of.'

'No, why should you be?' Ada agreed quietly. 'It's not your fault. Like it wasn't mine, but I've been called that name many times when I was a young girl, and felt ashamed.'

Beth was astonished. 'You mean . . .'

'Yes, I'm illegitimate, too, and I remember how it feels to be looked down on.' Ada shook her head warningly. 'But my family know nothing of it, and they never will. Understand?'

Beth nodded. 'Yes, Mrs Smart, and thank you for being sympathetic.'

'Gloria's a little monkey sometimes,' Ada said, tenderness in her voice. 'But she doesn't mean any real harm.'

Beth thought otherwise but didn't blame Ada Smart for being blinded by motherly love.

'The thing is,' Ada went on thoughtfully, 'she won't keep her mouth shut now. You're a good worker, Beth, and I don't want to see you go, but I'll understand if you feel you must.'

Beth swallowed. 'I don't want to leave this job,' she said. She smiled at the older woman. 'I'm quite happy here, really.'

Ada smiled back faintly. 'It won't be easy for you, Beth. People are very cruel. I know that better than most.'

Beth shrugged, knowing she had little choice. 'Then I'll have to put a brave face on it, won't I?' she said. 'You managed it somehow, Mrs Smart.'

Ada studied her for a moment. 'Yes, I think you *will* manage. You've got guts, Beth, and you are going to need them.'

13

———◆◆◆———

Knowing she had nothing to be ashamed of was one thing, but Beth found she had to gather her courage about her like a suit of armour when facing everyone at Windsor Lodge over the next few days. If she wanted to keep her job then she knew she must hold her tongue, no matter what insults were thrown her way.

Thankfully, none of the salesmen taking breakfast the next day gave her a second look, either being unaware of her supposed shame or else indifferent.

Mrs Russell, on the other hand, went out of her way to show her disapproval. 'You're that illegitimate girl, aren't you?' she asked loudly, giving Beth a contemptuous stare. 'Degrading! But I daresay you don't feel it as others would. *You* people have hides as thick as a rhinoceros,' she went on disparagingly. 'Nothing embarrasses you.'

At a table nearby Major Boyd guffawed in what Beth thought was a most ungentlemanly way, although he looked the part in grey flannel trousers and a black blazer with the badge of the Glamorgan Cricket Club on the pocket. She shot him a look, and was disconcerted to see him leer back at her, eyes glittering. He had hardly given her a second glance before today, always acting aloof with the paid help.

His insulting smirk was too much for her. 'And you people need a lesson in manners,' she muttered quietly, unable to hold her tongue.

'What was that?' Mrs Russell's eyes were popping.

'I said, I'd better mind my manners when I'm with my betters,' Beth fibbed quickly, realising she could get into hot water with Ada for cheeking her star boarders.

'I should think so!' Mrs Russell said with a toss of her head. 'Now fetch me more toast, girl – and wash your hands first!'

Beth departed, fuming. Illegitimacy was like a cloud passing overhead, darkening everything in her life. She would have to face up to it, and so would little Tommy. It broke her heart to think that he might be hurt this way too.

Bert and Gloria always had their meals in a small room adjacent to the dining room and it was Beth's duty to serve them there. She was apprehensive as she carried in Bert Smart's plate, laden with bacon, egg, sausage and fried bread, his usual breakfast. Sitting with her father, Gloria smiled mockingly as Beth appeared.

'Here she comes, Dad,' she said spitefully. 'I don't know how she can face us. You tell her, Dad, tell her what you think of her.'

Bert glanced up at Beth with a stretched smile, cigarette dangling from his lips. 'Fetch more toast, love, will you?' he said mildly. 'And bring a fresh pot of tea. This one has gone cold.'

'Dad!'

'Yes, Mr Smart,' Beth said, relieved that he appeared not the least interested. She couldn't resist sticking her tongue out cheekily at Gloria behind Bert's back as she left the room, and was rewarded with a furious squeal.

Syd Woods was back in the kitchen when Beth was alone there later that afternoon. He sidled up quietly behind her as she washed pots at the sink. When he placed his hands on her hips and drew her sharply against him, Beth let out a scream of fright and whirled to face him, pushing him away roughly.

'What do you think you're doing, Mr Woods?'

'Don't be like that, Beth.' He grinned. 'It's only a bit of fun.'

'I don't like it. Don't ever touch me again,' she warned him furiously. 'No matter what Gloria has told you, I'm no cheap flighty piece.'

'Never thought you were,' he said seriously. 'She told me about the letter, but I don't hold it against you, Beth. You're still the girl for me.'

'I'm not your girl,' she said sharply, quickly moving out of reach, disturbed by his words and that look on his face. Syd Woods was so sure of himself, and so sure of her. 'Nor ever likely to be, Mr Woods.' She stared at him. 'Don't you realise Gloria is mad jealous, and she'll make trouble for me whenever she can? Please keep away.'

'I never promised her anything, so she's got no reason to feel she's exclusive,' he said angrily. 'Look! I'm thinking of leaving Swansea soon. Come with me, Beth,' he said eagerly now. 'You've seen I've got plenty of money, and I can get more. I'll take care of you. You'll never have to work again, and never want for anything, I swear. I'll buy you nice clothes, anything you like.'

'No!' Beth shook her head emphatically, made uneasy by the fervour in his voice. 'It's out of the question. I'm not interested in you, and what's more, I'm not that kind of a girl. Please don't pester me like this.'

'I'll marry you if that's what it takes.'

Beth stared at him astounded, lifting a hand to her breast. 'Marry me?'

'If there's no other way I can have you,' he said candidly. 'Listen, I've never been stupid enough to say this to a girl before, but I'm pretty crazy about you, Beth, honest I am.'

She was speechless, not knowing what to say. Her first proposal of marriage! Maybe it would be her last, too.

'What do you say?' he asked hopefully. 'We'd be great together.'

'But for how long, Mr Woods?' Beth asked soberly.

'Until you've found another girl to be crazy about?'

He straightened. 'I'm not like that.' He looked hurt and she found she was sorry she had spoken so insensitively. She didn't like him but that didn't mean he didn't have genuine feelings.

'I'm sorry,' she said quickly. 'But the answer is still no, Mr Woods. I'm afraid I don't feel the same way about you.'

To her dismay he stepped forward quickly and grasped both her upper arms, as though to embrace her. 'I could make you care,' he said huskily. 'Give me a chance.'

'Let me go, Mr Woods!'

He looked defiant for a moment, and Beth struggled in his grasp. Then heavy footsteps could be heard, coming down the stairs, and she realised it was Ada. So did Syd. He moved away quickly, but spoke to her as he did so.

'You'll change your mind about me, I know you will. We were meant for each other, Beth.'

Syd's proposal had been an eye-opener, although Beth wasn't sure she was flattered. She hadn't liked the certainty in his voice in those few seconds before Ada appeared. She'd have to be very careful from now on not to give him another opportunity to repeat his offer. Something told her he was a man who didn't take no for an answer. Whatever Syd Woods wanted, he got.

Beth decided she would have to grow a thick skin when dealing with Mrs Russell's prejudice, the older woman never failing to get a dig in, especially in front of others, and seeming to take pleasure in causing Beth as much embarrassment as possible. If Ada noticed she said nothing.

But it was Major Boyd's changed attitude towards her that caused her much more unease. Previously she had been almost invisible to him, now his sly lingering glances as she served his meals were discomfiting, even disrespectful. But he was no brash salesman like Ralph Dawson, so she saw no real danger. The Major was somewhere in his fifties and inclined to be corpulent. He could leer all he wanted, but she judged he would do no more than that.

One morning a few days after Syd's proposal, Beth went up to the second-floor bathroom to clean it. Ada was furious that one of the salesmen had left a greasy ring around the bath.

'You could fry chips in it,' she had told Beth. 'The dirty devil! I expect he keeps coal in his own bath at home.'

As Beth reached the top of the second flight of stairs she saw Major Boyd further along the passage. His room was on the first floor next to Mrs Russell's, so she was startled to see him there. Besides, he usually went for a walk along the prom this time each morning.

He seemed startled to see her, too. 'Thought I smelled smoke,' he said gruffly as he pushed past her to go downstairs.

'I'll check on it, Major,' she said, relieved to see his retreating back.

She could smell nothing untoward herself and went further down the passage to the bathroom. The bath wasn't as bad as Ada had made out. Beth set to with cloth and scouring powder and in no time it was gleaming.

She was just about to turn and leave when the bathroom door opened and Major Boyd stood there. His small pink mouth was slack under his moustache, and his normally pale face was heightened with colour. He was breathing heavily, and there was a glow in his eyes which made Beth's muscles tense. She was suddenly conscious of his bulk and the smallness of the room.

'Did you want something, Major?' she asked nervously.

'Yes, you, you witch,' he said thickly, closing the door and slipping the bolt home. 'You've been giving me the glad eye for days. I don't approve of street drabs, never did, but a man can only stand so much.'

'What are you talking about?'

'Huh! You know full well, you little tart,' he rasped. 'I suspected it all along, you know. Then when I heard about your background, I knew I was right. You're easy meat.'

'How dare you?' Beth was appalled. 'Get out of my way!' she shouted loudly, only too aware that the rooms on this floor were all empty, the salesmen having gone about their business in the town. No one would hear her screams.

'Oh, come on, you don't fool me,' he said thickly. 'I can spot a willing piece like you a mile off.' His hand went to his fly buttons. 'Seen plenty of 'em when I was in the army. Come on, get that skirt up around your arse. Let the dog see the rabbit.'

'I'm a decent girl!' Beth cried, backing away, terrified. But there was nowhere to go. 'You've got no right to molest me like this. Get out of my way, Major.'

He guffawed, fingers pausing on the second button. 'Oh, I get it. You want to see the colour of my money first. A sharp one, aren't you? All right, then.' He put his hand in his trouser pocket and brought out a palm full of coinage. 'What's your charge? Half a crown? Five bob?'

He looked her over in a way that made Beth's skin crawl. 'You're a nice little bit of stuff, though. Clean. I'll go as far as ten bob.'

'Open that door and let me out!' Beth cried. 'I'll report this to Mrs Smart.'

'Like hell you will,' he said huskily. 'You like to tease a man, don't you?' He reached out a hand to grasp at her breast. 'Let's find out what you've got inside that blouse for a start. A man likes to see what he's paying for.'

Beth slapped his hand away. 'Don't you dare touch me, you horrible filthy beast!' she cried. 'I'll have the police on you.'

'Hey! Now that's no way to talk to a customer,' the Major said harshly. 'We both know what you are.' He edged closer. 'Come on now, give! I've got a nice crisp ten-bob note in my pocket. It's all yours when we've had our fun.'

'Help!' Beth screamed. 'Help me, someone!'

'Shut up, you silly bitch! Somebody will hear us.' Major Boyd lunged at her, grasping her in a bear hug. 'You won't up the ante by playing hard to get. Ten bob is the most I'll go. I can get it down on the museum steps for two.'

She felt his hand grasp the material at the front of her skirt to drag it up over her thighs. Beth couldn't believe this was happening to her and struggled like a wild animal to free her hands to claw at him.

'Stop it! Stop!' She punched his shoulder wildly.

'Oh, you like a bit of rough stuff, do you? Good! I like that myself.'

Without warning he leaned back and slapped her across the face. For a moment the force of it stunned her, but the feel of his fingers closing brutally around her breast brought her senses to full alert. The sweet cloying scent of the cologne he used made her feel sick as he pressed his body against hers.

Terrified of what could happen next Beth flexed her knee and then brought it up powerfully between his open legs. He gave a strange squeal, like a pig stuck through the throat with a knife, and doubled over, going down on his knees, cursing and groaning loudly and clutching at his groin.

'I hope that hurt,' Beth blazed at him as he knelt before her with head bowed. 'I hope it hurts for a long time. You deserve it. You're no gentleman. You're an animal!'

He was groaning in agony, but Beth felt no pity. She stepped around him quickly and, unbolting the door, rushed into the passage, gathering her torn chemmy and open blouse about herself.

'Don't you ever come near me again,' she said from the safety of the doorway, her voice shaking. 'And don't think you've heard the last of this, either. I'm going straight downstairs to tell Mrs Smart that her precious gentleman boarder is nothing but a dirty old man!'

Beth's terror had given way to anger by the time she rushed down to the kitchen, determined the Major would pay for what he had done to her, the humiliation he had put her through.

Flossie was at the sink and Ada Smart was just putting the second of two steak and kidney pies into the big oven.

'I hope I can see my face in the gleam on that bath,' Ada said acidly over her shoulder as Beth stumbled down the last of the steps to the kitchen. 'You've been long enough at it.'

'Major Boyd has just assaulted me in the second-floor bathroom,' Beth burst out loudly. 'For two pins I'd report him to the police.'

'The dirty old bugger!' Flossie exclaimed, turning from the sink, her eyes like saucers.

Ada spun around from the oven to stare at Beth, her mouth gaping. '*What* did you say?' There was disbelief on her face.

'He called me a prostitute,' Beth insisted heatedly, clutching the front of her blouse to her heaving bosom. 'He grabbed me, ripped my chemmy and tried to . . . to . . .' She couldn't even say the word, it was so horrifying.

'I don't believe it for a minute,' Ada declared stubbornly, fists on hips, nostrils flaring. 'A gentleman the Major is. He wouldn't do anything like that.'

'He just did!' Beth cried forcefully. 'It was awful. His hands were all over me and he said some horrible things, too.' She tossed her head indignantly. 'He insulted me and I don't have to put up with anything like that, Mrs Smart. This is your house, you should tell him off, give him a warning.'

Ada pulled back her chin, looking furious. 'I'll do no such thing,' she exclaimed, and wagged a finger at Beth. 'Now look here, miss, I stood by you over the illegitimacy thing because that isn't your fault, but now you're trying to pull a fast one.'

'A fast one!' Beth cried angrily, astonished at Ada Smart's self-deception. 'Why should I lie about it? Look at my blouse and chemmy. Do you think I did that myself?'

'You might've.' Ada's cheeks puffed out. 'And don't you use that tone with me, my girl. I don't know what your game is, but it won't wash.'

'This isn't a game, Mrs Smart,' Beth said seriously. 'Major Boyd attacked me and tried to force me to . . .'

'Be quiet!' Ada shouted. 'Had enough of this, I have,

and I've just about had enough of you too, Beth Pryce. It was bad enough you accusing that salesman back along, but doing the same with the Major is going too far. You're trying to get more money out of me, aren't you? But you can think again.'

'Why won't you believe me?' Beth flared.

'The Major pays his rent on time, never in arrears. He's the perfect gent,' Ada insisted acerbically. 'I've no intention of upsetting him on account of your say so.'

Beth was indignant. 'Are you calling me a liar, Mrs Smart?'

'That's your word, not mine,' Ada retorted quickly. 'What I'm saying is this: either you stop this nonsense and get on with your work, or you can pack your bag and get out.'

'You're going to let him get away with it, then?' Beth queried in consternation . She couldn't believe it. 'What if he does it again?'

Ada's face took on a hard look, her glance challenging. 'Either you shut up about it or you're out,' she snapped belligerently. 'What's it going to be, Beth?'

She was dumbfounded. What could she do but keep quiet? Losing this job would also lose her a bed. She had settled nicely in the little room behind the kitchen. The thought of being thrown out filled her with dread. Dan had stolen Tommy from her and her life was poorer for the loss. If she lost her job and the roof over her head as well, it would be the end. She must keep earning until an opportunity presented itself of getting Tommy back, because somehow or other she would.

'Got no choice, have I?' she said dispiritedly, and then straightened her shoulders in resolve. Next time it wouldn't be just her knee bone the Major would feel. She would mark his face with her fingernails. Let him explain *that* to Mrs Smart.

Ada sniffed and pulled in her chin with satisfaction. 'Well, I'm glad you realise which side your bread is buttered,' she remarked. Her hard glance lit on Flossie. 'And don't you open your gob either,' she said to the thin woman. 'Or your job will be down the pan as well.'

It was as much as Beth could do to serve the Major his meals after that, but now he looked right through her as though she wasn't there, and that made her feel easier. Obviously he had been shocked by her violent reaction, and she guessed he wouldn't approach her again in a hurry.

But her relationship with Ada Smart over the following weeks remained prickly. It was Ada's guilty conscience, Beth decided, certain that her employer knew the accusation against the Major was true. But Ada's attitude was that nothing must stand in the way of business, and Beth found that hard to forgive. It reminded her too much of Dan Henshaw's cold and calculating philosophy.

The beginning of October brought colder weather and Beth was glad of the warmth of her room. She usually fell asleep while making wild plans for how to snatch Tommy back, but this Saturday night she could not. There had been a new batch of commercial travellers booking into the boarding house that day, and some of them, having travelled a fair distance, arrived too late for the evening meal. Whereas the last meal was normally served at six o'clock at the latest, cooking and serving had gone on until eight tonight. Ada had kept her so busy afterwards Beth had not had time to have a decent meal herself and now felt ravenous.

Lying in bed she couldn't stop thinking about the

remnants of that veal and ham pie sitting on a shelf in the larder. The battered alarm clock supplied by her employer told her it was gone midnight. She would never sleep with her stomach rumbling so much, so getting up she slipped into her old dressing gown, wishing she had some warm slippers to put on, but she would never spend Mam's money on herself. That was meant for Tommy's future. One day she *would* get him back.

Deciding against lighting a candle, she padded down the passage to the big kitchen, trying to ignore the discomfort of the cold stone flooring on the soles of her bare feet.

It was a bit eerie with the bright October moon shining through the back window overlooking the yard, casting strange shadows in the room. Everything looked different. It was hunger exciting her imagination she told herself, her mouth watering at the thought of the pie. Ada would never miss a slice.

Beth fetched a knife from the box and a plate, and was in the big walk-in larder cutting herself a generous slice when there was a sound in the kitchen that made the hairs on the back of her neck stand on end. Someone was trying to get in through the back door!

Burglars! But how? There was no access at the rear of the house, the properties and yards on Oystermouth Road and St Helen's Road being back to back, so the door was never locked.

Beth stood stock still in the larder, the slice of pie in her hand, listening in horror as the back door opened and feet scuffled on the flagstoned floor.

'Don't slam the bloody door, for Gawd's sake,' a familiar voice gasped. 'The bobbies might hear it. They'll be after us.'

With astonishment Beth recognised the speaker as Bert Smart.

'That was a damned close call,' another familiar voice said. 'They nearly had us then, mate.'

Syd Woods! What was going on?'

There was some choice cursing from Bert in a breathy voice as though he'd been running. 'I'm getting too old for this lark. Climbing over all those bloody garden walls in the dark has nearly done for me,' he wheezed. 'This is my last job.'

There was a snigger from Syd. 'Sez you!'

'Shut up!' Bert hissed. 'That girl Beth is sleeping down the passage out by there. We don't want her coming in here to investigate.'

'Oh, I don't know,' Syd said. Beth could tell by his tone of voice that he had a leer on his face. 'I bet she's fetching in a nightie.'

'You clever-arse!' Bert exclaimed irritably. 'Did you have to bash that night watchman? He was only an old bloke.'

'He asked for it!' Syd snarled. 'Besides, he recognised you. I had to do him.'

'Oh, Gawd!' Bert whined. 'They'll have us for murder if he's kicked the bucket.'

'Nobody knows it was us,' Syd said with confidence. 'And God help anybody who finds out.'

'Ever heard of fingerprints?' Bert asked sarcastically. 'Oh, Gawd! Ada will kill me when she finds out what I've been up to. Why the hell did I listen to you? Easy job, you said. A piece of cake. And now you've killed a man.'

Beth froze behind the open larder door, afraid to take a breath. If either of the men walked to the other end of the kitchen they would be bound to see her standing here. What would they do to her when the realised she had heard everything? She was afraid even to imagine.

'Stop whingeing. I only tapped him on the head,' Syd

snarled. 'What are we going to do about this here loot?'

'Chuck it in the Tawe,' Bert said despairingly. 'It'll hang us.'

'Don't be daft! Worth a bit is this,' Syd said. 'I could cut along to old man Dodds right now, see what he'll pay us for it. He'll still be up.'

'Are you mad?' Bert exclaimed excitedly. 'We don't want to show anybody we had anything to do with that job, at least not for a long time. And old Dodds would sell us down the river if he could make a penny on it.'

'What are we going to do then?'

'We'll hide it,' Bert said. 'Let the heat cool down a bit.'

'That's no bloody good to me,' Syd rasped. 'I need the money now. I'm buggering off from Swansea. Bigger things up the Smoke.'

'You're not taking our Gloria with you?' There was a warning note in Bert's voice.

'Don't worry, your Gloria is safe enough. She's the last one I want. I've got my eye on something sweeter.'

Beth felt a shiver go up her spine, remembering his proposal. Her instinct about him had been right.

'Listen to me,' Bert said. His voice was steadier now that he was safe. 'We'll do this my way. The stuff will be hidden, and it won't come out until the time is right. Go up the Smoke if you want, I'll send your share to you.'

'What do you take me for?'

'A bloody young fool, that's what,' Bert hissed. 'I've warned you time and again about the violence, haven't I? Now you've landed us in it good and proper. Well, I'm not getting my neck stretched because of you, you lame-brain.'

'Now, watch it, Bert!' Syd snarled.

'Shut up!' Bert was in control again. 'Let me think. Where's the best hiding place?'

There was silence for a moment and Beth waited, not daring to move a muscle, even though the coldness of the stone floor was rising up through her bare feet and making her legs numb.

'How about the larder?' Syd suggested.

He moved suddenly, footsteps approaching the larder door, and Beth nearly bit her tongue with terror. Syd fancied her, had asked her to marry him, but that wouldn't carry any weight if he discovered her now. He would turn on her like a snake. After all, what she knew could send him to the gallows. It wouldn't matter how many people he'd killed, the result would be the same.

'Don't be a fool,' Bert said. 'Put it there and it'll be found straight away. Ada's no mug and neither is that Beth. Too bloody bright that girl is, I'm telling you.'

'Well, where then?' Syd snapped. 'I'm not walking through the streets with it at this time of night.'

'Huh! I wouldn't trust you anyway,' Bert retorted craftily. 'I think I've got it. Until I can find a better place, I'll put it in the back of that big wall cupboard in Gloria's room, where Ada keeps odds and ends of bedding.'

'What if she's not asleep?'

'She will be,' Bert said confidently. 'Sleeps like the dead our Gloria does.' Shoes scuffed on the floor. 'Come on,' he went on. 'You get off home. And keep your mouth shut.'

'Am I likely to rat on myself, mun?'

'Huh! I don't know what you're likely to do next, that's the trouble,' Bert said sarcastically as they shuffled up the stone steps.

Beth waited until all the sounds had died away before venturing to come out of the larder, the slice of pie forgotten. Her one thought was to get back to her room and safely into bed, although there would be no sleep for her tonight.

What should she do? She ought to tell someone about Syd Woods, but who? Would anyone believe her? Certainly not Ada, who had scoffed at her accusation against Major Boyd. Her thoughts went to Peggy and Elias Morgan. They were good people with plenty of common sense. She would ask their advice, knowing she could trust them not to betray her confidence.

But what about her employer? Beth suddenly thought. Ada clearly knew nothing about the illegal activities of her husband, and Beth didn't want to be the one to tell her, either.

By early dawn she had managed to doze off, mainly because her mind was made up to slip around to see Peggy and Elias after she finished work that evening.

In the meantime she must say nothing of what she knew. Instinct warned her it wouldn't be safe while Syd was still around. He would be leaving Swansea soon, or so he'd said. She wouldn't feel out of harm's way until he was gone.

Beth rose reluctantly from bed when her alarm rang at six o'clock, viewing the hours ahead at Windsor Lodge with trepidation. Both Bert Smart and Syd would be nervous and wary from now on. How could she face them day in, day out, without showing that she knew something? She had no skill in disguising her thoughts, and if she gave herself away, dreaded to think what would happen. Syd Woods was a very dangerous man, dangerous and unpredictable. Beth began to feel very frightened indeed.

'Murder? *Duw annwyl!*' Elias exclaimed when Beth had finished relating what had happened in the kitchen of Windsor Lodge the previous night. 'Who'd have thought Bert Smart had it in him?'

'But what should I do?' Beth asked, twisting her hands anxiously. 'Should I go to the authorities?'

'No, no, *cariad*,' Peggy exclaimed. 'You keep quiet, my girl. Don't get involved. The police might decide you were an accessory or something.'

'Oh! They wouldn't, would they?'

Peggy twisted her lips in derision. 'You never know with them coppers.'

14

Beth scanned any newspapers left lying around by the salesmen over the next few days. There was no mention of a night watchman being attacked or murdered, although there was a report of a large sum of money being taken from a safe in a warehouse in nearby Lower Fleet Street, but she didn't know whether Bert and Syd were responsible for that. Perhaps the old man hadn't been killed after all. She hoped not.

Nothing was seen of Syd Woods at Windsor Lodge that week to Beth's relief, and she wondered if he had left Swansea as he had said. She fervently hoped so. She couldn't bear him to come anywhere near her again, knowing what he was capable of.

Now all she had to worry about was Bert. She kept out of his way as much as possible, and avoided looking directly at him when serving his meals, fearing he would read something into her nervous glance. But she had a shock the following Friday morning when she took in breakfast for him and Gloria.

The girl jumped up from the table when Beth came in with their plates, mouth twisted with anger.

'What have you said to Syd?' she demanded to know. 'He hasn't been near us all week.'

'I've said nothing,' Beth said, bewildered. 'I haven't seen him, not since . . .' She faltered and Gloria was on it in a moment.

'You've been meeting him on the sly, haven't you?' She was furious. 'You bitch! I warned you to keep away from him.'

Beth dumped the plates on the table.' Don't call me names,' she said, furious herself. 'I won't take it from you.'

'Now, now, girls,' Bert said soothingly. 'Let's not get aerated, especially before I've had my grub. Sit down, love,' he said amicably to his daughter. 'Syd will turn up when he feels like it.'

'It's her, Dad,' Gloria whined. 'She's driven him away. He's fed up with her chasing him like a street woman.'

Beth could have smacked her face, and struggled to hold on to her temper. 'If Syd Woods hasn't been around,' she said incautiously, 'it's probably because he's left Swansea.'

Bert's head lifted abruptly. 'What makes you say that?' he asked, his tone sharp.

Beth swallowed, realising her anger with Gloria had made her careless, but now she had no option but to explain. 'He said he was going up the Smoke, wherever that is.'

'London,' Bert said, and sounded surprised, though by what Beth could not determine.

He put down his knife and fork and looked up at her, a flash in his eyes. Beth began to tremble. She put her hands behind her back to hide it.

'When did he tell you that?' Bert asked.

Her breath caught in her throat with fright, but she had to answer. 'The other week.'

'I knew it!' Gloria interrupted, her face turning red. 'She's been after him like a bitch on heat. It's because he's got a bit of money, isn't it? A little gold-digger, she is.'

'Shut up, our Gloria!' Bert snapped. 'So, Syd is going

away, is he?' he went on to Beth in a level tone. 'Well, well, fancy that.'

His surprised tone confused her. Syd had made his intentions clear enough in the kitchen that Saturday night.

'But I thought you knew, Mr Smart,' she said, and then could have bitten off her tongue.

'How would I know his plans?' he asked, eyes narrowing to slits.

Beth felt trapped and shuffled her feet nervously. 'I don't know,' she murmured nervously, longing to get out of the room. 'I just thought . . . as you seem to be friends with him.'

He looked at her keenly. 'I'm no friend of Syd Woods,' he said. 'He has nothing to do with me and I have nothing to do with him. I don't know what he gets up to.' He turned to his daughter. 'And I don't want you seeing him any more either.'

'But, Dad, Syd and me are almost engaged,' Gloria said peevishly.

'Over my dead body,' Bert Smart remarked.

'Now see what you've done,' Gloria spat at Beth.

'Shut up, our Gloria, and eat your grub,' Bert said firmly.

Father and daughter began a heated argument and Beth slipped away unnoticed. She felt very shaken as she ran back down to the kitchen, resolving not to be so careless in future.

Neither Gloria nor her father said anything further to her about Syd Woods, and Beth thought it best to try and put the whole thing out of her mind. She was more or less succeeding until a fortnight later when, answering a ring at the front door, she found a young police constable standing on the step.

Beth gulped guiltily and nearly choked with fright as he politely touched his forefinger to the brim of his helmet.

'I'm looking for a Mrs Ophelia Russell, miss,' the constable said in a very official tone. 'Does she live here?'

Beth nodded, unable to speak for a moment. He stepped forward purposefully, and Beth moved aside for him to come in. She stared up at him as he stood there expectantly.

'Well?' he asked pompously. 'Can I see her? She has sent for the Law.'

'Why?' Beth blurted without thinking.

The constable sniffed and looked stern, although he was hardly much older than she was. 'That's none of your concern, miss, at present,' he said. 'But I may want to question you later. Now take me to her.'

Beth was flummoxed. 'I'd better call Mrs Smart first,' she said.

'Who's she?'

'The landlady,' Beth explained. 'I think I'd better call her. Mrs Russell is a very important boarder.'

'Well, be as quick as you can, my girl,' he said abruptly. 'The Law don't wait for no one.'

Beth scurried down to the kitchen. Flossie and Ada were there and so was Gloria.

'Mrs Smart, come quick,' Beth urged breathlessly. 'There's a policeman upstairs, and he's asking for Mrs Russell.'

Ada stared. 'What the heck for?'

'He won't say. I think Mrs Russell has sent for him.'

'What?'

Ada bustled up the steps and everyone followed, but Beth, her guilty knowledge weighing on her like a ton load, hung back a little, not wanting to get involved in whatever was wrong because clearly something was.

Ada Smart's face was red as she confronted the police-man in the hall. 'What's this all about, Constable? I don't want my boarders put to any inconvenience.'

The young constable looked down his nose at her. 'I'm here to see Mrs Russell because earlier this morning she sent a young boy around to the police box near Swansea Public Baths to report the theft of a valuable brooch.'

Ada's jaw dropped. 'What? She never said nothing to me.'

'Yes, well, she wouldn't, would she?' he said airily. 'Everyone is under suspicion.'

'I know who stole it,' Gloria announced with triumph, pushing her way to the front of the group. 'It was her.' She pointed an accusing finger at Beth. 'She's got sticky fingers, she has. She's a sneak thief.'

The constable looked startled at Gloria's outburst and stared hard at Beth.

'I've stolen nothing!' she cried out, aghast at the accusation. 'How dare you accuse me? There are others in this house . . .' She stopped and folded her lips, realising she was saying too much. 'I'm innocent,' she went on lamely.

'Well, that's as may be,' the constable said carefully. 'But there will have to be an investigation.'

'I bet she's got it on her,' Gloria insisted. 'Strip-search her. Go on! She's nothing more than a little tart anyway.'

'Touch me,' Beth screeched at him, affronted, 'and you'll get the back of my hand across your face, policeman or no policeman.'

The constable's face reddened. 'I don't think a strip-search will be necessary, for the moment. I shall have to speak with my superiors.'

'You can't accuse me on her say-so,' Beth flared, trembling with rage. 'She could've taken it herself for all we know.'

'Ooh!' Gloria was fuming. 'The lying cat!'

'Well! It's about time you turned up,' a commanding voice said from the landing above. Mrs Russell stared down at them, a sour expression on her face. 'My husband was a Town Councillor, you know, Constable. I'm used to better service.'

The young policeman began to climb the stairs towards her.

'Mrs Ophelia Russell, I take it?' He took a notebook and pencil from his breast pocket. 'Now I want a full account.'

Everyone traipsed up the stairs in his wake. This time Beth was well in front, furious with Gloria for her un-warranted and spiteful accusation. Mrs Russell led them to her two rooms on the first floor, the best rooms in the house Beth always thought whenever she cleaned them.

'Now then, madam,' the constable began importantly when they congregated in the bedroom. 'Where was the purloined brooch before it was . . . er . . . purloined?'

Mrs Russell pointed to the dressing table where a jewellery box stood. 'I keep it in there,' she said.

'How valuable is it?'

'Oh, very valuable,' Ada cut in enthusiastically. 'Always talking about your best bits of jewellery, aren't you, Mrs Russell? A collection to be proud of, I always say. Very ladylike pieces.'

Mrs Russell smirked and touched her hair. 'Very generous man, my husband was. Only the best for me.' Her face clouded. 'Now someone has taken my prize piece.'

'So most everyone knew it was there, then,' the constable remarked. 'Do you keep your door locked?'

Mrs Russell looked cross for some reason. 'Of course not,' she said testily. 'How would the girls get in to clean and light the fire? Use your head.'

The constable looked put out at her disparaging tone.

'There has been an accusation already,' he said stiffly.

'I didn't do it!' Beth shouted.

Mrs Russell stared stonily at her. 'She's illegitimate, you know, Constable,' she said arrogantly. 'These people are capable of anything.'

The constable looked sceptical but said nothing.

'Well, if you can't search her, search her room,' Gloria demanded loudly. 'She's got it hidden there, I know she has.'

'You can't search my room,' Beth stormed. 'I won't have it!'

The constable looked severe. 'Have you got something to hide, miss?'

'Certainly not!'

'Then I suggest you agree to a search,' he said. 'It'll clear the matter up once and for all.'

Beth had not been so insulted since Major Boyd took her for a prostitute, but she saw the sense of what he said. 'Oh, very well! But I want it on record that I protest strongly.' She pointed to his notebook. 'Write that down, Constable. I protest!'

Everyone had crowded into Beth's room behind the kitchen, jostling in the doorway as the constable made a methodical search of the chest of drawers and under the thin mattress.

Well,' he said, straightening up after being on hands and knees, looking under the bed, 'the stolen object is not here.'

'That doesn't mean she didn't take it,' Gloria persisted. 'She could've hidden it elsewhere.'

'I'll give you such a slap in a minute, Gloria Smart,' Beth threatened wrathfully. 'I am not a thief.'

Gloria opened her pouting mouth, but her mother cut her short.

'There's something I have to tell you, Constable,' Ada said hesitantly, and everyone stared at her. 'This isn't the first theft. There have been others, but all of them occurred long before Beth came to work here.'

'Mam! You never said.'

'I didn't want it to get out, did I?' Ada said sorrowfully. 'Cigarette cases and lighters were taken from the commercial travellers, but most of the thefts were cash. I had to reimburse them from my own pocket. An initialled gold banknote clip with ten pounds in it was taken, too. That cost me a pretty penny to replace, I can tell you.'

'There, you see!' Beth stormed. 'I've been insulted for nothing.' She glared at Ada. 'Why didn't you say something before, Mrs Smart? You could've saved me a lot of embarrassment.'

Ada looked unrepentant. 'I'm sorry, Beth, but I had the reputation of the business to think of.'

'Oh, I see,' she snapped. 'Never mind my reputation, is it?'

'I'll make it up to you,' Ada said.

'But that doesn't get my brooch back, does it?' Mrs Russell exclaimed loudly. 'I demand an investigation and a thorough search.'

'Yes,' Beth agreed, feeling vengeful. 'I've been humiliated and I'm innocent. I, too, demand a search of other rooms. It's only fair.'

'What the hell's going on here?' a new voice asked, and Bert Smart appeared in the passage, his flat cap on the back of his head and a cigarette dangling from his lip as usual. He caught sight of the policeman and his face paled. 'Oh, my Gawd! It's the Old Bill!'

'And who might you be?' the constable asked in a heavy tone.

'My husband,' Ada answered for him. 'And don't go thinking *he's* taken anything because I know he didn't.'

'Taken anything?' Bert repeated weakly. 'What are you on about, Ada?'

'My beautiful emerald and diamond brooch has been stolen,' Mrs Russell told him loudly. 'The house must be searched.'

'Now hold on a minute, boyo,' Bert said, his face reddening. 'You need a search warrant for that.'

The constable's eyes were suddenly watchful. 'You seem to know a lot about the law, Mr Smart. Had some dealings with us before, have you?'

'No, he hasn't,' Ada exclaimed brusquely. 'And don't start accusing him. He's a good husband is my Bert and honest as the day is long.'

Beth didn't know where to look.

'Well, everybody is suspect,' the constable declared stubbornly. 'I have to inform my superiors of the situation.' He cast a glance around the group and then pointed to Flossie, which made her nearly jump out of her thin frame. 'You!' he said forcefully. 'Run down to the police box and get my sergeant along here.'

'Why can't you go yourself?' Flossie managed to squeak at him.

The constable's glance flickered over Bert Smart. 'I'm not budging from the scene of the crime,' he said. 'Vital evidence might be moved.'

'What's that supposed to mean?' Bert spluttered. 'Here! I've got rights, I have. You can't go accusing a bloke out of the blue like that. I never set eyes on this woman's bloody brooch.'

Mrs Russell spluttered with disapproval.

'No one is accusing you, Mr Smart,' the constable said. 'I've got my duty to do, see. And I'm not budging from

by here. So, off you go,' he said to a wide-eyed Flossie.
'The Law hasn't got all day.'

When she had darted off, the constable herded
everyone back up to the hall, including Mrs Russell, even
though she protested loudly.

'You can't keep us idle by here,' Ada stormed. 'I've got
a business to run, meals to prepare.'

But everyone had to be patient for the next half-hour
until three more policemen arrived at Windsor Lodge, a
burly red-faced sergeant accompanied by two constables.

The first constable, who told Ada his name was PC
Lewis, immediately went into a whispered consultation
with his superior. Eventually, the sergeant stepped
forward.

'I'm Sergeant Slade. My constables will now make a
thorough search of all rooms, guests' as well as staff's.'

'You can't search the guests' rooms, not without their
permission,' Ada said.

'If they are in their rooms we'll ask them,' Sergeant
Slade said confidently. 'And if we need a search warrant
we can get one easily enough, but if no one has anything
to hide why do we need one?' He looked hard at Bert.
'Any objection . . . sir?'

He looked nervous, his face paling. 'Do as you bloody
like,' he murmured, turning to walk away out of the front
door. 'But I've got work to do.'

'No,' Sergeant Slade said firmly. 'You stop here. I want
everyone to wait in the dining room until the search is
finished. PC Thomas will remain with you.' He pointed
at Beth. 'You come along with us, if you please, miss.'

She stared. 'I haven't done anything, I tell you!'

'I wouldn't argue with the Law if I was you, miss,' PC
Lewis said darkly.

Beth had no choice but to accompany the policemen

upstairs again. They began the search on the second floor, where the commercial travellers had their accommodation. Beth found she was expected to match each room number to a guest's name while one of the constables wrote the details laboriously in his notebook.

She was confused when they went down to the first floor.

'But these are Mrs Russell's rooms,' she said. 'You can't search here. She wouldn't steal her own brooch.'

'Huh! Funnier things have happened,' the sergeant exclaimed. 'And anyway, there can be no exceptions made.' He gave her a hard look. 'For instance, Lewis has made a search of your room but I intend to go through it again with a fine-tooth comb, my girl.'

'You've got no right!' Beth objected, but was ignored. The Law apparently was a law unto itself.

When the search of Mrs Russell's room was complete the sergeant paused outside in the passage, which led to the back of the house, and peered down the length of it. 'Where does this go?'

'To the family's quarters,' Beth said miserably. 'A living room and two bedrooms.'

The sergeant turned to PC Lewis. 'Right oh! Lewis, off you go, and every cubbyhole, mind. I'm going to get to the bottom of this.' He turned back to Beth. 'Now, my girl, whose room is this?'

'Major Boyd's,' she said. 'He won't like it, you know,' she warned. 'Mrs Smart believes he is a very important man.'

'Oh, an army man, is he? Well, he'll understand such things must be done,' Sergeant Slade said confidently. 'I was in the army myself, see. Fought in the thick of it in France.' He gave her a sideways glance, as though expecting her to be impressed. 'One of the lucky ones I was; got out alive and well. Now all I need is a good wife.'

Beth stared stonily at him and he gave a little cough. 'Yes, well, we must get on with the search.'

The Major's room was entered, and as with the others Beth was told to wait outside while the search was in progress. She fidgeted as she waited, and worried, remembering the sergeant's words that he would search her room again. Suppose someone, like Gloria, had hidden the brooch in her room, just to get her into serious trouble. There was no one she could turn to for help. Certainly not Dan Henshaw or Aunt Mae.

Beth was nibbling her thumbnail with worry when the sergeant's shout startled her. 'Girl! Come in here.'

Her heart in her mouth, Beth did as she was told. The sergeant and constable were standing at the chest of drawers.

'Come here,' Sergeant Slade commanded her, a hard edge to his voice. 'I want you to witness this.'

The top drawer was open, and Beth looked in. All she could see were the Major's pristine shirts folded neatly, some white handkerchiefs and several pairs of socks rolled up.

'Now my girl,' the sergeant went on heavily. 'I want you to answer truthfully. Who brings the Major's clean laundry up to his room?'

Beth swallowed. 'I do.'

'And who puts it away in the chest of drawers?'

'The Major always does that,' Beth said. She didn't add that, being afraid of him, she usually dumped his clean linen on the bed and departed as quickly as possible just in case he caught her unawares.

The sergeant nodded. 'Right, Constable. Let's see what our Major Boyd has hidden here, shall we?'

The shirts, handkerchiefs and socks were taken out.

Underneath was a length of cardboard covered with tissue paper. When that was removed Beth gasped with surprise to see a collection of objects. Cigarette cases and lighters, wristwatches, a man's signet ring with a large white stone in the centre, and several rolls of bank notes in rubber bands.

The sergeant put a hand in the drawer and picked up something. 'The initialled banknote clip,' he said, examining it carefully. 'This'll take a bit of explaining.'

'And what's that, Sergeant?' the constable asked, pointing to something wrapped in tissue paper.

Sergeant Slade lifted it out, and when the wrapping paper was folded back a magnificent brooch with green and white stones glistened in his hand.

'So, there was a brooch,' he said, chuckling. 'I wouldn't have been surprised if the old girl was having us on.' He looked at Beth. 'Where is the Major now?'

'I don't know exactly,' Beth said, wondering what Ada Smart would say when she knew one of her star boarders was a common thief. There would be fireworks because she wouldn't believe it. 'He usually goes for a stroll on the Prom about this time to give himself an appetite for luncheon.'

'He doesn't work for a living, then?'

'The Major is a man of means,' Beth said confidently. 'A gentleman, so Mrs Smart says.'

'I'm anxious to meet him,' Sergeant Slade said. 'I suspect I'm going to feel his collar.' He looked around the room. 'Get me a pillowcase,' he told Beth. 'I'm taking these stolen things into safekeeping.'

As she and the two policemen returned downstairs, Beth was aware that PC Lewis had not reappeared from the Smarts' family quarters. She had a strange crawling sensation at the back of her neck as though aware of impending disaster. Major Boyd had been found out, but

Beth, knowing what she did about Bert, realised there was more to be revealed. What would the police do to her if they found out she had known all along about his activities and had said nothing?

Back in the dining room, Beth went and stood next to Ada Smart. Everyone's glance was glued on the sergeant as he came in after her, carrying the bulging pillowcase.

'The stolen items have been recovered,' he announced importantly. There was a babble of voices as everyone began to speak at once.

'I'll take my brooch, if you please, Sergeant,' Mrs Russell said imperiously, stepping forward.

'Sorry madam,' he answered. 'But it's evidence now. Anyone seen Major Boyd?'

'What do you want him for?' Ada asked irritably.

Beth touched her arm. 'Mrs Smart, listen,' she began. 'They found all those stolen things in the Major's room.'

'What?'

'That's enough, my girl!' Sergeant Slade exclaimed angrily. 'This is police business now. We want Major Boyd for questioning.'

At that moment the front door opened and someone came in whistling. Beth gave a sharp intake of breath, recognising the newcomer as the Major. Taking one alert look at her, the sergeant turned and dashed into the hall, followed by the constable.

'What the hell?' Beth heard the Major exclaim loudly, and the next moment there was the sound of scuffling feet.

'What's going on, Beth?' Ada asked dazedly. 'They can't treat the Major like this. He's a gentleman.'

The policemen reappeared in the dining room, Major Boyd struggling between them. He stared around wildly, his face red.

'Get your hands off me,' he yelled. 'I've done nothing.'

'Hold on a minute!' Sergeant Slade said, looking keenly into his face. 'I know you! It's Billy Boyd, isn't it? And you should know me, Billy. I pinched you back in 'thirteen, before the war. A little matter of safe-cracking, as I remember.'

'You've got the wrong man,' the Major shouted loudly, pulling frantically against the hands that held him. 'I'll have your badges for this.'

The sergeant shook his head, smiling like a Cheshire cat.

'Come off it, Billy,' he said triumphantly. 'We've had a look in the chest of drawers. It's all up, boyo. We've got you bang to rights. I'm arresting you, Billy Boyd, for theft. Now come along quietly with us.'

'This is terrible!' Ada cried, wringing her hands. 'You can't treat the Major like a common criminal.'

'That's what he is, missus. He's no more a major than I am,' the sergeant said. 'Never even seen the outside of an army barracks, our Billy hasn't, never mind been inside one. He spent the entire war in clink.'

'Oh, heavens above!' Ada looked gutted.

'I haven't stolen a damned thing,' Billy Boyd blustered again. 'Somebody must've dumped that brooch on me, I tell you.'

'You impostor!' Mrs Russell exclaimed indignantly. 'And to think we took sherry of an evening together. Oh!'

'Come on,' the sergeant began, as he and the two constables bundled Billy Boyd towards the hall. But just at that moment PC Lewis rushed down the stairs, shouting excitedly.

'Sarge! I've found something!' The young constable burst into the dining room, his youthful face alive with excitement. 'A sack full of banknotes. Could be from that warehouse job . . . you know, Perrot's.'

'What?'

'Hidden in the back of a cupboard, it is,' PC Lewis went on, pointing up the stairs.

'Show me,' the sergeant said to him. He nodded at the two constables holding a wriggling Billy Boyd. 'Hold him!' he commanded, his face grim. 'And no one leaves this room, got it?' With that he dashed away after the scurrying constable.

The wait seemed interminable. An agitated Ada kept shaking her head and muttering. Beth sat next to her, but kept her eye on Bert Smart. He paced up and down before the window like a caged animal, his face pale and tense, puffing away at one cigarette after another. He clenched his fists from time to time, while stealing covert glances at the two constables. It looked as though he was waiting for a chance to bolt.

She felt bewildered, wondering what she should do for the best. Should she tell them what she knew about Bert and Syd? She ought to, she knew, but Syd was still at large and he was a dangerous man, probably a killer. If she spoke up he might come after her to take terrible revenge. She quivered at the thought.

Beth stole a glance at her employer's worried face and felt sorry for her. If she kept quiet it would be for Ada's sake. Beth weighed up the consequences of keeping her mouth shut. It was unlikely that the police would ever find out that she had overheard Bert and Syd's conversation. On the other hand, suppose that somehow or other they *did* discover she had deliberately withheld information, she could find herself in serious trouble, perhaps go to prison. The thought sent chills of horror up her spine.

And if she did end up in prison, what would happen to Tommy? He would be condemned too, to a lonely and unhappy childhood with Dan Henshaw who could feel love for no one. Tommy might even grow up to be as cold and heartless as their father. She must save him from that if she could.

The constables had forced Billy Boyd to sit on a straight-backed chair on the other side of the room. He was handcuffed now, but their large hands gripped his shoulders tightly. He was scowling, yet his nose and mouth were pinched white with fear. Even though she had no sympathy with him, Beth had some idea how he felt. Very soon she might find herself in the same boat.

There was a lot of activity in the hall as more policemen were sent for, and finally Sergeant Slade came back accompanied by a tall, spare man wearing a long black coat and a bowler hat.

'I am Inspector Watkins,' the newcomer told them in measured tones. 'We have identified the money which my constable has just found as that which was taken from a safe at Perrot's Warehouse over a week ago. There is no mistake. I must caution you all that this is a very serious matter.'

'It was him!' Bert Smart jumped forward suddenly, flinging up his hand to point at Billy Boyd. 'You said he was a safe-cracksman. He stole that money and hid it in my daughter's room.'

'You lying toad!' Boyd roared, and got to his feet, only to be pushed back down by the constables. 'It was more likely you and that little sod Syd Woods.'

'Syd Woods?' Inspector Watkins looked interested and stared keenly at Bert Smart. 'I've been after him for a while. Has he been in this house?'

'He's here all the time,' Billy Boyd butted in. 'He's mucking about with their daughter.'

'Here, you leave my daughter out of this!' Bert rushed forward, but PC Lewis barred his way.

'No rough stuff, Mr Smart,' he said. 'By the way, Inspector, I never mentioned which room the money was found in. As it happens it was the daughter's room. I wonder how Mr Smart knew that?'

Bert looked from one to the other, his face puckering as though he were about to burst into tears, then suddenly, head down, he tried to dash towards the open door. Many heavy hands grabbed him, and he was hauled before the Inspector.

'Hey!' Ada jumped to her feet. 'What are you doing to my husband?' she cried. 'What's going on, for the love of Mike?'

'I'm taking you in,' Inspector Watkins said gravely to Bert. 'On a charge of robbery. You may also face a charge of murder.'

'Murder?' Ada and Gloria screamed together.

'Dad! What's he talking about?'

'I didn't do it, Ada,' Bert said, straining against the constables' grasp to look back at her. 'I swear I didn't.'

'It wasn't Mr Smart that killed the night watchman,' Beth burst out, unable to keep quiet any longer despite her fear of retribution from Syd Woods. She clapped a hand to her mouth as everyone turned to stare at her and there was a deep silence for a moment.

'How do you know a night watchman was killed, Miss . . .' The inspector's eyes narrowed suspiciously. 'What's your name?'

'I don't know that anyone was killed,' Beth stammered, avoiding his question and wishing fervently that she had held her peace.

Inspector Watkins looked stern. 'I warn you, young woman,' he said in heavy tones. 'If you have information about this serious crime and are keeping quiet, you'll be in very hot water.'

'I don't know anything!' Beth insisted, beginning to panic. 'I mean, only what I heard.' She was making things worse for everyone but especially for herself. 'There was nothing in the papers afterwards.'

'Afterwards?' Inspector Watkins frowned grimly. 'After what?'

'She's mixed up in this,' Gloria cried out furiously. 'I knew she was no good. Arrest her! Go on,' she urged the inspector. 'She's been helping the Major with his thieving.'

Beth shook her head vigorously. 'I've done nothing wrong. It's just that one night last week in the kitchen downstairs, I heard Syd Woods admit he had assaulted a night watchman somewhere that night. Mr Smart had nothing to do with it. It was Syd.'

'You're a liar!' Gloria shouted. 'Syd wouldn't do that.' She turned to the inspector. 'Don't listen to her. She's out to get Syd because he wouldn't give her the time of day.' She gave Beth a venomous look. 'The little tart that she is!'

Inspector Watkins turned his gimlet eyes on Beth. 'You've got some explaining to do, young woman, and you'll do it down the station. Sergeant! Call for the Black Maria for three passengers, Boyd, Smart and this here girl.'

The sergeant gave quick instructions to one of the constables, who dashed away.

'You can't lock me up!' Beth cried out in terror. 'I haven't done anything wrong.'

'That remains to be seen,' Inspector Watkins said firmly. 'Get your hat and coat. Constable, go with her. We don't want her making a dash for it, too.'

'You're not going to put me in handcuffs, are you?' Beth asked, almost in tears.

'Only if you give me trouble,' the inspector said. 'So come along quietly.'

★

Beth had never been more terrified in her life. The inside
of the Black Maria was dim and stuffy, and smelled of
every rascal and degenerate it had ever carried. Beth
huddled in one corner as far away as possible from the
two arrested men and a watchful constable. The wooden
bench on which she sat was hard under her bones, and
every time the horse pulled the van over cobbles or other
rough surfaces, Beth thought her skeleton would fall apart
with the vibrations.

She was feeling sick by the time they reached the police
station at the centre of town. When the back doors were
opened she wanted to rush out into fresh air, but was
afraid to move a muscle until told to do so, for fear of
being put in handcuffs.

Climbing out of the van last Beth realised they were in
a back courtyard behind the station, and was thankful that
members of the public could not see her disgrace. Billy
Boyd and Bert Smart were led away in a different
direction, while she was escorted along several corridors
to a small room with bars on the windows and containing
nothing but a table and two chairs. There she waited . . .
and waited.

Finally Inspector Watkins arrived with another
constable.

'Now then, young woman, what is your name?' he
asked, sitting himself at the table opposite her while the
constable took up position behind her chair.

Beth told him her name in a hushed voice.

'Well, Miss Pryce, what do you know of the murder of
a night watchman at Perrot's Warehouse last week?'

'Absolutely nothing!' Beth cried, twisting her hands in
agitation. 'You must believe me.'

'Come along now!' the inspector said sharply. 'You're

not helping yourself by lying. Are you Syd's woman?'

Beth's mouth dropped open. 'Certainly not!' she exclaimed, affronted. 'I wouldn't have anything to do with a man like that.'

'All right then,' the inspector said. 'Start from the beginning.'

And Beth told him all that she had seen and heard between Bert Smart and Syd Woods in the kitchen of Windsor Lodge that night. But the questions continued until her head ached.

'So you knew a man might have been killed and that the proceeds from the robbery were hidden in the house, and you did nothing. Why not?'

Beth swallowed hard, fear gripping her heart. She said the first thing that came into her head. 'I was afraid of Syd Woods. I was afraid he would harm me. I still am.'

To her surprise, the inspector nodded. 'You were probably right. It's likely he would have done you in, too. Syd Woods is a vicious criminal. I hope for your sake he has left the area.' He stood up. 'All right, Miss Pryce. You can go.'

Despite his remark about Syd Woods, relief at escaping prison flooded through Beth like fresh mountain water and she jumped quickly to her feet, anxious to go. But what about Bert Smart?

'Mr Smart had nothing to do with that man's death,' she ventured to remark.

'He robbed the warehouse,' the inspector said grimly. 'And he was accessory after the fact in the murder. Bert Smart will go to prison for a long time.'

It was early evening when Beth walked into the hall of Windsor Lodge, wondering what sort of reception she would get from Ada. When she went down to the kitchen

Flossie was alone, looking hot and flustered. She seemed startled to see Beth.

'I thought you was behind bars,' she exclaimed. 'What happened?'

Beth shook her head. 'I don't want to talk about it,' she said weakly. 'It was the worst experience I have ever had. Where's Ada?'

'Flat out on her bed,' Flossie said, 'leaving me to do everything. I'm no bloody cook!'

'I'll go and see her,' Beth said. She might as well get it over and done with.

'You won't get much sense out of her,' Flossie warned. 'What with Bert nicked and facing clink, and now Gloria gone . . .' She paused, seeing Beth's puzzled expression. 'You know what Gloria's done, don't you?'

'No, what about her?'

'Hopped it, she has, the little hussy!' Flossie exclaimed with fury. 'Left a note. Done a bunk with that swine Syd Woods. Now Ada's all alone.' Flossie shook her head. 'Knocked her for six it has, mind. Never seen such a change in a woman.'

Beth was sorry for Ada, losing the daughter who was the light of her life. But she was also very thankful to know Syd Woods had gone for good.

15

Bert Smart was to be charged with robbery alone, the murder charge having been dropped much to Ada and Beth's relief, and his trial was to take place within a few weeks. The papers were full of it, and everyone was of the opinion that he would cop a long stretch in prison. Syd Woods had disappeared into the woodwork completely, taking Gloria with him, and Ada was devastated.

Tearfully, she told Beth that she would give up the boarding-house business, having no heart to carry on alone and fearful of notoriety. Beth did her best to dissuade her against such a hasty decision.

'But how would you live, Mrs Smart, and where?' she asked her employer. 'Jobs are very hard to come by just now.'

'I'll scrub floors if I have to,' Ada said miserably.

'Oh, buck up,' Beth urged. 'Within a few months the trial will be over, and people soon forget.'

'But with my Gloria gone, what's it all for?' Ada's haggard face was wet with tears. 'Besides, my reputation is finished. No one will want to stay here.'

Beth wondered if that were really true. For the first time since she had been at Windsor Lodge every room was taken, and quite a few callers had been turned away. People could be so ghoulish.

'Stick it out, Mrs Smart,' Beth urged again. 'Flossie and

me will stand by you. We'll work extra hard, won't we, Flossie?'

She smiled half-heartedly, her red hands immersed in soda and water in a sink full of crockery.

'Besides,' Beth went on encouragingly, 'I'm sure Gloria will come back. Once she realises what Syd Woods is really like, she'll be home like a shot.'

'If he will let her.'

Beth shook her head. 'I can't see anyone making Gloria do something she doesn't want to do.'

'You're right,' Ada agreed, wiping her nose on the edge of a tea towel. 'She's a chip off the old block, all right.' She gave a weak smile. 'You're a good girl, Beth.'

Ada's prediction that the business would suffer because of the trial proved wrong. Business was booming, so much, that Beth suggested to her she should take on another pair of hands, recommending Cissie Morgan for the job.

The weeks that followed were hard for Ada, Beth knew. Bert was convicted, which wasn't a surprise to anyone, but the ten-year prison sentence was a shock.

'I might as well be a widow,' Ada told Beth tearfully. 'I could be dead and gone before he comes out.'

One morning towards the end of August, Cissie came lumbering down the steps to the kitchen, calling loudly for Beth.

'You'll never guess who's in the hall asking to see you. Guess, go on, guess!'

Beth laughed, shaking her head. 'I give up, Cissie. Who is it?'

'Old Wilky, and she's looking real sour as usual.'

Beth almost dropped the china tureen she was holding, and began to shake. 'Mrs Wilks? Oh, no! Something has happened to Tommy.'

It was her daily dread, for never a day went by without thoughts of him, wondering how he was, missing him with an aching heart. Every night he was in her prayers. And now Mrs Wilks was here to see her.

'Tommy must be ill!' she cried and dashed upstairs, her heart in her mouth, thinking of the terrible brain fever that had taken Freddie.

Mrs Wilks was in the hall and turned as Beth's running footsteps approached. Cissie was right, the older woman's expression was disagreeable and her eyes hostile, and Beth had the impression she was here under protest.

'What is it?' Beth panted. 'What has happened to my brother?'

'Nothing. His nursemaid takes good care of him, I'll give her that,' Mrs Wilks said grudgingly. 'No, I'm not here about him. It's madam.' Her eyes snapped. 'Well, you know full well she's ill, don't you? Very ill she is, and asking to see you.'

'Aunt Mae wants to see me?' Beth was astounded, wondering if she had heard right.

'Are you deaf or what?' Mrs Wilks snapped. 'You have to come with me now. Bring a bag to stay for a time.'

Beth was nonplussed. 'What does my . . . Dan Henshaw say about this?'

'He doesn't know yet. Madam sent me to fetch you after he left for work,' Mrs Wilks said irritably. 'She's the one who wants you back.' She looked down her bony nose at Beth. 'I don't approve of you returning, but I'm doing this for Madam.' She sniffed. 'After all, I'm quite capable of seeing to all her needs. You can't do more for her than I do.'

'I'm family,' Beth said quietly.

Mrs Wilks sniffed. 'Well, are you coming or not?'

'Of course I'm coming if Aunt Mae needs me,' Beth said sharply. 'But I have to explain things to my employer, Mrs Smart. Things are difficult for her at the moment.'

'Well, I haven't got all day, and neither has your aunt. In fact . . .' Mrs Wilks bit her lip. 'I don't know how much longer she does have. The doctor said . . .' She shook her head. 'She's very poorly.'

An expression of genuine sorrow creased Mrs Wilks's face, and Beth was distressed to hear her words. There was no doubt in her mind that she must go to her aunt, no matter what animosity there had been between them in the past. 'I won't keep you long,' she said. 'Sit in the lounge for a while.'

Ada looked panic-stricken when Beth explained. 'You can't go and leave me in the lurch like this! You promised you'd stick by me,' she exclaimed, her broad face creasing, and Beth thought her employer was about to burst into tears. 'Your aunt has treated you shabby in the past. I need you here, Beth.'

'I know what I promised, but she needs me more, Mrs Smart,' Beth said gently, laying a hand on her arm. 'And she is my own flesh and blood.'

'What will I do?' Ada said, flopping on to a kitchen chair.

'You've got Flossie and Cissie,' Beth reminded her. 'They're both good workers, and loyal. If anything should happen to my aunt, I'll come back here, if you'll have me.'

To Beth's astonishment Ada jumped up and, taking her by the shoulders, planted a kiss on her cheek. 'There will always be a place for you here, Beth. You have stuck by me through thick and thin. Like a daughter to me you've been,' she said, a catch in her voice. 'Truer than my own girl.'

'It's good to have real friends,' Beth said quickly, feeling overcome by Ada's words. She patted the other woman's arm comfortingly. 'And don't blame Gloria. That Syd led her astray, but she won't forget her mother, I know she won't.'

Ada smiled faintly. 'You have more faith than I have, Beth.' She sighed. 'Well, off you go then. You're right. Blood is thicker than water, and your aunt needs you. But don't forget us, will you?'

As they hurried to Brynmill, Beth was excited by the prospect of seeing Tommy once again. It had been such a long time, and her heart ached at the thought that he wouldn't know her. She was a stranger to her own brother, but if she were to stay at Brecon Parade, she would see him every day, get to know him again, take care of him perhaps. If Dan Henshaw didn't forbid it.

The house seemed very quiet when Beth and Mrs Wilks arrived, too quiet, as though death had already visited and the place itself was in mourning.

'Where is my brother?' Beth asked hastily. 'Where's Tommy? I want to see him.'

'You're here to see your aunt,' Mrs Wilks said snappishly. 'Besides he's not here at present. His nursemaid is looking after him at her family's home.'

'What? He's been moved to live with strangers? This is unforgivable,' Beth exclaimed angrily. 'I should have been told.'

Dan had berated her for leaving him with Cissie, but now her brother had been bundled off to stay with strangers, like an unwanted dog.

'It's not like that at all,' Mrs Wilks said. 'They are very respectable people by all accounts.'

'They're not family!' Beth protested loudly.

Mrs Wilks gave a disparaging sniff. 'This house is no place for a child at the moment, is it? Mr Henshaw decided to send him away until . . .' There was a catch in the housekeeper's voice. 'Until it's all over.'

Beth swallowed hard against a rising sob. How could Dan bear to be parted from his son if he really had any feelings for him? Her own heart ached with the disappointment of still being parted from Tommy when she had so looked forward to being with him. But she couldn't argue against this reasoning.

'Is it that bad, then?'

'Oh, yes.' Mrs Wilks shook her head sadly. 'Madam is not expected to live.' Abruptly she lifted a handkerchief to her nose, her tone rising. 'I don't know what he'll do without her.'

'Where is Dan?' Beth asked, dreading to come face to face with him before she had had time to speak with her aunt and assess the situation.

'Still at the yard,' Mrs Wilks said. 'I made sure he was gone before I left. You had better go straight up to see Madam. She's anxious. I'll make some tea, and it's time for her medicine again.' She sighed. 'Not that it does much good, but it helps with the pain a little.'

Beth went upstairs to her aunt's room, afraid of what she would find. It was dimmed in sharp contrast to the bright sunshine outside; the contrast between life and death, Beth thought, and shivered at the notion. She expected to see her aunt sitting near the window as before, but today Mae was in bed, a thin outline beneath the bed sheets. And so still!

Beth crept silently and fearfully to the bed and peered

down at the shrunken figure, holding her breath. A wave of relief swept through her to see the gentle rise and fall of Mae's chest. Her aunt was asleep. Beth turned and was about to creep away when there was movement from the bed and her aunt spoke her name.

'Beth, I'm so glad you are here.'

Mae's voice sounded so weak, Beth felt shaken and a surge of deep pity engulfed her. She was at Mae's side in a moment, taking her cold, white hand in her own.

'Aunt Mae,' Beth whispered, a sob in her throat, 'I'm so glad you sent for me. I'll do anything I can to help you.'

'No one can help me,' Mae said quietly. 'I'm in God's hands, now. But you must stay with me, Beth. I want you here. I have so much to make up for.'

Mrs Wilks came into the room at that moment, carrying a tray.

'I've brought you some tea, Madam,' she said, her voice hushed. 'And it's time for your medicine.'

'I don't want it,' Mae said. 'I must stay awake to talk to Beth. There is so much to explain . . .'

'You must take it,' Mrs Wilks interrupted, sounding worried. 'How will you stand the pain otherwise?'

'Aunt Mae,' Beth said gently, 'I'm here to stay as long as you want me. We'll have plenty of time to talk.'

'No, my girl, we won't,' Mae said with some of her old spirit. 'My time on this earth is short. The doctor knows it, I know it, yet there's so much that still has to be put right. I can't go from this life until I have made amends.'

'Please take your medicine,' Beth pleaded.

'I will later,' Mae agreed. 'Now please, the pair of you, prop me up with extra pillows. My need to talk is greater than any relief from pain.'

With Beth's help Mrs Wilks got Mae sitting upright in bed. Now more light fell on her face, Beth was once again shocked by her aunt's changed appearance. Her features were much thinner, smaller, cheekbones more prominent, while her eyes seemed enormous in her face.

Emotion stirred in Beth, pity and compassion making her eyes brim, but she struggled to hide it. Her relationship with Mae had been stormy from the start. Now all that was forgotten, seeing the devastation her aunt had suffered. She sensed Mae wanted forgiveness, and Beth was ready to grant anything she wanted.

'Shouldn't you rest?' she asked gently, seeing her aunt's difficulty in breathing.

She was surprised to hear a faint laugh from Mae. 'I'll rest long enough when the time comes.'

Beth's heart ached at her aunt's bravery. 'What can I do?'

'Sit with me,' Mae said. 'Have some tea. Let's talk properly. We've never done that, Beth, and that was my fault. I was full of self-pity and resentment, and I took it out on you. But when we have talked perhaps you'll understand and find it in your heart to forgive me.'

Beth gently squeezed the hand that still lay in hers. 'I bear you no grudge, Aunt Mae.'

Mae looked at her, her large eyes glittering with an unnatural brightness. 'You are so like your mother, Beth. Esme was lovely as a girl of your age. All the young men of the chapel gathered around her like moths to a flame. She could've had her pick of any of them. But instead she chose to . . .'

Mae abruptly withdrew her hand from Beth's grasp and turned her head to gaze away towards the window, where the drawn curtains showed only a chink of the sunshine outside.

'I can't bear the sunlight any longer, isn't that strange?' Mae went on in a different tone, as though she had forgotten what she had been saying about Esme. 'It hurts my eyes.'

She seemed suddenly aware of Mrs Wilks hovering nearby.

'That will be all, Mrs Wilks,' she said in a stronger voice. 'I'll ring if I need you.'

'Your medicine . . .' Mrs Wilks began, but Mae lifted a hand languidly to wave her away.

When the door had closed on the housekeeper's heels Mae turned her gaze on Beth again. 'She means well,' she said. 'But she fusses so.' She gave a little laugh. 'Anyone would think she was my mother.'

'She's concerned,' Beth said. 'And in her way she is fond of you. She was almost in tears earlier.'

'Yes, she is loyal, I suppose,' Mae said, and then her voice took on a scathing tone. 'And, of course, she worships Dan.'

'You were telling me about my mother as a girl,' Beth reminded her. 'I'd like to know more.'

Mae smiled at her. 'I've been told you work in a boarding house,' she said. 'Esme and I ran a boarding house in Picton Place in the Hafod when we were girls. And very successful we were, too. We had some very nice lady boarders with us for years.'

'Windsor Lodge takes mostly commercial travellers,' Beth said. 'I expect you did the same.'

'Oh, no,' Mae said firmly. 'I wouldn't tolerate men on their own at our place. Asking for trouble that is.' She paused, looking thoughtful. 'And then Dan Henshaw came along.'

Beth had the impression there was so much more Mae wanted to say about Dan, but her aunt fell silent as though deep in thought.

Beth was about to mention Tommy, but decided

against it. Mae might have temporarily forgotten his existence, and Beth didn't want to rake up ill feeling again.

'Do you miss your mother?' Mae asked suddenly.

'Every moment of every day,' Beth confessed. 'Mam and me were close.' Her voice faltered. 'Very close at one time,' she added, and smiled then, remembering how cosy things used to be before Percy died. 'We had to be, in a house full of men.'

'Percy Pryce was good to her, was he?'

'He was the best of men,' Beth said proudly. 'A good father and husband. I wish to heaven he was my real father.'

Mae suddenly grasped her hand. 'Oh, Beth, I am so full of remorse for the way I treated Esme,' she blurted. 'I was too filled with pride when I was young, and I was resentful and bitter at the disgrace I believed she had brought on us.' She smiled ruefully. 'But at least she had a child who grieves for her. No one will grieve for me.'

Beth gripped Mae's hand tightly. 'That's not true, Aunt Mae,' she exclaimed. 'If anything happens to you, I will grieve, and so will Dan.'

Mae shook her head. 'No, not him. He never loved me the way I wanted, wholeheartedly. In fact, I doubt he can love anyone.'

Beth had to ask the question which had been burning in her mind since reading Esme's letter. 'Not even my mother? Not even while he fathered a child with her?'

And what about Tommy? she asked herself silently. Was there no love in his creation? Surely there had been on Esme's side. Beth had forgiven her mother, but hoped love was the excuse for what she had done.

Mae gazed at her pityingly. 'My poor Beth. It's been hard on you, hasn't it, losing your mother, only to discover you are not who you thought you were?'

'I still think of Percy as my father,' she said loyally. 'He's the only one I am ever likely to know.'

Mae nodded. 'Unfortunately, you are probably right. Dan Henshaw is a hard and devious man, if a charming one.' There was that faraway expression in her eyes again. 'He charmed us both all those years ago – married me for my little bit of money and took Esme's innocence.' She looked back at Beth. 'But she and I were not the only women Dan wronged.'

Beth drew in a breath. 'What?'

Mae suddenly put both hands to her breast, eyes squeezed tight, features contorted in agony. 'My medicine!' she gasped. 'Call Mrs Wilks. I need my medicine. I must sleep to get away from the pain.'

Beth was in the kitchen when Mrs Wilks came down later from seeing to Mae's needs.

'How is she now?'

'Asleep, thank God,' Mrs Wilks said. 'Hopefully she'll have some hours yet.'

Beth frowned. 'It must be very strong medicine.'

'Yes, it is.' Mrs Wilks glanced at her. 'The doctor says she could become addicted to it, but since she won't live much longer we aren't to worry about it.'

Beth put a hand to cover her mouth, upset at the thought.

'I've taken good care of her, you know,' Mrs Wilks went on belligerently as though Beth were questioning it. 'I've not neglected her for a minute.'

'I know,' Beth said. 'And thank you.'

'It's not your place to thank me,' the housekeeper said sharply, her eyes flashing. 'I don't know why you're here. What can you do that I can't?'

'As I said before,' Beth answered, 'I'm family. Look, Mrs Wilks, can't we be friends . . .'

The housekeeper stared.

'All right,' Beth said quickly. 'Perhaps friends is too strong a word, but could we at least call a truce while my aunt is so ill?'

Mrs Wilks looked down her nose. 'I know what you're after,' she said. 'You're hoping she'll leave you something in her will.'

Beth was appalled at the idea. 'No such thing!' She was momentarily very angry with the housekeeper, but the thought of the dying woman upstairs drained her of indignation. 'Come on now, Mrs Wilks,' she said more calmly. 'Nothing much escapes you in this house. You know Dan is my natural father, and you know Aunt Mae and I have been at loggerheads in the past. But she wants to make her peace with me, and that's why I'm here.' She shook her head. 'I have no expectations.'

Mrs Wilks glanced away, looking contrite. 'Yes, well, I'm hurt that she should need anyone else to care for her.'

'You have no need to be,' Beth said gently. 'You must take care of her as you've always done. I won't interfere. My role is very different.'

It was true. She sensed she was here to listen to Mae's confession and to give forgiveness, which she would be glad to do wholeheartedly. Who could bear malice against the dying?

'I'm moving my things to the dressing-room next to Madam,' Mrs Wilks said challengingly. 'I'll be on hand there in case she needs anything.'

'Of course,' Beth agreed.

'To save opening up another bedroom, which would need airing anyway,' Mrs Wilks went on, 'you can use my room, if you like. I don't know how long . . .' She paused, lifting a handkerchief to her mouth.

'Thank you,' Beth said simply. 'I'm very grateful.'

*

It was early evening when Dan Henshaw came home
from the yard. Beth was in the kitchen doing what she
could to help Mrs Wilks prepare his evening meal. She
knew she had to make her presence known to him, but
was dreading the moment when she must face him. She
decided to wait until he had eaten, but it wasn't to be.

He came marching into the kitchen unexpectedly.
'How is my wife today, Mrs Wilks?' He stopped and
stared on seeing Beth. 'What the devil are *you* doing
here?' he exploded.

Beth was determined to stay calm. She glanced apolo-
getically at the housekeeper. 'I won't embarrass Mrs
Wilks by explaining here in the kitchen,' she said firmly.
'We'll talk in your study . . . *Father.*'

He darted an embarrassed glance towards Mrs Wilks,
his face suffused with fury, then turned immediately and
marched out. Beth followed quickly, her mind racing to
find the words to convince him she must stay for her
aunt's sake. But did he really care about his wife's
wishes?

He flung the study door open and strode in, going
immediately to his desk. But he didn't sit. Instead he
stood leaning over it, palms flat on the polished surface,
glaring wrathfully at her.

'Explain yourself,' he barked. 'And it had better be
good, because you're not welcome in this house.'

'Aunt Mae sent for me.'

'What? Preposterous!' He straightened. 'Mae can't
bear the sight of you any more than I can.'

Beth felt the words like a slap in the face, but braced
herself for more abuse. 'She did, Father,' she said
stubbornly. 'It's her dying wish that we should mend our
differences.'

He brought his fist down on the desk with a thud. 'Don't call me that, damn you!'

His violence made Beth blink, but she had made up her mind she wouldn't be intimidated. 'Aunt Mae has asked me to stay here until . . . the end,' she went on doggedly. 'And I intend to, unless you throw me out.'

Her challenging tone made him look uncertain for a moment. 'I don't know what you think you'll get out of it,' he said harshly.

'I want nothing!' Beth burst out. 'Aunt Mae treated my mother badly but . . .'

'Rubbish!' Dan interrupted brusquely. 'If you think there's any money in this, you're mistaken.'

'Money?' Beth flared angrily. 'Your wife is upstairs dying and you talk of money?'

'Why else would you be here?'

'I came at Aunt Mae's request, and because I wanted to see my brother, of course,' she retorted. 'Now I understand you have fobbed him off on strangers. How typical! I demand to know where he is and that he is all right.'

'He is not your concern any longer.'

'You keep telling me that, Father, but I don't agree,' Beth blazed at him, furious at his arrogance. 'I am his sister, the only person who loves him by the look of it. I have a right to be kept informed.'

'You have no rights,' Dan said. 'I have legally adopted Thomas. He is now my lawful son and heir.'

Beth stared, disconcerted. 'Adopted him?' Now he had the law on his side, would she ever see Tommy again? Her dream of getting him back suddenly seemed completely unobtainable. Dan had triumphed again.

'How did you receive this alleged request from Mae?' he asked, pulling out the chair and sitting.

'She sent Mrs Wilks to fetch me from my place of work.'

Dan scowled.

'Don't blame Mrs Wilks,' Beth went on hastily. 'She's very loyal to Aunt Mae, and knows how serious her condition is. Do you, Dan? Do you even care? Or are you too wrapped up in building up your precious business to give *any* thought to your wife and son?'

He looked furious. 'How dare you ask me that?'

But Beth didn't care about his anger. She had an urge to provoke him further. 'Where is Tommy anyway? I want to see him.'

'I've already said, you no longer have any say in his life. Stay away from him and this house if you know what's good for you.'

'It's a cruel thing to do, splitting up brother and sister,' Beth cried. 'He'll grow up a lonely little boy.'

'I should throw you out now for your interference,' her father rasped in fury. 'You are a troublemaker and I have no time for you.'

'Then why *don't* you throw me out?' Beth challenged. 'Are you so contemptuous of Aunt Mae's feelings you would brush aside her dying wishes?'

He hesitated. 'Of course not. I am not an ogre.'

He straightened the blotting pad on the desk and fussed with the inkwell. He had to climb down, and Beth could see it burned him like acid.

'I don't know how long Mae has to live,' he said quietly. 'But I want her last days to be as happy and comfortable as possible. If your presence in this house can bring her any relief then I won't oppose it – for now.'

'Thank you,' Beth said simply.

'Don't thank me,' he retorted harshly. 'And don't read anything into this decision. It's not made from weakness.'

'Huh!' she said disparagingly. 'I never thought it was.'

'Understand this: I'll tolerate you for Mae's sake, but when she has gone, you go too. You will not spend one night here after her funeral, is that understood? And you will take nothing from this house, either. If you do, I'll have the law on you, make no mistake about it.'

'I want nothing from you except my brother,' Beth cried defiantly. 'Why are you so afraid to let me see him?'

'Damn you!' Dan roared, jumping to his feet. 'You push me too far. The child is perfectly healthy and safe. That's all you need to know. I won't have you poisoning his mind against me.'

'He's only a baby,' Beth said scornfully. 'He doesn't understand anything yet.'

Dan's eyes narrowed as he stared at her. 'I know you hate me,' he said, 'and want my son to hate me too. *That's* why you will never see him again.'

'Oh, but I will, Father, I will! And *you* won't stop me.'

'You ought to know better!' Mrs Wilks's lips were a thin line as she glared at Beth. 'All this talking is exhausting her.'

Beth had been at Brecon Parade almost a week, and each afternoon her aunt had asked her to sit and listen while she talked.

'It's what she wants,' Beth protested, trying to be patient, knowing the housekeeper meant well. 'She needs to get things off her chest. She needs forgiveness.'

'Huh! I've never heard such claptrap,' Mrs Wilks exclaimed. 'We were doing very nicely before you came.'

'Yes, I expect you were,' Beth said sharply, not liking the other woman's tone. 'Making yourself indispensable to a dying woman.'

'Ooh!' The housekeeper recoiled and put a hand to her mouth, her face crumpling.

Beth realised she had been too sharp and insensitive. 'I'm sorry, Mrs Wilks,' she said. 'I didn't mean that the way it sounded. I know you are devoted to my aunt.'

'Well, don't try to make out you feel the same way because I know different,' Mrs Wilks retorted. 'I can see right through you, just like Mr Henshaw can.'

Before Beth could respond a bell sounded upstairs.

'I'll go to her,' Mrs Wilks said quickly, jumping up.

Beth glanced at the clock. Half-past three. 'No,' she said firmly, moving to the door. 'You know she usually wants me to sit with her around this time.'

'She may need some more medicine,' Mrs Wilks said, twisting her hands together. 'I'm worried about her. She's gone downhill these last few days.'

Mrs Wilks was right. Mae's weakened condition was very obvious. Beth found it distressing but tried not to show it in front of her aunt.

'I'll call you if she needs anything,' Beth promised. 'Look, Mrs Wilks, I thought we had agreed on a truce for the time being?' She shook her head sadly. 'We're all going through a difficult enough time without this animosity between us.'

Mrs Wilks lifted her chin, giving her a challenging look. 'I'm not the interloper here, mind.'

With a resigned sigh Beth went upstairs to her aunt's room. Despite her growing frailty Mae had been pouring out her heart over these last few days, but it was mostly family history. Beth was learning things about her maternal grandparents she had never known before. Esme had never talked much about her father, and Beth had often wondered why.

She was very surprised to find Mae sitting near the window with the curtains open today, the sunshine streaming in. It seemed to shine right through the skin on her aunt's face as though through tissue paper.

Her aunt turned towards the door as Beth came in, and she was distressed to see the dark ominous shadows lurking in Mae's face, now gaunt with suffering. But her eyes were brighter today, and she smiled to see her niece.

'Sit down, Beth. You're a breath of fresh air in this house.' Mae gave a weak laugh. 'I thought that from the first day you ever came here,' she admitted. 'But I wouldn't let myself acknowledge it. It was like seeing Esme young again.'

'Mam never talked about your father much,' Beth said. 'Didn't she get on with him?'

'Of course she did,' Mae assured her quickly. 'He thought the world of her, his baby. But Esme was always woolly-minded, had no head for business, whereas I took to it like a duck to water.' Mae's face clouded. 'Her reluctance to talk about our father was my fault perhaps.'

Beth said nothing and waited. Mae shifted uneasily in her chair, and Beth wondered if she were in pain. 'Shall I ring for Mrs Wilks to fetch your medicine?'

'It's not pain that troubles me but my own guilty conscience,' Mae admitted. She leaned forward and clasped Beth's hand. 'I regret so much about the way I treated Esme, and most of all I regret withholding our father's inheritance from her.'

'What?'

Mae withdrew her hand uncertainly. 'I thought she didn't deserve it after what she did – disgracing herself and me. I know now the money might have eased her hardship.'

Beth nodded. 'Mam's life was never easy,' she said sadly. 'There was never enough money, but she was a wonderful manager. We never went short, Freddie and me, and she made sure Gwyn and Haydn weren't hungry either. Mam never appeared woolly-minded to me. Quite the opposite, in fact.'

'She had to grow up quickly,' Mae agreed. 'I grieved for her, you know,' she went on. 'Grief and guilt, they are a terrible mixture.'

'Didn't you ever think about reconciliation?'

'Yes, and for selfish reasons,' Mae admitted. 'Dan and I had been married six years when I had a miscarriage, and the doctors told me I would never have another child.'

'Oh, I'm so sorry,' Beth blurted.

'So was I,' her aunt confessed. 'I thought about Esme and her child then – you, Beth – and I wanted a child in my life even if it was just a niece.'

'But you never contacted my mother?'

'No.' A darker shadow crossed Mae's face. 'For a long time I couldn't bring myself to make the first move, and then just as I was about to go and see Esme, I learned about Daphne Prosser-Evans . . . learned about her the hard way.'

'I don't understand?'

Mae turned weary eyes on her. 'Daphne was the other woman in Dan's life of whom I spoke before. I learned about her affair with him when her grieving husband came here to this house and told me face to face that his young wife had just died giving birth to Dan's child.'

'Oh, Aunt Mae!' Beth was aghast. 'How terrible!' She hesitated. 'But how could he be sure Dan was responsible?'

'Daphne confessed all to him before she died,' Mae said. 'Probably the only time she was ever honest with him.'

Beth sat back in her chair feeling shaken to the core. Her own father was a man without principles. Was he any better than Syd Woods or Bert Smart? They were out and out criminals, but perhaps the way Dan conducted his life was even worse.

He took what he wanted without any thought for the feelings of others. He had betrayed Mae twice, had ruined Esme, and the most shocking thing of all was that he wasn't in the least repentant, arrogant in his refusal to accept his own wrongdoing. And now Tommy was under the control of this heartless and immoral man.

Beth felt a sob rise in her throat. Tommy! She had betrayed her baby brother by allowing him to fall into their father's hands. How could she ever forgive herself?

'I remember Daphne when she was just fifteen,' Mae recalled suddenly, breaking into Beth's misery. 'Her grandmother, Mrs Arnold, was a boarder with us at Picton Place. Daphne was back and forth, always making eyes at Dan – the little madam!'

Beth swallowed down the sob, even more scandalised. 'A girl of fifteen? What kind of a man *is* my father, for heaven's sake?'

'Oh, no, no!' Mae said, shaking her head at Beth's expression of revulsion. 'He took no notice of her at that time. No, it was years later when he ran into her again. She was already married to Jarvis Prosser-Evans by that time, his second wife, a man almost old enough to be her father but wealthy. And that was Daphne all over, always after the main chance.'

'You don't mean Jarvis Prosser-Evans, the wholesale provisioners in High Street?' Beth asked, astonished.

'The very same,' Mae confirmed. 'He also owns a building contractor's, and has a thriving money-lending business as well.'

'He's a gentleman, then?'

Mae gave a faint derisory laugh. 'He dresses and lives

as a gentleman, with a fine house on Gower Road, but there's nothing gentle about Jarvis Prosser-Evans. He came up the hard way. It's common knowledge his father Dai Evans had a greengrocer's stall in Swansea Market for years. Jarvis has gained wealth and many powerful friends in this town. He's not a man to get on the wrong side of, as Dan will learn one day.'

'What do you mean?'

'Jarvis swore to me the day he came here that he would ruin Dan eventually. He's just waiting his chance.' Mae shook her head. 'That was thirteen years ago, but men like Jarvis can afford to be patient.'

Beth was thoughtful. Dan Henshaw's hostile attitude to her had made it impossible for her to have any feelings for him except dislike, but now he was revealed in an even harsher light, she wondered at those women, like her mother, who must have loved him. How could they have been so blind to his true nature?

'It was after Daphne's death that I began to wonder about Esme,' Mae went on. 'Although Percy Pryce admitted responsibility for her condition I was never really convinced, but their marriage was a convenient way out of a scandal.'

Beth stared at her aunt, and Mae smiled bitterly.

'Your mother's letter was no shock to me. All along I knew in my heart you were Dan's daughter.'

'How could you stay with him after that betrayal?' Beth asked with distaste.

'I didn't,' Mae said. 'We occupy the same house, but that is all. I kept a close grip on my majority shareholding in the business.' She paused, looking at Beth keenly. 'I have a feeling that after my death Jarvis will take his opportunity to destroy Dan. He probably held off till now so as not to hurt me further.'

Beth was startled. 'What makes you say that? Is there something you're not telling me, Aunt Mae?'

'You know all you need to know,' she said. 'But remember this, Beth. Dan Henshaw is your father, your flesh and blood, even though he has denied you.'

'You sound as though you still love him, as if you have forgiven him despite his treachery?' Beth said accusingly. 'Are you asking me to forgive him, too, Aunt Mae?'

She smiled sadly. 'You must decide that for yourself when the time comes.'

Beth thought about her previous quarrel with her father, when he had forbidden her ever to see Tommy again. He was cold and unloving, did not deserve her loyalty.

'I'll never forgive him!' she said with conviction.

16

November 1921

It was mid-November when Mae Henshaw died quietly in her sleep.

Although the doctor had told them to expect it, at any time over the last few weeks, Beth was devastated when a tearful Mrs Wilks woke her early one morning to bring the sad news. Beth and Mae had become very close towards the end, and now her aunt was gone she felt a growing void in her life, a void that only Tommy could fill. As far as she knew she had no living relative except him. She didn't count Dan.

And he lost no time in putting Beth straight about her future. 'Mae is gone and you're finished here, too. I want you out,' he told her harshly that same afternoon. 'You can pack your bag now.'

Beth was aghast at his callousness. His wife's body was barely cold, yet already he was taking his revenge.

'You can't send me away before the funeral!' she exclaimed. 'She was my aunt. And besides, how will it look to all your smart friends if Mae's only living relative is turned out? They might realise you cared nothing for her.'

His expression darkened. 'How dare you?' he thundered, rising from his chair in his study. 'How dare you even mention my feelings?'

'I know everything . . . Father,' she said, deliberately provoking him. 'I know about your affair with that woman Daphne. I know she died because of you.'

'Be quiet, damn you!' he snarled. 'Mae had no right to reveal anything concerning me.' He wagged his finger at her. 'And I warn you now: if you repeat anything she told you, you'll find yourself in deep trouble.'

Beth shook her head vehemently. 'Oh, believe me, I have no interest in you or your sordid affairs. You'll be glad to see the back of me? Well, let me tell you, the feeling is mutual. I'm ashamed to admit that *you* are my father.'

She turned and walked from the room, leaving him fuming.

Beth remained at Brecon Parade for the funeral on which Dan spared no expense. A draped carriage drawn by two fine black horses carried Mac to her final resting place in Dan-y-Graig cemetery. Beth was astonished at the number of people who attended the service. Although womenfolk were not expected to go, she was determined to be present despite Dan's disapproval, and persuaded Mrs Wilks to go with her.

'Mr Henshaw won't like it,' the housekeeper had said uncertainly.

'You were Aunt Mae's friend as well as her employee,' Beth pointed out. 'You have a right to pay your last respects.'

Quite a few mourners, many of them well-dressed businessmen by appearance, came back to the house, and Dan had hired some women to help Mrs Wilks with the spread. Beth assisted in passing out the food for a while until he appeared at her side.

'You can leave that,' he said quietly to her, his voice hard. 'It's all over now, you can clear out.'

Beth swallowed down the lump rising in her throat. 'Very well,' she said, resigned to the helplessness of her situation. 'But I still demand to see my brother, no matter what you say. You can't keep us apart.'

'You have no brother,' he told her harshly, and strode away.

There was nothing else to do but leave. Beth went to the room she was using and got out her small suitcase. There wasn't much to pack. She sat on the bed for a while, thinking about Dan's severe pronouncement, reluctant to leave the house just yet despite her father's orders.

She would *not* give up. Tommy would be brought back now, with any luck. Beth was determined to keep watch close by whenever she had the chance. Sooner or later an opportunity would present itself, but whether she could find enough courage to act, she did not know. She must at least see her brother to reassure herself that all was well with him.

She was still in the room when the mourners began to drift away, and was about to pick up her suitcase and follow them, when Mrs Wilks came in, her expression animated.

'Good job you haven't gone yet,' she said somewhat breathlessly. 'Mr Carradog-Jones is here.'

Beth shook her head, not really interested in any of Dan's friends. 'Who is he when he's at home?'

'He's your aunt's solicitor. He wants you to come down to the sitting room. Mrs Henshaw's will is about to be read.'

Beth was startled. 'Her will?'

She didn't know whether she could face Dan's animosity again. Her aunt's passing and the funeral had left her exhausted. She had little fight left in her.

'I don't think that's necessary,' Beth said tiredly. 'I'm going to slip out through the back door. Tell the solicitor I've already gone.'

'But you can't do that!' Mrs Wilks exclaimed. 'He says you are in the will. You are a beneficiary, like me.'

'A beneficiary!' Beth was astonished. She had not expected her aunt to remember her in that way. 'Are you sure?'

'Yes, come on,' Mrs Wilks urged. 'He's waiting and he's a busy man, so he said.'

When Beth entered the sitting room she saw Dan pacing up and down before the windows overlooking the gardens. He glanced at her, his expression thunderous, and she realised he had had no idea that she was to receive anything in Mae's will.

Beth looked away from the enmity in her father's eyes to the other man standing before the fireplace, examining some legal-looking papers, wearing a disagreeable expression on his bony face. Mr Carradog-Jones was a tall, angular man dressed in a dark jacket and pinstripe trousers. He looked up impatiently as she approached, regarding her over the top of his spectacles.

'You are Miss Bethan Pryce, lately of Libanus Street, I take it?' he asked in clipped tones. It sounded more like an accusation than a question.

'Yes, I am,' she said nervously. Since her previous brush with the police, she was wary of anyone connected to the law. 'Why do you want to see me?'

'Sit down,' the solicitor commanded bluntly. He glanced at Dan with a frown. '*Everyone* sit down. This process is taking far too long already.'

'Why must *she* be here?' Dan asked nastily, indicating Beth.

'If you'll sit down, Mr Henshaw,' Mr Carradog-Jones said impatiently, 'everything will be revealed.'

Everyone sat.

'Now,' the lawyer began, 'I won't waste any more time on preliminaries but will get to the bequests immediately.' He glanced at the paper before him and then at Mrs Wilks. 'I quote: "to my devoted housekeeper, Mrs Wilks, I leave the sum of five hundred pounds".'

She gave a gasp of satisfaction.

' "And also to Mrs Wilks",' the solicitor continued in his droning voice, ' "I leave my diamond and emerald brooch which she has admired for so long." '

'Oh!' Mrs Wilks appeared overcome, and lifted a handkerchief to cover her mouth. 'Oh, the dear woman.'

The solicitor gave a cough of irritation at the interruption and then continued to read from the document. ' "I leave this house and all it contains, including furniture, fittings and my remaining jewellery, to my husband, Daniel Henshaw." ' The solicitor cleared his throat before continuing. ' "To my niece, Bethan Pryce . . ." '

'Just a minute!' Dan interrupted brusquely. 'There must be more for me than that. My wife had financial resources of her own, and then there's her share of the business. You haven't mentioned that.'

Mr Carradog-Jones pursed his lips, looking thoroughly cross at this further interruption. 'If you'll allow me to continue,' he snapped, 'I was just coming to that portion of her estate.'

'I don't like the way you are conducting this reading,' Dan said rudely, and Beth wondered why he appeared so agitated. No outsider could guess he was so recently bereaved. She could see no pain or grief in his handsome face.

'Oh, really?' Mr Carradog-Jones retorted sarcastically.

'Well, may I remind you I am acting for your late wife, not you, and she was more than happy with the way my firm attended to her legal business. Now, please let me get on with the reading.'

Dan gave a contemptuous grunt and the solicitor rustled the papers in his hands angrily, giving Dan a long hostile stare. 'As I was saying, and I quote: "To my niece Bethan Pryce I leave the residue of my estate . . ."'

'What?' Dan exploded and jumped to his feet. 'What the hell is going on here, Jones?'

' ". . . the residue of my estate," ' the solicitor quoted, doggedly ignoring the outburst, ' "which includes the sum of ten thousand pounds and . . ."'

'I don't understand.' Beth sat forward with a start, unable to believe what she was hearing.

'Understand, be buggered!' Dan turned on her. 'You understand all right, you conniving little hussy,' he snarled. 'You talked her into it, don't deny it. Every afternoon you worked on her, didn't you? Cajoling, persuading, until the poor broken woman didn't know fact from fantasy.'

Mrs Wilks gasped and looked shocked.

'That's not true!' Beth protested hotly. 'I had no idea Aunt Mae had left me anything. She never mentioned it.'

'Now just a minute, Henshaw!' Mr Carradog-Jones stood up abruptly, two red spots appearing on his gaunt cheeks. 'Are you suggesting there is misconduct here, and that my firm, Carradog-Jones and Furlong, is involved?'

'Misconduct is your word, Jones. I'm saying my wife would not have left anything to Bethan Pryce,' Dan shouted. 'Mae hated her, like she hated Bethan's mother before her. There's trickery here, and I won't stand for it.'

'Trickery!' Spittle appeared at the corners of the solicitor's mouth, and his hand shook as he held up the document and then waved it under Dan's nose.

'I draw your attention to the fact that this will was drawn up last March, and so dated,' the lawyer said heatedly. 'Your wife came to see me at that time. She told me her sister had recently died, and that she bitterly regretted their quarrel. She wanted to make amends and so issued new instructions regarding her will, leaving the bulk of her estate to Miss Pryce as her sister's sole heir.'

'The bulk of the estate?' Dan's face paled as he stared at the solicitor.

'That's what I said,' Mr Carradog-Jones told him emphatically. 'As well as the ten thousand pounds, Miss Pryce also inherits Mrs Henshaw's fifty-one per cent shareholding in the company trading as Dan Henshaw, Coal Merchant. Miss Bethan Pryce is your new partner, Henshaw.'

Beth lost track of the next few minutes, her mind reeling with shock. She was vaguely aware of Dan's curt dismissal of Mrs Wilks from the room, and then the voices of the two men raised in furious argument.

She distanced herself from them as she struggled to make sense of what the solicitor had said. Aunt Mae had left her some money and what else? Part of Dan's business? It could not be! Her aunt knew the way she felt about Dan Henshaw; knew full well that Beth wanted nothing to do with the man who had fathered her so shamefully.

She felt betrayed. Why had her aunt put her in this impossible position? She became aware that her very thoughts were being shouted aloud by someone else.

'Mae can't do this to me!' Dan was bellowing. 'It's preposterous, I won't have it. My wife must have been out of her mind, or else she was bullied. I'll contest the will.'

'There was nothing wrong with Mae Henshaw's mind,' Carradog-Jones expostulated angrily. 'You can contest it if you wish, but I warn you, Henshaw, it will cost you money and you'll lose. This will is watertight.'

'Damn Mae to hell then,' Dan howled in fury. 'She has done this for revenge.'

'I don't want any part of it,' Beth burst out, jumping to her feet. 'I just want to be left alone to get on with my life. And I want my brother Tommy back with me, where he belongs.'

Carradog-Jones turned to her. 'You have the opportunity of beginning a new life,' he said gruffly. 'You should be grateful, at least. You are now a wealthy young woman.'

'I don't want to be part of *his* business,' Beth blurted, pointing a shaking finger at Dan. 'I despise him!'

'Then sell up,' Carradog-Jones suggested quickly, 'it's a thriving company, by all accounts. There are plenty of men in this town who would like to take the lion's share of it.' The solicitor's eyes gleamed with malice as they were turned on Dan. 'And some who would cheerfully see Henshaw ruined altogether. I can easily arrange the sale for you, Miss Pryce.'

Beth saw her father's face had turned deathly pale. Obviously his feud with Jarvis Prosser-Evans was common knowledge.

'I'll buy her out myself,' Dan said hurriedly, a quiver in his voice.

Carradog-Jones sat down, very calm all of a sudden. 'Well, let's talk about this,' he said evenly. 'I estimate Miss Pryce's share of the business to be worth in the region of, say, fifteen thousand pounds. Can you come up with that kind of money, Henshaw?'

Beth stared, open-mouthed, astounded at the sum of

money mentioned, while Dan seemed to totter and sat down heavily.

'All my assets are tied up in the business,' he said in a strangled voice. 'It was always Mae who had the money.'

'Too bad,' Carradog-Jones said in an offhand tone, gathering up papers to put them in his briefcase. 'If you wish to give me your instructions now, Miss Pryce, I can spread the word that you are willing to sell.'

'Wait a minute!' Dan exclaimed. 'I'm not done yet, and I demand first refusal. I'll mortgage this house to raise the money and meet her price. You must give me time.'

'My client, Miss Pryce, may not wish to wait,' Carradog-Jones said in a hard voice. 'You heard her say she wants to get on with her life.'

Beth couldn't take her eyes from Dan's face. He looked panic-stricken, and the echo of Mae's words to her rang in her mind.

Dan Henshaw is your father, your flesh and blood.

She could take her revenge on him now for the way he'd treated her mother, for his callous denial of her. It would be so easy, but she was sure Mae had not wanted her to do that. Besides the solicitor was trying to push things along too quickly and she wasn't ready. She needed time to get to grips with her new situation, and not only that but an astonishing idea had come into her mind on how she could best use her legacy.

'You are mistaken, Mr Carradog-Jones,' Beth said firmly, surprising herself by speaking so confidently to such an important man. 'I am not your client, and I have no intention of selling my share of the business – at this time.'

'But, Miss Pryce . . .'

'I'm sure Mr Henshaw and I can work something out between us without your help. And that is all I have to say on the matter.'

No one spoke for a few moments and finally the solicitor got to his feet. 'Very well, Miss Pryce,' he said stiffly. 'I'll have some papers for you to sign within a day or two. I can bring them here, if you wish?'

'I won't be here,' she said quickly. 'I'll call at your office in town one day next week.'

'Of course, but if you change your mind . . .'

'It's unlikely,' Beth said shortly.

Carradog-Jones glanced helplessly at Dan, who was sitting silently, eyes downcast. 'I'll see myself out,' the solicitor said, and left.

The tension in the room did not leave with him. Beth sat quietly, trembling, waiting for her father to speak. She had saved his bacon, and he must know that. After a moment Dan got up and walked to the sideboard to pour himself a small glass of whisky.

'I suppose you expect me to thank you?' he asked bitterly over his shoulder. 'But I won't because I suspect your motives are self-serving.'

'I've told you before, I don't expect anything from *you*,' she said sharply. 'And I have no hidden motive for saving you. And save you, I did, Father, whether you like it or not.'

'Out of the goodness of your heart, I suppose? Huh! No one is *that* generous.' He turned to look at her. 'I can't believe Mae would do this to me without some persuasion from you.'

'Your arrogance is amazing!' Beth exclaimed, rising to her feet. 'You repeatedly betrayed her, yet you think she didn't want revenge?'

She stared at him. Tall and handsome, a hint of silver at his temples, he was still a very attractive man. She wondered if there were other women in his life whom Aunt Mae had known nothing about, even someone ready and waiting to step into his wife's shoes.

'Actually, you are right,' she went on, disturbed by the notion. 'I think Aunt Mae still loved you despite everything. She wouldn't want me to sell you out, even though I think you deserve it.'

He swallowed back the whisky in one throw. 'I'll get the money,' he said confidently. 'Just give me time.'

'Don't bother,' Beth retorted brusquely. 'As I told the solicitor, I don't intend to sell my share, not even to you. I am your partner, Father, and will be for a long time to come.'

'What?' He took a step forward. 'What the devil are you playing at, you little minx? If you believe you can prise more money out of me, think again.'

'I'm not the devious one in this family, Father. But rest assured,' Beth went on, enjoying the consternation showing in his face, 'like Aunt Mae I'll be a silent partner and won't interfere with the day-to-day workings – at least, not for the time being.'

'You're no family of mine,' he rasped, fury in his eyes. 'You think you've got me over a barrel, don't you? But I'm no one's fool. I'm not taken in by your little game, whatever it is.'

'My game, as you put it, is to make you sweat, Father,' Beth returned heatedly, infuriated by his continued denial of their kinship. 'I'm not as forgiving as Aunt Mae. You won't know from week to week what I intend to do with my shares.' She gave him a look of derision. 'I certainly could not stomach working alongside you day after day. I have no love for you, you see.'

He scowled. 'If you hurt me, you'll hurt your own brother, too,' he said nastily. 'Destroy me and you destroy him. Thomas is my heir. Are you going to take away his birthright?'

'His *birthright*! Oh, you hypocrite!' Beth shouted.

'Your only concern is for yourself and your own survival.'

His lips tightened. 'Well, *partner*, what are you going to do next?'

'Bide my time,' she retorted. 'And while I'm doing that, I'll be taking care of a business of my own.'

'Huh!' He sent her a mocking look. 'You don't know the first thing about running a business.'

'I know about hard work, though,' she said. 'I did enough of that here in this house when I first came to Brecon Parade. I skivvied for you until my hands were raw, your own daughter.' She would never forgive him for that.

'And what is this business?' he jeered.

'Boarding-house keeper,' she said triumphantly. 'I'll go into partnership with my former employer, Mrs Smart. I have a feeling she'll welcome me and my money with open arms.'

'A boarding house?' He looked startled, and Beth smiled scornfully.

'Yes, ironic, isn't it?' she said. 'I'm following in the footsteps of my own mother and Aunt Mae. But unlike them I will not fall in love with the first handsome, scheming face I see.'

17

Beth smiled at Ada Smart's astonished expression when she arrived at Windsor Lodge later that day, carrying her small case.

'Never thought to see you again, Beth,' Ada said as they took tea in the kitchen. 'I heard you'd come into a barrel-load of money. Thought you'd be planning to move up the Smoke or somewhere like that to live the posh life.'

'My goodness!' Beth said, her turn to look astonished. 'News travels fast in this town. I only just heard myself a few hours ago.' Mrs Wilks's tongue had been wagging overtime obviously, she thought.

'It's true then?' Ada said. 'Well, well. We'll have to make an appointment to talk to you soon.'

Beth grinned. 'I'm the same old me, Mrs Smart,' she said. 'How have you been these last few months? How is Mr Smart?'

Ada's face crumpled, and Beth was sorry she had mentioned him yet genuinely anxious to know how he was coping with life behind bars.

'He's awful miserable inside,' Ada said. 'It breaks my heart to visit him, but he's got no one but me. No word from our Gloria,' she added before Beth could ask. 'Dropped off the face of the earth, she has. I do get lonely when Flossie and Cissie have gone home at night.'

'I want to come back,' Beth told her quickly. 'Come back to stay.'

'Back here?' Ada looked astounded. 'What for?'

'Well, it's the only place I can call home,' Beth said simply. 'I miss my cosy little room here.' She paused, realising there was no other way to approach the subject than by asking straight out. 'Mrs Smart, how would you like a new business partner?'

Ada's eyes opened wide. 'How do you mean?'

'I'd like to come into the business with you. Now I've got this money we could expand. Windsor Lodge over-looks the Bay. We could cater to summer visitors as well as commercials.'

'Expand?'

'I notice there's a "For Sale" sign up next door,' Beth said. She had noticed it in passing, and it had given her an idea.

'Yes, Phoebe is giving up the business,' Ada said forlornly. 'So the landlord has decided to sell off the property.'

Ada and Phoebe Palmer who ran the boarding house next door had been close friends for years.

'That blighter of a husband of hers left her flat,' Ada went on. 'Ran off with one of the guests. The stinker! Took the heart out of her, it did.' Ada sighed. 'Know how she feels, I do. I worked my fingers to the bone, all for Bert and our Gloria, and now they are gone, I have to ask myself, why go on? What's it all for?'

'For yourself,' Beth said firmly. 'Let's work together, for our own sakes. What do you say?'

Beth was due to see Mr Carradog-Jones the following day to sign the necessary papers regarding her inheritance. She needed a solicitor now and decided he was as good as any. Ada went with her to put their new relationship on a legal footing.

With the solicitor's help Beth arranged to put in a reasonable offer for the property next door, and instructed him to approach the landlord with a view to purchasing Windsor Lodge as well. She also clarified her position as Dan's partner.

'As I understand it, Mr Carradog-Jones,' Beth said firmly, 'since I own fifty-one per cent of Dan Henshaw's business, shouldn't I be in receipt of some sort of income from that?'

The solicitor's glance at her was sharp, and he almost smiled. 'You most certainly should, Miss Pryce, and don't let Henshaw tell you any different. As long as the business is doing well, and in profit, you should see a return. Of course, you could plough it back into the business . . .'

'Oh, no,' Beth said quickly. 'I want whatever is due to me.'

She had no intention of making things easy for Dan.

'I'll inform him of that,' Carradog-Jones said, and actually smiled.

Beth came away from his office feeling more elated than she had done for many a year. At going on for nineteen years old she was already a businesswoman, a woman of property, or would be soon. She was sure her mother and Percy would be proud of her. It was certainly a step up from a humble seamstress. She was making her way in the world, despite a father who denied her and losing most of her family. Ada was her family now, and so were Cissie and Flossie.

But Ada was very quiet as they walked back along St Helen's Road towards Oystermouth Road, and Beth wondered what was on her mind.

'You're not having second thoughts, are you, Ada?' she asked gently.

'No,' the woman said. 'But when you own Windsor Lodge, will I be working for you instead?'

Beth laughed and linked her arm through Ada's as they walked. 'We are equal partners, Ada, and we are going to do well. I can feel it in my bones.'

'I hope so,' Ada said, her tone gloomy.

Beth wanted to cheer her up and give reassurance, too. 'Why don't you ask Phoebe Palmer if she would like to come and work for us as she is on her own now? She knows the business inside out, and the both of you are such friends. She could live in. It would be company for you.'

Ada beamed. 'Oh, Beth, what a wonderful idea!'

As they had expected Christmas was quiet, and Beth used the time to think and plan ahead. By the second week of January 1922 the sale of both properties was completed, and she was the proud owner of two substantial houses on Oystermouth Road.

Business picked up again with the New Year, and they were full to capacity with commercial travellers. Beth didn't have time to feel any qualms about the responsibilities she had taken on, what with the reorganisation of the business, engaging more staff and the general day-to-day grind.

It was only at night when she lay in her bed in the little room behind the kitchen, which she insisted on keeping for herself, that she wondered what had happened over the intervening months since Aunt Mae died. It was her aunt who had made it all possible, and she hoped Mae approved of what she had done with her inheritance so far.

At the end of January she had a surprise visitor. Cissie showed Dan Henshaw into a room at the back of the house that Beth had made into an office. Astonished to see him stride in, she half rose from her chair and then sat down again, annoyed at herself for reacting.

'What's happened? Is Tommy ill?' she asked quickly, her heart almost stopping in dread.

'No, this is business,' he said abruptly. 'I want you to countersign a document.'

'What is it for?'

'That doesn't matter,' he retorted offhandedly. 'It won't mean a thing to you anyway.'

'Well, in that case, I shan't sign it,' Beth said angrily. 'Now, if there's nothing else on your mind, Father, please close the door on your way out.'

'How dare you speak to me in that tone of voice?' Dan blustered. 'And don't call me Father.'

She stood up and faced him fearlessly. 'No, you're right,' she snapped. 'There's nothing fatherly about you. As for my tone, I'll say and do as I like in my own house.'

He stared and Beth nodded. 'Yes, that's right,' she went on proudly. 'I own this house and the one next door. I'm already in business so if you're not prepared to explain yourself properly, perhaps you'd leave and let me get on with my work.'

His mouth was set in a hard line as he stared down at her.

'Very well,' he said harshly, and she could see he was holding on to his temper with great difficulty. 'It's an insurance claim.' He paused, obviously reluctant to say more.

Beth waited, deliberately keeping her gaze steady on his. Dan Henshaw's days of browbeating her were over.

His mouth worked furiously for a moment as he stared at her and she realised his anger was not so much against her as the circumstances that had forced him to come here.

'One of the coal drays was deliberately damaged,' he

said at last, his voice tense. 'The horse was lucky to escape serious injury, not to mention Elias Morgan.'

'What?' Beth was startled. 'Is Elias all right? What happened?'

'He'll live,' Dan said callously. 'But the dray is useless. Someone sawed through the back axle. The load was spilled in the road and most of the sacks split open. One hell of a mess it was.'

'But who would do such a thing?' Beth asked, wondering why Cissie had said nothing of this.

'I lost a lot of business that day,' Dan said, ignoring her question. 'Customers I've had for years. They looked elsewhere for delivery, and who can blame them? Sabotage, that's what it was, pure and simple. If it happens again it could put me in serious financial trouble.'

'But who did it?'

Dan turned his gaze away, looking obstinate, and Beth realised he knew who was involved. She could guess, too.

'So, it's come at last,' she said quietly. 'Jarvis Prosser-Evans has made his first move against you.'

'What do you mean by that?' His eyes flashed with fury.

'Don't pretend with me, Dan, or deceive yourself,' Beth retorted impatiently. 'He's waited long enough. It's thirteen years since Daphne died, isn't it?'

Dan flinched as though he didn't want to be reminded. 'Damn him to hell!' he shouted. 'I wasn't responsible for that. There were other men in her life. I wasn't the only one.'

'Blackening her name won't help,' Beth said. 'You should try to meet him. Make him see reason.'

'Damned if I will!' He stared at her challengingly. 'I need the money Mae left you, Beth. I need it to survive if Prosser-Evans steps up his campaign against me.'

Beth shook her head, 'Oh, no!' She was astonished that he should ask that, and realised he was frightened of the future.

'It should've come to me,' Dan insisted with a snarl. 'I was her husband.'

Beth smiled at the irony of it. 'You're not going to beg me, are you?' She shook her head. 'Don't bother. You betrayed Aunt Mae, and you would betray me too, if I let you. You've already denied our kinship more than once. You're not trustworthy, Dan.'

The muscles in his jaw worked as he strove to control his temper. 'What does a girl like you want with all that money, anyway?'

'I'll sign your insurance paper,' Beth said, ignoring the jibe. 'And that's all you'll get from me.'

'You're a hard, grasping little bitch!' he snarled.

Beth glared at him. 'It's in our blood then, Dan. Like father, like daughter, as Aunt Mae told you, remember? I hate the thought that I might be like you, but maybe she was right.'

Beth sat in her little office for a long time after Dan had left, feeling very miserable and lonely, and for some reason thought about her future. It seemed very bleak at the moment. Would she ever meet a man she could love, who would love her in return and be true to her? Would she ever belong to a family again and be happy?

She understood Ada's feeling of despondency and uselessness now her loved ones were taken from her. It was hard to fight on alone.

She had just begun to revive her spirits when Cissie came to tell her that a gentleman had called and wanted to see her.

'It's not Dan Henshaw again, is it?' Beth asked irritably.

She had a feeling she hadn't heard the last of his demand that she should hand over Aunt Mae's inheritance to him.

Cissie shook her head. 'No. This gent has a very posh horse and trap outside, with a driver as well.' Cissie paused, frowning. 'Mind you, although he's dressed up to the nines, he doesn't talk posh.'

Beth was intrigued. 'I'd better see him, then.'

She stood up hurriedly as a tall, fashionably dressed man strode in. Beth's experience in handling cloth as a trainee seamstress told her that his dark grey three-piece pinstripe suit was of the finest quality, as was the grey Homburg he wore at a tilted angle. He was probably in his late-fifties, she judged, though well preserved. His florid craggy features seemed at odds with his elegance, yet there was an air of supreme confidence about him. With a sudden flash of insight, Beth thought she could guess who he was.

'You are Miss Bethan Pryce?' He had a strong local accent, and she thought she recognised it as belonging east of the river.

'Yes,' Beth admitted. 'And you are Mr Prosser-Evans,' she added, guessing.

He raised his brows, obviously surprised. 'You know me then?'

'No,' she said. 'Just a shrewd guess.'

'Shrewd, eh?' He looked her up and down speculatively. 'Perhaps you also know why I'm here?'

'No,' Beth said again. 'Please sit down and explain.'

She was astonished at her own presence of mind. This man was her father's enemy. The smell of money exuded from him, along with power and strength of will. A self-made gentleman, the most dangerous kind perhaps. He might well prove to be her enemy, too. She must tread carefully.

'I won't beat about the bush, Miss Pryce,' Jarvis Prosser-Evans said importantly. 'I'm here to do business.'

It was Beth's turn to be surprised. 'What business can you possibly have with me?' she said sharply. 'I run a boarding house.'

'And so young, too,' Jarvis said, his astute gaze searching her face as though he expected to find a clue there to her nature. 'I understand you own the house? Very unusual these days, especially for a female of whatever age. You have courage and a flair for business, I judge.'

Beth pursed her lips angrily at his arrogance and patronising tone. 'I'm sure you haven't come here to exchange compliments, so perhaps you will get to the point, Mr Prosser-Evans.'

'Certainly.' He crossed his long legs. 'You hold the major shareholding in the company known as Dan Henshaw, Coal Merchant. I'm here to buy you out.'

'What?'

'I'll give you a fair price.'

'You can whistle against the wind!' Beth exclaimed heatedly. 'I've no intention of selling.' She frowned at him. 'How do you know so much about my personal business anyway?'

Jarvis Prosser-Evans was silent for a moment, as though weighing up what he should say next. 'A certain Mrs Wilks has kept me informed of matters in the Henshaw household for some time,' he admitted, and smiled widely. 'For a generous consideration, of course. A mine of information she has been, too, over the years.'

Beth blinked, unable to believe Mrs Wilks's duplicity. According to Mae, the housekeeper had worshipped the ground Dan walked on, but all along she had been betraying him to his most bitter enemy.

'Thanks for telling me. I'll see to it she is sacked forthwith,' Beth said bluntly.

Jarvis shrugged. 'She has served her purpose anyway,' he said callously. 'Do as you like.'

Beth stood, holding her head high. 'I think you had better go, Mr Prosser-Evans. We have no more to say to each other.'

He sat forward, a hard expression in his eyes. 'Oh, I think we do,' he said resolutely. 'I intend to get control of Henshaw's business one way or another, and no one had better stand in my path. Do you understand me?'

Staring at the malevolent glare in his eyes, Beth felt a shiver of apprehension race up her spine. Could this man destroy her hopes and plans for the future, and all because of her father's betrayal? His eyes said he could and would.

'Are you threatening me?' she asked incredulously, trying to keep fear from her voice.

Jarvis's mirthless smile was jeering. 'You may take my words any way you wish, Miss Pryce. I've waited a long time. Mae Henshaw has gone now and I'm tired of waiting. I want justice.'

'You arranged for one of Dan's drays to be damaged,' Beth accused wrathfully. 'The driver, an innocent man, was nearly hurt. Where's the justice in that?'

Jarvis pursed his lips, and was silent for a moment. When he spoke again it was in a measured tone. 'That was unfortunate, I grant you.'

'Unfortunate!' she exclaimed angrily. 'I call it criminal.'

'Call it what you like,' Jarvis snapped. 'No one can prove I had any hand in it.'

'What kind of a man are you?'

'A wronged man!' he declared. 'By your father. But I assure you I want no one hurt, except Henshaw,' he went on, his face darkening. 'I'll see him grovel in the gutter yet.'

'Then you'll do it without my help,' Beth burst out. 'Now please leave my house.'

'Now look here, young woman,' Jarvis said in a dangerous voice, rising to his feet. 'I intend to bring Henshaw to his knees, and anyone who stands with him. It would be a pity if that happened to you, Miss Pryce. You show such promise.'

'You have a long way to go before you bring Dan Henshaw to his knees,' Beth said, in raised tones. She was beginning to feel really frightened, but wouldn't show it. 'I have resources, Mr Prosser-Evans. I'm sure Mrs Wilks told you that, too. I have a mind to put them at Dan's disposal.'

'Then you'd be a fool to do it, and I don't think you are,' he snapped. 'I'm prepared to offer a fair price for your shares. And I would promise to keep the business going so the employees would not lose their living.'

'Your promise!' Beth exclaimed in disgust. 'Is that worth anything? Anyone who stoops to sabotage is obviously totally untrustworthy.'

His eyes narrowed, and she could see he was trying not to lose his temper again. Obviously Jarvis Prosser-Evans was not used to people defying him. 'Despite what you say,' he said evenly, 'I have the power to ruin the business altogether.'

'The answer is still no,' Beth said loudly.

'I'm not a man to be thwarted,' he said angrily, his face turning more ruddy than before. 'I don't take kindly to people being uncooperative.'

'You can't ride roughshod over me,' Beth cried. 'I'll have the law on you.'

He stared at her, and she could see puzzlement in his gaze.

'You are prepared to stand by Dan Henshaw, after he has denied fathering you? You have more forgiveness in you than most people in such circumstances. I thought you hated him.' He raised his eyebrows. 'I know you have sworn to make him pay. Now is your chance, Miss Pryce. Dan Henshaw has wronged both of us.'

Beth stared at him silently for a moment. Was there nothing this man didn't know about her?

'He is my father after all,' she said at last. 'I thought I wanted revenge, but now I'm not so sure.'

'Then you'll go down with him!' Jarvis shouted. 'Because I am sure about winning my revenge. Thirteen years ago he took my wife from me and with it my chance to start a new family. I can never forgive that.'

He stood glowering at her for a moment, and Beth could see he was shaking with fury.

'Be warned, Miss Pryce,' he went on in a heavy voice. 'Think carefully before you choose sides in this fight, because as Heaven is my witness, I will prevail, and I'll trample your business and you underfoot along with your damned father.'

18

Beth didn't waste any time after Jarvis Prosser-Evans had stamped out of Windsor Lodge. Quickly struggling into her coat and hurriedly clapping her hat on her head, she made her way up to Dan's yard in Brynmill.

Her father's expression wavered between surprise and irritation at the sight of her. 'If you have come to pester me about Thomas, you are wasting your time,' he rasped as she was shown into his office. 'With one dray short we have a crisis on our hands at the moment. I haven't got time or patience to waste on you.'

'You'd better listen!' Beth rapped out, thoroughly annoyed at his tone when she had come to do him a favour. 'You may not have a business to run at all. In fact, Dan, it's entirely down to me whether you sink or swim.'

'You're talking drivel.' He looked impatient.

'I've had a visit from Jarvis Prosser-Evans.'

'What?' He jumped to his feet, his expression agitated. 'What the hell did he want with you?'

'My fifty-one per cent of all this,' she said, waving a hand around. 'At a handsome profit to me.'

Dan sat down heavily, his face turning deathly pale. 'You treacherous bitch!' he exclaimed loudly, glaring at her. 'You've sold me out to that bastard and now you've come to gloat.'

Cut to the quick, Beth stared silently at him for a moment, unable to reply immediately. Did he really believe she could be so disloyal? 'You don't think much of my principles, by the sound of it,' she said at last, not able to keep the hurt from her voice despite trying.

'Huh! Principles!' he sneered. 'I'm still not entirely convinced you didn't dupe Mae into leaving you that money. With your background you might be capable of anything.'

'*I* have done nothing shameful. *You* are my background, Dan, as well you know,' she snapped. 'But don't judge me by yourself. I didn't sell out to Prosser-Evans, nor was I tempted to do so.'

He sat forward, colour coming back into his handsome face. 'You refused him? How much did he offer?'

'I didn't let him get that far,' Beth said. 'And he wasn't at all pleased. He more or less admitted he was behind the damage to the dray, and implied that wouldn't be the last of it.' She sat on a chair before the desk, her legs suddenly feeling shaky. 'He threatened us both,' she said, unable to keep a tremor from her voice. 'Swore he'd ruin me, too, because I wouldn't give way.'

'Prosser-Evans is all talk,' Dan said, looking away, but Beth saw a film of sweat on his upper lip. He was as frightened of the man as she was.

'I can't take that chance.'

He glanced back at her, fear plain in his eyes. 'What do you mean? What are you going to do?'

'I'm not going to do anything. You are, and quickly. You must talk to the man, reason with him,' Beth said firmly. 'I've just started my business. I can't afford trouble from the likes of him. I tell you, Dan, he frightens me.'

'It'll blow over,' her father said in a casual tone that didn't deceive her. 'If we just sit tight.'

'You coward!' Beth cried, jumping to her feet. 'I won't

put my future at risk because of you. Why should I? You deny me, so maybe I'll deny you by giving Prosser-Evans what he wants – your head on a block!'

'You can't do that to me!'

'Why not?' she asked quickly. Would he finally call himself her father?

'Because . . . I'm your uncle by marriage. You owe it to Mae's memory to protect the business, any way you can.'

Beth stared at him for a moment, disappointment slicing through her like a sharp knife. He didn't deserve her loyalty, and she suddenly felt bitter and vengeful towards him.

'I take it the profits will be down this quarter because of the damaged dray,' she asked grittily.

He looked surprised. 'What's that got to do with anything?'

Beth set her mouth in a firm line. 'Just this! That loss is not coming out of *my* share of the dividends,' she warned. 'This feud with Prosser-Evans is all your fault, so you'll bear the brunt of the loss.'

Dan gave a bitter laugh. 'Dividend? What makes you think you'll get any?'

'My solicitor will see that I do,' she said. 'And if you don't cough up, you will be dealing with Prosser-Evans as a partner instead of me. And I don't think you'll like *that*.'

'This is blackmail!' Dan stared at her as though seeing her for the first time. 'How can you do that to one of your own family?'

'Family?' Beth exclaimed wrathfully. 'You don't know the meaning of the word, Dan. You could've had family around you, standing by you, but you've thrown that away. So be it. Whatever happens next is your own fault.'

Feeling suddenly weary, she rose to leave. She should

have known it would be useless to expect him to do anything to help her.

He jumped up. 'Wait a minute! What the hell are you going to do? You can't go back on your word about selling out. Prosser-Evans will see me in the gutter or the workhouse before he's finished with me.'

Beth turned to him, her tone bitter. 'You should have thought of that before you stole his wife.'

'That's none of your damned business,' Dan shouted. 'Whatever happened in the past is private to me.'

'Nothing you do outside or inside your house is private,' Beth said. 'You've been betrayed, Dan, but not by me.'

'What are you getting at?'

'Jarvis has been paying Mrs Wilks to spy on you for years. He bragged about it to me.'

Dan stared at her, mouth open, obviously knocked back by the revelation.

'Apart from little Tommy, you really are alone now, Dan,' Beth went on quietly, although inside she was fuming. 'With no one you can trust. I hope you're satisfied.'

Beth still fumed as she made her way back to Windsor Lodge. It was plain her father did not care one jot what happened to her. He would never stand between her and the vengeful wrath of Jarvis Prosser-Evans. Not for the first time she wondered why she was protecting Dan at all. After he'd denied her, callously stolen her brother from her and refused even to let her glimpse Tommy – after all that, she continued to stand by him. She must be a fool! And he was taking her for one, laughing up his sleeve.

Passing the entrance to the park, Beth paused. It was

merely a stone's throw to Windsor Lodge but she did not want to return just yet, feeling shaken and disturbed by Dan's hostile attitude.

It was cold but the sun shone brilliantly and Beth was tempted to spend a few moments resting on a park bench to get her emotions under control. Making the decision, she passed through the gates and strolled aimlessly along the main path. There were quite a few mothers and children around the duck pond, braving the cold and enjoying the winter sunshine.

A middle-aged woman in a nanny's uniform sat on a bench with an infant on her lap who looked to be around Tommy's age. The child was wrapped warmly against the cold and wore a little knitted cap. Beth's heart contracted at the sight. She was painfully reminded of her brother. This child could be Tommy for all she knew. She could walk past without ever knowing it was he.

On impulse Beth sat on the end of the same bench. The nanny was throwing bread to the ducks and encouraging the child to watch their antics. Hope suddenly filled Beth's breast. Perhaps this nanny was acquainted with Tommy's nursemaid. Maybe she could discover something about him, she thought, and attempted to start a conversation.

'Nice day for January,' Beth observed chattily.

The woman glanced at her and smiled faintly, then turned to the child and murmured something, pointing to the squabbling ducks. But there was no enthusiasm in the child's glance at the birds, no happy animation in his features. For an electric moment the child's gaze fixed on her own, and Beth felt a great shock go through her system. Something about those wide-spaced eyes and the up-tilt of the nose reminded her of Esme.

'A little boy, is it?' she asked, struggling to catch her breath. 'What's his name?'

'Thomas,' the woman answered grudgingly, turning her shoulder away.

Beth swallowed hard, scarcely daring to believe it was true, that she had found him at last. 'Would that be Tommy Henshaw of Brecon Parade? Dan Henshaw's son?'

The woman looked startled and stared at Beth, a frown creasing her brow. 'I don't know you,' she said accusingly. 'You're not from around here.'

'That's my Tommy you've got there, isn't it?' Beth cried, edging closer. 'That's my brother!'

The woman clutched the child to her, looking alarmed, and stood up abruptly. 'Now I know who you are,' she exclaimed loudly. 'You're that Bethan Pryce who's always causing trouble. Mr Henshaw warned me about you, said you'd be up to no good.'

'Warned you?' Beth stared. 'What do you mean?'

'He said I must be careful if you ever approached the baby while we were out,' the woman answered, edging away. 'He said you might try to steal Thomas away. You are not to be trusted anywhere near him.'

'But I've a right to see my own brother,' Beth said, jumping to her feet. 'And you can't stop me.'

'Brother, my foot!' the woman said angrily. 'You don't fool me with that one. Mr Henshaw has only one child and this one's adopted.' She turned towards the pram standing nearby and placed the child in it, covering him with a blanket.

'It's true!' Beth said forcefully, taking a step towards the pram. 'My mother died last March giving birth to Tommy.'

'I don't believe you,' the woman retorted angrily. 'What a wicked thing to say!' She gave Beth a haughty look. 'Mr Henshaw confided in me that you have a grudge against him for some reason. Unbalanced, he said you are. He said you would steal Thomas just to get money out of him. That's criminal, that is.'

'That's a lie,' Beth cried desperately. 'It's Dan who's the criminal for stealing Tommy from me. I just want to spend time with my own baby brother.'

'Huh!' the woman was scornful. 'He said you were a liar and no good, as well as being half off your head. You keep away from us, I'm warning you.'

She turned the pram and began to walk hurriedly towards the park gates.

'Just a minute!' Beth exclaimed. 'Don't you walk away like that! I haven't finished. I won't let you go until I've seen Tommy properly, seen that he's all right. Let me see him!'

Beth grabbed at the handle bar and there was a sharp tug of war with the pram. Tommy began to cry with fright. She felt desperate, yet did not know what she intended to do if she managed to wrestle the pram from the woman's grasp. She could hardly run off with the baby, yet she longed to.

'Get away!' the woman screamed at the top of her voice. 'Help! Help, someone! She's trying to kidnap this baby. Help!'

People began to move uncertainly towards them, and then Beth spotted the park keeper striding purposefully in their direction.

'Hey, you!' he bellowed at her, waving his stick. 'I want a word with you. What's your game?'

'Call a policeman,' the nanny shouted to him. 'There's a mad woman here, trying to take this baby.'

Her attention distracted, Beth felt the pram being wrenched from her grasp, and the woman began to walk quickly away pushing the pram before her. Beth stood stock still for a moment, watching the approaching park keeper who had broken into a run now, still waving his stick threateningly.

Suddenly afraid of being arrested again and falsely accused, Beth turned tail and ran off in the opposite direction, almost in tears. Dan Henshaw was poisoning people's minds against her to stop her having any contact with Tommy. It was all part of his denial of her. Why did her father hate her so much? She thought she could guess. He couldn't face his own shame at what he had done to her mother, and he was taking it out on her.

She stopped running at last when Windsor Lodge was in sight, although still in shock at what had happened. But at long last she had glimpsed Tommy. He had looked well and cared for but not very happy, she thought, a sob in her throat. He had no one really to love him except her. They were in the same boat. Would she ever find someone to love her? She fervently hoped so, because no one can live without love.

'Burning the midnight oil again, Pa?'

Jarvis Prosser-Evans glanced up from studying some papers on his desk to see his son Eynon stroll into the study, immaculate in evening dress.

'And you are still enjoying yourself, I see,' Jarvis said irritably. 'What was it this time? Another damned party.'

Eynon walked in leisurely fashion to the sideboard where the decanters stood.

'I took the Dewhurst twins to hear the Welsh Opera Company give a performance of *La Bohème* at the Grand Theatre,' he said in his fine cultured voice that tended to make Jarvis feel inferior sometimes, despite himself. 'Wonderful!' Eynon went on, pouring out a measure of whisky and throwing it back immediately. 'As good as anything I've heard at Covent Garden.'

Jarvis felt his facial muscles tighten in a scowl. He had never been to an opera in his life, and didn't understand the attraction. 'You're seeing a lot of those Dewhurst girls lately,' he said sullenly. 'I hope you haven't done something stupid, like proposing marriage to one of them? They haven't one brain between two.'

'Marriage? Not very likely!' Eynon laughed. 'Besides, it's not their brains I'm interested in. But I haven't managed to get either of them alone yet to try my luck. That formidable mother of theirs watches them like a hawk.'

'Wise woman.'

'Yes, she has managed to outwit me so far.' His son sighed. 'They're beginning to bore me anyway. It's time I looked for easier prey.'

'It's time you settled down with a sensible wife, that's what!' Jarvis said forcefully. 'Raise some children. You're twenty-seven now. Don't leave it too late.'

Eynon shook his blond head. 'Too many beautiful women out there I haven't met and wooed yet. Marriage can wait. I'm in no hurry.'

'It's a pity you don't devote as much time and energy to business as you do to chasing skirts,' Jarvis said acidly. 'My God, Eynon, you make me despair for the future.'

'Don't blame me, Pa.' Eynon poured himself another whisky then lowered his tall elegant frame into a leather armchair before the ornate white marble fireplace. 'It's not my fault you gave me a gentleman's education, and a gentleman's tastes to match,' he said evenly and without rancour. 'It's what you wanted in a son.'

Jarvis ground his teeth with ire. It was true. He had wanted his son to be something he himself could never be, despite money and fine living. But he had come to realise to his cost that gentlemanly sensibilities and

manners did not stand up well in the harsh dog-eat-dog
world of commerce. Eynon displayed little of the ruthless
instinct a man needs to succeed in trade. He had had
things too easy and now was complacent.

'More fool me!' his father said resentfully.

'I say, Pa, what's the matter?' Eynon asked from the
depths of the armchair. 'Some deal go wrong, did it? Lost
a quid or two, have you?'

Jarvis threw down his pen on to the blotting pad, feeling
disgust at his own shortsightedness. 'I made a very grave
error of judgement today,' he said. 'I used heavy-handed
tactics with someone when I should've used charm.'

'Charm!' Eynon laughed and sat forward. 'I'm afraid
you're a bit short of that commodity, Pa. That's my
department.'

'Yes.' Jarvis looked at his son thoughtfully. 'Perhaps I
should've sent you, at that.' He shook his head. 'But I
wanted to see to it myself as it is something very dear to
my heart.'

Eynon's mouth tightened in sudden disgust. 'Not the
Henshaw business again?' he said in consternation.
'You're living in the past, Pa. Daphne is long dead, let her
rest in peace.'

Jarvis jerked to his feet, and strode angrily to the fireplace. 'You always hated her,' he said morosely. 'For
taking your mother's place.'

'I didn't hate her,' Eynon denied strenuously. 'But even
as a fourteen-year-old I could see she was the wrong sort
for you. She was flighty, Pa. Maybe Henshaw wasn't
totally to blame for what happened.'

Jarvis rounded on him, his face turning even redder.
'Take that back, damn you!'

'Oh, for God's sake, Pa!' Eynon exclaimed, standing
up face to face with his father. 'You've made Daphne into

a plaster saint when clearly she wasn't. And thirteen years ago you could've married again if you'd really wanted a new family.'

Yes, Jarvis thought, he could have remarried, but it would have meant nothing. He'd never thought he could love again until Daphne came along. Irreverent, boisterous, sparkling-eyed Daphne. His money had been the attraction for her, of course, he knew that very well, but they could have been happy together if she had lived. Damn Dan Henshaw to hell!

'Yes, I wanted more sons to inherit my businesses,' Jarvis shouted wrathfully as a renewed sense of loss swept over him. 'And I wouldn't have made the same mistake with them as I did with you. No more fancy manners and fancy talk.'

Eynon's face was impassive and his voice quiet as he answered. 'Like I said, Pa, I am what you made me.'

'Yes, yes,' Jarvis answered in disgust, turning away, his shoulders drooping. 'I'm well aware of it.'

'I'm going to bed,' his son remarked after a moment. 'You ought to do the same.'

'I won't sleep,' Jarvis said, sitting down again behind the desk. 'I can't get that girl's face out of my mind.'

'What girl?'

Jarvis ran his thumb along his jaw line, seeing again in his mind's eye the quick defiance flashing in Beth Pryce's glance and that firm young chin jutting at him belligerently. He'd known in that moment he had made a big mistake in threatening her. He was used to bullying and browbeating men. Those tactics wouldn't work with her, and perhaps he had already spoiled his chances of getting at Henshaw through his daughter.

'When she more or less told me to go to hell,' Jarvis went on thoughtfully, 'I saw something in her eyes that I recognised. She has steel in her backbone, that one. Guts and drive. I was reminded of myself when I was that age, with nothing but determined to be someone. She's on the first rung of the ladder and she'll climb to the top, and no one had better try to stop her.' Perhaps not even himself, he thought ruefully.

'What are you talking about, Pa? Who is this paragon of female virtue you so obviously admire?' Eynon uttered an oath. 'Hell's teeth! You haven't fallen in love with another chit of a girl, have you?'

'Don't insult me, Eynon, and don't be more of an idiot than you already are,' Jarvis snapped. 'And certainly don't make the mistake of taking me for one either.'

'Then what is it?' his son asked impatiently. 'Who is this girl who has got you so wrought-up?'

'Bethan Pryce, Dan Henshaw's illegitimate daughter who he has denied. The fool!' Jarvis said disparagingly. 'She had recently inherited a fifty-one per cent share of his business from her Aunt Mae.'

He paused a moment, remembering. He had taken no pleasure in telling Mae Henshaw of her husband's treachery thirteen years ago. He had wanted to punish Henshaw, not her, yet Jarvis knew he had finished her marriage. It came back to haunt him from time to time that he had had no right to do it. And Mae Henshaw had taken her revenge by leaving everything to the girl.

'Such an adversary is no match for you then, Pa?'

Jarvis glanced at his son, aware of the irony in those words. A chit of a girl would hardly be seen as a worthy adversary for a wily and ruthless businessman of his standing, yet she had him worried.

'You wouldn't think so, would you?' he said. 'Yet when I tried to buy her out, she sent me packing with a flea in my ear.'

'Well, well!' Eynon said, and grinned widely. 'Perhaps she *is* the wife for you after all.'

'Be serious, Eynon, for once in your life.' Jarvis looked up, annoyed. 'I tell you this,' he rapped out, 'she's the kind of girl you need for a wife.' He looked past his son's shoulder to another place and time. 'By God! I wish she was *my* daughter.'

'You'll never be satisfied with me, will you, Pa?'

Jarvis detected an edge to his son's voice, and suddenly regretted his earlier harsh words. 'You are my son, Eynon, and I love you,' he said simply. 'But heaven help the business when I'm gone.'

'That's years off,' Eynon said offhandedly. 'You're as fit as a fiddle. And I need more time to sow my wild oats.'

'You'd better come to your senses soon,' Jarvis retorted harshly, annoyed at such flippancy. 'I could easily sack you from the board, you know. You're not pulling your weight, and I want things to change.'

Eynon looked sceptical. 'Threats? Oh, really, Pa!'

'I mean it,' Jarvis said ominously. 'I want you to go and see Beth Pryce and talk her around. Practise some of that charm you're so proud of. Get her to sell us her share of Henshaw's business.' He paused. 'I'll tell you what, Eynon, if you can carry this off, I'll see you get an increase in salary.'

'It's a deal!' his son said with enthusiasm. 'Piece of cake.' He laughed confidently. 'And I'll have her eating that cake out of my hand before the week is out.' He paused, suddenly uncertain. 'By the way, what's she like? Built like the back of a tram, I expect, with a face to match?'

Jarvis shook his head thoughtfully. 'Far from it. She's a beauty but unaware of it.' He looked at his son's grinning face, and his eyes narrowed. 'You treat her with respect, mind. No funny stuff, or you'll answer to me.'

Eynon looked puzzled. 'She really has got to you, hasn't she?'

'It's the father I'm out to destroy, not the daughter,' Jarvis said, and realised he meant it. 'I may have other plans for her.'

It was very late but Beth was still in her little office catching up with all the work she had neglected earlier in the day. It was hard to concentrate on bills and invoices after what had happened in the park. She had no doubt Tommy's nanny had reported the incident to Dan by now. He would not let that pass unchallenged. She could expect a visit from him within the next few days. She hoped he would not turn vindictive and make it a police matter. He had witnesses on his side who would probably believe the lies he told them.

Beth was sitting with her head in her hands when Phoebe Palmer came into the office, carrying a cup of tea. She was already attired for bed, and with a thick hair net protecting her blonde Marcel wave. She was a slim handsome-looking woman, and Beth had to wonder at Ted Palmer's folly in deserting her.

'Do you know what time it is, girl?' Phoebe asked, putting the cup and saucer on the desk. 'It's nearly midnight, that's what.'

Beth picked up the cup gratefully. 'Thanks for this, Phoebe. I'll be going to bed soon. Why are you still up anyway?'

'I've been to bed once, haven't I?' she said, pursing her lips. 'But I knew you were still down here.' She shook her head. 'You are doing too much, Beth kid. You'll make yourself ill, and where will we all be then?'

Beth sipped the tea, and then smiled. 'You'd all manage somehow.'

'No, we wouldn't,' Phoebe said emphatically. 'We'd be all at sea, kaput. You're the backbone of this place, Beth. Poor old Ada isn't the same since Bert went into clink and that Gloria deserted her.' Phoebe's lips tightened. 'Oh! I'd give that little hussy a good hiding if I could get my hands on her.'

Phoebe was very protective of her friend Ada, and Beth could understand her sentiments. She drained her cup, surprised at how thirsty she was. 'I'll take this down to the kitchen on my way to bed,' she said, standing up and stretching. 'You go on up now. It'll be time for breakfast soon.'

Phoebe wished her good night, or what was left of it, and disappeared upstairs. Beth was just about to switch off the last light in the hall when she was startled by the sound of pounding on the front door. Not the police! But who else could it be? The boarders were all in, she knew they were. Nervously, Beth edged towards the door as the din continued.

'Who is it?' she asked, her heart in her mouth.

'Dan Henshaw!' a man shouted back, and she recognised her father's broad accent. 'Open this bloody door now.'

Astonished, Beth quickly unlocked the door, withdrew the bolts and opened the door. 'What do you want at this time of night?' she asked, but could guess. 'Decent people are in bed.'

'You are up, so that's saying something,' Dan retorted savagely. He pushed past her without being invited and strode into the hall, but Beth held the door wide open.

'Get out! Whatever you've come to talk about, it can wait until morning,' she said testily. 'How dare you barge in here so late?'

'I'm not leaving until I've had an explanation of your

outrageous attempt to abduct Thomas in the park today.'

'That's a lie!' she cried. 'I didn't try to abduct him. All I wanted was to see him and hold him a minute, but that stupid nanny made such a fuss.' Beth's eyes flashed. 'But, of course, the woman believes all your terrible lies about me.'

'Mrs Tate was given her orders. She did the right thing. I don't want you anywhere near my son, understand?'

Beth was suddenly conscious of the open door and the light flooding out on to the pavement. She was also conscious that their raised voices must be carrying to the street. Reluctantly she closed the door, and then faced him.

'Why?' she asked, shaking her head wonderingly. 'Why are you so set on keeping Tommy and me apart? I wouldn't do him any harm, you must know that.'

He was silent, his face tense, but his gaze slid away from hers as though he were feeling uneasy, or perhaps guilty.

'It's part and parcel of your denial of me, isn't it?' Beth said, seeing the truth. 'Even to let me see Tommy would be a public admission of my kinship to him, that we both have the same father.'

'Be quiet! It's you who is in the wrong here, Bethan,' Dan barked. 'I could bring a charge against you, you know. I'll speak to the park keeper. I've no doubt he'll be willing to testify.'

'Testify to what?' she blurted. 'Anything you *tell* him to believe, I suppose.' There was silence for a moment and then she went on in a different tone. 'This isn't fair on Tommy, Dan. He'll need his family around him when he is growing up or later, when he is more aware, he'll be very lonely.'

'That's not for you to comment on.'

'Do you plan to marry again, raise more children?'

Dan stared, outraged. 'How dare you ask me that, you impertinent hussy?'

'I'm trying to understand you and your motives.'

'Well, understand this,' he said tersely. 'I don't want you near Thomas because I never want him to know about his ignominious origins. He is my heir, and will have a proper standing in the community in time.'

Beth stared open-mouthed at his audacity and self-deceit. 'But his origins, as you call them, are of your making. It was you who fathered him out of wedlock.'

'Of course he will know I'm his father, and as far as he is concerned I am his legitimate father,' Dan said testily. 'But he must never learn about his mother and what she did. That's why there must be no contact between you. His mother died in shame, but he must never suffer for it.'

Beth felt hot blood scald her cheeks. 'You speak as though my mother seduced *you*.'

Dan's lips twisted. 'Huh! You didn't know your mother as well as you thought you did,' he rasped. 'Seduction? Oh, yes. She was capable of that all right.'

For a moment Beth was stunned, and then red rage engulfed her. She stepped towards him and, swinging up her arm, struck him full force across his face with her open palm. 'You swine!'

He rocked back, clutching at his reddening cheek, seemingly stunned as much by her action as the force of the blow.

'I hate you for that, Dan Henshaw,' she gasped. 'You're a sanctimonious coward, blaming my mother for your own wrong-doing.'

'You little hellcat!' He sounded winded. 'That was a vicious assault.'

'I'm giving you warning, Dan,' she blazed. 'No one, no threat, will stop me from seeing Tommy. Maybe you can keep me from your house, but you can't keep me away from public places. Wherever Mrs Tate takes him, I'll follow. The park, the beach, wherever. I'm my own boss now. I can take as much time off as I like. So, what are you going to do about it?'

They stared at each other for a moment, eye to eye. She saw a hard steely glint in his eyes, and hoped he saw the same steel in hers. After a long moment he looked away.

'I'm willing to compromise, provided you obey my rules,' he began. 'You may see Thomas on neutral ground, in the park, once a week. Mrs Tate will always be there. She will be in control, and you will behave towards Thomas exactly as she says. Do you agree?'

Beth swallowed hard, unable to believe his climb-down. It seemed almost too easy, and she wondered what he hoped to gain by it, but she would not question him in case he changed his mind. 'Yes, I agree, I swear.'

He stared at her for a moment longer. 'Don't think you have scored a victory, here, Bethan, because you haven't,' he said. 'Thomas must never know you are his sister and you must never speak of Esme to him.'

'But he will want to know about his mother when he grows up.'

'He will know only what I choose to tell him,' Dan rasped. 'You must agree to this or the arrangement is off. I hold the upper hand, Bethan. He is *my* legitimate son now. You are nothing to me – or to him.'

19

'Mr Prosser-Evans is waiting in the guests' sitting room, Beth,' Flossie said the following morning. 'Wants to talk to you.' She grinned. 'My word! Gents calling on you, left, right and centre. You've gone up in the world, haven't you?'

'Jarvis Prosser-Evans is no gent,' Beth said irritably, feeling a shiver of fear go up her spine. 'He's next down to a scavenging hyena, and I wish he'd leave me alone.'

Flossie looked startled. 'Well, I never! Shall I tell him to push off?'

Beth hesitated. She had had little sleep after her confrontation with Dan, and regretted striking her own father, but the awful insult to her mother had been too much to bear at the time.

'No, it's all right,' she sighed, making up her mind that she could not shirk this new encounter.

Her small victory in being allowed to see Tommy once a week had set her mind racing all night, tired though she was. And now Jarvis Prosser-Evans had come to annoy her again.

'I'll have to face him,' she went on, removing her pinafore.

She was shaking with fatigue and apprehension as she approached the sitting-room door. If he had come with a new ultimatum or fresh threats, how could she defend herself? She decided attack was the best defence and, throwing the door open, marched in boldly.

'Now look here, Mr Prosser-Evans,' she began in a strident tone, 'I'm not afraid of you and I won't be threatened . . .' She stopped, staring at a complete stranger.

The young man who had been gazing out of the sitting-room window whirled round to face her, startled by her abrupt and noisy entrance.

'Oh, I'm sorry!' Beth said haltingly, feeling her face flush with embarrassment. 'I thought you were someone else.'

'Heaven help him then,' the young man said without a smile.

Beth didn't know where to put herself. 'Please accept my apology, Mr . . . er . . .'

'Prosser-Evans,' the young man said, stepping forward with an outstretched hand. 'Eynon Prosser-Evans. I believe you have already met my father?'

'Your father!' About to take his hand, Beth sharply withdrew her own, furious. 'Has he sent you here?'

'As a matter of fact, he has,' Eynon said frankly. He held up a hand in warning. 'But before you kick me out, hear what I have to say.'

'Oh! I know what you have to say,' Beth exclaimed angrily. 'And the answer is still no.'

'I don't blame you,' Eynon said quickly. 'And I certainly agree with you, Miss Pryce. It's a disgraceful business altogether. I've told my father so in no uncertain terms.'

'What?' Beth felt confused at the sincerity in his voice; a beautiful voice, too, so cultured and refined. Intrigued, she looked more closely at him. His facial features had none of the cragginess of Jarvis, but were finely chiselled. A very handsome man indeed: tall, blue-eyed, blond hair neatly cut and styled close to his well-shaped head, with none of the excesses of brilliantine used by many young men these days. He was smiling at her.

'It was all so long ago,' Eynon went on smoothly. 'I have advised my father to let things lie. My stepmother, God rest her soul, was no saint. In my mind she was as responsible for what happened as your father.'

Beth blinked, at a loss. 'Well, I'm glad someone in your family sees a bit of sense,' she said lamely. Then a thought struck her. 'But, wait a minute, you said your father had sent you here today.'

'Yes, he did.' Eynon looked around. 'Can we sit down?' he asked. 'So much more civilised, don't you think, Miss Pryce?'

'By all means,' Beth said, annoyed that she had been momentarily bowled over by his looks and fine manners. 'But it won't make a jot of difference. I won't sell.'

'Of course not, why should you?' he said, and Beth felt confused again that he agreed with her. He shrugged. 'I pointed as much out to Pa,' he went on. 'But he insisted I came along anyway.' He smiled at her. 'I'm glad I did, Miss Pryce. I wouldn't have missed meeting you for the world.'

'I beg your pardon?'

'You have made a very big impact on Pa, don't you know,' Eynon said. 'And he's not a man who is easily disturbed in his business dealings, I can tell you. But you have him rattled.'

'I see.' Beth stared at him. 'Should you be telling me this, Mr Prosser-Evans? I am, after all, your father's adversary,' she said frankly.

'How strange! That's exactly how he described you,' Eynon exclaimed with equal candour. 'But it is so absurd and such a waste of everyone's time and money. It's high time this feud was brought to an end.'

Pleased, Beth raised a hand to her throat. 'I was saying a similar thing to my own . . . to Dan,' she said hesitantly. 'I suggested he should meet your father and talk this thing through. But . . .' She hesitated, unwilling suddenly to make Dan look small by revealing his cowardly attitude. 'But he wouldn't hear of it.'

'Huh!' Eynon said. 'Each as bad as the other. But something must be done.'

'Oh, yes.' Beth nodded enthusiastically. 'What?'

Eynon smiled. 'We must work together, Miss Pryce, to find a way.'

'Perhaps we could contrive a meeting between them,' she suggested eagerly. 'Do you think your father would call at Dan's office on some pretext? With both of us there to mediate, perhaps we could reach some kind of understanding.'

He looked at her steadily for a moment. 'You should be in politics, Miss Pryce. The country could use some of that clear thinking at present.'

Beth stared back at him, suspecting he was laughing at her. 'This is no joking matter, Mr Prosser-Evans,' she said severely.

'Oh, please call my Eynon,' he said quickly. 'There is no quarrel between us. I'm sure we can be friends.'

Beth felt her face flush again. She liked his easy manner, and his tone sounded genuine. Suddenly she wanted very much for him to be her friend.

'Very well, Eynon,' she said pleasantly. 'I'm Beth. How do you suggest we proceed to put an end to this feud?'

'Well, I'll certainly talk to my father again and try to make him see reason,' Eynon said soberly. 'You do the same with Henshaw, then we can meet again tomorrow to compare notes and see what other plans we can devise.'

'I hope there will be no more sabotage in the meantime,' Beth said cautiously.

Eynon Prosser-Evans was a very presentable and charming young man, and although his easy manner was a pleasant surprise she wouldn't be taken in if she could help it. Could she really trust him? He'd said he wanted the feud to end, but was that true or was it merely some kind of a ruse to trick her and damage Dan?

'I think it unlikely,' Eynon said. He stood up and reached for his hat, gloves and steel-topped walking stick. 'But it might be wise to meet elsewhere to discuss this matter further, Beth. I don't want Pa to know we're seeing each other again.'

She looked at him with raised eyebrows. 'Why not?'

Eynon inclined his head knowingly. 'He sent me here to try to persuade you to sell. He has no idea I . . . we . . . are plotting against him, and if we have to meet frequently, he might guess. Let me take you to luncheon tomorrow. The Baltic Lounge in High Street is quite discreet.'

This suggestion sounded underhanded for some reason and she was dubious. 'I don't know, Eynon,' Beth said hesitantly.

'Why ever not?' He smiled. 'It's perfectly respectable for us to meet there for lunch.' He hesitated, looking serious. 'There isn't a young man in your life, is there, who might misunderstand?'

'Of course not!' she said, and then was ashamed of her flushed cheeks. He must think her gauche and naïve. Yet still she hesitated to agree. She had nothing to wear to such a posh place, and didn't want to make a fool of herself especially in front of him. 'Why can't we meet here?'

He reached forward suddenly and grasped her hand.

'Please, Beth,' he said sincerely. 'I would feel much more comfortable meeting on neutral ground. You don't know my father as I do. He's suspicious of everything and everyone.'

'You make it sound as if we're conspiring,' she said, laughing despite her uncertainty.

'Well, we are, aren't we?' he answered. 'But in a good cause.'

Eynon left after that, arranging to meet Beth in town the next day.

'What's the matter?' Ada asked anxiously when Beth returned to the kitchen. 'Has the old bugger made more threats against us?'

'It wasn't Jarvis, it was his son,' she said thoughtfully. 'And he has invited me to luncheon tomorrow at the Baltic Lounge.'

'What?' Ada stared. 'What's he up to?'

'I don't know yet,' she said seriously. 'But I'd like to find out.'

'Luncheon, is it?' Flossie said. 'He's a very handsome chap, mind. Perhaps he fancies you, Beth?'

'More like he fancies I am a nincompoop who will fall for smooth talk,' she said, while hoping deep in her heart she was wrong. She shrugged. 'I can't go anyway. I've got nothing to wear.'

'Now look here!' Ada said severely. 'You never spend anything on yourself and you should, a girl of your age and with your looks. Get up to town now and buy yourself an outfit for tomorrow.'

'It would be a waste of money,' Beth said dourly. 'Just for one occasion.' She never seemed to meet any young men who might ask her out, certainly no one remotely like Eynon. And the business kept her so busy these days anyway. She shook her head. 'No, I'm not sure it's a good idea at all.'

'Of course it is,' Ada persisted. 'He's young, good-looking and well off. It'll do you no harm to be seen out with a chap like that. You ought to get about a bit, enjoy yourself. You work hard enough, Beth.'

'I – I don't altogether trust him,' she admitted. The truth was, she couldn't believe that a toff like Eynon Prosser-Evans really wanted to be seen in her company in such a swanky place as the Baltic Lounge. Only people with plenty of money could afford to dine there. Of course, she reflected with amusement, *she* had plenty of money now. Nevertheless, she wasn't used to the high life and might embarrass herself. 'It might be a trick,' she went on thoughtfully. 'And I don't want him to make a fool of me.'

'Huh! He will have to get up very early in the morning to make a fool of you, Beth.' Ada nodded. 'You've got your head screwed on the right way, you have. I wish my Gloria was as smart.'

Beth was pensive. If she didn't go she might regret it. There was something about Eynon Prosser-Evans that intrigued her. 'Well, I am curious to know what he's up to – if anything.'

She had never met anyone like Eynon. Even while uncertain of him, she liked his smile, and she liked his eyes, and the way he looked at her as though he were really interested. Somehow he made her feel special, like an attractive woman.

'Then put your hat and coat on and off you go,' Ada said firmly. 'Ben Evans' store has some lovely stuff, or Lewis Lewis. Don't come back without something bang up to the latest fashion, mind.'

*

Beth finally made her choice of outfit in Ben Evans. It was just a little more than she'd intended to pay, but recalling Eynon's fashionable appearance and remembering where he would take her, she decided she owed it to herself to dress the part. Besides, knowing she looked good would give her more confidence when dealing with him, for as yet Eynon was an unknown quantity.

She didn't go straight back to Windsor Lodge but took a tram to Brynmill, to see Dan and inform him of this new development, confirm his promise of the night before and make arrangements to see Tommy.

He was in the outer reception office when she got there, talking with his clerk. Dan gave her the usual greeting, a bad-tempered frown. 'Not now, Beth,' he said gruffly. 'I'm busy.'

'I've got news about our problem,' she said quickly, eyeing the clerk who was watching her with avid interest. 'We'd better talk.'

Dan gave way with bad grace, and let her walk before him into his office. 'Well, what is it now?'

'I've had another visit from the Prosser-Evanses,' Beth began. 'The son, Eynon, came to see me. He wants this feud to end, too. He's going to help me to find a way to persuade Jarvis to give way. I know we can work this out, Dan, if only you will co-operate.'

'Oh, really?' he exclaimed grittily. 'Then perhaps you'll explain why Jarvis has recently taken over Carwyn Davies the coal merchants in St Thomas, and refitted them?'

'What?'

Dan nodded, his expression savage. 'He's brought in two of those new motorised lorries, and two new drays. Three days ago he moved into my territory. I've already lost several customers to him because he's undercutting me on price. Not only that, he has poached two of my best drivers, offering them nearly twenty per cent more wages.'

'This is awful!'

'Awful? It's disastrous!' Dan said wrathfully. 'He's obviously operating at a loss, but his other businesses will soak it up so he won't be badly hurt.'

'You didn't mention this last night.'

'I had other things on my mind then, remember. Like your attempted abduction of my son.'

Beth decided to let the jibe pass. 'I'll have a word with Eynon . . .'

'Don't be such a bloody little fool,' Dan exclaimed angrily. 'He's no different from his father. They're playing you for a dupe, softening you up before getting you to sell me down the river.'

Beth felt a shaft of disappointment lance through her. Her mind had been filled with thoughts of Eynon since their meeting earlier, and she had so longed for him to be genuine. Now she realised Dan was probably right. Eynon was waiting to make a fool of her. But forewarned is forearmed.

'Two can play at that game,' she said, trying to hide the deep hurt she felt.

'Huh!' Dan scoffed. 'You're no match for him. You had better make your inheritance over to me immediately before it's too late.'

'I'm certainly a match for *you*, Dan,' Beth snapped. 'And now I know where I stand with Eynon, I can manage him and his father, too.'

'You had better leave these things to those who understand them,' he said derisively. 'Women have no real sense of business.'

'Then why didn't you marry my mother instead of Aunt Mae?' Beth asked angrily. 'Aunt Mae was a clever businesswoman, wasn't she? That's why. And you knew you could profit from the marriage. You're despicable!'

'Oh, get out!' he thundered. 'You sanctimonious little witch. Only out for your own ends, you are, like everybody else.'

'Why are you being so pig-headed?' Beth shouted, not caring whether her voice carried outside the office. 'I'm trying to help you as well as myself.'

'You must think I'm going soft in the head,' Dan bellowed back. 'Do you think I don't see what's going on? You and the Prosser-Evanses ganging up against me, putting on the pressure, thinking I'll sell to you just to get out of the financial mess you have forced me into.'

'That isn't true!'

'You hate me enough! You demonstrated that last night.'

Beth shook her head. 'I don't hate you . . . Father.' She paused, a sob constricting her throat. 'If there is any hate it's on your side. And . . . and I am sorry that I struck you. If only you hadn't said what you did about my mam! How could you besmirch her memory like that?'

'I don't want your apologies, damn it! Get out, go on!' Dan shouted. 'Run back to your cronies and tell them there's no sale. I'm not finished yet.'

'About Tommy . . .' Beth began defiantly.

'What?'

'What day can I see him?'

'God in Heaven!' He raised his hands to his head. 'Haven't I enough to put up with, without you badgering me?'

'You did promise, Dan. And I won't give up.'

'All right, confound you!' He sat down at his desk, shuffling the blotter and repositioning the inkwell. 'Two o'clock every Wednesday afternoon in the park,' he conceded, and then looked up at her sharply. 'For an hour only, mind. I'll instruct Mrs Tate. She is not to let you take advantage. Understand?'

Beth felt quite the young lady about town as she went to meet Eynon the following day. She was nervous about her new appearance and unused to the admiring glances she received from passers-by as she walked along Castle Street. She was relieved to see Eynon standing outside the entrance to the Baltic Lounge. If he had not been waiting she had made up her mind to turn tail and scuttle back home. But he was there, smiling, his eyes telling her in no uncertain terms that her appearance met with his approval.

The meal was wonderful and Eynon's company so absorbing she wanted to forget the reason they were there and just enjoy herself, but Dan's predicament had to be discussed.

'You must get your father to stop persecuting Dan,' Beth said firmly as they were just finishing coffee. It would be time to go soon, but she didn't want the afternoon to end.

'What?' Eynon looked blank. 'What are you talking about, my dear Beth?'

'The feud,' she reminded him.

'Oh, that!' he said, and looked pained. 'Must we talk about it? I'm having such a wonderful time here with you, I don't want to think of anything else but the colour of your lovely eyes.'

Beth couldn't stop colour flooding her cheeks at the unexpected compliment. 'But the feud is why we're here,' she said. 'Jarvis is poaching Dan's customers, not to mention his employees. It's got to stop, Eynon.'

He looked discomfited for a moment. 'I have a confession to make,' he said, leaning across the table towards her. 'I don't give two hoots about the feud. Our respective fathers can tear each other to pieces for all I care. I just want to be with you.'

'Eynon!'

'When I met you yesterday I was up to no good, I admit it,' he said, trying to take her hand across the table. Beth, shocked at his words, took her hand quickly out of his reach. 'But when I saw you, everything changed,' he went on eagerly. 'It was like a bolt of lightning.' He gazed at her longingly. 'Oh, Beth, you are so adorable I just had to see you again, take you out somewhere, just to be with you. I've been waiting for you all my life.'

'You lied to me!' she flashed at him. 'I trusted you.'

'You *can* trust me, my dear Beth,' he said, looking surprised at her flare of anger. 'You can trust me with your life, I swear it.'

'Huh! I wouldn't trust you with a twopenny tea-cake!' she said crossly, and tossed her head so sharply her smart new cloche hat, that was meant to hug her head lovingly, twisted on her glossy hair and almost fell over her eyes.

She pulled it more securely on to her head, glaring at him. She had done the very thing she'd sworn she would never do – fall for a handsome face. She had tumbled into his trap like a brainless blockhead.

'I'm off!' she said, rising.

'No! Don't go, please.' Eynon rose too. Several diners turned to stare and Beth felt even more humiliated. She had no idea where the exit was and so sat down again quickly.

'Take me out of here,' she demanded in a brittle voice. 'I won't stay in your company for another minute.'

'Please, Beth, you must listen,' he said earnestly. 'I

didn't mean to lie. I was just looking for an excuse to see you again.'

'Do you realise your father is out to ruin my business because of this stupid feud?' Beth hissed at him across the table. 'This may be a joke to you, but I assure you, *Mr Prosser-Evans*, I take it very seriously, as does Dan Henshaw.'

'Let's not quarrel, Beth,' he urged desperately. 'Look, I'll do something about the situation between Jarvis and Dan, I promise. I'll straighten it out somehow.'

'But your promises are worth nothing,' Beth objected tartly. 'Why should I believe you?'

'Because I desperately want to see you again,' he said. 'I can't lose you now. Please give me another chance?'

Beth gathered her bag and gloves. 'I don't think so.'

'You won't get rid of me that easily.'

She looked across at him. His blue eyes were fixed on her face, his expression earnest, and she did so want to believe in him, but common sense told her to stop being a silly young fool.

'What will you do about Jarvis then?' she heard herself ask, and was astonished at her own weakness in forgiving him.

Eynon hesitated. 'He's not an easy man to deal with,' he said slowly. Beth ground her teeth, feeling cheated again, and seeing this he hurried on, 'But I will tackle him. Or at least . . . why don't you tackle him yourself, my dear? Come to dinner at my home tomorrow evening.'

She laughed in disbelief. 'I hardly think Jarvis would want me at his table,' she said. 'Not after the things I said to him the last time we met.'

'You're wrong. My father admires you, Beth,' Eynon said. 'He thinks you are a better businessman than I am.' He nodded at her astonished look. 'He told me so himself.'

She considered. Perhaps it wasn't such a bad idea after all, if she could find the courage to face Jarvis Prosser-Evans again on his own ground. But Eynon would be there too, at her side. He had disappointed her, but at the same time she took comfort from realising he thought well of her.

'All right, I will!' she said, nodding. 'But I have no dress suitable for dinner.'

'Come as you are,' Eynon said, smiling widely now that she had agreed. 'Pa doesn't stand on ceremony. He's a plain man. And don't let him bully you, either. He has a soft side which he tries to hide because, as he says, it's fatal to be soft in business dealings.'

'I'll certainly remember *that* advice,' Beth promised with raised eyebrows.

As Eynon escorted her from the dining room, he talked about the new automobile he was expecting to take possession of shortly, and about the trips they could take in it together.

But Beth only half listened, her mind filled with planning strategy for the coming confrontation with Jarvis Prosser-Evans. He would give no quarter, she knew that, but neither would she. No, in the vein of her wily adversaries, Jarvis and Dan, she would take no prisoners.

20

———◆◆◆———

Beth was in the park waiting well before the appointed time. She sat on a bench that gave her a clear view of the gates and everyone who came and went, making sure she did not miss Mrs Tate's arrival. She did not trust her father, and suspected he might renege at the last minute.

But promptly at two Beth spotted the nanny pushing the pram along the path towards her. She stood up quickly and came forward to meet her. Mrs Tate's expression was set and stony.

'Good afternoon,' Beth began. 'Cold isn't it? I'm glad to see you both.'

Mrs Tate sniffed disdainfully, but said nothing.

'Shall we sit over by there, out of the wind in the shelter of the hedge?' Beth asked. 'We'll get most of the sun there.'

Mrs Tate pushed the pram in the direction suggested. Beth was so eager she felt like an excited puppy, looking expectantly into the pram. Tommy was well wrapped up and appeared to be asleep. She felt a quiver of disappointment. But she must not be impatient, she told herself, she must take things slowly. One false move would give Dan an excuse to ban her altogether.

'How is Tommy?' Beth asked. 'Has he had any problems? He seemed to catch colds quickly when I had him.'

'Huh!' Mrs Tate tossed her head. '*I* take great care of Thomas,' she said haughtily. 'He has the best of everything. Mr Henshaw insists on it.'

'But does my father . . . does Dan ever nurse him or play with him?' Does he ever set eyes on the child from one day to the next? she wanted to ask, but didn't want to get Mrs Tate's back up.

The nanny hesitated. 'Well, Mr Henshaw is a busy man, mind,' she said defensively. 'He's got a business to run.'

That told Beth all she wanted to know, and she felt anger rise. Dan was not the least bit interested in Tommy as a person, nor even as a son. He was simply an heir, the beginning of a dynasty perhaps, which was probably the way Dan looked at it.

'Shall we take him out of the pram?' Beth asked hopefully, swallowing her anger. She was here to see her brother and wanted to make the most of it.

Mrs Tate looked annoyed. 'No. Thomas usually naps at this time of an afternoon,' she said irritably. 'Mr Henshaw shouldn't have suggested . . .' She hesitated, slanting a glance at Beth.

'Dan knows very little about Tommy, does he?' Beth said quickly. 'I don't know why you want to shield him.'

Mrs Tate hesitated again. 'Well, Mr Henshaw is my employer, after all,' she said. 'I must look after my job.'

'Of course,' Beth said. 'I wouldn't want you to do anything to jeopardise that. But Tommy is my brother, and I have a right to be part of his life.'

Mrs Tate nodded. 'Look, I had to tell Mr Henshaw about you approaching us in the park the other day,' she said, giving Beth a direct stare. 'It was only right. If I hadn't, and he'd found out, well . . .'

'I don't blame you,' Beth assured her quickly. She felt Mrs Tate's attitude was thawing a little. 'He lied about me,' she went on. 'You must know that now.'

Mrs Tate looked ready to argue, then obviously

changed her mind. 'I put it off as long as I dared,' she said. 'I waited until he was on the point of going up to bed. I thought he would've cooled down by morning, having slept on it.' She blinked. 'I never dreamed he would go round to see you at that time of night.'

'I'm very glad he did,' Beth said. 'It brought matters to a head, and now he has agreed I can see my brother once a week.' She touched Mrs Tate's arm. 'We can make it three o'clock in future, so as not to interrupt Tommy's nap. Dan needn't know. I certainly won't tell him.'

Mrs Tate nodded, a faint smile on her face. 'Yes, three would suit us just fine.'

Eynon came to fetch her in a trap that evening, and Beth was glad of the warm rug he wrapped around her legs against the chill air as the pony clip-clopped its way to Jarvis's house on Gower Road.

'I'll have my motorcar soon,' Eynon told her cheerfully as he flicked the reins gently against the pony's rump as encouragement. 'Then you'll see some speed.'

'Have you warned your father that I'm dining tonight?' Beth asked nervously. She was half expecting to be ordered out the moment Jarvis set eyes on her, and viewed the coming meeting as an ordeal.

'Pa is looking forward to it,' he said.

Somehow Beth could not believe that. She lifted her chin defensively. 'If he expects to wear me down about selling out, he'll be disappointed,' she said frankly.

She was duly impressed when a deferential butler took her new warm coat and gloves, and looked around her with awed curiosity. It was a far cry from the humble and cramped terraced house in Libanus Street where she was born. As a dinner guest in this very grand house, she felt out of place.

But she wouldn't be intimidated, she told herself sternly. She was a businesswoman in her own right now, and was as good as anybody. Nevertheless, she felt the need to straighten the long jacket of her new two-piece suit and adjusted her snug little hat as Eynon, taking her by the elbow, led her towards the sitting room.

Jarvis Prosser-Evans rose to his feet as she entered, and to her astonishment came to greet her, hand outstretched.

'Good evening, Miss Pryce,' he said in an even tone. 'And welcome to my house. An apéritif perhaps?'

It wasn't the greeting she was expecting, and she nodded and smiled at him uncertainly as he handed her a glass of sherry.

'How is business?' Jarvis asked, and Beth glanced up at him with a frown. Was that a veiled threat?

'My business is doing very well,' she answered tartly. 'So long as I am left alone to get on with it.'

'Quite!' he said with a wry smile. 'No one bears you any grudge, Miss Pryce.'

'Pa!' Eynon said edgily. 'Must we talk shop? Beth is our guest. Let's be civilised.'

'I might be a rough diamond, Eynon,' Jarvis retorted gruffly, 'but I know how to behave towards a guest.'

The butler announced dinner was served and they went in. Jarvis sat at the head of the table with Beth on his right-hand side and Eynon opposite her. Jarvis was a plain man with no side, but being with him at his own table, Beth felt the full force of his presence. Seeing father and son together, it struck her that she did not sense the same authority in Eynon. He was attractive and charming but would never command the same power or respect perhaps. He would never be dangerous in business. He would always be the gentleman first.

Eynon began to talk about his new motorcar again but

she could see Jarvis wasn't much interested, and neither
was she. There was no point in wasting time. Despite
Eynon's protest she was here to talk shop and to make
Jarvis see some sense regarding Dan Henshaw, so she
might as well strike first.

'What are your views on unfair trading, Mr Prosser-
Evans?' she asked boldly.

Eynon was obviously dismayed by her candour and
Jarvis looked startled. He stared at her for a moment and
then said, surprising her: 'Since we are being so frank,
you had better call me Jarvis.' He paused, pushing some
food on to his fork. 'Unfair trading?' he went on. 'I don't
hold with it.'

'Oh, really?' Beth couldn't keep the anger from her
voice. 'Then why are you moving into Dan Henshaw's
territory west of town? Carwyn Davies has always oper-
ated east of the river. A gentlemen's agreement, I
understand.'

Jarvis raised his brows. 'Gentlemen? I doubt that.
Besides, business is business, Beth, and business must
expand or go down. Unfair trading has nothing to do
with it.'

'Then what do you call poaching Dan's drivers?'

'I say, Beth, steady on!' Eynon looked crestfallen. 'Pa
wouldn't do a thing like that.'

'He would and has,' she stated emphatically, staring at
Eynon, astonished that he knew so little of his father's
dealings. 'And for no other reason than twisted revenge.'

Jarvis threw down his fork, looking angry. 'You are a
very outspoken young woman.'

'I certainly am when it comes to *my* business,' she said
bluntly. 'As you know well enough I own over half of Dan
Henshaw, Coal Merchant. I won't see it destroyed on a
whim.'

'Then sell to me,' Jarvis urged quickly. 'Wash your hands of it. I'll pay you a fair price.'

Beth put down her fork carefully. She had eaten hardly a thing and had no appetite anyway. 'I think I had better leave,' she said quietly.

'Oh, no, Beth, please,' Eynon exclaimed, agitated. 'You're rushing things. I want the two of you to get to know each other better . . . I mean . . .' His words petered out and he looked embarrassed. 'Diplomacy, you know. What?'

Jarvis was staring at him, a curious expression on his face. 'I think I understand,' he said slowly. 'Yes, I believe I do.'

'This was never a social occasion, Eynon,' Beth said bluntly. 'I came solely to persuade your father to give up his vendetta against Dan. Obviously, I've failed. There's no reason for me to stay any longer.'

Jarvis turned his gaze on her. 'I wouldn't say that, Beth,' he said quickly. 'Please don't leave yet. I find you an interesting, if somewhat stubborn, young woman. I believe we may have more in common than you think.'

Beth recognised this as an olive branch, and decided to accept. She had to, for Dan's sake as much as her own. 'Very well,' she agreed solemnly. 'But no more talk of me selling.'

The rest of the evening went reasonably well. Jarvis had many more interests than business alone. It appeared he was somewhat of an authority on local bird life, and had written a slim volume on the subject. Also, to her astonishment, she found he was an accomplished pianist with a good baritone voice, and was content to sit with Eynon enjoying the entertainment.

'You must dine here again, Beth,' Jarvis said when she was leaving. 'I suspect you'll be seeing a lot more of

Eynon over the coming weeks.' A little smile played around his mouth. 'And I heartily approve.'

Beth gave a half smile in return, uncertain what he meant.

'As for unfair practices in business,' he went on, 'I think you'll find there'll be no more of that. In fact, I guarantee it.'

Beth blinked, astonished. 'Well, thank you, Jarvis, for being so reasonable.'

His father was still up having one last brandy in the sitting room when Eynon returned from taking Beth home, and felt like celebrating.

'Join me,' Jarvis invited as he came in.

'I think I will,' his son said cheerfully. 'Well, what do you think of her now, Pa?'

'An admirable young woman,' Jarvis said carefully. 'Perhaps a little strong-willed, but that may not be such a bad thing.'

'She's wonderful! Intelligent, exciting . . . and yet so earnest,' Eynon said, and sighed. 'I've never met anyone like her.'

'I hope you are not philandering, Eynon,' Jarvis said sternly. 'I'll not allow it. She's worth more than that.'

'Good God, no!' his son exclaimed adamantly. 'In fact, I'm thinking of asking her to marry me.'

Jarvis almost gasped in astonishment, but controlled himself. It was more than he'd hoped for. Seeing Eynon settled with a good wife was the one pleasurable prospect left to him, and Beth Pryce would be the making of him, Jarvis was certain. If only she would consent.

'You've known her such a short time,' Jarvis reminded him, reluctant to cast doubts yet wanting no mistakes. 'Are you sure you want this? Only a few days ago you were adamant you wanted to sow more wild oats.'

Eynon leaned forward, his expression more solemn than Jarvis had ever seen it before. 'Pa, I've never been so sure of anything in my life. I knew as soon as I saw her, she's the one I've been waiting for. And I knew then why I'd been waiting. She's unique. The only one. And I want her, badly.'

Jarvis felt a warm glow inside and it wasn't only from the brandy.

'Well, you have my approval and blessing, my boy,' he said happily. 'But I wouldn't rush her. Take your time. I sense she's not ready for such a commitment yet. Make her love you first.'

Eynon grinned widely, and Jarvis raised his eyebrows. 'What's amusing you?'

'Pa, I've wooed more women, and successfully too, than you've had good cigars.'

'Yes, but you've never wanted to marry any of them. Don't let this one slip away by being brash.'

Jarvis eyed his son's happy face and was content. There was another aspect of this marriage that pleased him, too. He might not be able to buy his way into Dan Henshaw's business, but if he could marry his son into it, that might do just as well. As Eynon's wife, Beth might be inclined to make her shares over to him. What could be more natural as a show of love and confidence in her new husband?

Beth found Jarvis was as good as his word over the following weeks, and Dan looked relieved when she went to see him towards the end of February. The incursions into his territory had ceased. He had hired two more drivers and there had been no more damage.

'Prosser-Evans has thought better of it,' Dan said to her confidently.

'I talked to him,' Beth said frankly. 'He saw reason. He's a sensible man underneath.'

Dan looked sceptical. 'I hardly think he would take notice of a chit of a girl,' he said scathingly. 'No, the man realises that in me he has a hardheaded businessman to deal with. I knew I could out-wait him in the end.'

It was no good talking to him, Beth decided, and could not help comparing Dan's arrogance with Jarvis's willingness to listen to her views with something like respect. And she was beginning to respect him, too, even though she knew he was a ruthless businessman.

The weeks had flown by with Beth seeing Tommy every week and steadily gaining Mrs Tate's trust. She was even allowed to cuddle him on her lap for a while each visit, and was much happier about him if still longing to have him all to herself.

Eynon's new motorcar proved exciting, and she couldn't resist accepting when he invited her on weekends out motoring in the Gower, even though the weather was cold and the motor was an open tourer. But she felt guilty leaving Ada to cope without her.

'Listen, Beth love,' her partner assured her, 'make hay while the sun shines.'

'Sun?' Beth laughed. 'It looks more like snow.' It might snow but that would not keep her from Tommy. 'I think we're mad going down the Gower at all. But I love it, riding in that contraption. I wish Eynon would let me drive it one day.'

'Oh, my Gawd!' Ada exclaimed clapping her hands to her face. 'You'll end up in a ditch! Oh, for heaven's sake, don't!'

'Don't worry,' Beth said glumly. 'Eynon treats that motorcar like his baby. He won't let anyone touch it.'

★

It was a crisp morning in mid-March when Eynon Prosser-Evans called on Dan Henshaw at the coal yard. Dan was in his office when the clerk came in to announce the visitor.

'Who did you say?' Dan stared in disbelief, reaching for his handkerchief to wipe away the sweat that came immediately to his top lip.

'It's the son, not the father,' the clerk said slyly.

'What the hell does he want around here?'

The clerk shrugged. 'I dunno.'

'All right,' Dan said, rising to his feet. 'Show him in.'

For several weeks things had been quiet and business was beginning to recover. Dan had felt sure he had heard the last of the Prosser-Evanses. Now this visit. What in Hades did it mean? He had no doubt some trick was involved. Well, they would have to get up early in the morning to dupe *him*.

He wasn't quite ready for the tall, elegantly dressed young man who strode confidently into the room. He had expected to see a copy of Jarvis's rough-hewn features, and was struck by this man's handsome looks. Suddenly Dan felt more confident. This was no business rival. He looked more like some fashionable man-about-town, completely out of place in these surroundings.

'It's good of you to see me,' Eynon Prosser-Evans began pleasantly. He held out his hand and Dan reluctantly stretched out his own to shake it.

'Why are you here?' he asked bluntly. He was not deceived by pleasantries.

Eynon smiled at his directness. 'Well, it's not in the way of business, I assure you,' he replied lightly. 'Though it is a serious matter, something very close to my heart.'

Dan hid his confusion. 'You'd better sit down,' he said,

giving himself time to think. He waited until the young man was seated before sitting himself. 'Now what's this all about if it isn't business?' He didn't believe that for a minute. 'I don't doubt your father sent you here.'

'Actually, I am here to speak to you about your daughter,' Eynon replied.

Both astonished and angry, Dan's hackles rose. 'I have no daughter,' he said harshly.

His young visitor looked taken aback. 'Really? I refer, of course, to Miss Bethan Pryce. I've been given to understand you are her natural father and only relative.'

'I don't know what slanderous rubbish the little minx has been telling you but Bethan Pryce is no child of mine,' Dan snapped.

'I do not like to hear her referred to in those terms,' Eynon said severely, frowning, then rubbed his chin thoughtfully. 'That makes it dashed awkward,' he said. 'I mean, I came here this morning to ask your permission to marry her, but if you are no kin then I've made an ass of myself.'

'Marry her?' Dan jerked to his feet. 'What the hell are you talking about?'

Eynon rose too. 'Well, of course, I wish to do things the proper way,' he said pleasantly. 'I have been seeing Beth for some weeks now, and have grown extremely fond of her. I had hoped to make it a June wedding.'

Dan felt floored. 'She has accepted your proposal?' Had Beth betrayed him after all? He had allowed her to see Thomas against his better judgement mainly to keep her sweet and off his back, but perhaps his ploy had not worked. His mind was a whirl of chaotic thoughts as he tried to see what really lay behind this new tactic of marriage and how he might fend it off. One thing he was sure of: Beth must not marry Eynon Prosser-Evans. Jarvis lay behind this move, he was certain.

'As a matter of fact, I haven't asked her yet,' Eynon confessed, throwing Dan even more off balance. 'I thought it proper to get your permission first.'

Dan felt fury rise in his chest, as he believed he saw Eynon's true game. 'Damn you!' he burst out. 'She won't sell so you think you can get her share of my business through marriage. Very neat! But it won't work.'

Eynon shook his head. 'I assure you, Mr Henshaw, this has nothing to do with business.'

'Like hell it hasn't,' Dan stormed. 'What would a gent like you want with the likes of her, with her questionable background?' he went on scathingly. 'This is a filthy trick but I'll scuttle it. Beth is underage and can't marry without my say so, as you so rightly point out. I'll be damned if I'll give that permission, so you're wasting your time.'

Eynon raised his brows. 'But you say you are *not* her father. She is therefore an orphan and doesn't need anyone's permission.' He picked up his fedora, gloves and walking stick. 'I will ask Beth to marry me at the earliest opportunity,' he said firmly. 'Nothing now stands in our way.'

'I forbid it!' Dan shouted. 'You stay away from her. You are not to see her again. There'll be no marriage between you, and that's final.'

'There's not a lot you can do about it,' Eynon replied. His face had flushed up and Dan could see he was on the point of losing his temper. He turned to leave the room. 'Beth will be my wife before the summer is over.'

'You won't get away with it!' Dan shouted. 'I'll see my

lawyer today. He'll put a stop to this shoddy ruse of yours, good and proper. I warn you, Prosser-Evans, you and that father of yours are risking legal action.'

'Let's go for a drive on Sunday afternoon,' Eynon suggested to Beth when they next met. 'There's something important I want to ask you.'

'Can't you ask me now?'

It was Thursday afternoon, half-day in town, and although she had spent the previous afternoon with Tommy and Mrs Tate in the park, Beth had given herself this afternoon off, too. They were strolling in Singleton Park, and had paused to watch the ducks dabbling in the pond.

'The ambience isn't right,' he said, swinging his walking stick at a clump of turf. Beth was puzzled by his choice of words. 'I thought we might take a leisurely lunch at one of those little country inns in the Gower,' he went on. 'Somewhere romantic.'

Beth was reluctant, all at once uneasy as to what lay behind his mood. 'It's still too chilly for Gower,' she said feebly.

It wasn't much of an excuse, she knew. Eynon was around at Windsor Lodge most days, and Beth felt they were seeing too much of each other. During the past week she had been wondering where their friendship was leading, uncertain of what she wanted from it and how she felt about Eynon. Perhaps she should ease out of it a little, she thought, until her feelings were clear.

'Besides,' she went on, 'I'm taking advantage of Ada with all these days off, to see my brother and to spend with you. It's not fair on her.'

'Don't you want to be with me?' he asked suddenly, his voice faltering, taking her by surprise.

'Yes, of course,' she answered quickly. 'I value your friendship.'

'Is it no more than friendship to you?'

She stared up at him, struck by the tense timbre of his voice. He was usually so light-hearted. 'Eynon, what are you trying to say?'

'Beth, listen.' He took hold of her arms and turned her to face him, looking down on her so earnestly her heart turned over in her breast. 'This isn't the way I planned it,' he said. 'But I'm asking you to marry me.'

'Marry you?' Beth found she was breathless and could not say more.

He raised his brows, a half-smile on his lips. 'You sound astonished,' he said. 'I thought you would have guessed my intentions by now. I doubt I could've made my feelings plainer.'

'I'm not in a position to expect anything from you,' she said, feeling her face flush. 'Least of all marriage.'

'I love you, Beth,' he said earnestly. 'Really I do. I want you to be my wife. Please say you will?'

Beth hesitated, doubts growing in her mind. She didn't know what to say to him. What did she feel for Eynon anyway? She liked him a great deal, liked being in his company. He was exciting . . . but she wasn't in love with him, was she? She really did not know what she felt.

'What about Jarvis?' she asked by way of gaining time to think.

'He's all for it.'

She could hardly believe that. Eynon had had an expensive education. He was a gentleman from a well-to-do family. Jarvis Prosser-Evans would want much more than a boarding-house keeper for his son's wife.

'Why?'

'Because he respects you, Beth, and thinks you'll make

me an admirable wife.' Eynon grinned boyishly. 'You'll make a businessman of me, Pa says.'

A notion came into her head then and she had to voice it. 'Has this offer anything to do with Dan Henshaw?'

'Beth!' He looked aggrieved. 'I'm hurt that you would think me so devious. You know how I feel about the stupid enmity between our fathers. I love you, Beth, and want you desperately.' He shook his head. 'I've never felt this way before, never, and it is wonderful. I never knew what being in love was. Please say you will marry me?'

Beth stood on the turf, looking up into his blue eyes, aglow now, and she knew he *did* love her. A chill March wind cut across the pond, rippling the water and slicing through the material of her coat, and she shivered.

'Eynon, I am very fond of you. I've been really happy these last weeks,' she said. It was true. Eynon was wonderful to be with. He was full of life and laughter, and he had lavished so much attention on her. 'You've been so good to me,' she went on. 'I meant it when I said I value our friendship, but I don't love you, Eynon. And so it wouldn't be fair to agree to marry you.'

His handsome face fell. 'But, Beth, I thought we both felt the same way.'

She touched his arm. 'Oh, I'm sorry if I have given you the wrong impression, Eynon. I hope you don't feel that I've led you on.'

'Of course I don't feel that. You are not that kind of a girl, Beth.' He hesitated. 'Perhaps I *have* chosen the wrong time and place?'

'No, it's not your fault,' she said quickly. 'It's me. I'm young yet and not ready for marriage. I have plans for the business.'

His face tightened. 'You're not letting your father influence you, are you?'

Bridling, she stared up at him, and spoke with bitterness. 'I have no father. Dan Henshaw has denied me for the last time. He couldn't care less what I do. Why do you think he would have any objection to my marrying you?'

Eynon turned his head away to stare at the ducks. 'I can't believe you have no feelings for me,' he murmured, and sounded so miserable her heart ached.

'I didn't say that,' Beth answered quickly. 'I have deep feelings for you, as a friend, and that's why I know you'd come to regret taking me as a wife. It wouldn't work, Eynon, believe me. We are from very different backgrounds.'

He turned his gaze back to her face. 'I suppose you don't want to see me again, under the circumstances, to avoid embarrassment?'

'You are my friend,' she said simply. 'Of course I want to see you, but perhaps not so often. I don't want to hurt you, Eynon.'

She turned to continue their walk and he stepped along beside her. 'I won't give up, you know,' he said more cheerfully. 'Pa thinks I'm unreliable, and perhaps I am where business is concerned, but when it comes to love I am steadfast, unswerving. I won't rest until you are my wife, Beth.'

She felt sad at his words and unsettled, too. She had found real happiness and enjoyment in Eynon's company these last weeks, but now everything had changed.

A fortnight later Beth was busy in the kitchen preparing breakfast for the guests with Cissie Morgan helping her.

'Hey! Have you heard about poor old Ben Barton?' Cissie asked cheerfully. 'In hospital he is, with two broken legs.'

'What?' Beth was shocked. Ben had worked for Dan for years as a dray driver and she knew he was nearing retirement. 'What happened?'

'Dirty work at the crossroads, my dad says,' Cissie answered. 'One of the drays has been got at again. Wheel came off, old Ben was thrown in the road, and the load – tons of coal, mind you – fell on him. Lucky he didn't peg out, my dad says.'

'Oh, no,' Beth exclaimed. 'It's started again! And he promised faithfully . . .'

Cissie was staring at her curiously but Beth had duplicity on her mind. Why had Jarvis deceived her? Why go back on his word? She had not seen him for some weeks, not since she and Eynon had cooled their relationship. She should go and see Jarvis, and confront him about his broken promise, but having refused Eynon's offer of marriage, she felt embarrassed and uneasy.

But the next day Cissie brought even more startling news.

'There's been a terrible fire,' she exclaimed as soon as she arrived.

'Good heavens, where?' Ada asked, looking frightened, and Beth felt a chill run up her spine, too.

'Up at Henshaw's yard last night,' Cissie told them, struggling out of her coat and hat and throwing on her wraparound pinafore. 'Mr Henshaw's offices have been gutted. Nothing left. Good thing the whole factorage didn't catch light,' she went on. 'The coal would've burned for weeks, maybe months, my dad says.'

'Was anyone hurt?' Beth asked.

'No, but my dad says Mr Henshaw is in one hell of a mess. All the accounts went up in flames. Lost hundreds of pounds, see, because now he doesn't know who owes him money. All of it will have to be written off, Dad says.'

Cissie looked suddenly mystified. 'What does written off mean?'

'It means going bust by the sound of it,' Ada opined. 'Oh, Beth, I am sorry, girl. You'll lose money as well as him. It's too bad. Let's hope Henshaw's insurance is paid up to date.'

Beth debated with herself all morning whether she should go and see Dan and try to find out how much their loss was. But she also wanted to confront Jarvis.

It was just before luncheon when Dan called at Windsor Lodge demanding to see her. She took him to her small room behind the kitchen away from prying eyes and ears.

He looked around with distaste. 'Why are you living like this?' he asked sullenly. 'You have all of Mae's money.'

'And I'm holding on to it, too,' Beth retorted sharply. 'Just in case you think I'll make good your losses, Dan.'

He looked sour. 'They are your losses too,' he said. 'Your fifty-one per cent represents very little now. One more dirty trick by Prosser-Evans and I'm really finished. But I think I know how to stop him now.'

'Jarvis gave me his word,' Beth said despairingly. 'I don't understand why he has broken his promise.'

'You were a fool to trust him,' Dan snapped. He sat on the bed, rubbing his thumb along his jaw. 'But I was a fool, too,' he went on thoughtfully. 'I know why he's continued his campaign against me. It's out of revenge because I refused my permission. I acted too hastily. I should've agreed to the marriage straight away. The lesser of two evils . . .'

'Marriage?' Beth stared at him. 'What are you talking about?'

Dan stood up. 'Eynon Prosser-Evans came to see me a

few weeks ago to ask my permission to marry you. I refused. I saw straight away it was a trick to get your shares.' Dan shook his head. 'But now I realise it could save me – us.'

'What?'

'Don't you see?' he went on persuasively. 'As Eynon's wife your interest would be protected, and mine along with it as your business partner.' He shook his head, a cunning smile on his handsome face. 'Jarvis wouldn't allow my business to go under, not when there was a good chance he could get hold of it through you. Keeping it in the family, like. Protection, that's what this marriage would be. Protection.'

Beth could hardly believe his utter selfishness, and her lips were tight as she stared at him. 'You want me to marry Eynon to save you? You're prepared to sacrifice the rest of my life and my future happiness for your own ends? You're unbelievable!'

'I'm fighting for survival,' Dan snarled. 'I'll do whatever I have to. And so must you, Beth. You own half the business. You have an obligation to me, and to Mae, too. She trusted you with it.'

'Don't try that emotional blackmail on me,' Beth snapped. 'I won't be used as a pawn by you of all people. You denied me, remember? It's too late anyway,' she went on quickly when she saw he was about to argue. 'I've already refused Eynon's offer of marriage.'

'What?' he shouted savagely. 'You little fool!' Dan's face was dark with wrath. 'Tell him you've changed your mind. Tell him anything, but you've got to put things right for me.'

'I will not.' She lifted her head defiantly in the face of his growing anger. 'And that's an end to it, Dan. You'll have to find some other way to survive.'

He looked shaken and his anger seemed to drain away at her stubbornness. 'But you *must* accept,' he said, a desperate edge to his voice. 'You must go through with this marriage. It's the only way left, Beth.'

She frowned at his words. 'No,' she said firmly. 'I need do no such thing. I don't owe you a farthing, Dan, not a bean. I certainly don't owe you gratitude or duty. You are no kin of mine remember?'

He looked angry again. 'But why are you so against the marriage?' he asked loudly. 'Eynon Prosser-Evans is a good catch, especially for a girl with your dubious background. He's good-looking and well off. What the hell more do you want?'

'I want happiness when I marry,' Beth shouted, furious that he should hint at her illegitimacy in such a callous way. 'Illegitimate I may be, but I have integrity, thank Heaven. I don't love Eynon. I won't tie myself to someone I don't love.'

'Love!' Dan's voice was laced with scorn. 'What the devil has love got to do with anything?' Tight-lipped, he studied her face closely. 'Is there another man?' he asked in a harsh voice. 'Is that it?'

Suddenly, from nowhere, an image of a face came unbidden into her mind, a strong smiling face from the past, and her heart was stabbed through with longing. She had loved that good-natured face and still did. Whereas in the past she had not understood such feelings for what they truly were, now she knew why she had refused Eynon. Her heart belonged to someone else, and always had.

But it was too late. Years had gone by, and that love could never be rediscovered. It was lost to her forever.

'Well, is there someone else?' Dan asked again impatiently.

'No,' she said reluctantly. 'There's no one.'

'Then there's nothing to stop you marrying Prosser-Evans, is there?'

Beth didn't answer, still stunned by the realisation that love had been almost within her grasp, but death and fate had robbed her of it.

'Answer me, damn you, Bethan!' Dan demanded wrathfully. 'You could save my business just like that.' He snapped his fingers. 'And you should! I am family, after all.'

'Family?' Beth was scornful in her turn. 'You've turned your back on family, Dan. You can't have it both ways.'

'But you must help me.' He was whining now he was losing the argument. 'It's only right you should.' He hesitated as though reluctant to utter his next words. 'You have a filial duty towards me.'

'*What?*' Beth laughed with utter disbelief, and the bitterness that was in her heart rang through it. 'You denied and rejected me, made me a skivvy, bad-mouthed my mother and stole my brother from me. Give me one good reason, Dan, why I owe you my filial duty?'

'Because you are my daughter, Bethan, my flesh and blood. I am your natural father.'

21

Early the following morning, after making an excuse to Ada for her absence from the kitchen during the preparation of breakfast, Beth began the long walk to Jarvis Prosser-Evans's house on Gower Road, hoping to catch him before he left for business. She had a score to settle.

She was still stunned at the way Dan had finally acknowledged paternity of her, and had hardly slept for thinking about it. She had waited so long to hear him admit it, but now could find no satisfaction and was bitterly disappointed. The admission had been wrung from him by dire need and not affection, and was therefore worthless. Besides, it had come too late for her to feel any real affection towards him.

It rankled with her that he was using their kinship as a bargaining point only, and had no real fatherly feelings for her. But knowing he *was* her father, her own flesh and blood, and that her mother must have loved him at one time, her conscience was stirred, and despite struggling against it she became aware of a growing sense of filial duty which lay heavily on her shoulders.

And there were other factors to consider. Her fortunes and those of Tommy were irrevocably linked to Dan's, and she could not let Jarvis destroy all of them. She was forced to rethink Dan's solution. Perhaps marriage to Eynon would not be such a sacrifice after all, if it would save them all from ruin. She might even learn to love him in time.

She thought briefly of the past and the love that had slipped through her fingers then, but pushed it out of her mind. It was gone forever, and she had to think of the future: hers, Dan's and little Tommy's.

But, in the meantime, she must face down Jarvis, and confront him with his duplicity.

He was already seated in his trap outside the house when Beth hurried up the driveway. She heard him give an order to his groom. The man was about to set the horse in motion, but loosened the reins and lowered the whip, seeing Beth.

'I want a word with you, Jarvis,' she panted. 'It's important.'

'I have a meeting in town,' he said curtly, although he raised his hat politely enough. 'Your word will have to wait.'

Beth put one hand firmly on the trap. 'No, it won't,' she said pithily. 'Not after I've walked all this way. Common courtesy, Jarvis, surely even *you* can rise to that.'

He stared at her, his mouth twitching. 'I'd forgotten what a forthright young woman you are,' he said sardonically. 'Very well, I'll give you five minutes only. I'll even take you back in the trap.'

He led the way into the house, leaving his hat, gloves and cane on the hall table. 'Come into the study,' he said. 'There's always a fire lit there because I usually have work to do in the mornings before I leave. I doubt Eynon is even out of his bed at this hour.'

'That work wouldn't involve arranging sabotage and wilful damage, would it?' Beth asked boldly as she followed him across the hall. 'I think you know what I'm talking about.'

In the study Jarvis walked to the mantelpiece and

turned to look at her, his expression grim. 'There is a thin line between being forthright and being impertinent,' he barked. 'And you have just crossed it, young woman.'

'You won't browbeat me, Jarvis. I'm not afraid of you,' Beth said defiantly, sitting on a nearby chair without waiting for an invitation. Her feet were aching from the long and hurried walk. 'I may be Dan Henshaw's daughter,' she went on, 'but I draw strength from another branch of my family.' She was thinking of Aunt Mae whom no one had ever bettered, except perhaps Dan.

'So you are prepared to cross swords with me, are you?' Jarvis exclaimed, and smiled thinly. 'Many a man has regretted that.'

'Even Eynon, perhaps?' Beth said, then immediately regretted her words as a shadow passed across her opponent's face. 'I'm sorry, Jarvis,' she said, and meant it. 'That was unforgivable, but I am angry, you see, angry because you've gone back on your word to me. You have attacked Dan Henshaw again, and done serious damage to our business this time. You have even put an innocent man in hospital.'

He frowned, and pursed his lips. 'I am sorry about the driver,' he said. 'It was not intended.'

'I had begun to respect you, Jarvis,' Beth said, her lips tightening. 'But I see you have no more principles than Dan Henshaw.'

'I resent that!'

'Was the fire intended?' Beth blared back at him. 'Someone could have died.'

Jarvis turned his glance away and was silent for a moment. 'I had taken on a new man to harass Henshaw,' he said at last. 'I was – still am – very angry, and wanted to put pressure on Henshaw, but the new man overstepped the mark. I have now sacked him.'

'But why take any action against Dan at all?' Beth asked. 'I thought we had reached an agreement.'

'So did I, but things have changed again,' he said irately. 'Henshaw had the effrontery to refuse your hand in marriage to Eynon. How dare he!?' he added, raising his voice. 'Damn him to hell! I'll break your father this time.'

'Then you must break me too,' Beth exclaimed loudly. 'For I also refused Eynon's offer.'

'Yes,' Jarvis thundered, 'and I'm certain Henshaw was behind that refusal.'

Beth jumped to her feet. 'You underestimate me, Jarvis. I'm not some feeble-minded girl who needs others to make life-changing decisions for her,' she retorted angrily. 'Dan had nothing to do with it.'

Quick steps sounded in the hall, and then Eynon appeared still in his dressing gown. 'What's all the shouting about, Pa?' He stared in astonishment to see Beth. 'Beth, my dear girl, what are you doing here so early in the morning?'

She was suddenly embarrassed to see him. 'I've come to take your father to task,' she said weakly, feeling guilty, knowing her purpose was more devious than that.

Eynon nodded. 'The fire,' he said. 'I made sure the wretch who perpetrated that outrage was sacked immediately.' He glanced angrily at his father. 'I was all for calling the police too, but Pa persuaded me against it. However, I'm sure nothing like that will happen again. Isn't that right, Pa?'

Jarvis scowled. 'I've not finished with Henshaw, not by a long chalk. He has a lot to answer for, so I will not promise anything.' He strode towards the door. 'I'm off to business. If you want to ride into town, Beth, you had better come with me now.'

Eynon gently took her arm, holding her back. 'No, stay, Beth,' he said earnestly. 'I must speak with you. I'll take you back in the motorcar.'

She was eager to stay and talk to him so shook her head at Jarvis, who shrugged and strode out.

'Have you had breakfast?' Eynon asked, smiling. 'You look famished.'

She had to admit she had had nothing since rising, and he led her into the breakfast room, and indicated a laden chiffonier.

'There's kedgeree, scrambled eggs, toast. Have what you will. I'll ring for more tea.'

'I don't deserve this,' she ventured as she sat at the table, buttering a piece of toast. 'Not after the way I have treated you.'

She wanted to broach the subject of marriage yet was at a loss to know how to begin. She felt she was acting underhandedly, about to deceive him.

'I've missed you,' he said wistfully, reaching a hand across the table to touch hers briefly.

'I've missed you, too, Eynon.' That was very true. At least her affection for him was genuine, she told herself as a salve to her sore conscience. 'And – and I am filled with regret,' she went on hesitantly.

'Regret?' His expression was quickly alert. 'What do you regret? Not that we ever met, I hope?'

'No, of course not.' She shook her head, and couldn't help smiling at his expression of mortification. 'I will never regret that. You are the best of men, Eynon.'

He looked down at his plate. 'But not the best of men to marry, apparently.'

'You are putting words into my mouth,' Beth exclaimed, touched by his look of desolation. He did love her, and no woman could wish for a better husband. She gathered her courage about her before rushing on. 'My regret is that I refused you.'

He sat up straight. 'What? You mean, you've changed your mind?'

Beth swallowed hard, feeling ashamed of what she was about to do. 'I have thought a great deal about it since.' She raised a hand as he started to his feet. 'I'm not madly in love with you, Eynon,' she went on quickly, gazing up at him. 'I think you should know that. But I am very fond of you.' She had to be honest with him, no matter what. 'I don't know whether you would be satisfied with mere fondness in a wife?'

'Beth! Are you saying you'll marry me?'

She felt her mouth go dry, knowing that she was about to commit herself to a lifetime as his wife. No matter what she had felt about anyone else in the past, she would now be true to Eynon. He deserved no less.

'Yes, Eynon, I will marry you if you still want me.'

'Still want you?' He darted forward, his face wreathed in smiles, and taking her hand, drew her to her feet. 'Oh, Beth my darling, you've made me the happiest of men.'

Gently he pulled her into the circle of his arms, and bent his head to kiss her for the first time. Beth didn't know what to do or how to behave. No man other than Percy Pryce had ever given her a kiss, and that was always fatherly. Now in Eynon's arms she felt a new and pleasant sensation as his mouth pressed lovingly against hers.

She had made up her mind to marry Eynon Prosser-Evans in the early hours of that morning, and had no doubt that they would get on well together, but she had had some qualms about the physical side of marriage. Now, as his mouth tenderly explored hers, she was surprised at the way her body responded with its own yearning to be loved, and knew everything would be all right. The past was gone. There was only the future.

Eynon insisted they marry in June, and wanted the ceremony performed at St Mary's Church in the town centre, but Beth begged to be married at Libanus Chapel in Cwmbwrla where she was born and brought up. He conceded this as long as the wedding breakfast could be held at the fashionable Mackworth Hotel in the High Street. Although Beth wanted to keep her wedding day as simple as possible, she agreed, realising that coming from very different backgrounds, their life together would probably be a series of compromises anyway.

Acknowledging that Dan must be the first to hear the news, Beth called at his house in Brynmill later that day, hoping to catch a glimpse of Tommy, only to be told by Dan's new housekeeper, a Mrs Davies, that the boy had been put to bed by his nanny for a nap and was not to be disturbed.

Dan received Beth in the sitting room, reluctantly putting aside his newspaper as she came in, and staring sullenly at her without a word of greeting.

She felt piqued, not only at his lack of interest but also at not seeing her brother. 'Why can't I see Tommy now? Would it hurt if he missed his nap this once?' she complained.

'You know what we agreed, and I've kept my word,' Dan said irritably. 'Why can't you be content with that? I've been very generous, I think, letting you see Thomas at all.'

Beth was incensed by his unreasonable attitude when she was prepared to change her whole life solely for *his* benefit. 'Am I to be treated like some poor, disgraced relation you are ashamed of?' she demanded loudly.

'Keep your voice down,' he snapped. 'Servants talk. Why are you here anyway?'

'I came to tell you that I am to be married in June,' she began, trying to control her anger. 'I've accepted Eynon's proposal as you asked me to.'

Dan jumped to his feet, his expression elated. 'That's excellent!' He rubbed his hands together as though extremely pleased with himself. 'I'm glad you've come to your senses, my girl.'

Beth stared at the tall handsome man standing before her and felt nothing but contempt for him. He would use anything and anyone to save himself. Acknowledging her as his daughter was merely a means to an end, and the knowledge left a bitter taste in her mouth.

'I think I've seen the last of any trouble with Jarvis,' Dan went on, and then glanced at her, his expression hardening. 'As long as you don't double-cross me,' he said savagely. 'If you are planning to hand over your shares to your new husband, you'd better think again.'

'I have no such plans, but don't strain yourself thanking me, Dan,' she said scathingly. 'You are all take and no give, you are. I don't know what my mother ever saw in you, or Aunt Mae either. A handsome face with no heart.'

'I don't waste my time with sentimentality,' Dan muttered brusquely. 'And you will get plenty out of this marriage, too, a rich husband and good life, so what are you complaining about?'

'All I want is a little bit of happiness,' Beth said, and suddenly felt she was doing the right thing for the wrong reasons. But the die was cast and she wouldn't go back on her word.

'If it's thanks you want,' he snapped, 'I'll say thanks for letting me know I'm in the clear. Now, if there is nothing further you have to say, perhaps you would leave.'

'Gladly,' Beth flared. 'If it wasn't for Tommy you would never see me again. But you can't keep controlling my time with him forever. One day I'll find a way to get him back, adoption or no adoption. He belongs with me.'

'You used to know the Pickering family up in Cwmbwrla, didn't you?' Flossie asked Beth one morning the following week.

She was startled. 'Nothing has happened to Mrs Pickering, has it?'

'No, no.' Flossie shook her head. 'Maudie Pickering as was has had another baby, that's all. I was talking to a neighbour of hers in the market yesterday.'

'Oh, there's lovely,' Beth said, relieved. 'They were so good to me when my mam died. Like family, they were,' she went on. 'I must go and see them.'

So far most of the wedding guests were from Eynon's side. Beth had no family to invite to her wedding, only friends. All the staff at Windsor Lodge were invited, and Beth had sent invitations to Elias and Peggy Morgan, too. It would be nice to have Mrs Pickering, Maudie and her husband Teifi there as well. She decided to visit Libanus Street, see the new baby and take the invitations in person.

That afternoon she walked into town and then caught the tram from High Street. Libanus Chapel, standing on the corner of the main road, looked as impressive as ever, and Beth was glad she had chosen it for the ceremony. As she walked up her old street she had a sudden vision of little Freddie running to meet her on his spindly legs, and felt a longing to enter the house where she was born once again and find her mother busy at the stove, making her mouth-watering Welsh cakes. Those days had been so happy she'd never dreamt they would end in tragedy.

When Beth knocked at Mrs Pickering's there was no answer and so she tried next door, her old home. Maudie answered, looking plump and very healthy, with a cheerful smile on her face.

'Beth! Oh, there's lovely to see you, kid.' Maudie pulled her into the passage and gave her a warm hug. 'Hey! You're looking smart. There's lovely that suit is.'

'And you look blooming,' Beth said with a laugh. 'Motherhood suits you.'

'Oh, yes.' Maudie nodded, beaming from ear to ear. 'Come and see my new little one.'

The house smelled of new baby, and Beth felt a quiver of longing. Perhaps she would be showing off her own baby by this time next year.

Mrs Pickering was in the scullery rinsing nappies in the stone sink when Beth walked in. 'Well, well, there's nice to see you again, Beth,' the older woman said cheerfully. 'Oh, my word! You look the toff these days. I heard you came into some money, and you've got your own business as well.'

Beth didn't reply, feeling awkward for a moment, as though her new prosperity was forming an invisible barrier between her and her friends.

'Here he is,' Maudie said quickly, holding up a baby wrapped in a shawl. 'Here's my precious Gareth. He's the image of Teifi, isn't he?'

'Yes, he is. Can I hold him?' Beth asked.

Maudie handed the baby over and Beth sat down to nurse him.

'I don't suppose there's a cup of tea going, is there?' she asked with a grin at Mrs Pickering.

Perhaps she did have more money than most people around here would see in a lifetime, but inside she was the same girl she had always been, and she needed her friends close to her now more than ever.

'Of course there is,' Mrs Pickering said, and immediately put the kettle on the gas ring. 'Old friends are always welcome.'

Beth praised baby Gareth up to the skies, and Maudie simpered with pleasure and pride.

'Well, Beth girl, what's been happening to you then?' Mrs Pickering asked as they sat sipping hot tea later, with baby Gareth safe in his cot nearby.

Beth told them about Aunt Mae and Windsor Lodge but didn't mention Dan, feeling ashamed. 'And I've got some other news,' she said. 'I'm getting married next June.'

'Oh, Beth love!' Maudie exclaimed, clapping her hands. 'Oh, I'm so happy for you. After all you've been through you deserve a bit of something good.'

'Who's the lucky man?' Mrs Pickering asked practically.

When Beth mentioned Eynon's name, mother and daughter exchanged glances, obviously astounded.

'Prosser-Evans, the provisioners in High Street?' Mrs Pickering asked, looking impressed. 'My word, you've done well for yourself, kid.'

'How did you come to meet him?' Maudie asked, eyes wide.

Beth hesitated. 'Through business, really,' she said lamely. In a way it was true. She forced a smile and a cheerful tone. 'And I want you all to come to the wedding.' She opened her handbag, took out the invitation cards and handed them over. 'I hope Teifi can get time off.'

Mrs Pickering gaped at the cards. 'There's posh!' She

ran gnarled fingers over the gilt lettering, and then gave Beth a startled glance. 'I'll have to have a new frock.'

'Me, too,' Maudie said. 'Ooh! There's exciting.'

'I tell you what, Maudie,' Beth exclaimed impulsively, 'I'd like you to be my matron of honour so I'll have an outfit made for you especially, something that will complement my wedding dress. You can choose your own colour.'

Maudie gaped in astonishment. '*Duw! Duw!* That would be wonderful.' She sat forward excitedly. 'Listen, I've always fancied myself in lilac.'

'I'll get some material swatches from the dressmaker and bring them around one day next week,' Beth suggested, feeling some of the excitement herself. 'You can choose what you like.'

She came away from Libanus Street in a happier frame of mind. She was getting married and might as well enjoy all the fuss and preparations as though she were really in love. After all, the prospect of having a child of her own, starting a family, was something to be joyful about. She made up her mind that this marriage would be as happy as she could make it.

Beth called on Maudie again a few days later, bringing the swatches of material, but there was no reply to her knock. Mrs Pickering came out on to her own front step as Beth was about to turn away. 'Maudie's gone to the clinic,' she explained. 'She'll be back soon. Come on in and have a cuppa with me while you wait.'

Beth was pleased to do that. The idea that her newfound wealth could separate her from old friends was worrying.

Over tea she showed Mrs Pickering the swatches.

The older woman fingered them with enthusiasm.

'Lovely quality,' she observed. 'Our Maudie will look like a princess.'

As they bent over the swatches there was a thud upstairs, as though a shoe had been dropped on the floor, and Beth glanced up at Mrs Pickering, startled.

'What was that?' she whispered. 'Someone is upstairs.'

To her astonishment, Mrs Pickering's cheeks turned pink, and she looked discomfited. 'It's all right,' she said. 'It's only one of my lodgers. He works nights, and is just getting up for a meal.'

Relieved, Beth put a hand to her breast. 'Goodness! I thought you had burglars.'

'If burglars can find anything of value in this house,' her old friend said flatly, 'I'll help them look for it.'

'Perhaps I had better go,' Beth said, suddenly feeling uncomfortable. 'You'll be wanting to make some food and I'll be in the way.'

'No, I think you should stay a bit,' Mrs Pickering said firmly. 'Maudie will want to see you. She's looking forward to her new outfit.'

Footfalls were heard on the stairs and the next moment a tall broad-shouldered young man came into the living room. Beth glanced up at the newcomer and then got the shock of her life to see a face she'd never thought to look on again.

'Haydn!' Her heart turning somersaults in her breast, she jumped to her feet, staring at him open-mouthed. 'Haydn! Where did you spring from?'

He stared down at her, his face turning pale, obviously deeply disconcerted to meet her. 'Beth, I didn't know you were here.' He glanced at Mrs Pickering with the suggestion of a frown. 'You never said Beth was calling, Mrs P?'

'Makes no odds, does it?' she asked, looking perplexed.

Her heart still shuddering at the shock, Beth stepped towards him, her eager gaze fixed on his well-remembered features: the gentle grey eyes and the wide generous mouth that was always smiling in the old days. The old days! It was only two years since she'd seen him last yet he appeared much older somehow. That boyish look she recalled with love and warmth was gone.

'How have you been, Haydn?' Beth asked, feeling her lips quiver. 'I had no idea you were back in Swansea.'

The face that had haunted her recently, the face that she loved and had thought never to see again, was before her, and she struggled to hide her feelings, wanting to go to him and hug him.

He turned his eyes away as though embarrassed, and pain pierced her heart. She felt rejected.

'Been back a month or two now, I have,' he said awkwardly, sitting down at the table. 'Never expected to see you again, Beth.'

'Why not?'

'We move in different circles now, mun. I hear you've got your own business, like.'

'But we are family, Haydn.' Beth sat down too, looking at him earnestly, unable to believe he was here in the same room with her after all this time while other feelings too fluttered about inside her like a bird trapped in a barrel. 'You should've let me know you were home,' she went on. 'I might've been able to help.'

He didn't answer, and Beth became anxious. 'You don't blame me for what happened do you, Haydn? I didn't drive you away, mind. I wanted you to stay.'

He looked up at her then, that wide familiar smile curving his mouth. 'Of course I don't blame you, *cariad*,' he said. 'It was Gwyn's doing, mun.' He shook his head. 'I should never have gone with him. It didn't work.'

Beth hung her head as painful memories flooded through her mind. 'When Freddie died and then Mam it was awful, Haydn,' she murmured, reliving the anguish of those times. 'I missed you. I was wishing all the time you were here.'

'I wish I'd been here, too,' he said. 'I was fond of little Freddie and your mam. Our own mother couldn't have treated us better, but Gwyn being Gwyn, he's never satisfied.'

'Where did you go when you left us?' Beth asked. She wanted to know everything about him, feeling she had been cheated in being separated from him. If Haydn hadn't gone away, who knows? They might have been sweethearts now and then she wouldn't be engaged to marry a man she didn't love.

'Up to Bristol first, found good jobs in an engineering works,' he said, picking up the mug of tea Mrs Pickering had placed in front of him. 'But Gwyn wouldn't fit in. Always quarrelling with the other workmen, he was, and finally he got the sack and pushed off to London.'

'Is that where he is now?' Beth asked hopefully. Gwyn's bitterness towards Mam had been hard to bear, and Beth would never forgive his selfishness when Percy died. She couldn't help feeling he had broken up the family by deserting them. His was one face she never wanted to see again.

Haydn gave her a quick embarrassed glance and lowered his head.

Mrs Pickering cleared her throat. 'Gwyn is lodging here, too, kid,' she said, and then sniffed. 'And he owes me two weeks' rent. He's out of work again, so I don't know when I'll see it.'

Beth felt momentarily disturbed at the news, but then her glance fell on Haydn and her heart sang with joy.

Looking at him across the table, she wanted to stroke his cheek and kiss him, but all she could do was gaze at him helplessly.

'Why did you come back, Haydn?' She wanted him to say he had yearned for her, too, but perhaps that was too much to hope for.

He looked at her, his face wistful. 'Nowhere felt like home without you . . . I mean . . .' He flushed and looked away. 'I couldn't settle in Bristol. I've got my old job back at the tinplate works.'

'Oh, Haydn, I'm so glad you are home.' Beth reached a hand across the table to clasp his. 'Don't ever go away again.'

'Beth is engaged to be married, mind,' Mrs Pickering announced suddenly. 'Next June it is. Marrying into money, too. The Prosser-Evans family are filthy rich. Isn't that right, Beth?'

The smile left Haydn's face. He stared at her, and Beth felt as though someone had thrown a bucket of cold water over her.

'Is it true, Beth? Are you to be married?'

'Yes, I am engaged.' Beth glanced at Mrs Pickering. She wanted to tell Haydn everything: about Dan, about the feud with Jarvis, about the promise she had made under duress which she now bitterly regretted, but she hesitated to reveal all in front of Mrs Pickering. If only she and Haydn could be alone.

'I see,' he said shortly, and stood up.

Beth rose too. 'I don't think you do, Haydn. There's so much more I have to tell you about what's been happening to me . . . who I am . . . I need to explain.'

'You don't owe me any explanation,' he snapped, his face white. And she wondered why her engagement to another man was such a shock to him if he had no feelings for her. 'I'm not even family really, am I? Not any more.'

'I need to talk to you, Haydn!'

He shook his head. 'I doubt we have anything to say to each other. We've grown apart over the last two years, Beth.' He looked her up and down. 'I don't know you, with your fancy clothes and such. You're not the girl I once . . .' He stared at her. 'If you must know, I didn't get in touch with you because of the money you inherited. I didn't want you to think I was cadging.'

'I would never think that,' she exclaimed, feeling that a wedge of mistrust was splitting them asunder when they had only just found each other again.

'Others would,' he retorted, and turned away to march into the passage. 'And I won't have that. A man's got his pride if nothing else.'

'Haydn, please!' Beth ran after him, but he went back upstairs and she couldn't follow.

Mrs Pickering was watching with open curiosity when Beth returned to the living room. 'Everything all right, is it, kid?'

Beth nodded. 'Never expected to see Haydn again, that's all,' she said quietly. 'We were close. I was always fond . . .'

She could not say any more, and Mrs Pickering patted her arm.

'You'd better pop off now, kid,' she advised. 'Before Gwyn comes home. He'll have been drinking somewhere, as usual, and he gets nasty with it.' She sniffed. 'I wouldn't have taken him in if it weren't for Haydn pleading for him. He's loyal to his brother, although I don't know why. Gwyn doesn't appreciate it.'

'Poor Haydn.'

Mrs Pickering sniffed. 'Different as chalk and cheese,

them two. Between you and me he's a bad lot, that Gwyn is.'

'He's out of work, you say?' Beth asked. Gwyn could be bitter and quarrelsome when short of money. She remembered the savage way he had tried to take Percy's savings from Esme.

'Oh, aye.' Mrs Pickering shook her head. 'He got into some bother in his last job. Bit of a coincidence, really,' she went on thoughtfully. 'He was working for Prosser-Evans. I don't know what he did, but from the stories I've heard, he was booted out sharpish. There were whispers the police could be involved.'

'The police!' Beth felt fear clutch at her heart. Was Gwyn the man responsible for the fire at Dan's yard?

'Criminal doings, so they say,' Mrs Pickering said. 'If it wasn't for Haydn, I'd ask Gwyn to go, but I don't want Haydn leaving with him. He deserves better.' The older woman put a hand on Beth's arm. 'Mark my words,' she said in a hushed voice, 'Gwyn will get himself and Haydn into serious trouble one of these days.'

22

Beth found it hard keeping her mind on her wedding preparations after seeing Haydn again, torn in two by her aching longing for him and her pledge to Eynon. But how could she renege on her promise to wed him when there was so much at stake, not only for Dan but little Tommy, too?

She had not felt so miserable and helpless since her mother died. Her feelings for Haydn had been just about bearable while he was out of reach; now he was back she was tormented by them. And it was made worse by the fact that, contrary to what he had said, her womanly instinct told her he felt the same way, yet he must surely believe she had deliberately put herself out of his reach by marrying for money.

She could not ignore her yearnings, no matter how hard she tried, and no matter how wrong it was to feel such deep love for a man other than the one she had promised to marry.

By the middle of the following week, she could stand it no longer and knew she must see Haydn once more; make him speak his heart, despite the consequences. And if he did love her, then she must beg his forgiveness for what she had to do.

Of course, she was putting everything at risk. Her even seeing Haydn again might seem like a betrayal to Eynon, if he ever found out.

As Beth made her way to Cwmbwrla, she rehearsed excuses she might make to Mrs Pickering to persuade her to leave them alone together, without arousing her suspicions. But when she knocked at her former neighbour's door there was no reply.

She was about to turn away, bitterly disappointed, when the sound of the sash being raised at an upstairs window made her step back and look up. Haydn peered down at her, his hair tousled as though he had just risen from bed, and she remembered he was working shifts.

'Beth?'

'Let me in, Haydn.'

He hesitated. 'Mrs Pickering isn't home.'

'I've come to see you.'

'Beth, please!' He glanced up and down the street as though fearful of being seen and heard. 'You mustn't come here again. Please go now.'

'I won't!' she said. 'I can't!' She was past caring whether anyone was observing them. 'I'll keep knocking until you let me in.'

Hastily he withdrew his head and after a few minutes the door opened. He stood there in his vest and trousers, shrugging into his shirt.

'Beth, what possessed you to come here today?' he asked, a tremor in his voice. 'It isn't fair on either of us, not to mention the man you are to marry.'

That was something she didn't want to be reminded about. Without a word, she pushed past him and walked down the passage to the living room. He followed her and she stood at the far side of the table, facing him.

'There's something unfinished between us,' she said tremulously. 'Something left unsaid. My life can't go on until it's settled.'

'I don't know what you mean.'

'Haydn! Don't make this difficult for me.'

'What do you want from me, Beth?' He sounded exasperated.

'Honesty.'

'Honesty! Ha!'

She shook her head. 'Don't accuse me of anything, Haydn,' she begged. 'I've had to make my own way as best I could after you and Gwyn left us all stranded.' She bit her lip. 'If you had stayed Mam would never have sent me away, I'm certain of it. Freddie might not have died . . .'

'You can't lay that at my door,' he exclaimed angrily. 'Esme made it plain she didn't want either of us there.' He hesitated, looking at her, the anger draining from his face. 'I'll never forget that day as long as I live, Beth,' he went on softly, shaking his head. 'I had to leave behind everything I loved.'

She caught her breath. Was this the moment she had been waiting for? 'The same was true for me, too, Haydn,' she breathed. 'But I was too young and inexperienced to realise it.'

'So was I.' He nodded. 'You were like a sister to me in those days, and I got it into my head that what I felt for you was wrong, bad. I was ashamed of it. That's why I chased after Maudie and other girls.'

'But I'm *not* your sister,' Beth cried desperately. 'There is no relationship of blood between us, no barrier.'

'Of course there's a barrier,' Haydn said quickly. 'You're promised to another man.'

She waved a hand dismissively. 'Put that aside for the moment.'

'Put it aside?' There was a quaver in his voice and he stared at her in disbelief. 'How can I put it aside?' He looked angered. 'What is it you're trying to do to me, Beth?'

'I only want to know what is in your heart, Haydn,' she said gently. 'I need to know how you feel.'

'And will it make any difference?' he asked raggedly. 'Will you change your plans about marrying him?'

Beth's mouth trembled so much she couldn't speak. She longed for him; yearned for him to say the words, tell her how much he loved her. She wanted to be in his arms, know the thrill of his loving, but his questions hung between them like a dark miasma.

'Don't ask me that,' she murmured at last.

'Why not, Beth?' he asked. 'That's the whole point, isn't it?' His hand trembled as he raised it to his brow. 'You want me to bare my soul, but what will be my reward?'

She was dumb again at the look of despair on his face.

He turned away. 'Anyway, I haven't the right,' he said, and pointed at her hand. 'Not while you are wearing that ring.' He hesitated, looking at her, pain etched in his face. 'Do you . . . do you belong to him, Beth, body and soul?'

She gazed at him, not understanding his meaning for a moment. Something flashed in his eyes then and she realised it was jealousy. She shook her head vehemently.

'No! How could you ask that?'

'I'm sorry!' he exclaimed. 'It's just the thought of you and him together . . . it drives me crazy.'

Beth darted around the table and ran to him, placing her hands against his chest, looking up into his face.

'I'm not marrying Eynon for love,' she said. He stared, bewildered, and she rushed on. 'And certainly not for his money. I'm doing it for my father – Dan Henshaw. I'm marrying Eynon to save Dan from Eynon's father's revenge.'

'Revenge?' He shook his head, perplexed. 'You're not making much sense, Beth *cariad*.'

She wetted her lips nervously before explaining,

knowing it would sound cold and calculating.

'Eynon wants me,' she said simply. 'And Jarvis Prosser-Evans wants the marriage too. He says Eynon has changed since he met me; he's taking his responsibilities to the business much more seriously. Jarvis is convinced I'll be the making of his son, and that's all-important to him.'

Haydn winced. 'You make it sound like a business arrangement,' he said disparagingly. 'Worse! It's as if you are being procured.'

Beth was horrified. 'That's a dreadful thing to say,' she gasped. 'Eynon truly loves me. And I might've gone very happily into marriage with him . . . if you and I hadn't met again, Haydn.'

'Huh! So, it's *my* fault?'

'Don't twist my words!' Relenting, she raised a hand to touch his face, her heart aching at his dismal expression. 'And don't let's quarrel, Haydn. I love you.'

He grasped her hand. 'Beth, it's not too late. Tell Eynon it's over. Don't marry him.'

She bit her lip. 'If I back down now, Jarvis will think Dan is behind it and will ruin him.'

'Ruin him?' Haydn shook his head impatiently. 'What are you talking about?'

She hesitated, reluctant to reveal Dan's faithlessness.

'My father did something wrong years ago,' she said at last. 'He took something precious from Jarvis – I can't explain – you must trust me.'

'Trust you to do what?' He shook his head. 'This isn't right, Beth. You can't love me and marry Eynon. My God! It's dishonest.'

'No! No!' She was distressed. 'Please understand! I have to do this for my father.' It was her duty. She had to put family before her own feelings.

'So there's no hope for us, then?'

'I'm being selfish, Haydn,' Beth admitted. 'I can go through with this, but I need to know you love me. If I know that for certain, I'll put up with anything.'

'And what about me?' His voice held a hollow tone. 'What am I supposed to do with the rest of my life?'

She wanted to burst into tears at the pity of it. How many lives must her father spoil?

'You're a strong man, Haydn,' she whispered. 'And you'll go on being strong, and survive, because you will always know I love only you.'

'But it's more than a man can stand, Beth. I'm only human.'

With a groan, he gathered her in his arms and kissed her. Beth eagerly wound her arms around his neck, clinging desperately to him. Tides of desire surged through her, but she stifled them, knowing there could be no more than this moment for them.

After a long moment he released her. 'I love you, Beth,' he said fervently. 'I've loved you since forever. I'll always love you.'

'Oh, Haydn, my darling!'

They clung together, their lips eager. This was all they would ever have.

'Oh, what a touching scene!' a harsh voice said from the doorway. 'Love's young dream, is it?'

Haydn and Beth sprang apart to see Gwyn leaning against the doorjamb, his flat cap pushed back from his forehead, a mirthless grin on his face.

'Gwyn!' Beth gasped, taken aback that he had witnessed their tender moment.

'Didn't think you'd ever see me again, did you?' he sneered.

'No,' she flared, hating the look of triumph on his face. 'No one wants to see the return of a bad penny.'

'Beth!' Haydn's tone was reproachful. 'I know there's been bitterness between you in the past, but Gwyn doesn't deserve that.'

Beth stared at him. 'Oh, yes, he does,' she said with conviction. 'And more besides. Obviously you don't know why he lost his latest job.'

Gwyn pushed himself away from the doorjamb, his colour darkening. 'Keep your mouth shut, you hussy,' he snarled.

'Hey!' Haydn snapped. 'Watch your lip, Gwyn. Don't talk to Beth like that.'

She told him, 'I've recently found out Gwyn was working for Jarvis Prosser-Evans, doing Jarvis's dirty work for him in an attempt to ruin my father.'

'You lying bitch!' Gwyn snarled.

'He wrecked one of my father's drays and put the driver in hospital. He didn't care the old man was an innocent party,' Beth cried. 'And then he set a fire in Dan's coal yard which destroyed the offices.'

'What?' Haydn stared at his brother. 'What the hell is she talking about?' He shook his head. 'You weren't involved with that, were you, Gwyn?'

'Jarvis turned a blind eye,' Beth rushed on. 'But Eynon isn't ruthless like his father. He did the right thing and sacked Gwyn.' She turned to glare at him. 'You're lucky you're not in prison.'

'I only did what I was told to do,' he snarled. 'I was made the scapegoat.'

'That's no excuse, Gwyn, for breaking the law,' Haydn said impatiently. 'What's got into you, mun?'

'Nothing has got into him,' Beth snapped, impatient with Haydn for his blindness to Gwyn's treachery. 'He's always been the same, always selfish and money-grabbing. Look how he tried to rob Mam.'

'Huh! Look who's talking,' Gwyn bellowed. 'You're carrying on with our Haydn by here and all the time planning to marry that bloody posh-boy, Eynon Prosser-Evans.' He gave a disdainful laugh. 'He doesn't know what a little tart he's marrying, though, does he? But he soon will, because I'll tell him.'

'Now that's enough!' Haydn stormed, taking a step towards his brother. 'You'd better shut your dirty mouth, Gwyn, or I'll do it for you.'

'Oh, yes! You and whose army?' he taunted. 'You could never lick me and you know it.'

With an angry snarl, Haydn darted at him, but Beth clung to his arm, holding him back. 'No, don't, Haydn, mun,' she cried desperately. 'He's not worth it.'

'That's right,' Gwyn taunted again. 'Listen to her and save yourself a good hiding.'

'You insult Beth again and I'll bloody flatten you!' Haydn yelled, struggling to free himself from her grip, but she hung on like grim death. Haydn being hurt because of her was the last thing she wanted, and it wasn't right that brother should fight brother.

'She'll have more than insults to worry about from now on,' Gwyn rasped. 'It'll give me great pleasure to tell Eynon all about the dirty double-crossing little slut he's got himself engaged to.'

'You bugger!' Haydn shouted, and wrenching himself free, flew at his brother, swinging a wild punch at Gwyn's head.

Beth screamed as the two men exchanged punch for punch in the confines of the small living room.

'Stop! Stop, for God's sake,' she pleaded, but they were too incensed with each other to listen, and slugged it out, fists swinging, arms grappling and pushing, finally barging into Mrs Pickering's Welsh dresser, sending china crashing to the floor.

'Oh, my God!' Beth shrieked. 'Help me, someone!'

Suddenly Gwyn got in a lucky blow. Haydn's head sank on to his chest and he went down on his knees amidst the broken china. With a gloating shout Gwyn moved in, his fist raised, but Beth dashed between him and Haydn.

'Get away from him, you beast!' she screamed. 'Get away!'

She saw temptation flare in Gwyn's eyes and thought he would strike her, but then he lowered his fist and stepped back.

'Let that be a lesson to him,' he panted. 'I'll crack open his skull next time.'

'You madman!' Beth shouted, terrified. 'You should be behind bars.'

Gwyn bent and snatched up his cap from the floor nearby and put it on his head. His right eye was already swelling, and his lip was split and bleeding, but he grinned insolently at her.

'I'll fix you as well,' he promised. 'Eynon Prosser-Evans won't want soiled goods, so you can say goodbye to your big house and posh lifestyle.'

'Why are you doing this, Gwyn?'

His eyes glittered with enmity as he wiped blood from his mouth on to his sleeve. 'I haven't forgotten the way Percy Pryce favoured you over me,' he said sourly. 'Favoured Dan Henshaw's bastard daughter over me!'

Haydn struggled to his feet. 'I'll smash you for that, you swine,' he gasped.

His nose was bleeding and he had a deep gash through his right brow where Gwyn's signet ring had cut him. He came after his brother again even though he was unsteady on his feet, but Beth flung her arms around his neck to hold him back and shield him.

'Get out!' she shouted at Gwyn. 'Get your things together and go. Mrs Pickering won't have you here after this.'

'Huh!' He gave them both a contemptuous glance. 'I'm buggering off anyway. I've found a nice little widow woman in Caer Street. She'll suit me for the moment.'

With one final glance of hatred, he turned and left them.

Haydn flopped on to a nearby chair, blood pouring from his nose which was beginning to swell.

'That was terrible!' Beth gasped. 'I thought he'd kill you.'

She rushed into the scullery to fetch a basin of water and a towel to bathe his face.

'It'll take more than a couple of lucky punches to see me off,' Haydn muttered, but he hung his head and Beth knew he was in great pain.

She had just finished bathing his face when Mrs Pickering returned. The older woman shrieked when she saw the broken china.

'What happened?'

Beth told her about Gwyn. 'He's gone so don't worry,' she said. 'And I'll pay for all the damage, Mrs Pickering.'

'Some of that china belonged to my mother,' she said tearfully. 'It can never be replaced.'

'I'm so sorry,' Beth said. 'I'll make it up to you somehow.'

Mrs Pickering went upstairs to lie down after the shock, and Haydn and Beth looked at each other.

'Gwyn knows about us and that changes everything,' he said, his tone earnest. 'Now you'll *have* to call off the marriage.'

'Eynon will never believe his lies,' Beth said confidently. 'He knows what a nasty piece of work Gwyn is.' She was convinced Eynon would send him packing with a flea in his ear. 'And we've done nothing wrong,' she went on, shaking her head. 'Nothing has changed.'

Haydn stared at her, astonished. 'You can't really believe that?' he said. 'Surely you don't mean to go on with this charade? You have to tell Eynon the truth.' He grasped her hand. 'Call it off, Beth, I beg you.'

She pulled her hand free. 'I can't do that, Haydn,' she whispered miserably. 'I've explained why.'

'You're putting Dan Henshaw before me, before our love?' Haydn said loudly. His expression darkened and she could see he was angry at her stubbornness. 'Or perhaps you don't really love me at all?'

'I do!'

'Then leave Eynon.' He looked at her eagerly. 'I'll get a special licence,' he went on. 'We'll be married as soon as you like.'

'It's impossible.' Beth put a hand over her mouth to prevent sobs of deep unhappiness from bursting out. 'Jarvis will destroy the business if I go back on my word. Dan will be ruined and that means Tommy's future will be blighted as well.'

'So what if Dan is ruined?' Haydn shouted. 'He's hardly been a proper father to you, has he? Why do you care so much what happens to him?'

'Because no one else does,' Beth sighed. 'He's my own flesh and blood, Haydn. I can't ignore that. I wish I could.'

His expression hardened. 'So it *is* about money after all, isn't it? You own more than half Dan's business, I've been told. If he goes down the drain, so do you.' His lips tightened. 'What's the matter, Beth, afraid of being poor again if you marry me?'

'Haydn! How could you?' She was cut to the quick. 'You know me better than that.'

He shook his head. 'I *used* to know you,' he said, sadness in his voice. 'Five minutes ago I thought we might have a future together, but now I can see what a stupid fool I am.' He stared at her coldly. 'You've changed, Beth. Perhaps you're more like Dan Henshaw than I thought.'

'That's unfair,' she cried. 'I didn't know my aunt intended to leave her share of the business to me. I didn't want it or ask for it. But she did and now I'm doing what I think is right.'

Haydn stood up. 'This is getting us nowhere,' he said shortly. 'I'm getting out too. We won't see each other again, Beth.'

'Oh, please!' she pleaded. 'We can't part like this. I do love you, Haydn. Can't we be . . . friends?'

He drew in a sharp harsh breath as if she had struck him, and without another word or glance, turned to stride out of the room. She heard his feet pound up the stairs.

'It's too late for us, Haydn,' she murmured quietly to herself. 'And my heart is breaking.'

The dining room at Windsor Lodge had been extended by taking down the wall separating it from the premises next door, and opening the enlarged space to the public, hoping to attract passing holidaymakers. At noon the following day Beth was supervising the serving of the midday meal, instructing the new waitresses she had taken on for the season, when Phoebe came and touched her arm.

'You're wanted in reception, Beth.'

'Oh, rightho!' She removed her apron. 'Listen, see to it that Mrs Russell gets an extra helping of gravy.' She sighed and rolled her eyes to the ceiling. 'You know what she's like.'

'Leave the old boot to me,' Phoebe chuckled. 'I'll have her swimming in the stuff.'

In the hall Beth stared in consternation at the man lounging against the wall, fingering leaflets on the notice board.

'Gwyn, what do you want?'

His bruised and broken lips twisted in a sneer. 'You're doing all right by here, aren't you?' he observed. 'Trust you to fall on your feet.'

'I work hard for everything I get,' Beth snapped back. 'And I don't whinge and whine when things go wrong like you do, Gwyn, always ready to blame someone else for your mistakes – or should I say crimes?'

'You've always had it easy, you mouthy piece,' he rasped back. 'Now it's my turn.'

'What do you mean?'

'You owe me, Beth Pryce, owe me plenty, and I've come to collect the debt.'

She shook her head, frowning. 'I don't know what you're talking about. I owe you nothing.'

'Don't play stupid,' he said angrily, taking a step towards her. 'I'll keep my mouth shut about you and our Haydn, for a price. I want a hundred pounds up front – now, today.'

Beth gave an astonished laugh. 'You're out of your mind, you are, Gwyn. Where would I get a sum like that?'

'Oh, you've got it all right, tucked away in a bank somewhere.'

'I'm not paying you a penny, you rotter!' she snapped angrily. 'Now get off these premises.'

'I'm not going anywhere until I'm paid,' Gwyn exploded.

A couple with two children had come in from the street and were looking at the menu and tariff displayed on the notice board. They appeared startled by Gwyn's loud voice and walked out.

Beth was dismayed. 'Look what you've done,' she cried. 'You're frightening trade away.'

'Then pay up and I'll be off.'

'Come into my office,' she said. 'We can't argue the toss here.'

He followed her down the passage to the office at the back. Beth shut the door and faced him, although she felt intimidated by his presence in the small room. 'I don't know what you're playing at, Gwyn. You've no business coming here,' she began angrily. 'There's nothing between Haydn and me, and you know it.'

'I saw what I saw.'

'You saw a kiss between . . . friends, nothing more.'

Gwyn's smile was scornful and he shook his head. 'It doesn't matter, you stupid woman. I can say anything I want to, and I will. A few juicy lies should do the trick. I'll tell your husband-to-be I caught you and Haydn rolling around between the sheets.'

She was appalled. 'You lousy swine!'

His expression darkened and she saw him clench his fists, clearly wanting to hit her.

'And I won't stop at Prosser-Evans either,' he snarled. 'I'll blacken your name about this town, make it stink to high heaven. Before I'm finished I'll have people believing you're running a knocking-shop here. What will that do for business, eh?'

Beth felt trapped. How could she fight such vicious lies? Perhaps Eynon would not believe them, but many people would only be too glad to pass on Gwyn's filthy rumours.

'I haven't got anything like a hundred,' she told him sullenly. 'And I don't know when I can get it either. You'll have to wait.'

'I'm sick of these bloody games you're playing,' he snarled. 'Eynon Prosser-Evans will hear from me today, and so will others. I don't care what I have to do or say.'

'He won't believe you,' Beth said emphatically. 'He knows what an evil rat you are, Gwyn.'

'Perhaps he won't believe me straight away,' Gwyn said with a nasty smile. 'But I'll have sown the seed. It'll make him think twice.' He raised his brows. 'Are you willing to take that risk?'

Biting her lip in consternation, Beth took a tin cash box out of the desk drawer. It held the takings for the week so far.

'There's twenty-five pounds here,' she said with a tremor in her voice, conscious that half of it was Ada's. 'That's all I can lay my hands on.'

Gwyn's eyes gleamed with greed as he looked at the cash in her hand. He grabbed it from her. 'That'll do for a start, but it's still not enough.'

'That's all you're going to get,' Beth snapped. 'So take it, Gwyn, and get out of Swansea. Get far away from me and Haydn.'

'You bitch!' he exclaimed with fury. 'You've driven a wedge between my brother and me, but you'll pay for it.'

'I've already paid,' Beth said miserably. 'Haydn has gone away.'

'No, he's still at Ma Pickering's,' Gwyn growled. 'Always her favourite, Haydn was.' He grinned nastily. 'Of course, you know what this means?' He held up the money. 'It's an admission of guilt, that's what it is. Or that's how Eynon will see it.'

Beth was aghast. 'Now, look here . . .'

'I'll be back for more in a few days,' he sneered. 'Say another twenty-five, and don't fail or else.' He grinned. 'I'll be a regular caller, Beth. You'll see a lot of me in future.'

23

July 1922

The interior of Libanus Chapel, Cwmbwrla, gleamed in the sunlight streaming in through its high mullioned stained-glass windows. Flowers were everywhere. Their scent seemed almost overwhelming to Beth as she began the long walk down the aisle to the altar. She almost stumbled, but Elias Morgan's strong arm held her firm.

'You all right, my good girl?' he asked in an undertone.

'Just nerves,' Beth whispered, and prayed she would have the strength not to faint and make a spectacle of herself.

Ahead of her she saw Eynon turned towards her, waiting, his handsome face beaming, his eyes aglow. Perhaps he had enough love to last them both for the rest of their lives, Beth thought, and hoped it was true.

When she reached his side, his gaze was fixed on her face.

'You are so beautiful,' he murmured so that only she could hear. 'And I love you so, Beth.'

Beth thought the wedding breakfast at the Mackworth Hotel would go on forever. Jarvis's many business friends and acquaintances were present, and every one of them seemed intent on making a long speech.

She breathed a sigh of relief when finally Eynon

whispered that they could leave. They made their escape, retiring to a room upstairs to prepare for their departure on honeymoon to Italy.

Alone with Eynon for the first time as his wife, she did not know what to expect and was shaking with nerves as he closed the door behind them. She stood facing him, her hands clasped together before her breast, and couldn't stop trembling. He looked at her, smiled and shook his head.

'I'm not going to pounce on you, my darling,' he said gently. 'We have a lifetime before us. Let's get ready to catch that boat train. I'm longing for you to see Italy. I know you'll love the country as much as I do.' He tilted his head. 'I still wish we were going for a whole month.'

Feeling a little more confident and reassured by his gentleness, Beth relaxed. 'No, Eynon,' she said firmly, 'two weeks will be enough. I can't be away from the business too long, and neither can you. Goodness knows what mischief Jarvis could be up to while we're gone.'

Eynon made a comical grimace. 'Oh, so, it's going to be nose to the grindstone for the next forty years, is it?' He grinned at her. 'Meanwhile, can I beg one kiss from you, Mrs Prosser-Evans?'

It was the beginning of August when Beth and Eynon returned to Swansea. The two weeks in Italy had been idyllic, and Eynon had proved himself to be a considerate husband and patient lover. Their nights together had been a time of discovery for Beth, when she realised the joys of being a woman.

But now it felt strange, returning to Jarvis's house on Gower Road, strange and restricting. She felt she had to be on her mettle at all times, as though Jarvis were watching her, and wished they had a house of their own, away from his influence over Eynon.

On the Monday after their return Beth rose early, prepared to take control of her business at Windsor Lodge once again.

Eynon regarded her from the bed with a surprised expression.

'My darling, I'm not sure it's quite proper for my wife to conduct a business, especially that of a boarding house. You know, you do have a social position now.'

Beth was surprised. It was the first time he had used a reproving tone with her, but her mind was made up. She had no intention of lounging about like a bored society lady.

'I wouldn't fit in with your circle of friends, Eynon,' she remarked dryly, 'and I won't begin to try.'

'They'd adore you, as I do.'

She smiled at his words. 'I must be busy and useful,' she went on firmly, 'and I owe it to Ada Smart to continue to be her partner. It's the height of the holiday season now. She must be rushed off her feet.'

'You could put in a manager instead,' Eynon pointed out. 'Heaven knows, we can afford the salary.'

'No, Eynon,' Beth retorted with some energy. 'I intend to continue earning my own living.'

He laughed. 'Earning your living! But that's absurd. You have a rich husband. Ask me for anything, my darling, anything, and I'll gladly give it to you.'

Beth stood with hands on her hips, looking down at him. 'What I want can't be bought,' she cried. 'Independence, Eynon, that's what I want.' She paused a moment and stared at him. 'Something your father would take from me if he could.'

'That's nonsense!' he said, throwing back the

bedcovers to swing his long legs over the edge of the bed. 'The very opposite is true.'

He slipped on his dressing gown and came over to her where she stood before the ornate mahogany dressing-table.

'Pa admires your drive and determination,' he went on. 'I believe he's seriously considering you for a directorship of Prosser-Evans Provisioners. The first time in the history of our firm that a place on the board has been offered to a woman.' He put his arms around her waist, lowering his head to kiss her neck. 'It's an honour, Beth, and a privilege,' he said in her ear. 'What do you say to that?'

She eased herself gently from his embrace, her mind on business not on marital duty. She was not over-impressed by Jarvis's decision to 'honour' her, knowing her father-in-law did nothing without a very good reason.

'And what do I have to give him in return?' she asked dryly.

Beth was soon to find out when she went down to breakfast. Jarvis was all smiles when she came in to the breakfast room. She helped herself to scrambled eggs and toast, while the butler, Stark, brought her a fresh pot of tea.

'Has Eynon told you about the directorship?' Jarvis asked bluntly when the butler had retired. 'You have a good mind, Beth, for a woman, and a keen business sense. I'd like to see you on the board.'

She buttered some toast. 'Let's not beat about the bush, Jarvis,' she said just as bluntly. 'What are you after?'

He gave an amused grunt. 'Sharp as a tack, aren't you?' He glanced at her, his eyes hard despite his amusement. 'All right then. It's time you made your share of Dan

Henshaw's business over to your husband.' He lifted a hand to silence her as she opened her mouth to protest. 'I'll have nothing to do with it, I swear it,' he went on. 'You know you can trust Eynon not to harm Henshaw in any way.'

'I trust Eynon. I don't trust you,' Beth snapped. 'The answer is no, I won't be bought out, so don't dangle any more carrots before my nose.'

His eyes narrowed and his mouth set in a thin line. 'I will have my way in this, Beth,' he said heavily. 'Perhaps you thought marrying Eynon would put an end to it, but I have no intention of letting Henshaw off scot-free. If I can't ruin him then I will absorb him. I'll have him working for me before I'm through.'

'I'll fight you to the last ditch, Jarvis,' Beth hissed at him. 'You won't wear me down so easily.'

One thing she had learned about herself since Percy Pryce had died and Esme had pushed her aside was that she was resilient, and no one could take that away from her.

Jarvis's expression darkened even more. 'I could force you, you know. Eynon has certain rights as your husband, and besides he has enjoyed a fancy lifestyle all these years. But I control his salary as a director, I could soon curtail it.'

Beth stared at him aghast. 'You would do that to him?' she said, unable to believe such callousness. 'What kind of man is prepared to put that sort of pressure on his son just to get his own way in a pointless feud? You're despicable!'

Jarvis was furious. 'How dare you speak to me like that? You are under my roof, and therefore under my control.'

'I'm under no one's control. I'm my own woman, and always will be,' Beth cried out, rising from the table. 'This is the twentieth century, not the Dark Ages. And not even you are above the law, Jarvis.'

'A stubborn, self-opinionated young woman, that's what you are,' he shouted. 'You know nothing of life, but you'll soon learn it is cruel. It gives and it takes away, as it took my Daphne from me.'

'And for your long-dead wife you would sacrifice a son's pride and independence?' Beth asked scornfully. 'Eynon admires and looks up to you. Listen to your own bitter words, Jarvis,' she urged desperately. 'Your enmity towards Dan is eating you alive. Don't let it destroy Eynon, too.'

'That's up to you,' he retorted.

She was shaking from head to foot, realising Jarvis Prosser-Evans was implacable in his hatred of Dan. She had thrown Haydn's love away for nothing.

'I had hoped you were a better man than this,' she said tremulously. 'You led me to believe Dan's business would be safe if I married Eynon, but that was solely to enable you to win through. But you won't defeat me,' she cried. 'Not after all I have sacrificed.'

He looked puzzled. 'What do you mean?' When she didn't answer he lifted both hands as though in a plea. 'I'm not your enemy, Beth, despite what you think,' he said, changing tactics in a flash. 'You're part of my family now. We should be allies, especially in business. I look forward to grandchildren.'

Beth felt her face flush up. Why did that simple sentiment sound so threatening coming from him?'

Jarvis wasn't ready to leave for business when Beth was so Stark drove her into town, dropping her outside Windsor Lodge.

'Pick me up at six o'clock this evening, please,' she said

to him, feeling awkward at giving instructions to a servant with such dignity and poise as Stark. She was more used to dealing with chattering waitresses.

'Very good, madam.'

She watched him drive away, and then glanced up and down Oystermouth Road, already busy with holiday-makers intent on having a good time in the morning sunshine.

Suddenly her attention was caught by a figure lounging against the railings of a house a few doors away and with a shock she recognised Gwyn Howells. She stared in consternation as he raised his cloth cap in greeting, an insolent expression on his face. Beth hesitated a moment, expecting him to approach her, but suddenly he turned and swaggered away.

She saw his sudden appearance as a new threat. She had been paying him weekly for months. It had been difficult keeping the truth from Ada. Obviously he intended to prise even more money from her now that she was married. Fear touched her heart. Gwyn would bleed her dry if she let him.

24

September 1922

'You're looking pale and sickly this morning,' Ada said, a quizzical light in her knowing eyes. 'Anything you want to tell me?'

Startled, Beth looked up from scrambling eggs at the stove. She was persevering with her duties in the kitchen even though the smell of bacon frying made her feel queasier than ever.

'How did you guess?'

Ada put her hands on her hips. 'I've been through it myself remember? I know all the signs. When are you due?'

'April.' Beth pushed the pan away from the gas flame and thankfully sank on to a chair at the table. 'I've been meaning to tell you all week. I'll have to start thinking about training someone to replace me when the time comes.'

Ada wiped her hands on a tea towel and took a seat too. 'If you don't mind my saying so, Beth,' she went on in a kindly tone, 'you don't seem very happy at the prospect of motherhood.'

'Oh, I am happy!' she exclaimed, appalled that Ada might believe she didn't want her own baby. 'It's so wonderful I can hardly believe it. To think I'll have a child of my very own to love.'

'Then why the long face?'

'I'm worried about you and the business, and how you'll manage, that's all,' Beth said. 'And other things.'

'How does your hubby feel?'

Beth looked down at her hands. 'I haven't told him yet.'

'What?' Ada sounded puzzled. 'But if you're happy, Beth kid, surely this is something you want to share with him?'

She knew her attitude must seem strange to the older woman.

'Eynon will be ecstatic,' she said. 'But I worry about his father's reaction. He'll be more than pleased, of course, but he might use the child as a lever against me, force me to do something I don't want to, make me break a solemn promise.'

'Jarvis is still dead set against your father then?'

Beth nodded.

Ada lifted her chin. 'Tsk! That Dan Henshaw has brought you nothing but trouble,' she said brusquely. 'It's about time you let him sink or swim.' She leaned forward and patted Beth's arm. 'Tell your husband the good news straight away, love,' she advised sagely. 'Think about yourself for once.'

'Dinner will be served soon,' Eynon remarked to her that evening in their bedroom. 'You know how Pa hates to be kept waiting.'

Beth slipped into a dress of fine strawberry-coloured linen, wondering how much longer it would fit her. 'Must Jarvis always be running our lives?' she asked a little tetchily. 'I wish we had a house of our own, Eynon.' She did not say a home where he could be his own master.

Eynon rubbed his jaw. 'Buying property might be tricky at the moment,' he said. 'Pa informed me today that I need not look for a rise in salary for another two to three years. We're ploughing all profits back into the company or some such.' He shrugged. 'I don't understand that side of the business. Wish I did.'

'Well, I understand it!' Beth exclaimed angrily. 'And I understand your father only too well.' So Jarvis had started to implement his threat. She snatched up her wrap from the bed. 'But he'll have to think again, because changes are coming.'

Eynon frowned. 'What do you mean, darling?'

Beth relented, throwing off her anger, and went to him, looking up into his face and placing her hands against his chest. He was a good man and a good husband to her. He deserved her loyalty even if her heart belonged to another.

'Eynon, my dear, I have some news,' she said gently. 'I am expecting a baby in April.'

Eynon stared at her for a moment, his eyes round, his mouth agape, and then with an excited yell he gathered her into his arms, planting kisses on her face.

'Oh, Beth, my wonderful, clever girl! I'm to be a father!' He laughed as though astonished. 'Wait until Pa hears about this. He'll be proud of me then. He'll be overjoyed.'

Beth reached up and kissed him, pleased that he was so happy at the prospect of fatherhood.

'And you must make him see that an immediate raise in your salary is essential,' she said persuasively. 'Press him, Eynon. Press him hard. Surely even Jarvis won't see his only grandchild go in need?'

Eynon laughed out loud. 'When he hears our news he'll grant you anything, my darling Beth,' he said joyfully. 'And I'll be a hero!'

'It will be a boy!' Jarvis exclaimed loudly, raising his glass. 'Eynon, congratulations, my dear chap! I am so proud of you at last.' His eyes twinkled as he glanced at Beth. 'I knew Beth would be the making of you.'

She eyed him over the rim of her glass. Jarvis was all happiness and geniality now, but she still remembered how threatening he had been, and how implacable he really was.

'The boy will be brought up to take charge of the business, and will be educated with that end in mind,' Jarvis decreed. 'No public school for him. A gentleman's education never did a man any good.'

Beth saw Eynon's lips tighten. 'A moment ago you said you were proud of me.'

'I am,' Jarvis acknowledged. 'You have achieved something at last. But your son will achieve far more, I'll see to that personally. I'll engage a private tutor. From the off the boy will learn how to be a hard-headed businessman.'

Beth waited a moment for Eynon to challenge his father, but he sat there, eyes downcast. As ever it was up to her. She lifted her chin and straightened her shoulders, trying not to show her anger.

'*If* we have a son,' she said resolutely, 'his future will be in the hands of his parents. Eynon will decide upon his child's education. You are *not* to interfere, Jarvis.'

He flashed her a glance of astonishment, obviously taken aback at this tone of rebellion.

'This is my house,' he thundered, bringing his fist down hard on the table, making the port decanter rattle alarmingly. 'I'll decide what goes on under this roof.'

'And it is *our* child,' Beth retorted hotly, unable to contain her anger any longer. 'You have no right to make decisions about him or her.' She rose stiff-legged from the table. 'I'll leave you both to your cigars and port,' she said more calmly. 'There are other important matters at stake.' She sent a meaningful glance at Eynon. 'You will want to discuss them in private.'

Beth was very pleased when her husband told her Jarvis had caved in to his demand for an increase in salary. The money meant nothing to her, she was simply proud that her husband had stood up to his intimidating father for once. Perhaps by being fearless in the face of Jarvis's iron will she had shown Eynon the way.

Now she could give herself over entirely to enjoying the prospect of motherhood, and dream of the time when she would hold her child in her arms. Despite still loving Haydn and her deep hidden longing for him, she felt she was as happy as any woman in her position could expect to be.

Beth felt it was time to see her father and break the news to him. She hardly expected any show of enthusiasm, given his usual lack of interest in her or family matters. However, he surprised her by smiling good-naturedly when he was told.

'That's the best news I've heard in a while,' he said with satisfaction. 'Jarvis will dote on a grandchild, especially if it's a boy. The bond is complete.'

'It will be your grandchild, too,' Beth pointed out.

'I am aware of that,' he snapped. 'But I am not in Jarvis's happy financial position, able to shower a child with benefits.'

Beth gazed at him, her heart filled with sadness at the gulf that remained between them, and always would. 'All a child wants is love,' she said quietly. 'To know she is wanted and needed.'

Dan looked away abruptly. He knew she was talking about herself, and also knew he was quite unable to give those things to anyone, even Tommy. Beth had finally gleaned from Mrs Tate that Dan paid little attention to his son, sometimes not seeing him for days. Her heart ached for her little brother, growing up without the reassurance of love from his father.

If only she could find a way to force Dan's hand, and take custody of her brother. She was just about to ask to see him when her father spoke again.

'I'm glad you came today,' he went on, obviously determined to change the subject. 'Whereas I am not a wealthy man, I am now in a position to be able to buy you out, Beth. I want your share of the firm, I think you owe me that.'

'What?' She rose to her feet. It flashed into her mind that she could perhaps bargain her shares for custody of Tommy, but she did not trust Dan enough to suggest it. After the exchange he might well find a legal loophole enabling him to take the boy back. He was devious enough.

The shares were her ace-in-the-hole, a bargaining point against her father, and she had the notion that one day they would be all important. Besides, if she exchanged Tommy for the shares, her marriage to Eynon would have been in vain, and she could not bear the idea of that.

'I admit, your news of the coming child certainly eases my mind as regards Jarvis's intentions,' Dan went on conversationally. 'But I'd feel even safer as sole proprietor of the business. Ten thousand was the price mentioned, I think?'

'A million couldn't buy me out,' Beth said angrily. She had done what he wanted by marrying Eynon; now he was ready to abandon her. 'I married a man I don't love for *your* sake, Father. You won't be rid of me as a partner that easy.' She wanted to hurt him as he was hurting her. 'Besides,' she went on coldly, 'Jarvis still badgers me to sell. I'm considering what I should do for the best.'

Dan's face fell. 'So you do plan to betray me?'

'Betray you?' Beth was furious. 'I hardly think I could beat you at your own game, Father.'

On the next Saturday afternoon, Beth was in Swansea Market, looking at skeins of wool, planning what she would knit for her baby, when someone touched her arm and a familiar voice called her name.

'Bethan kiddo, there's lovely to see you.'

Beth whirled round to see a smiling Maudie, toddler in arms, and another child tugging at her sleeve.

'Oh, Maudie!' Beth was delighted to see her old friend, and kissed both children. 'Listen, I've so much to tell you,' she went on. 'Let's go into the Market Café and have a pot of tea. These two can have an iced bun each.'

Maudie squealed with delight when Beth told her the news.

'I'm so glad you are happy,' she said. 'To tell you the truth, Beth love, I thought you had made a mistake in marrying Eynon. Haydn Howells was sweet on you, you know, all those years ago. I was sure you two would end up together.'

Beth felt a shock go through her at the words, and for a moment didn't know what to say.

'He's still at my mam's place, see,' Maudie went on, cutting an iced bun in half, oblivious to the turmoil she was causing in Beth's mind. 'He's not like he used to be, mun. Never goes out these days.'

'Is he working?' Beth almost choked on the question.

'Oh, aye! Still at the tinplate works. Spends most evenings out the shed, trying to make one of those cat's whiskers wireless things. He can get chamber music, so he says. I tell him to find himself a nice girl instead.'

The idea of Haydn with another woman sent pain stabbing through Beth's heart, and suddenly she understood only too well how he felt about Eynon. She had to see him again. She could not help herself.

'I would like to see him,' Beth said. She knew it was madness even to think of meeting him again, but her growing hunger for a glimpse of him was becoming an obsession.

'Well, why not come up to the house then?' Maudie suggested, looking surprised.

Beth swallowed, feeling guilty. 'No, I don't think that would be a good idea. I don't want to run into Gwyn.'

'Oh, him!' Maudie pulled a face. 'Him and Haydn don't see much of each other any more, not since that day they smashed up Mam's china. Gwyn's living with some fancy piece down in Caer Street.'

'Ask Haydn to meet me somewhere,' Beth said impulsively. She looked around at their surroundings. This café was as good a place as any. No one could read anything bad into two people sharing a pot of tea together. 'Ask him to meet me here next Saturday afternoon, about two o'clock.'

Maudie was staring at her and Beth felt the colour flooding her cheeks. 'Is anything wrong, Beth love?' Maudie asked.

'Of course not,' she said quickly. 'You're forgetting, Maudie, Haydn is my stepbrother after all.'

She couldn't believe he might really turn up, but got to the café early just in case. At two o'clock exactly when the café was beginning to empty after the midday rush, Haydn walked in and looked around.

Beth lifted a hand tentatively and he threaded his way past the tables to come to a halt near her chair, taking off his flat cap, a solemn expression on his face as he looked at her.

'Sit down, Haydn,' she invited with a smile, but he remained standing, his eyes full of pain.

'What's the point of this meeting, Beth?' he asked in a dull voice. 'I don't know why I came. I'm a bloody fool for punishment.'

She tried to smile cheerfully. 'I wanted to see you,' she said lightly, but could not maintain this false cheerfulness and shook her head, feeling her throat choke up with unshed tears. 'Oh, Haydn, I've tried not to think of you,' she exclaimed. 'But I can't help myself. I want you.' She wasn't ashamed to say it frankly. 'I need to talk to you, reassure myself you still love me.'

His sombre expression remained unchanged. 'Aren't you being selfish, Beth?' His tone was harsh.

That hurt, but she knew it was true. 'Yes! Yes, I am being selfish,' she burst out. 'I love you, Haydn, and I want to be with you.'

He glanced around, obviously embarrassed by her rising voice, and hurriedly sat, leaning across the table to speak in lowered tones. 'You can't be with me, Beth. You're a married woman.' He spoke brusquely. 'Aren't you happy in your marriage? Or perhaps it isn't exciting enough for you? You've got to have a bit of rough on the side?'

'Haydn!' Beth was shocked. 'How could you say that to me?'

'I say it because I don't understand what's going on in your mind,' he answered impatiently. 'Maudie told me your good news.' His mouth turned down at the corners. 'I suppose it *is* good news?'

'Of course it is!' Beth bit her lip. They were quarrelling when she wanted the very reverse.

'You can't have it both ways,' he said. 'You made your choice a long time ago. You chose Eynon, so where do I come in?'

Beth countered with another question. 'Why *did* you turn up today, Haydn?'

He put his hands palms down on the table and stared at them silently for a moment. They were large, roughened by hard work. She couldn't help comparing them to Eynon's fine manicured hands. Yet it was Haydn's she longed to feel caress her.

'Because I'm a fool,' he said in a tone of self-mockery. 'I love you, Beth, but I know I've lost you. I feel as though I'm in limbo. Nothing matters any more.'

'My poor darling,' she murmured gently.

'Don't call me that!' he retorted angrily. 'Not when you're carrying another man's child.'

'Don't let's quarrel,' Beth implored. 'Let's just enjoy being together.'

He gave a derisive laugh. 'This is insane! What's the point of it?' He gave her an intense glance, his eyes burning into hers. 'Have you any idea what it's like for me sitting here near you, wanting you, yet unable even to touch your face?'

Beth nodded slowly, sadly. 'Yes, Haydn, I have.'

He sighed deeply. 'I had better go,' he said dejectedly. 'Someone might see us.'

She grabbed at his hand. 'Not yet. I have so much to say to you.'

He squeezed her hand suddenly in both of his until it hurt, but Beth didn't care. The feel of his flesh against hers sent spirals of electricity through her, making her heightened senses reel.

'Oh, Beth *cariad*!' he exclaimed. 'That should be *my* baby you are carrying. You should be *my* wife.' He let her hand go abruptly, and drew back. 'I had no right to say that. I'm sorry.' He rose to his feet. 'Goodbye, Beth.'

She jumped to her feet, too. 'Haydn, meet me here next Saturday, same time. Please!'

'Why torture ourselves?'

'Please!'

His face softened. 'Do you think anyone would notice if I kissed you here and now?' he asked with a wry smile.

Beth looked at him through her tears. 'We could meet somewhere less public next time.'

He started. 'What are you suggesting, Beth?'

She shook her head. 'I don't know. But I must see you again, if only for a moment or two.' She stepped a little closer to him. 'I'll be here waiting next Saturday, Haydn. Don't disappoint me.'

'What about your husband? He'll wonder where you are.'

'I've told him I'm shopping.'

'I hope we won't both be sorry, Beth.'

She waited in trepidation the following Saturday, but felt her heart swell with joy at the sight of Haydn weaving his way between the tables. They managed to clasp hands under cover of theirs, but she could see Haydn was on edge.

'We can't meet here again,' he said when it was time for him to leave, and Beth felt her heart would burst with grief at this parting. 'We're sitting ducks.'

'We can meet near the Cenotaph on the Prom,' she suggested. 'Crowds go there on a Saturday afternoon. We wouldn't be noticed.'

'It's getting colder,' Haydn said doubtfully.

'We won't feel it.' She smiled at him. 'We can stroll, keep moving. I *must* see you.'

They met at the Cenotaph the following weekend and walked along the Prom, even daring to go arm in arm for a while. After that Haydn suggested they vary their meeting place as much as possible: a bench in Victoria Park or a café on the edge of town. Beth lived for Saturday afternoons, trying to draw as much pleasure as she could from the meetings, realising that when her baby was born the following April she might never see Haydn again.

25

Christmas 1922

It was cold sitting on the bench by the small pavilion in Victoria Park, but Beth dismissed the discomfort. The chill air meant there were fewer people around to observe them.

Christmas Day was the day after tomorrow, and she would have to give all her attention to Eynon for a while. Today might be the last time she would see Haydn for weeks, and she waited on tenterhooks for him.

But he was late. He had never been late before. She glanced at the little watch Eynon had given her to celebrate her happy condition. She would give Haydn another five minutes then she must go.

She was about to rise from the bench when she heard the sound of heavy boots on the flagstones on the other side of the pavilion, and her heart leapt with joy. He hadn't let her down.

A figure rounded the corner and her smile froze as she saw Gwyn Howells standing there, grinning at her mockingly.

'Surprised, eh?'

'Where's Haydn?' She clutched at her handbag and jumped to her feet. 'What have you done to him?'

'Your precious Haydn is all right,' he muttered. 'Ma Pickering took a tumble down the stairs this morning, the spiteful old bat,' he added callously. 'Haydn took her to the casualty department at Swansea Hospital. Pity she didn't break her scrawny neck!'

'Oh, I'm sorry about Mrs Pickering,' Beth said. 'Is she badly hurt?'

'How the hell would I know, or bloody care?' Gwyn growled.

'Didn't Haydn send you here?'

'Don't be stupid, will you!' he said disparagingly. 'Of course he didn't. We're not on those terms.' His face darkened. 'And that's your fault, you interfering bitch!'

'Don't call me names, Gwyn. I'm not one of your fancy women.'

'Get off your high horse, missus,' he snarled. 'I can see through you like a pane of glass, and always could. Little Goody Two-shoes you were when Percy was alive, staying in his good books, making sure you got the benefit of whatever money he had.'

'That isn't true, Gwyn. You and Haydn were more Percy's favourites than me.'

'Dah!' Gwyn made an exclamation of disdain. 'I don't want to hear any more from you. Listen to what *I* have to say instead.'

'How did you know I was here if Haydn didn't tell you?'

'I've been following you both for weeks,' Gwyn said. 'I know most of your little meeting places and I know what's been going on behind the scenes as well. And soon that husband of yours will know as much as I do. So will everyone else. You'll be the talk of every chip shop in town by the time I'm through with you.'

'You've been spying on us?' The thought turned her stomach, and suddenly Beth felt frightened.

'That kid you're having,' Gwyn said, 'it's Haydn's, isn't

it? Oh, come on! Don't pretend to be so shocked. I saw what I saw at Ma Pickering's that time. I caught you both, remember?'

'Haydn and me have done nothing wrong!' Beth cried. 'You should know that if you've been following us. We've talked, that's all.'

'You're brazen, you are,' Gwyn sneered. 'Standing by there like butter wouldn't melt in your mouth. I know you met him at Ma Pickering's often when the old girl was out, both before and after you were married. You can't tell me you didn't get up to a little bit more than slap and tickle. What do you take me for?'

'We kissed. And I met him twice, that's all.'

'I don't believe you,' Gwyn mocked. 'And neither will anyone else, especially that snob of a husband of yours. Passing off another man's kid on him, eh? He'll have you out on the pavement, bag and baggage, before you can say bastard.'

Furious, Beth stepped forward and slapped Gwyn as hard as she could across his smirking features. He stepped back, fury in his eyes.

'You dirty little tart!' he yelled. 'That'll cost you, that will.' He took his hand away from his cheek, which already showed the reddening imprint of Beth's fingers. 'I want two hundred pounds by tomorrow.'

She was stunned. 'That's impossible!' she panted, appalled. 'It's a fortune. You might as well ask for the moon.'

'Then do like you did before. Get what you can – for now.' His lips curled into a snarl as he saw her hesitate. 'You'd better if you don't want every man-jack sniggering over the juicy bits in every pub back-parlour hereabouts.' He grinned nastily. 'People like to believe the worst, Beth. It makes them feel good about themselves.'

Remembering how some people had reacted to news of her illegitimacy, she knew that was only too true.

'Tomorrow is Sunday, Christmas Eve,' she said miserably, knowing she had to resign herself to paying up. 'I can't get hold of any money for days. Use your common sense, Gwyn, if you've got any.'

'That's enough lip from you,' he retorted in a dangerous tone. 'All right, then. I'll take it the day after Boxing Day, without fail.'

'*No!*' Suddenly Beth felt her stubborn streak coming to the fore. Why should she give in? She had been a coward for too long, afraid of Gwyn's lies, but enough was enough. She would not allow him to take anything more from her. 'There's no more money, Gwyn. You've had too much out of me already.' Her heart was racing as she saw fury in his eyes. 'You'd better get out of Swansea,' she warned nervously. 'Because when Haydn hears about this, he'll kill you.'

'Don't make me laugh!' he sneered. 'My little brother couldn't fight his way out of a brown paper bag.'

Now she had made a stand she was determined to be strong. Let Gwyn do his worst. She would face it, head held high. It was better than bowing down to blackmail. 'You'll get nothing from me, so push off!'

His expression darkened. 'I'm warning you, Beth. I'm determined to get what I should have had years ago, and would have had if it weren't for you.'

'I'm sick of you blaming me for your own short-comings,' she snapped. 'Perhaps if you had shown more respect and love for Percy it might have been a different story. You've got no one to blame but yourself, so live with it!'

'You hard-faced little hussy!' He stared at her for a long moment, vexation in his eyes. 'I'm going straight to your husband this very day,' he said at last. 'I'll tell him everything.'

'Eynon won't believe a word,' Beth said, although she could hardly breathe for fear. 'He knows what a rotten swine you are. He'll throw you out on your ear.'

'Are you so sure of that?' he asked mockingly. 'Are you prepared to take that chance?'

Beth lifted her chin defiantly. 'Yes, I am. You're all talk, Gwyn, and people, especially Eynon, know you for a loser and a cringing coward.' She shook her head. You won't tell Eynon any of your filthy lies. You haven't the guts to face him.'

Rage in his eyes, Gwyn took a step towards her, his fist raised. 'I ought to smack you silly,' he rasped.

'Lay a finger on me, Gwyn, and I'll scream for a bobby.' Beth remembered that there was a police box just beyond the park hedge. 'How would you like to spend Christmas in Swansea Prison?'

He backed away. 'You're going to be bloody sorry for this, Beth, bloody sorry.' Then he turned and ran off.

As she walked away, Gwyn's parting words rang in her ears as though to torment her. 'You're going to be bloody sorry.' She had no inkling at that moment just how prophetic these words would prove to be.

Ada looked flushed and excited when Beth returned to Windsor Lodge. 'I've had a letter,' she began breathlessly. 'From our Gloria.' Her plain face was wreathed in smiles. 'She wants to come home.'

'Oh, that's wonderful, Ada. I'm so pleased for you.' Beth touched her arm, knowing how much it meant to her friend to hear at last from the daughter she had idolised. 'I know you have been lonely with poor Bert locked away for so long.'

Ada nodded, her eyes filling with tears. 'Yes, I have some of my family back at last. The only thing is . . .'

Beth's face fell. 'Oh, don't tell me Syd Woods is coming back, too? We must tell the police, Ada.'

She shook her head. 'Gloria says the dirty scoundrel abandoned her months ago, before her – before her baby was born.'

'Oh, Ada!'

She nodded mournfully. 'I'd have given anything to have spared her that shame. Her father will be heart-broken. He doted on her.' She gazed at Beth, deeply agitated. 'I know our Gloria was horrible to you, Beth, but can you find it in your heart to forgive her? Windsor Lodge belongs to you, but it's the only home our Gloria has ever known. You wouldn't refuse her a roof over her head, would you?'

'Of course not,' Beth said quickly. 'Write back straight away and tell her to come home.'

Ada gave a nervous titter. 'As a matter of fact, Beth love, I answered her letter last week. Our Gloria arrived here about an hour ago,' she said hesitantly. 'Up in my room, she is, and her baby with her. A little girl, four months old. A lovely little thing, mind, despite having a dirty dog for a father.'

With a laugh, Beth hugged the older woman. 'Your Christmas is made, then,' she said. 'You have your heart's desire. You've got your daughter back.'

'Come up and see her, Beth,' Ada begged. 'Show there's no hard feelings.'

Gloria looked at her apprehensively when Beth walked into the bedroom. She was thinner and her prettiness had lost its shine. Her blonde hair, once so bouncy and curled, was lank, pulled back in a bun at the nape of her neck. Beth felt only pity, seeing that the other girl had suffered.

'Hello, Beth,' she began hesitantly. 'I hope it's all right . . .'

'Welcome home, Gloria,' she said quickly to dispel any doubt, and then her gaze fell on the baby, such a pretty, doll-like creature that her heart was captured. 'Oh, the little darling!' Beth breathed. 'Can I hold her? What's her name?'

'Patricia,' Gloria, said, sounding a little more confident. 'Six pounds she was. Popped out like a pea. You're expecting, too. Married well-off, Mam says.' There was no rancour or challenge in her voice now. She certainly *had* changed.

Beth's smile was weak. 'Yes, but money isn't everything.'

That evening Beth sat for a while looking at the tall Christmas tree standing in the corner of the sitting room in Gower Road. If only Tommy could come and spend Christmas with them, it would be wonderful. Perhaps she would visit Dan tomorrow and suggest it. She would not mind if Mrs Tate came along too. Dan could hardly blame her for asking. It might be the beginning of a new and freer arrangement.

Beth gazed into the flames of the fire, trying to see into the future. There was one faint ray of hope – her child. This time next year would hopefully be a time of happiness, spent with her child, her husband and perhaps Tommy, too.

Beth felt a touch of sadness. Would another year as Eynon's wife help her to forget her love for Haydn? At the moment she could not envisage that, but the presence of a child in her life must help to ease her longing for such forbidden joys.

The house seemed very quiet suddenly. Jarvis was at

his gentlemen's club for the evening, while Eynon had reluctantly gone into town for a seasonal drink with friends.

With a sigh, Beth took up the book she had been reading earlier, glad of the peace and quiet, and had just turned the page when the door opened and Stark came in.

'Beg pardon, ma'am, but a person has called, insisting on seeing Mr Eynon,' the butler said in his measured tones. 'I have explained that he is out, but he refused to believe me.'

'Who is it?' Beth asked.

'Says his name is Howells, ma'am,' Stark said. 'Quite agitated, he is.'

Beth's heart turned over in her breast. Gwyn! He had come to carry out his threat. 'Send him away!' she cried, rising to her feet. 'Get rid of him, Stark. He is not welcome here.'

'Very good, ma'am.'

He disappeared, closing the door behind him, but Beth ran to it, opening it a crack to hear what was being said in the hall. Loud voices were heard, Stark remonstrating with someone, and then a voice called loudly, 'I demand to see Eynon Prosser-Evans, damn you.'

Recognising Haydn's voice, Beth rushed out into the hall. Stark was on the point of manhandling the visitor to the door with Haydn protesting loudly. She stared at him astounded.

'Haydn! What are you doing here?'

He turned to her, a stubborn expression on his face. 'I've come to face your husband and I won't go until I have,' he said gruffly, struggling in Stark's grasp. 'Tell this lout to take his hands off me before I do him an injury.'

'It's all right, Stark,' Beth said shakily. 'I'll deal with this.'

'With all due respect, ma'am,' he said to her huffily, 'I believe the master would prefer it if this man left now.'

'I'll see him myself,' Beth said more firmly. 'He's my stepbrother.'

Stark raised his eyebrows and stepped back. 'Very good, ma'am.' With that he turned and disappeared through a door at the back of the hall.

'You'd better come into the sitting room and explain yourself,' Beth said to Haydn, still feeling shaky at the shock of seeing him here. 'What do you think you're doing?'

In the sitting room she put another small log on the fire and then stood with her hands clasped in front of her, gazing at him expectantly. He had taken off his flat cap, and held it against his chest.

'Take your coat off,' Beth suggested, 'or you won't feel the benefit when you go out.'

'This isn't a social call so stop acting like the lady of the manor,' he snapped. 'I'm not impressed by all this.' He gestured with one arm. 'Grand pianos, butlers and God knows what. You were born in Libanus Street in a two-up, two-down. Or maybe you'd rather everyone forgot that?'

'There's no need to insult me, Haydn,' she said tightly. 'You weren't invited here, remember? I'm the one who should be angry, and I am.'

He paused, looking at her, and the tension left his face. He shuffled his feet. 'I'm sorry, and I can understand your anger,' he said awkwardly. 'After me not turning up in the park this afternoon, but there was a very good reason . . .'

'I know the reason,' Beth interrupted quickly. 'Gwyn

told me about Mrs Pickering's accident. He turned up in your place.'

'What?' Haydn started.

She nodded. 'He demanded money again . . .'

'Again? What do you mean?'

Beth's shoulders drooped. 'He's been blackmailing me for months. Now I'm expecting Eynon's child, Gwyn is demanding even more money. He threatened to tell Eynon that the baby is yours not his.' Beth spread her hands helplessly. 'I refused to meet his outrageous demands this afternoon, so I thought he'd come to carry out his threat.'

Haydn struck one fist forcefully against his other palm. 'The rotten swine. I'll kill him!'

'Oh, let there be no more violence between you,' Beth begged. 'I can't bear it.'

'He's got to be stopped . . .' Haydn began and then hesitated, staring at her wide-eyed. 'I can't go on with this game of hide and seek, Beth. We've got to settle it one way or another. That's why I am here. I came to tell Eynon the truth. We love each other and he *must* let you go.'

'Are you mad?' she asked in dismay. 'Eynon would never let me go, and even if he did, he would take my child from me. I couldn't go on living if that happened.'

'Isn't my love enough?'

Beth ran to him. 'Oh, Haydn, my darling, your love means everything to me, but no woman could bear giving up her child. It's unnatural, inhuman. You didn't really expect it, did you?'

He caught at her upper arms and drew her to him, holding her close. 'Of course I didn't,' he said raggedly, looking deep into her eyes. 'I'm not an unfeeling monster. But I want us to be together as a family, or else . . .'

'Or else what?'

'Or else it must end between us, Beth. I must go away and forget you, if I can.' He shook his head. 'The way we live now is tearing me apart. I came here tonight in desperation.'

Beth eased herself from his embrace and turned away. 'I am willing to endure it myself,' she said quietly. 'Just so long as I can see you sometimes, talk to you, hold your hand.'

'Yes, but you have a life apart from me,' he said bitterly. 'You have a loving husband and a child on the way. You already have a family. I have nothing.'

Beth whirled to face him, her heart aching for the despair in his voice. 'Oh, Haydn, forgive me for my selfishness.'

'I will if you come away with me, Beth, tonight,' he pleaded, seizing her again, holding her hard against his chest. 'Just give up everything, for the sake of our love. Can you do that?'

'Do you realise what you're asking of me?' she cried in distress. 'Everything I have worked for would be left behind – friends, family, my business . . .'

Abruptly he held her away from him. 'Yes, you're Dan Henshaw's daughter all right,' he said bitterly. 'Love must take second place to the almighty profit.'

'Haydn, that's not fair. I've put my marriage in jeopardy for you these last months, because I love you. I thought you understood my predicament.'

He stepped back, half turning to the door, his expression dark with anger. 'You want it all, Beth, that's your problem. A wealthy husband and me as a devoted would-be lover on the side. You carry on as if I have no feelings, as if you expect me to be content with the leavings from Eynon's table.'

'That's a horrible thing to say,' she cried.

'I'm going now, Beth,' he said, marching to the door. 'We won't be meeting again, I promise you.' He glanced at the glittering Christmas tree, the wrapped parcels at its foot. 'Enjoy playing happy families. Perhaps Dan Henshaw's philosophy is right: money is more powerful than love. Enjoy it while you can.'

He snatched open the door and strode swiftly across the hall. Beth ran after him. 'Haydn, don't go yet! Not like this, please.'

But in a moment he was through the door and gone, slamming it after him.

The taxi turned into the driveway of his house in Gower Road, and Jarvis Prosser-Evans gave a sigh of satisfaction. Evenings at the club were all very well, enjoying a joke and a drink with old friends, but he loved the quietness of his house. Next year things would be very different with a young one shattering the peace. But he looked forward to the prospect. Eynon's son – and the child would be a boy – would carry on the family name and business, and that was all he wanted out of life now.

As the taxi chugged up the drive Jarvis saw a man dressed in working clothes hurrying pell-mell away from the house. Jarvis thought, from the width of the man's shoulders, that it was that rascal Gwyn Howells, then realised that this man was taller.

Jarvis paid off the cabbie and went inside, glancing at his pocket watch as he stepped into the hall. Five minutes to eleven. Stark was there to take his coat.

'Someone's been here,' he said to the butler.

'A Mr Howells, sir,' Stark said. 'Asking for Mr Eynon. Mrs Prosser-Evans dealt with him.'

So it *was* Gwyn Howells, Jarvis thought. What the devil did he want with Eynon?

'Where's my daughter-in-law?' he asked shortly.

'In the sitting room, sir.'

Jarvis went into the room to find Beth sitting hunched in a chair, staring into the flames of the fire.

'You've had a caller, name of Howells,' he began questioningly.

To his surprise she jumped to her feet. 'Howells?' She shook her head emphatically. 'No, there was no one.'

Jarvis frowned. 'Stark was sure of the name.'

'No.' She shook her head again.

'There *was* a man. I saw him myself,' Jarvis rasped. 'It was Gwyn Howells, wasn't it? He's a nasty customer. I don't want him in my home.'

'It was no one.'

'Why are you lying, Bethan?' Jarvis snapped. 'Who are you protecting?'

'I'm not lying.' She sounded confused. 'Stark is mistaken about the name, that's all.'

She looked very pale and Jarvis was more puzzled than angry. Why would she dissemble for Gwyn Howells?

'What's the matter? What did he do or say? Did he make threats?' he asked. 'He must have said something. You look as though you've had a shock.'

'Shock?' Beth seized on the word eagerly. Her hands, clasped to her breast, were shaking. 'Yes, that's right. I've had a shock.'

'Do you want a brandy to steady your nerves?' He was suddenly concerned for the precious child she carried. His future depended on that child.

She shook her head. 'It was my friend Maudie's husband who just called,' she said rather breathlessly. 'Teifi Roberts. He came to tell me that Mrs Pickering, that's Maudie's mother, is in hospital after a bad fall.'

Beth turned towards the fire again. The movement of

the flickering flames on her face gave Jarvis the illusion that she was weeping. 'I must go and see her after Christmas.'

'You seem very upset over a mere fall.'

'She is my oldest friend,' Beth replied as though that explained everything. She moved towards the door. 'I won't wait up for Eynon tonight,' she went on, 'I have a headache starting. If you will excuse me, Jarvis?'

He watched her hurry from the room, his eyes narrowing. Beth was such a straightforward girl, yet tonight he was sure she was hiding something from him, lying even. He would talk to Eynon about it first thing in the morning. He would not tolerate being kept in the dark by his own family.

26

Eynon paused in the doorway of the fashionable Metropole Hotel in Wind Street, anxious to say good-night to the company and be on his way home to Beth.

He took his hunter out of his pocket and glanced at it. Ten-forty-five already. He had not wanted to leave her alone on this Saturday evening before Christmas but she had insisted he should meet his friends and business associates for a celebratory drink at the festive season as he had always done. Next Christmas he would have the duties of a father.

A young lawyer of his acquaintance, who was leaving at the same time, noticed the gesture with the watch. 'I'd be in a hurry to get home, too,' he said jocularly, 'if I had a wife like yours waiting.'

'Well said!' an older reveller remarked. 'I say, Prosser-Evans, you must bring that stunning little wife of yours to dinner at my place soon. My old girl is dying to meet her.'

Eynon touched his fedora in salute and stepped out on to the pavement. 'She's booked up for months,' he said cheerfully. 'Awash with invitations, don't you know.'

The two men followed him out, still chatting, and all three turned left towards the incline of Castle Bailey Street. Eynon walked with them a few yards before turning left again to walk through Salubrious Passage, making for the taxi rank at Rutland Street Station.

'I leave you here, gentlemen,' he said. 'Season's greetings to your families.'

Eynon swung his walking stick as he strode. He was lucky, he told himself. Beth was a girl in a million, and he shivered at the notion that he might never have met her if it hadn't been for his father's obsession with revenge on Dan Henshaw. So good can come out of evil, he thought.

Salubrious Passage was inadequately lit by one gaslight, suspended from a wrought-iron archway halfway down its length. In the faint light which hardly penetrated the darkness the alleyway seemed much longer and narrower than usual, and far from salubrious. He was just passing the doorway of a seedy back-alley pub when a figure stepped out in front of him and Eynon stopped in his tracks, lifting his stick to rest it against his shoulder as a warning.

'Out of my way, ruffian!' he snapped, thinking he had walked into the trap of a street-robber, possibly with a knife.

'You don't get rid of me that easy again.'

Something about the voice and the outline of the man was familiar and Eynon sidestepped to get a better view. The other man moved too and gaslight fell on his face.

Gwyn Howells! Eynon let out his breath in relief to see someone he knew how to deal with.

'Howells, if you are trying to get your job back, you are going about it the wrong way,' Eynon said testily. 'Besides, I wouldn't employ you again if you were the last man standing.'

'You can keep your stinking job,' Gwyn snarled. 'I'm not here for that.'

Eynon tensed. This man had a grudge to settle and had obviously chosen this very night to settle it.

'Don't try anything stupid, Howells,' Eynon warned.

'We're not all that far from Wind Street. It is teeming with revellers, and there are plenty of constables about, too. One yell from me and you are done for.'

'What's the matter, Prosser-Evans? Got the wind up, have you?' Gwyn sneered. 'You posh-boys have no guts for fisticuffs.'

Eynon laughed. 'I was boxing champion at my old school for three years running,' he said confidently. 'I did a bit of bare-knuckle on the side, too. I could punch your lights out in five minutes flat.'

Gwyn took a step back. 'No bloody need to get nasty,' he said, uncertainty in his voice. 'I'm here to do a bit of business.'

'Huh! What business could you possibly have with me?'

'I've got information to sell,' Gwyn said. 'Interesting information, but it'll cost you twenty pounds to hear it.'

Eynon guffawed. 'Twenty pounds? Like hell!'

'All right, a tenner then. It's worth it, I tell you.'

'Get out of my way, Howells.'

Eynon made to step past, but Gwyn moved quickly to bar his way.

'It's information about your wife. Do you want to know the truth about her? The fragrant Beth isn't so fragrant as you think.'

'What?' Eynon roared, and lifted his stick from his shoulder threateningly. 'I don't want to hear my wife's name on your lips again, understand?' he warned. 'Now get out of my way or you'll feel the steel handle of this stick on your skull.'

Gwyn took another step back. 'That kid she's expecting . . . it isn't yours, you blind fool,' he rasped. 'She's been meeting my brother on the sly, even before you were married. She's been in love with our Haydn all along. They've been at it behind your back like a couple of rabbits.'

'You foul-mouthed swine!' Eynon bellowed, lunging forward and swinging the stick at his adversary. 'I'll kill you for that insult.'

The end of the stick caught Gwyn on his upper arm and he yelled in pain. He stared malevolently at Eynon, rubbing his arm.

'You're married to a slut,' Gwyn snarled. 'I've been watching them meeting for weeks. You think you are so damned clever, but you don't even know you've been taken for a lily-livered booby.'

Eynon felt a red rage engulf him and swung wildly with the stick again, aiming at the other man's head. But somehow Gwyn grabbed the end of the stick and with a mighty heave wrenched it from Eynon's grasp, the force of the manoeuvre knocking his fedora from his head.

'The boot is on the other foot now, isn't it?' Gwyn taunted, brandishing the stick like a club. 'Not so brave now without a weapon, are you?'

'You low-life swine!'

'Better a swine than be married to a double-crossing little hussy like Beth,' Gwyn mocked. 'She's no better than a street-walker.'

With a howl like a demented wolf's, Eynon launched himself at Gwyn, attempting to connect his clenched fist to the other's chin. But Gwyn used the stick as a barrier, forcing him back. Eynon had the skill of a boxer, but at close quarters Gwyn's brute strength was telling on him.

Eynon panted as he began circling his enemy in the narrow alleyway. He was seized with a terrible wrath and wanted to kill this man, any way he could.

'I'm going to finish you, Howells,' he snarled as he watched Gwyn nervously turn and turn, keeping pace with his manoeuvres. 'You'll pay dearly for those filthy lies about Beth.'

Suddenly Eynon lunged again, throwing a powerful punch, his long arm reaching out for his adversary's head, bunched fist itching for contact with flesh and bones.

But before he could connect, Gwyn panicked, making a wild sweep with the stick. It caught Eynon on one shin. With a howl of pain, Eynon fell on to his knees. Gwyn stepped back a pace as Eynon looked up at him from where he knelt, straining to find the strength to regain his footing.

'If you survive the beating I'm going to give you tonight,' Eynon growled, drawing in a ragged breath from the pain in his shin, 'you'll spend time in jail, Howells. I promise you. And you'll rot there if I have anything to do with it, you snivelling coward!'

'I take that from no man,' Gwyn shouted. 'You think you are better than me, but you'll bleed just like a pig before I am through with you.'

Rushing forward, he struck viciously at Eynon's upturned face with the stick, the steel handle cutting a deep gash in his temple. Eynon stifled a scream of pain, instinct telling him that if he was to survive this, he must get to his feet. He made a valiant effort to rise, but at that moment Gwyn lunged at him again. Eynon tried to protect his head with his arms but Gwyn beat at him mercilessly, one powerful blow after another on his defenceless head.

'Take that! And that! You toffee-nosed bugger.'

Blows raining down on his head, arms and shoulders, Eynon tried to see through the blood that was pouring into his eyes, feeling a terrible weakness overcoming him. He glanced up in terror to see Gwyn holding the stick poised above his head with both hands, the gaslight glinting off its lethal steel handle. The expression on Gwyn's face revealed a man out of control, beyond pity, bent on murder.

As the stick came rushing down towards him through the cold night air, Eynon had one final thought and spoke it aloud: 'Beth, my darling, I love you.'

Enraged by the words, Gwyn struck again and again at the other man's head until, exhausted, he stepped back, panting.

'There, you prissy weakling!' he hissed in derision. 'Let *that* be a lesson to you. You'll think twice before you insult a real man again.'

His adversary lay stretched out face down on the cobbles of the alleyway, unmoving. He's faking it, Gwyn thought. He's had enough, the coward.

He was suddenly aware of movement at the Wind Street entrance to Salubrious Passage, where the new electric streetlights illuminated the wide roadway. People were coming out of the nearby pubs and hotels. Some might come this way.

'Get up, Prosser-Evans,' Gwyn said to the fallen figure. 'Face me like a man.'

But Eynon remained motionless. Impatiently, Gwyn stepped towards him and kicked at the prone body. 'Get up, damn you!'

He kicked again, and when there was no movement knelt down to turn Eynon over on his back. Gwyn flinched at the sight of his bloodied head and almost unrecognisable face illuminated in the gaslight, his own heart contracting with fear. The man couldn't be dead!

Suddenly, figures appeared at the entrance to the alleyway; two men with arms linked, singing a Christmas carol, staggered towards him. They were too far away to have spotted him yet, but within a moment they would be on him.

Gwyn jumped to his feet and, throwing down the stick, turned and fled, running pell-mell along the alleyway away from them towards York Street. He had to get away, well away. he must get to Caer Street as quickly as possible. His woman would vouch for him if it came to the crunch. She would swear he had been with her all evening. As he ran he felt sick to his stomach.

Duw annyl! He had killed a man.

Beth woke suddenly and sat up in bed, wondering what had disturbed her. She reached out a hand to Eynon lying beside her, only to realise he had not come to bed. Switching on the bedside lamp, she looked at the clock. It was gone midnight. What was keeping him downstairs? Jarvis must have waited up for him. They were probably talking together in the sitting room. But the room was in darkness when she went to investigate, as the rest of the house appeared to be, and it was obvious Stark had gone to bed, too.

Beth shivered as she stood in the silence. Eynon had promised he would not be late home. Perhaps he had gone to Jarvis's room.

Beth approached her father-in-law's door, expecting to hear conversation, but everything was silent. Her own apprehension growing, she knocked at the door and then, taking courage, opened it and walked in. The room was in darkness, and suddenly she felt a great fear engulf her.

Something was very wrong.

Stumbling towards the bed, Beth reached out and shook Jarvis by the shoulder, her panic rising. 'Jarvis! Wake up! Where is Eynon?'

It took a few seconds for her to rouse him to his senses,

and he was obviously confused at being woken so abruptly. 'Stark? Is that you, man? What the devil do you mean by it?' He sat up and switched on the bedside lamp to stare at her in astonishment. 'Beth! What are you doing?'

'Where is Eynon?' she asked, her panic growing. 'He hasn't come home. What's happened?'

He waved a hand at her, indicating she should turn her back as he got out of bed. The next moment he stood before her in his dressing gown. 'Now what is that all about, Beth?'

'Eynon hasn't come home,' she said breathlessly. 'At least, he doesn't appear to be in the house. Do you know where he might be?'

'You're panicking for nothing,' he said impatiently. 'Eynon is a grown man. He can stay out late if he wants to.' He glared at her. 'You're not suggesting he's with another woman, are you?'

'Something is wrong, I tell you. I can feel it,' Beth said in agitation, ignoring the remark. 'We must do something. Rouse Stark from bed, he must go to the police station. It's gone midnight. Eynon has never stayed out as late as this since we've been married.'

Jarvis looked sceptical but moved towards the door. 'I'm going downstairs for a brandy,' he announced. 'I'll have a hell of a job getting back to sleep now.'

They were both on the staircase when the front door bell rang.

'There, you see!' Jarvis said testily. 'That's Eynon now. Let him in.'

'But he has a key,' Beth said, fear engulfing her. 'He wouldn't ring the bell at this hour.'

It rang again and Beth hurried to answer it. Two men stood in the shelter of the porch. One wore a long black overcoat and a bowler hat while the other was in uniform. A police constable!

'What's happened?' she cried.

'Is this the residence of Mr Eynon Prosser-Evans?' the man in the bowler asked.

'Yes, yes.' Beth swallowed hard, her mouth suddenly dry with dread. 'I'm Mrs Prosser-Evans. What's happened?' she asked again.

'We'd like to come in, please,' the man said solemnly. 'I'm afraid we have bad news.'

Beth stood aside and the two men came in. Jarvis, standing at the foot of the stairs, stared at them, his face turning white. 'Oh, my God, what is it? I am Eynon's father.'

'Is there a room where we can talk, sir?' the older man said. 'I think you'd both better be seated.'

'What is it?' Jarvis shouted. 'Damn it, speak out!'

Beth took his arm. 'Jarvis, please!' She led him towards the sitting room. 'Come this way,' she said to the two policemen.

They both sat down while the policemen continued to stand.

'I am Inspector Edwards and this is Constable Baker.' The inspector cleared his throat. 'There was an incident in the town earlier tonight involving Mr Prosser-Evans,' he went on. 'He was attacked and beaten badly with his own walking stick. He was discovered almost immediately afterwards, it seems, but on arrival at the hospital was found to have died of his injuries. I am sorry.'

Beth sat feeling as cold as stone, one hand over her mouth, staring at the inspector. Eynon was dead? No! It couldn't be true.

'It's a mistake,' she blurted. He couldn't be dead. Their child would be born within months. 'It must be a mistake.'

'I'm sorry, ma'am,' the inspector said gently. 'He was identified by papers on his . . . person.' He paused, glancing at Jarvis. 'We thought at first it was a robbery, but nothing seemed to have been taken. He still had his wallet on him containing a large sum of money, and his hunter was still in his pocket. An expensive-looking watch it is, too. A thief couldn't fail to see its value.'

'Did he . . . suffer?' Beth asked, the horror of it making her skin prickle.

'It's hard to say, ma'am,' Inspector Edwards said carefully. 'I'd rather believe he died quickly.' He paused again. 'The thing is, since this crime appears not to be connected with a robbery, we wondered if Mr Prosser-Evans had any enemies who might wish to do him harm?'

'Gwyn Howells,' Beth blurted. The name popped out of her mouth before she could think straight, and she immediately regretted it. If Gwyn were questioned, Haydn might inadvertently be involved. That was the last thing she wanted.

'That's right,' Jarvis agreed emphatically. 'Eynon sacked the man for – misconduct at work. There was a great deal of bad feeling on Howells's part. In fact, he hated my son.' Jarvis turned to look at Beth. 'Howells may have come to the house earlier in the evening. A man did call asking for my son. Is that not so, Beth?'

'No!' she exclaimed vehemently, and shook her head. 'Gwyn Howells was not here last evening, I swear it!'

The three men stared at her, and Beth struggled to regain her composure, feeling guilty at the subterfuge. 'My friend's husband called, that's all.'

'What's his name, ma'am?'

Beth licked her lips, panicking. 'Is it really necessary for you to know? It has nothing to do with my husband.'

Inspector Edwards looked at her with narrowed eyes that were knowing and worldly wise. 'Your husband has been murdered, ma'am. I don't ask unnecessary questions.'

Beth swallowed, realising she was raising suspicion in his mind. 'Of course, Inspector. It's the shock, you see. I can't think straight.' She gave him Teifi Roberts's name and address, while praying he would not make enquiries. She was a fool to lie to the police but what else could she say in front of Jarvis?

'Were there any witnesses?' he asked. His voice was just a croak, and Beth knew he was barely keeping his self-control.

'A man wearing working-men's clothes was seen running into York Street from the direction of Salubrious Passage round about the time the crime occurred.' Inspector Edwards's glance flickered over Beth. 'We have a reasonably good description.' He paused. 'This Gwyn Howells,' he asked, 'where can we find him?'

She shook her head. 'I've no idea.'

Inspector Edwards looked impatient. 'The Christmas holidays will hamper our enquiries. I doubt we'll learn much before next Wednesday at this rate.'

Jarvis got shakily to his feet, trembling visibly. 'I want to be kept informed of every development,' he said. 'I want to know when that monster is caught.'

Inspector Edwards paused for a moment outside the house in Gower Road, fingers of one hand drumming on the roof of the new police motorcar he had recently been issued, complete with driver.

He glanced back at the house, all lights now blazing. 'You know, Baker,' he said slowly, 'whenever a woman lies to me I have a prickling sensation at the back of my neck, as my wife knows to her cost. I had the same feeling with Mrs Prosser-Evans.'

Constable Baker replaced his spiked helmet and adjusted the chinstrap. 'She looked devastated, sir,' he said sceptically. 'I can't believe she knows anything about this murder, a lovely young woman like that.'

'She's lying about something,' the inspector insisted. 'But I'll find out what it is, mark my words.' He climbed into the car. 'Get in, man!' he exclaimed impatiently to the constable, who had to take his helmet off again to do so. 'We must trace this Gwyn Howells, and sharpish.'

Beth and Jarvis continued to sit in silence after the policemen had left. He was slumped in an armchair, chin on his chest, and she knew he was weeping. She wanted to comfort him, but couldn't rise from her seat. She felt cold and numbed, as though in a terrible nightmare, unable to wake.

Eynon, the father of her child, was dead. She could not believe she would never see him again. She had lost a good, devoted husband who had loved her dearly and had been so generous. She had not been in love with him but she had become fond of him, and had begun to respect him even though he had been largely in the shadow of his father.

Jarvis was openly sobbing now and Beth forced herself to rise, realising Eynon's terrible death was a shock her father-in-law might never recover from. She must get him to his room.

At that moment Stark appeared, in his dressing gown, staring at them in astonishment. His expression turned to one of horror as Beth explained what had happened.

As Stark helped his master to his room, Beth followed up behind. She was worried for Haydn and about the way Inspector Edwards had looked at her when she'd lied about Haydn's visit. Something told her storms lay ahead. She had to weather them somehow, she and her father- less child.

Christmas came and went unnoticed at the Gower Road house. Jarvis refused to leave his room over the next few days, and turned away the trays of food Beth had sent up.

Arrangements for the funeral had to wait until the day after Boxing Day, Wednesday, when it was set for the following Wednesday. Despite her own grief, Beth saw to it all, as Jarvis seemed unable to accept that Eynon was gone from their lives.

She did not go to meet Tommy and Mrs Tate that Wednesday, being too upset at the tragedy that had befallen her, and knew she would be unable to see her brother the following week either because of Eynon's funeral. She fretted at what Dan would make of it all, and what the coming year would bring. What did the future hold for her and her unborn child now? She could not even guess, could only weep for Eynon and wait.

Caer Street was among the many higgledy-piggledy streets surrounding Cwmfelin Steelworks. The house Inspector Edwards was making for resembled a hundred others in the area, its once rich-coloured poll stone black- ened by decades of industry, but even that was hidden now by the early-morning darkness.

It was two days after the Christmas holiday, and Edwards was determined to catch Gwyn Howells before he left for his morning shift at the tinplate works. He could not help yawning as he got out of the back seat of the police motorcar. Not only was it far too early for him to be up, it was perishing cold, too.

At a nod from the inspector, Constable Baker gave the

doorknocker a good rat-tat-tat and kept on knocking. A blousy-looking woman, her blonde hair in curling rags, opened the door eventually, clutching her dressing gown close at the neck.

'What's the matter?' She peered at them suspiciously. 'What do you want at this hour?'

Constable Baker put his foot over the threshold. 'This is Inspector Edwards,' he announced. 'He wants a word with Gwyn Howells. Is he here?'

'He's shaving,' she said. 'Hey, hold on a minute!' She stared as the constable pushed his way into the narrow passage, followed by the inspector, forcing her to step back. 'Where do you think you're going?'

As they came into the passage, a man in hobnailed boots clumped down the stairs.

The woman turned to him. 'What's this, Gwyn, mun? Why are the police here at this hour?'

Gwyn Howells shrugged his shoulders. 'How do I know! Have you been shoplifting again, Gertie?'

'Hey!' She looked appalled, and swung around to give the inspector a frightened look. 'He's only joking, mind,' she said hastily. 'I've never shoplifted in my life.'

'Our business is a bit more serious than that,' Inspector Edwards said gravely. 'Where were you last Saturday night, Howells?'

Gwyn rubbed his jaw with his thumb. 'Let's see now.' He seemed to be trying to recall. 'Oh, yes, I remember. Gertie and me spent the evening at home.' He turned to the woman. 'Didn't we, Gertie?' He glanced back at the inspector. 'Got a couple of bottles of stout in, we did. Had a good night, too.'

'Is that right?' Edwards asked the woman.

She nodded eagerly. 'Yes, that's right. Played cards, we did, then went to bed early.'

Edwards felt the hairs on the back of his neck rise, and his skin prickled. 'I don't believe you,' he told her. She began to splutter indignantly, and he turned away to look at Gwyn Howells.

'A man named Eynon Prosser-Evans was murdered Saturday night,' he said to Gwyn. 'We know you had a grudge against him. You were seen running from the scene.'

Gwyn shook his head vehemently. 'It wasn't me. I was here with Gertie. She'll swear to it, I tell you, on a stack of Bibles if you like.' He hesitated as though reluctant to go on. 'Maybe it was someone who looks a lot like me, though,' he said.

Edwards laughed. 'That's rich.'

'No, listen!' Gwyn said. 'Yes, I did have a grudge against Prosser-Evans at one time because he sacked me unfairly. I wouldn't kill him for that, mind. But I know someone who would really like to see him out of the way.'

'Oh, yes. And who would this be?' Edwards was sceptical. Gwyn Howells looked big and strong enough to have carried out such a ferocious attack.

'My own brother Haydn,' he said, surprisingly.

Edwards was startled. 'What?'

'Haydn and Beth, that's Mrs Prosser-Evans, have been carrying on behind her husband's back since before she got married,' Gwyn said emphatically. 'She's expecting but it isn't Prosser-Evans's kid, see.' He shook his head, his smile triumphant. 'No, the real father is our Haydn. He and Beth want to get married, see. Now there's a good reason to want her husband dead, isn't it?'

Edwards was silent for a moment. He was certain Mrs Prosser-Evans had lied yet he would have sworn Gwyn Howells was the man they were after. But this new accusation needed looking into. 'You're giving your own brother up very easily, Howells,' the inspector said heavily.

'I don't want to,' Gwyn said with a shrug, 'but I can't condone what he has done.' He shook his head. 'Murder? No, I can't shield him any longer.'

Edwards looked at Gertie. 'Will you swear on oath that this man here was with you all last Saturday night?'

She lifted her chin and sniffed. 'Of course I swear it. I'm no shoplifter, and no liar either. Gwyn was with me all that evening, and all night as well.'

'Where does your brother live?'

'He lodges in Libanus Street.' Gwyn gave him the number of the house. 'Works in the tinplate, like me. I know for a fact that he's working nights this week.' He glanced at the clock on the mantelpiece. 'He'll be just getting home now.'

Beth was finishing her meagre breakfast on Friday morning when Inspector Edwards called with some news.

'I'll see the inspector in the sitting room,' she told Stark gravely. 'And then tell Mr Prosser-Evans that they're here.'

Jarvis had not been in to business or even about the house since the night Eynon had died, but she was sure he would want to be present to hear all that the police had to say.

Inspector Edwards strode into the sitting room followed by a constable. 'Good morning, ma'am,' the inspector began. 'I've called with important news.'

'Please sit down,' Beth said, taking a seat herself. 'My father-in-law will be here in a moment.' The inspector sat but the constable remained standing. 'I take it you've made progress?' she went on.

'We've made an arrest,' the inspector said, nodding.

'But there are more questions to be asked.'

Beth was disturbed by the look he gave her, but at that moment Jarvis hurried unsteadily into the room, unshaven and in his dressing gown. She was shocked to see how haggard he looked.

'Well?' he asked abruptly. 'Have you got the murdering devil?'

Inspector Edwards rose to his feet. 'We're holding a man in custody for the murder of your son,' he said gravely. 'The brother of Gwyn Howells was arrested earlier today. Haydn Howells is now in a police cell and has been charged.'

'Haydn!' Beth screeched, leaping to her feet. 'You've arrested Haydn? Are you mad, Inspector?'

'You know this man then, Mrs Prosser-Evans?'

'Of course I know him. He's my stepbrother, as is Gwyn.'

Inspector Edwards blinked, looking confused. 'Your stepbrother?'

'You fool!' she cried out passionately. 'You've arrested the wrong man!'

Edwards looked angry. 'I think not!' he said stonily. 'You lied to me, Mrs Prosser-Evans. Your butler has already told me that a man named Howells came to this house that night. Haydn Howells might well be your stepbrother, but I know for a fact he's also your lover!'

'What?' Jarvis shouted. 'What the hell is he talking about?'

'He's *not* my lover,' Beth said, panting in fright, staring wide-eyed at each man in turn.

'Haydn Howells came to this house on the Saturday night and you and he plotted together cold-bloodedly to kill your husband,' the inspector accused her loudly. 'You told him where Eynon Prosser-Evans could be found that night. Haydn Howells left here and went straight into town to lie in wait for his victim.'

'It isn't true!' Beth whimpered. 'Teifi Roberts called, not Haydn.'

'That's a lie,' Edwards thundered. 'I've questioned Mr Roberts. He was on afternoon shift at the tinplate works in the Hafod and did some overtime that night. He didn't leave until almost midnight. A score of people will vouch for him.'

'Haydn did *not* kill Eynon,' Beth cried shrilly. 'Gwyn must have done it!'

'He has a witness willing to swear on oath he was with her all night, whereas Haydn Howells has not. His landlady is in hospital. He has no alibi, and he has the oldest motive of all.' The inspector paused to nod solemnly. 'He *is* your lover, Mrs Prosser-Evans, isn't he? And he fathered your child. Did your husband find out? Is that why you wanted him dead?' He paused. 'This isn't the first time you've been questioned by the police about a murder, is it, Mrs Prosser-Evans?'

Beth stared at him, speechless with horror and shock.

Jarvis was staring at her open-mouthed, his face white. 'You treacherous bitch!' he bawled. 'It was you and your lover all along.'

He made a staggering lunge towards her, but the constable grabbed at him and held him fast. 'Let's not be hasty, sir.'

Beth put both hands to her throat, feeling her heart pounding, devastated by the look of hatred on Jarvis's face.

'You are completely wrong, Inspector,' she said, struggling to overcome the breathlessness of panic. 'Though I admit I was wrong to lie to you before. Yes, Haydn was here that night. He came to see Eynon.'

'Now why would he do that?' Edwards looked sceptical.

'Haydn isn't my lover, not in the sense you mean,' she insisted. 'But we do love each other, and he wanted Eynon to let me go.' She shook her head vehemently. 'But I would never have left my husband, who really *is* the father of my child.'

'You're lying, you trollop!' Jarvis shouted. 'Get out of my house tonight, you and your unborn bastard. Inspector, arrest her! She's an accomplice.'

'I can't arrest her,' Inspector Edwards said. 'Haydn Howells denies everything. There is no proof Mrs Prosser-Evans was his accomplice.' He paused. 'At least, not yet. Enquiries are continuing. We are arranging an identity parade . . .'

'Inspector, I beg you,' Beth interrupted, 'question Gwyn again. He's lying! He has made a false statement against his own brother. He is evil, he always was.'

'I am satisfied I have my man,' Inspector Edwards said firmly. 'I may have more questions for you in the morning.'

'She won't be here,' Jarvis shouted. 'I am kicking her out this very day.'

When the inspector and the constable had left the room Jarvis barred Beth's way, his face thunderous.

'You betrayed Eynon as Daphne betrayed me,' he hissed. 'You are as bad as that father of yours. It's in the blood. I should never have let my son marry you.'

'Eynon loved me,' she blurted. 'And I was faithful to him. He knew I wasn't in love with him, but I was very fond of him. He trusted me. I did not betray that trust.'

'No more lies!' her father-in-law shouted. 'Pack your bags. You won't stay another night under this roof. You're no longer family.'

'You've no right to treat me this way. I've done nothing

wrong,' Beth stormed, suddenly angry. 'Haydn and I love each other, yes, but we've not acted shamefully. I never betrayed Eynon. Never!'

Jarvis lifted a hand to silence her. 'I won't listen to any more confounded falsehoods, you Jezebel!' he shouted.

'If there's anyone to blame for Eynon's death, it's you,' she shouted back. '*You* brought Gwyn Howells back into our lives by employing him to do your dirty work – *criminal* work, in fact.'

'Silence, damn you!'

'I won't be silent,' Beth went on. 'Gwyn killed Eynon because of the grudge he held about being sacked, I'd stake my life on it.' She confronted him squarely. 'Face up to it, Jarvis. Your obsession about getting even with my father has killed your only son.'

'No! No, it isn't true,' he stormed. 'You and your lover are responsible.' He shook his fist at her. 'I'll see you both hanged for it.'

Beth was appalled at his malevolence, and trembled to realise he had become a dangerous enemy. Frightened as she was, her thoughts went to her unborn baby. It was unbearable to realise that Jarvis would deny this child as Dan Henshaw had denied her.

'I warn you,' she said solemnly, 'think what you will of me, but don't turn your back on your own grandchild or you'll live to regret it bitterly.'

'I have no grandchild,' he said with a sob. 'I no longer have any family, thanks to your treachery.'

27

Jarvis was implacable, so there was nothing left for Beth to do but take refuge at Windsor Lodge. To her distress, she realised that what had happened to Eynon, and the trouble she was in with the police, was already common gossip in the town. Ada had heard an embroidered version, and was thoroughly wrought up.

'Oh, the disgrace!' she wailed, almost as distressed as Beth was. 'Them coppers are persecuting us!'

'Now, now, Ada,' Phoebe said calmly, patting her friend's thick arm. 'Don't take on so. Beth has done nothing wrong, so the police can't touch her.' She gave Beth a confident look. 'You'll get through it, girl. You've got guts as well as brains, you have. You'll come out of it smelling like roses.'

Beth wished with all her heart that she felt as confident about the outcome.

Ada tutted with disapproval later when Beth insisted on taking up residence in the cosy bedroom behind the kitchen. 'It's a pokey little hole,' Ada exclaimed. 'There's a lovely room vacant on the first floor, overlooking the street. It'll be just right when you have your confinement.'

'My baby will be born right here when the time comes,' Beth said. 'Where I feel safe. In the meantime I need peace and quiet to think and plan. Haydn is innocent and I'll prove it.'

★

Peggy and Elias Morgan came around after tea, to offer their condolences and give what help and comfort they could. Beth could not help breaking down at the sight of their distress. It seemed like only yesterday these friends had shared the wedding feast with her and her groom. Now they spoke of his coming funeral, and Beth felt she would never get over the pity and waste of it all.

On Saturday morning she sent Flossie and Cissie in a taxicab to the house on Gower Road with instructions to bring all her belongings back. Jarvis might think he had finished with her, but she had not finished with him. But first she must await the birth of her baby. She was determined that, one way or another, Jarvis Prosser-Evans would acknowledge and accept Eynon's only child and heir.

A curt note was delivered by hand just after lunch on Saturday. It was from Dan, and Beth read it with dismay. In view of her notoriety in the town, her access to Thomas, his son, was withdrawn indefinitely. She must make no attempt to see him again.

After reading it several times, Beth was furious. Despite Ada and Phoebe advising caution, she hurried around to Brecon Parade to face her father down.

A stunned Mrs Davies answered her knock, and Beth guessed who had delivered the note. 'Mr Henshaw made it clear . . .' the housekeeper began.

'Where is he?' Beth demanded angrily. 'I want to see him now. Out of my way.'

She pushed past the startled woman and into the hallway, marching determinedly towards the sitting room. Dan was not there. Instead, she saw Tommy sitting on the mat before the fireplace, clutching a teddy bear. He looked up and blinked as she came eagerly towards him, obviously unsure who she was.

'Oh, Tommy, my little darling,' Beth burst out. Bending, she lifted him into her arms, held him tightly against her breast and kissed his soft cheek. 'No one will stop me seeing you.'

There were quick footsteps behind her and Mrs Tate appeared, carrying a baby's bottle with orange juice in it. 'Oh, heavens!' she exclaimed. 'I only left Thomas for a minute. Mr Henshaw will be furious to see you here, Beth.' She held out her arms for the child. 'Give Thomas to me.'

Reluctantly, Beth handed him over. 'I want to see my father, Mrs Tate. I know he's here somewhere. Is he afraid to face me?'

At that moment she heard a man's footsteps crossing the hall and the next instant Dan burst into the room, his face livid with rage.

'How dare you come here, bringing your disgrace to my house?' he burst out. 'Get out, before I call the police.'

'I'm not leaving until we settle the matter of my access to Tommy. You have no right to ban me. I've done nothing wrong.'

'That's not what I heard. You've been carrying on an illicit relationship with your own stepbrother. Disgraceful! Word is, you colluded in your own husband's death.'

'Ooh!' Beth was knocked back to hear her own father say such a thing. 'How could you even think that?' She paused, staring at him. His glance faltered, and then she understood. 'But you don't really believe that, do you? You're just using it as an excuse to stop me seeing Tommy. You've been waiting for something like this all along.'

He remained silent and Beth rushed on, 'You've already acknowledged to me that you are my father. Why can't you stand by that and publicly support me?'

He jerked his head in Mrs Tate's direction, indicating that she should leave the room. The nanny gave Beth an apologetic glance before hurrying out, taking Tommy with her. Beth thought her heart would break, not knowing if she would ever see her brother again.

'What I said to you in private about our kinship is just that – private between you and me. I'll deny it outside this room.'

'Huh! Everyone knows.'

'No one who matters does,' Dan rasped. 'Like friends and business acquaintances. I have my reputation to maintain – for Thomas's sake.'

'Your hypocrisy is monumental!' Beth shouted.

'Leave my house now,' he ordered wrathfully. 'Don't ever come here again. And never try to see Thomas or I'll be forced to take legal action. Your reputation is besmirched, Bethan. You contaminate anyone associated with you.' He shook his head. 'I always knew it would come to this. You are of weak moral character, like your mother. Now get out.'

With no ammunition left to fight him, Beth left Brecon Parade. In her time of trouble the one person who should have stood by her had turned his back, and grossly insulted her into the bargain. She could feel nothing but enmity for her father now, and a thirst for revenge.

On Monday she telephoned her solicitor, Mr Carradog-Jones. She guessed he was not a man over-fond of revelling, and so was not surprised to find he was at his desk New Year's Day, as any sober, hardworking man would be. She mentioned she might be in some difficulty with the police, and he arrived at Windsor Lodge within the hour.

'Haydn Howells is innocent,' Beth declared to the

solicitor. 'I want you to act on my behalf with the police. They suspect me, won't listen to a word I say in his defence.'

'It looks very bad against him, according to today's *Cambrian Leader*,' Mr Carradog-Jones said dubiously. 'Very bad indeed. And for you, too, Mrs Prosser-Evans, by association. My advice is to deny all connection with Haydn Howells.'

Beth was annoyed. 'I'll never do that! I won't desert Haydn. He's innocent.'

Mr Carradog-Jones's grumpy nature had not improved since she had seen him last. Now he sniffed with disapproval. 'Madam, if you won't take my advice, I see no reason to remain here.'

'You're here to take my instructions,' she told him, waving one hand impatiently. 'The police believe Haydn has no witnesses to his movements that night, but he has. Two very reliable witnesses: Jarvis Prosser-Evans and his butler, Stark.'

'The devil you say!' Carradog-Jones looked interested and took a fountain pen from his breast pocket.

'Stark saw Haydn arrive and leave, and Jarvis saw him go,' Beth went on as the solicitor made notes. 'Haydn left me in the sitting room just before five minutes to eleven that night. The police haven't told me exactly when my husband died.' She paused for a moment, a lump constricting her throat. 'But since I know Haydn is innocent, these witnesses must prove it. Find out the details, Mr Carradog-Jones. Make the police see sense. I believe Gwyn Howells killed Eynon.'

It was the following day when the solicitor called to see her again. 'The police are a stubborn bunch when they believe they have their man,' he said. 'However, I think there is every chance this new evidence will help free Haydn Howells.' He glanced at her cautiously. 'Are you up to hearing the details in your condition?'

'I'm not made of crystal,' Beth said. In fact she dreaded hearing the details of Eynon's death, yet feared Haydn's wrongful conviction even more.

'Eynon was found by two revellers badly beaten in Salubrious Passage that Saturday night,' Carradog-Jones said, eyeing her nervously as though he expected her to faint at any moment.

Beth swallowed hard. 'Go on, please.'

'They saw a figure ahead of them running into York Street,' he went on. 'They heard hobnailed boots striking the flagstones, so concluded it was a working man.'

Beth bit her lip. 'But what time was that?' Haydn's freedom depended on his answer.

'About five minutes past eleven, the witnesses stated.'

'That proves it!' she cried with relief. 'It couldn't have been Haydn. He couldn't travel the two or three miles into town in ten minutes, not even by tram.'

Mr Carradog-Jones held up one hand. 'Yes, but it actually depends on what Jarvis Prosser-Evans and Stark have to say. Haydn Howells's life hangs – if you will pardon the expression – on their testimony.'

Beth clasped her hands together in desperation. 'They *must* tell the truth.'

Surely Jarvis would not lie for spite, just because she loved Haydn? Surely he wanted his son's true killer brought to justice?

Although she knew Jarvis would not approve, Beth was determined to attend Eynon's funeral. She felt she had every right to be at the graveside when her husband was laid to rest. Ada and Phoebe insisted on accompanying her, and so did Peggy and Elias Morgan.

'I'm in my father's bad books at the moment,' Beth told them, understating the facts deliberately to save face. 'If he finds out you're supporting me, or even attending Eynon's funeral, he could make that an excuse to give you the sack, Elias. I don't want you to suffer because of me.'

'Then he can stick his job where the sun never shines,' Elias said rashly. 'I stand by my friends, I do.'

'That goes for me as well,' Peggy said staunchly. 'That man wants his head read, disowning you. I've never liked him, you know. Oh! Excuse me saying that about your father, Beth.'

Beth knew Eynon had been well liked, but was still astonished at the dense crowds of people who attended the funeral.

'It's because he was murdered,' Elias murmured darkly. 'Morbid, that's what I calls it.'

Perhaps Elias was right, Beth thought, but she was glad of the large numbers, among whom she was less noticeable. After the Reverend Thomas had spoken at the graveside, the coffin lowered into the ground and earth thrown down on to the nameplate, the crowds began to disperse. Beth spotted Stark standing alone and hurried to the butler's side.

'Stark.'

He looked startled to see her. 'Ma'am! I had no idea you were present.' He looked about him. 'If you'll pardon my outspokenness, ma'am, I don't think Mr Jarvis will like your being here.'

'I don't care what Jarvis likes,' Beth snapped. 'I want to know if you have spoken to the police? You know full well the time Haydn Howells was at the house that night. He did *not* kill my husband.'

Stark shuffled his feet on the turf. 'Mr Jarvis has forbidden me to speak,' he said. 'On pain of losing my position.'

Beth ground her teeth with fury. 'Is your position more important than a man's life? You must realise Haydn will be hanged if he is convicted. He is an innocent man.'

'Not so innocent,' a familiar voice rasped behind her. Her arm was gripped roughly and she swung around to stare into Jarvis's face. It was livid with fury. 'You have no right to be here,' he went on. His tone was subdued, but she could see his anger was barely suppressed. 'You fallen woman!'

'Your words can't hurt me,' Beth defied him. 'But your silence can kill an innocent man. Your thirst for revenge against Dan has already cost Eynon his life. Now you thirst for Haydn's blood. All for spite! Seeing Haydn hanged because he loved me won't bring your son back.'

'How dare you!'

'I'll dare anything,' she stormed. 'You are committing a crime by keeping silent. You know Haydn is innocent, you malicious old man!'

'It could've been anyone at the house that night,' he retorted. 'It was dark. I couldn't see properly.'

'It was Haydn!' Beth cried out in desperation. 'Let Stark speak out without prejudice.'

'Howells's own brother gave him up,' Jarvis stubbornly persisted. 'No man would do that unless he knew his brother was a killer.'

'Gwyn was saving himself! He's been blackmailing me for months. Had asked me for more money that very afternoon. He threatened to tell abominable lies about me to Eynon when I wouldn't pay up.'

'If that's true, why didn't you go to the police?' Jarvis asked mockingly.

But Beth wasn't listening, her mind travelling back to that awful night. 'It's clear to me now what happened,' she said quietly. 'Gwyn repeated his lies to Eynon there in that alley.' She stared wide-eyed at Jarvis. 'Don't you see! Eynon turned on him, and died defending my honour. He believed in me, Jarvis. Why won't you?'

He stared at her, his expression empty, and then without another word turned and walked away. With an apologetic cough, Stark followed. Beth stared after them, distraught. Her appeal had failed and with it went Haydn's last hope of release. There was nothing more to do but hope and pray for a miracle.

Peggy Morgan came and took her arm. 'Come away now, Beth *bach*,' she said gently. 'It's all over, and you can do no more here.'

'Shall I have a word with the stubborn old bugger?' Elias asked. 'I can talk to him man to man, get him to see sense.'

Beth put a hand on his arm, thankful and grateful for such a loyal friend. 'Thank you, Elias, but no. If Dan found out you had been talking to his arch enemy he would immediately suspect treachery. You would get the sack then for sure.' She looked at Peggy and Elias fondly. 'I don't want to drag you both into this awful mess.'

There was an agonising wait of two days before the solicitor called on her again. Beth wondered why the police had not been around to interview her in the interim. Was that good or bad?

When Mr Carradog-Jones strode into the sitting room, Beth jumped to her feet. 'Is there any news? Any hope?' she asked eagerly.

'Nothing definite,' Carradog-Jones said carefully. 'Prosser-Evans continues to keep silent. I don't think he will ever speak out. You are already condemned as guilty as far as he is concerned, I'm afraid.'

Beth sat down again, shoulders drooping. She had failed Haydn and she had also failed her unborn child. Jarvis Prosser-Evans was pitiless in his condemnation, as Dan had discovered before this. Now, so had she. Eynon's child would never receive his birthright and it was all her fault for loving too deeply. All at once she saw clearly that loving too much had been Esme's failing also.

'There is one development that's promising, though,' Carradog-Jones went on cheerfully.

Beth glanced up at him eagerly, suddenly hopeful, and he gave her one of his rare smiles.

'Gwyn Howells was brought in for questioning earlier today,' he said triumphantly. 'That widow he's living with was caught shoplifting. Apparently she's told Inspector Edwards she wants to give evidence against Gwyn in exchange for leniency with her own misdemeanours. She's admitted her previous statement was a pack of lies.'

'Oh, thank God!'

'Consequently, I believe Haydn Howells's release is a matter of hours away rather than days.' The solicitor paused. 'I've spoken to him. He knows the situation and that his freedom is now more or less assured. He has asked permission from you to come and see you.'

Beth longed to see Haydn again, but knew it was impossible now. Her love for him was just as strong as it had ever been, but Eynon's death had changed everything, overshadowing their love and all their hopes.

'Please tell Haydn I can't see him,' Beth said sadly. 'Tell him I am grieving for my husband.'

28

Mid-May 1923

'How's your mother after her bad fall at Christmas?' Gloria asked sympathetically of Maudie.

It was a Sunday afternoon and Maudie and her two children had come over to Windsor Lodge for tea in a room on the first floor that Beth had taken over for her own private sitting room. Gloria was there, too, with her sweet little girl Patricia, because although Maudie and Gloria were very different, the two young women had become firm friends since the year had begun.

Beth felt riddled with guilt when Maudie glanced in her direction as she answered. 'Much better, thanks.' She sighed. 'She walks with a stick now, though. Poor Mam!'

'Anyone for another cup of tea?' Beth asked hastily, lifting the teapot.

'She'd welcome a visit from you,' Maudie said wistfully, not letting her off easy.

Beth felt very uncomfortable, dumping the teapot back on the tray without a word. She longed to visit her old friend, but while Haydn still lodged there she had kept away. She yearned for a sight of his face, to hear his voice, feel his touch, but knew it would be too much to bear.

'Haydn is working afternoons next week,' Maudie volunteered persistently, her glance knowing as she looked at Beth. 'Mam will be on her own then, and she's longing to see your boy.'

Beth could not resist the appeal in her friend's voice. 'Of course I'll visit her,' she said. 'I should have done so before. Tell her I'll call on Tuesday, but she mustn't go to any trouble, mind.'

Maudie was all smiles, and then she screeched, 'Meirion! Now leave that alone, will you? Meirion!' She jumped to her feet and rushed across the room to her small son. 'Take your sticky little fingers off that vase.' She picked him up and carried him back to the settee. 'That belongs to Auntie Beth, not you.'

Maudie flopped back in her seat, her son clutched to her, but he wriggled free again, giggling happily, eyes gleaming with excitement and mischief, already anticipating his next adventure.

Beth's heartstrings were tugged. She could not help comparing him with her brother Tommy. Grudgingly admitting he had been in the wrong in judging her so harshly over Eynon's death, Dan had permitted her to see Tommy again when she had taken her baby son Rhodri to meet his Grandfather Henshaw the previous week.

Tommy was two years old now and should be full of mischief, but Beth was greatly disturbed to find him an unnaturally quiet and solemn little boy who sat on the rug before the fire, clutching a toy fire engine, staring at her and seeing only someone who called occasionally to see him. All the time she was there he never smiled and hardly moved.

Beth's heart ached for him now. Watching Maudie's energetic and lively son, she knew she must somehow rescue Tommy from her father's loveless household, and she must do it soon.

After her friends had gone she sat on for a while,

nursing Rhodri. He was so beautiful, and so like his father it was uncanny.

As she held him in the crook of her arm, he smiled at her, and her heart almost burst with joy.

Ada insisted that these smiles were the result of wind, but Beth knew better. Each time Rhodri smiled she saw Eynon beaming out at her through his son's eyes. If only Jarvis could see what she saw.

She had written hopefully to her father-in-law, telling him of his beautiful grandson, but had received no response. Jarvis's indifference made her sad at first and then angry. While Rhodri would never be short of anything while she lived, he should not be deprived of what was rightfully his birthright through his father. Jarvis must be made to acknowledge his grandson.

But there was another reason why Beth was determined to bring her father-in-law to heel. Cissie had told her that Jarvis had resumed his dirty tricks campaign against Dan, the episodes beginning directly after she had written to her father-in-law telling him about Rhodri. After all the tragedy that had befallen them Jarvis still had not learned his lesson.

Furious, Beth realised she must settle matters once and for all, and formulated a plan which she hoped would defeat two wily birds in one stroke, Dan Henshaw and Jarvis Prosser-Evans.

But the success of her plan depended on Haydn. Would he agree to what she proposed after the way she had kept him at arm's length since Eynon's death?

As promised she visited Mrs Pickering the following Tuesday, taking Rhodri with her, and was glad she had for her old friend looked much changed, and Beth knew she had suffered and was sorry for her previous neglect.

As she pulled on her gloves to leave, she spoke quietly

to Maudie. 'Would you ask Haydn to come and see me one day next week?'

Maudie looked astonished. 'I thought that was over.'

'It will never be over,' Beth said earnestly. 'I love him, Maudie, but I am also a grieving widow. No, this is a matter of business. Strictly business.'

'Haydn has changed, you know, kid,' Maudie warned. 'He's not the happy-go-lucky chap he used to be. Sometimes he looks – well – like his heart is broken, what with losing you and . . . Gwyn.'

'Oh, don't say that!' Beth exclaimed, aghast. 'What am I to do, Maudie? I can't afford to antagonise Jarvis further.'

It would be as much as she could do to repair the damage already done to their relationship. For Rhodri's sake she must not make things worse. 'I am sorry to my heart that I have hurt Haydn,' she went on.

Maudie touched Beth's arm, looking at her kindly. 'Don't deny yourself happiness, kid. Despite everything you and Haydn were meant for each other. I could see that years ago, even if you two couldn't.'

Beth dropped her gaze, pretending to adjust her gloves, not wanting Maudie to see the tears that were threatening. 'There's a lot at stake for Rhodri and Tommy. I must see them right first. One day, perhaps, Haydn and I will find each other again.'

'Don't leave it too late, Beth,' Maudie told her. 'That's all I'm saying.'

The following Wednesday Haydn came to see her as arranged. He stood just inside the sitting-room door, holding his trilby against his chest. Beth was shocked at the way he looked. He had lost weight and there were dark circles under his eyes. Obviously Gwyn's being convicted and hanged for Eynon's murder had hit Haydn hard. Beth had never seen him look so unhappy, and her heart ached at the sight.

'Come and sit down, Haydn,' she said. She longed to run to him, embrace him, and offer any comfort that she could, but held herself in check. There could only be business between them for the moment. 'Would you like some tea?'

He didn't move but looked at her, his eyes wary. 'Maudie made it clear that this visit was not to be a social occasion. What possible business can you have with me, Beth? Or is this some cruel joke?'

'You know me better than that.'

Should she speak to him about Gwyn? But his brother had cold-bloodedly tried to blame Haydn for the murder, so perhaps condolences were out of place. Yet it seemed hardhearted to say nothing, even if courage failed her for the moment.

'I need your help, Haydn,' she went on quietly. 'But I'll understand if you refuse. I've treated you badly.'

'As if I could refuse you anything,' he said, a tremor in his voice.

He put his hat on a chair nearby and came towards her. Beth trembled. If he tried to embrace her now she would be lost. She moved quickly to press the brass bell button near the fireplace.

'I think we'll have some tea anyway,' she said shakily.

He hesitated in his movement towards her, expression turning even bleaker, and instead sank on to a sofa nearby. 'I wouldn't blame you if you hated the sight of me after what my brother did,' he said miserably.

'I don't hate you, Haydn,' Beth burst out. 'My feelings haven't changed.'

His glance at her was sharp, even a little angry.

'Haven't they? I've seen no evidence of any love these past months.' His voice faltered. 'When I needed you most, Beth.'

'I'm sorry,' she said. 'I wanted to see you, of course I did, but it wasn't wise.'

'Wise?' His voice rose and he shook his head. 'What a cold, calculating way of looking at things. You're turning hard, Beth.'

'No!' She was hurt. 'I'm in a difficult position, but I love you and don't blame you for anything. What happened was Gwyn's doing, and he has paid for it with his life.'

Haydn sat forward suddenly and put his head in his hands. It was two months since Gwyn Howells had been convicted of the murder of Eynon Prosser-Evans and hanged for it. Beth could well understand that the pain and shame of it was still haunting Haydn as Eynon's terrible death still haunted her.

'Well, I can't help blaming myself,' he murmured. 'I should've done something. I should've saved him. My own brother.'

'Stop feeling guilty, Haydn,' she said. 'Gwyn killed my husband, and he was more than ready to see you hang in his place, remember that!'

She spoke more sharply than she'd intended, and he glanced up quickly, his expression darkening. 'Oh yes, I forgot. I am here on business only,' he said pithily. 'Hardly the time or place for sentiment or feelings.'

At that moment, to Beth's relief, Phoebe came in with a tray of tea and some cakes.

'Thanks, Phoebe,' she said gratefully, and the older woman smiled and nodded. Beth said nothing further until they were alone again, after pouring Haydn a cup of tea and handing it to him.

'Your brother is past help,' she said bluntly. 'But my brother isn't. I intend to get Tommy away from Dan, give him a proper life, and at the same time secure Rhodri's birthright. I owe it to Eynon. You must help me.'

'How?'

'I'll use my fifty-one per cent shareholding in Dan's business as bait. Both men desperately want control of it, but I have thought of an alternative.' She explained her plan to him in detail.

'A double bluff!' Haydn looked impressed.

'The first step is to hand the shares over to my son Rhodri, legally signed and sealed, making him Dan's new partner,' Beth said. 'But, of course, he needs someone trustworthy to act for him and look after his interests in the business until he is twenty-one. I don't trust my father.'

Haydn nodded but looked puzzled, obviously still wondering why he was here.

'For obvious reasons, that person can't be me,' she explained. 'I never wanted to work alongside my father in the business, knowing he would vigorously oppose what he would regard as interference from me. He would strongly object if I represented Rhodri now, and Jarvis might be suspicious of my motives, too. So I want you to undertake it, Haydn. Will you?'

'Me! Go into management?'

'Why not?' Beth urged. 'You have no axe to grind with either of them, and neither can object to you.'

'Jarvis might,' Haydn said quickly. 'My brother killed his son.'

'Please, Haydn. Do this for me?'

'But why me, Beth?' He laughed, and it sounded hollow and despairing. 'As a sop to my feelings for you?'

'You know it isn't that.' While she denied it, though,

there was a grain of truth in what he said. It was not a sop, but she knew he saw her money as a barrier between them. Haydn's self-respect was important to him. If he accepted this responsible position, with all the kudos that went with it, he might in time view any future relationship between them in a more favourable light, seeing himself as her equal.

'But I know damn' all about business,' he went on in agitation. 'I'm no more than a tinplate labourer.'

'You are only twenty-four, Haydn, and no fool. You can learn,' Beth exclaimed. 'I did!'

'Despite what you say, Dan will never accept me.'

'Oh, I think he will,' she said with conviction. 'He'll have no choice when he learns the alternative. The thing he fears the most: Jarvis Prosser-Evans gaining total control of his coal yard.'

Haydn looked dubious. 'How legal and binding is this, Beth?' he asked. 'The last thing I want is to find myself in trouble with the law again.'

'The arrangement is perfectly legal,' she told him. 'Carradog-Jones might be a proper misery in person but he is a very good lawyer. You should know that, Haydn. He helped get you free.'

'Yes, and I am grateful, I suppose.'

'Carradog-Jones has devised a loophole,' Beth went on. 'I'll offer each man an ultimatum, which I believe neither will dare refuse. If they do, or either one of them reneges on their agreement with me, I have the power to grab back the shares and dispose of them in any way I wish.'

Haydn shook his head. 'It's too much responsibility, Beth. I haven't the education for it.'

'Neither has Dan,' Beth said. 'Auntie Mae told me he had no more than his sharp wits and a ruthless streak when he came to Swansea looking to make his fortune.'

She rose to her feet and stood before him. 'You're a better man than he can ever hope to be. Please, Haydn. I can't trust anyone else.'

He stood up. 'Will we see anything of each other if I do this? You know how I feel, Beth. It'll be hard keeping my love for you in check.'

'We can't speak of love at present,' she said wearily, turning away. 'I mustn't offend Jarvis any more than I have to, for Rhodri's sake. He should be Jarvis's heir. I hope my plan will secure that for him.'

Haydn gave a grunt of censure. 'That sounds mercenary, Beth,' he said, his tone harsh. 'I thought better of you than to descend into money-grabbing.'

She swung back to flash an angry glance at him. 'If Gwyn hadn't killed his father, Rhodri would be in his rightful place in his grandfather's house right this minute.' She paused suddenly, regretting her sharpness. 'It's not the money, Haydn,' she said more patiently. 'All I want is for Jarvis to recognise Rhodri as his grandson. I won't have him denied, as my own father denied me. I don't care what I have to do.'

She stared at him challengingly, and he stared back, and then she saw his expression soften.

'I do love you so, Beth,' he said gently. 'Particularly when you are in a fighting mood. Your eyes flash like stars.' He nodded. 'I'll agree to take this job just because you ask me.'

Beth felt a great sense of relief flood through her. She wanted to throw her arms around him, but instead moved away to a safer distance.

'You must buy yourself a new three-piece suit and a pair of decent shoes,' she said, trying to control the tremor in her voice. 'Dan must see you as a businessman not a labourer.'

He laughed disparagingly. 'Shoes? A new suit? On the wages I get at the tinplate?'

'I'll lend you some money. No, don't look at me like that!' she exclaimed. 'This is a business arrangement. You can pay me back out of your salary from your new job. Don't forget,' she reminded him, 'as Rhodri's business representative, managing his shareholding, you'll earn almost as much as Dan does.'

The following Friday morning Haydn and Beth turned up at the coal yard. Dan jumped to his feet, scowling, when they came into his office unannounced.

'What the hell do *you* want now, Bethan?' He looked Haydn up and down. 'And who is this man?'

She flushed at the frosty greeting.

'You had better sit down, Father, while I explain,' she said more calmly than she felt, and sat down herself.

Dan waved one hand dismissively. 'Don't make yourself comfortable, Bethan. I've no time or liking for idle chitchat. I've a business to run.'

That was too much! 'Well, if you want to keep on running it,' she exclaimed brusquely, 'you'd better keep quiet and listen to me.'

'What?' Dan's eyes narrowed at her tone and his expression became wary.

Beth took a deep breath. 'I came to tell you I'm no longer your partner,' she said. 'I've disposed of my shares.'

Dan's clenched fist thumped the desk violently. 'I knew it!' he exploded. 'So you've finally sold out to Prosser-Evans? You scheming little bitch!'

'Hey!' Haydn stepped forward from behind her chair, his expression wrathful. 'You watch your foul mouth, mister. I won't have you speak to Beth like that.'

Dan jerked his head, his expression disbelieving. 'Who *is* this person, Bethan? And what's he doing on my premises?'

'This is Haydn Howells, Father,' she replied stolidly. 'Your new partner by proxy.'

'My new . . . !' Dan stared at her. 'Proxy?' He flopped on to his chair. 'What gibberish are you talking?'

Beth lifted her chin in defiance. 'I've made over my shares to my son Rhodri. He's now the majority share-holder.'

Dan blinked and then gave a disdainful guffaw. 'A baby holding shares! This is absurd, woman. Are you trying to make me a laughing stock?'

'There's nothing absurd about it,' Beth persisted. 'I've never wanted any part of this business. I kept the shares simply because they gave me a hold over you, Father. Now they belong to Rhodri and his interests must be protected. Haydn is here to do that. He will manage the shareholding in Rhodri's place until my son is twenty-one, and will act for him in all matters of business. That means, of course, he'll work here daily alongside you, so you'd better find him an office.'

'There's no need for this,' Dan bellowed. 'I won't do Rhodri down.'

'And I say there is every need,' Beth shouted back. 'I don't trust you, Father, not one inch. You'll accept my terms or suffer the consequences.'

Dan stared open-mouthed for a moment, looking from one to the other, temporarily bewildered, and then his expression darkened in fury. 'Like hell I will!' he stormed 'Get out, the pair of you. I'll see my lawyer today. I'll fight this. It's not legal.'

'Don't do anything rash, Father,' Beth warned in a hard voice. 'I retain the right to repossess the shares at any time. If you oppose this move in any way, I swear I will *give* control to Jarvis, unconditionally, and let him do his worst to you.'

Dan sat still, studying her for a long moment. She could almost hear the workings of his devious mind searching for a way out. Suddenly his glance darted to Haydn.

'I recognise you now, Howells.' He stood up, gritting his teeth and glaring at Beth. 'You're prepared to trust the brother of the man who killed your own husband?' he asked incredulously. 'Are you mad, woman?'

'Bluster all you want,' she said flatly, 'it won't change anything. Will you accept the change or not?'

Dan looked furious. 'No, I bloody well won't!'

'Very well,' she said, standing up. 'The shares will go to my father-in-law next week. I'll see my lawyer today. I know Jarvis is still after your blood. He's been sabotaging the rounds again. You're in trouble, Father, admit it.'

'I admit nothing!' Dan was furious, and stood up too. 'You're in cahoots with Prosser-Evans, aren't you? You're only doing this to avenge your mother.'

'You could be right,' Beth agreed. 'You treated her shabbily and you used her, so I don't care a farthing what happens to you from now on. I only married Eynon to save you. You begged me to, remember? I sacrificed my own feelings and those of the man I loved for your sake. But now I'll see you trampled underfoot if that's what it takes to ensure Rhodri and Tommy have the lives they deserve.'

'Tommy?' Dan sat down again, uncertainty in his voice. 'What's he got to do with it?'

Beth swallowed hard, dreading the outburst that was sure to come when he learned her plans for her brother.

'There is one more condition,' she said, trying to quell

a tremor in her voice. 'You won't like it, but I *will* have my way.' She hesitated a moment.

'Well, spit it out!' he demanded testily. 'What is it?'

Beth's hands trembled as she reached for her gloves on the desk. 'It concerns my brother's future upbringing.'

Dan's lips tightened. 'His upbringing? I don't like the sound of this.'

'He's a very unhappy child, can't you see?' she burst out passionately. 'You have no love to give him. You have no love to give anyone.'

'Tommy is my son,' Dan thundered. 'And no concern of yours, make no mistake, Beth.'

'I'm making him my concern,' she flashed back. 'Tommy will come and live with me. He and Rhodri will be brought up together in a loving home, instead of in isolation as Tommy lives now, with no one who cares a fig for him.'

'How dare you interfere?' Dan bawled.

Beth stood up. 'I'll do anything for Tommy!' she shouted back. 'I'll see you go under, Father! I'll see you ruined!' She gulped in a breath. 'I warned you, didn't I?' she went on. 'A long time ago I warned you I'd pay you back for stealing Tommy from me. Now is the time, Father.' She turned away from him, preparing to leave. She had said all she came to say. 'If you don't agree to my terms immediately, you can kiss your precious business goodbye.'

'If I lose out, so will you,' he reminded her. 'Your shares will be worthless.'

'But I'm not on my beam end, unlike you,' Beth exclaimed triumphantly. 'My business is not in financial trouble as this one is. I'll survive. But Jarvis will crush you. He'll make sure Tommy inherits nothing from you except debts.' She hastily pulled on her gloves over shaking fingers. 'You have until eleven o'clock tomorrow morning to decide.' She marched towards the door. 'Come on, Haydn. Let's get out of here.'

'Wait a minute!' Dan exclaimed, rising hastily to his feet.

Beth turned slowly back to face him, hearing the panic and desperation in his voice. 'Seems I have no option but to agree,' he hissed. 'You've got me over a barrel for the moment. Damn you!'

Beth walked back to the desk. 'I've no intention of taking your son from you completely,' she said. 'You can see him daily if you wish, but he'll live with me until he comes of age, starting from tomorrow. I'll come and fetch him myself. Make sure he's packed and ready. I mean this, Father.'

Dan's face was stony as he sat down again. 'I must have a guarantee that Jarvis will no longer be a threat to the business. Can you do that?'

'I believe I can.'

'That's not good enough!' he shouted.

'It'll have to be for the moment,' Beth burst out. 'You've no choice!' She paused a moment to compose herself. 'Haydn will begin work here next Monday,' she went on more calmly. 'I urge you to co-operate, Father. You will give him all the help you can in learning about the running of this business.'

'If he is up to it.' Dan looked Haydn up and down with disdain. 'He hasn't had much to say for himself so far, has he? He's left you to do all the talking.'

'I am a hard worker and a quick student,' Haydn said gruffly, obviously angry. 'But remember this . . . er . . . Dan, I control fifty-one per cent of this firm now, and I'm not afraid to throw my weight about just as long as Beth has faith in me.'

'Huh! How touching,' Dan sneered. 'Now, if you have no more demands, get out, both of you. I've had enough for one day.'

Haydn and Beth got out, but she did not feel at all triumphant. She still had to deal with Jarvis.

Beth's heart was pounding as she carried Rhodri down the driveway to Jarvis's house on Gower Road much later that same day. Stark opened the door and went so far as to crack a smile at the sight of the child in her arms, but straightened his face again as he stepped aside for her to come in.

'Mr Jarvis is in the sitting room,' he said, and then hesitated. 'Pardon my mentioning it, ma'am,' he went on, 'but I don't think he'll be too pleased to see you. He may refuse you admittance.'

'I won't leave until I've spoken to him,' Beth said emphatically.

Stark hesitated again, obviously uncertain whether to speak his mind. 'He's very lonely now, ma'am,' he said in a low voice. 'But stubborn as Old Nick himself – and about as friendly.'

'Then don't announce me,' she said quickly as the butler was about to walk into the sitting room. 'I'll do it myself.'

Beth didn't knock but walked straight into the room. Jarvis sat in an armchair turned towards the fireplace, a glass of port on a small table nearby.

'Damn you, Stark!' he bellowed without looking around. 'I don't want any dinner. How many more times must I tell you?'

'You should eat, Jarvis,' Beth said matter-of-factly. 'A man of your age needs to keep up his strength.'

'What the hell!' He leapt to his feet with remarkabl

agility. 'You!' he exclaimed. 'What do *you* want here?'

Beth was painfully reminded of her father's cold welcome earlier that day. 'I've brought your grandson to you,' she said.

He glanced at the shawl-wrapped bundle in her arms. 'I don't want to see it,' he barked. 'Take that bastard child out of my sight.'

Beth was cut to the quick, but held her tongue. Instead she lifted the folds of the shawl to reveal Rhodri, and pulled off his little knitted cap. Golden curls like spun silk were revealed and Beth heard Jarvis's deep intake of breath, which turned into a sob.

'My God!' His words were muffled. 'My boy . . . Eynon.'

'Yes, he's the living image of his father, isn't he?' Beth said, gratified at his reaction. 'This is Rhodri, your grandson, Jarvis. Your own flesh and blood.'

He looked shaken. 'It's like seeing my son as a child again.'

'Do you want to hold him?' Beth asked gently.

Jarvis seemed to stumble forward, arms outstretched.

'Sit down first,' Beth advised, and he sank back into his chair while she put Rhodri into the crook of his arm. Though he was just over a month old, Rhodri's eyes were already alert and enquiring, staring up fearlessly at the man who held him.

'Oh, Heaven be praised,' Jarvis murmured as though to himself, looking down at the child. 'And I thought my life no longer had meaning.'

'You see how mistaken you were about me,' she said.

Jarvis glanced up, startled, as though he had forgotten her. His arms tightened around the child, and an expression passed across his face which sent a shiver up her spine. Suddenly she was frightened.

'Yes, this is Eynon's son all right,' Jarvis said heavily. 'But that doesn't exonerate you, Beth. You betrayed him, carrying on shamelessly with that man Howells.'

'You can't still believe that!' She was astounded at his stubborn persistence in thinking the worst of her.

'I do believe it,' Jarvis exclaimed in a hard voice. 'Rhodri's place is with me. I'll take him and bring him up.'

'No!' Beth exclaimed, rushing forward to snatch her son from Jarvis's possessive grasp. 'No one will take my child from me.'

'I *will* have him,' thundered Jarvis, rising threateningly to his feet. 'You're not fit to be a mother to my grandson, tainted with adultery as you are.'

Beth grasped her child protectively to her breast.

'So you would believe a convicted murderer over me, Eynon's wife?' she asked. 'The perjured words of a man who would callously have seen his own innocent brother hanged in his place? You'd rather take the word of the man who murdered your own son?'

He started back as though she had slapped his face.

Beth shook her head, looking up challengingly into his eyes. 'Not even you would do such a terrible thing, Jarvis.'

'You admitted you loved this man Howells,' he said weakly.

'Yes,' Beth agreed. 'But even though I have feelings for him, feelings over which I have no control, I was never unfaithful and never would've been.'

Jarvis was silent for a moment, and suddenly his earlier expression of hopelessness returned. 'I suppose now you'll take the child away and never come back?'

'No, I won't do that,' Beth said earnestly. 'Eynon would want you to know and love his son, and to watch him grow.'

'What do you propose then?'

'Bringing Rhodri to meet you is not the only reason for my coming here this evening,' Beth said. 'I've settled my entire interest in Dan Henshaw's business on my son. He is now Dan's partner.'

'What!'

'If you continue to persecute Dan, you'll be ruining your own grandson as well,' she said and put a hand on his arm persuasively. 'It's all in the family now, Jarvis. Rhodri is Dan's grandson, too, you know. And while you and my father can never be friends . . .'

'My God!' Jarvis hooted. 'That's the understatement of the century. The man is an unmitigated scoundrel!'

'And you are a devious and ruthless rascal, Jarvis,' Beth retorted hotly. 'You are each as bad as the other.'

'You insolent madam!' he exploded.

'Oh, stop being such a stubborn old fool!' Beth exclaimed impatiently. 'The vendetta between you and my father is over. It is now a matter of family – Rhodri's family and his future.'

'Henshaw took my wife . . .'

'And Eynon and I have given you the heir you wanted,' Beth said. 'A grandson who will follow in your footsteps. You won't die alone and unloved.'

Jarvis was silent and thoughtful. He was obviously mulling over her words and Beth began to feel hopeful. But there was still Haydn's role to discuss.

'I will defer to you about Rhodri's schooling and training,' she went on gently. 'I know he must be brought up to take over the reins of the business in due course.'

Jarvis looked sober. 'You swear to that, Beth?'

'I swear.'

He sniffed, and pushed his thumbs into his waistcoat pockets. 'You and Rhodri had better move back into this house,' he said with studied care, as though she might refuse. 'Unless you didn't mean what you said?'

Beth was touched. She had thought it might take him longer to accept things, but Jarvis was no fool.

'Yes, thank you. We'll do that.'

He cleared his throat. 'Rhodri's interests must be safeguarded at the coal yard,' he said too casually. 'I'll appoint a man of my own to do that.'

'Jarvis! The feud is over!' Beth exclaimed heatedly. 'I've already appointed my own man. Haydn Howells begins work there next Monday. He's Rhodri's manager.'

'Howells! That murdering swine's brother? I won't have it.'

It's done,' she said emphatically. 'All wrapped up by my lawyer.'

He stared at her, eyes full of suspicion and hostility again. 'There's more to this than meets the eye.'

'You're right,' Beth admitted, deciding to be open about her future plans. 'I am in mourning for my husband at the moment, but that will pass in time. I'm only twenty years of age, Jarvis, and have my life before me. I want happiness again.'

'I don't doubt it.' His tone was harsh. 'But what has that to do with Haydn Howells?'

'Some time in the future, Haydn and I will be married.'

'I forbid it!'

'If you put obstacles in my way,' Beth said evenly, 'I'll have no option but to take back the shares from Rhodri and give them outright and unconditionally to my father. Not only that, I'll settle the residue of my aunt's legacy on him, which will make him financially secure for years to come, and further out of your reach.'

'Huh!'

'And that's not all,' she threatened bravely, although

her heart was in her mouth. 'I'll take Rhodri away from Swansea. You'll never see him again.'

He stared at her for a moment, his gaze searching her face while Beth maintained a determined expression.

'I believe you would at that,' he said in an astonished tone, although she thought she heard admiration in there somewhere. 'My God!' He nodded in bemusement. 'You hardheaded madam! You're Henshaw's daughter all right. As tricky as a wagon load of monkeys.'

29

April 1924

Beth smiled at Rhodri, standing up in his cot, gripping the rail with both hands and jigging up and down on his plump legs. He gave her a gummy grin in return, dribbling enthusiastically on to his clean bib. One year old today and already he was a heart-stealer.

'Who is my birthday boy, then?' Beth cooed at him, bending to kiss the top of his downy head while he gurgled merrily, attempting to grab the strap of her slip with wet fingers. She could not resist lifting him out of the cot for another cuddle. 'Who is a lovely boy for his mam?' she asked, nuzzling the soft skin of his cheek. 'Who is going to have jelly for tea?'

The bedroom door burst open and Tommy rushed in with not a stitch on. 'Me! Me!' he yelled at the top of his piping voice. 'I want jelly, Beth, and ice cream as well.'

A girl in a navy overall followed him in, looking flustered.

'I'm sorry, Mrs Prosser-Evans,' she began. 'I was trying to get Tommy in the bath but he escaped.'

'It's all right, Freda,' Beth assured her, trying not to laugh. 'I know he is a busy handful these days.'

And she was thankful for it. Her three-year-old brother had lived with them for a year, and the change in him was miraculous. He was now as noisily normal as any other boy of his age.

'I was wondering if Rhodri and Tommy could go in the bath together, to save time, like?' Freda said.

'Oh, I don't know,' Beth said dubiously. 'Tommy is very boisterous.'

'I'd be very careful of Rhodri,' Freda promised. 'Really I would.'

Suddenly Beth felt a stab of jealousy that Freda, their young nanny, would have the pleasure of the children's company throughout the day while she had to go to Windsor Lodge as usual. Perhaps she should give up her active role in the business, as Jarvis wanted her to do?

Something needed to change. Eynon had been gone sixteen months. It was time for her to come out of mourning, time her life began again. She had been lonely for too long.

'I'll give you a hand bathing them,' Beth said impulsively. 'I won't go to work today. I'll take the children out instead.'

The corners of Freda's mouth drooped. 'I can be trusted, you know, Mrs Prosser-Evans.'

Beth patted her arm. 'I know, but today is special,' she said.

After the bathing, while Freda was giving the children their breakfast, Beth put on a lavender two-piece suit. It was a size too big since she had lost weight, but it would do for a start.

Jarvis was already at breakfast when she went into the dining room. He stared at the suit, his face clouding.

'In my day women showed their respect and sorrow at losing their husbands by keeping in mourning clothes for eighteen months to two years,' he said tetchily. 'I think you should show a little more restraint, Beth.'

'I am twenty-one years old,' she retorted angrily. 'Not an elderly matron. I need to think about life, not death.'

'What does that mean exactly?' he snapped.

She sat down at the table. 'I don't know,' she said with a sigh. 'But I do know Eynon wouldn't want me to mourn for the rest of my life.'

'Have you been seeing anything of that man Haydn Howells?' he asked suspiciously.

Hearing his name spoken aloud for the first time in over a year, Beth's heart contracted with a longing that was more difficult to suppress with every passing day.

'No, I've kept my word, Jarvis,' she said. 'I've not spoken to or even glimpsed Haydn for almost a year. I don't know if he still has feelings for me. But I love him and I intend to see him today.'

'What?'

She was angered at his tone. 'I've waited as you wanted,' she flared. 'But I can wait no longer. I've a right to love and be loved, and I want more children.'

'Associating with the brother of the man who killed your husband will only encourage talk.' He put down his knife and fork with a clatter. 'Damn it! I'm not totally against your marrying again, Beth, but not *that man.*'

'Don't, Jarvis!' she cried in distress. 'Don't start again. You've held a grudge against my father for years which almost destroyed us all. If you begin another useless feud with the man I love, you'll bring only misery and loneliness down on yourself.'

'What do you mean by that?'

'Do you love your grandson?'

'Of course I do, woman,' he growled. 'What're you getting at?'

'If you really love Rhodri, have a care. You could lose him as you have lost your only son.'

His face turned chalky-white and Beth was immediately filled with regret for her harsh words. She jumped to her feet and went to his side to put a hand on his arm, which was trembling.

'I am sorry, Jarvis,' she said quickly. 'That was a cruel thing to say to you. Please forgive me?'

His lips tightened. 'You're threatening me in my own home, Beth. I won't have it.'

She snatched her hand away. 'And you are trying to rule my life, like you ruled Eynon's.'

'Eynon was his own man,' Jarvis told her. 'I never dictated the way he lived or who he associated with.'

'You tried to,' Beth insisted. 'Now you're trying to come between Haydn and me. I won't let you do that. If I can't live the rest of my life as I want, love who I want, then we must part company, Jarvis, and you'll see little of your grandson, I promise you.'

'I'm a very rich man, Beth. I could take him from you even now.'

She looked at him for a moment. 'No, you won't,' she said confidently. 'The true measure of a man is his capacity to pity others. You are a hard man, Jarvis Prosser-Evans, and a ruthless one, but you are not evil. And taking my son from me would be an evil act.'

His shoulders drooped. 'The loss of *my* son has taken the heart out of me,' he said wearily. 'I have nothing left.'

'That isn't true. You have Rhodri and you have me. We're your family now, and you should treat us right. Let me live and love again without having to fight you every inch of the way.'

Beth pushed the pram with Rhodri in it along Marlborough Road in Brynmill, making for her father's coal yard in the next street. Tommy toddled alongside, hanging on to her free hand.

'I want to go to the park and see the ducks,' he said eagerly.

'Another time,' Beth told him. 'We are going to see your dad today.'

Tommy pulled up short and tugged at her hand. 'Not to stay, Beth,' he said, his face puckering. 'I don't want to stay with him.'

'We're only visiting,' she assured him. 'Your dad hasn't seen you for over a week and he misses you.'

'Does he?'

'Of course he does. Your dad loves you.'

Beth's heart was fluttering as she pushed the pram through the wrought-iron gates and into the yard. The office door stood open. She lifted Rhodri out and, taking Tommy's hand again, walked through the door. There was no one tending the outer office. She decided not to walk straight in, but instead tapped the brass bell that stood on the counter.

'I'll be there in a minute,' Haydn called from somewhere beyond. 'Take a seat, please.' A thrill ran up her spine at the sound of his voice.

Tommy immediately scrambled on to one of the chairs and sat down. Beth suddenly felt shy and silly, and wished she had put on a flowery dress instead of the formal lavender suit, and had taken more care with her hair. What would he think of her after all these months?

Brisk footsteps came along the passage and Haydn's tall figure loomed into sight. He was examining some papers and didn't look in her direction straight away.

'Now then, madam, what can I do . . .' He stopped and stared at her, his mouth open. 'Beth!'

'Hello, Haydn.'

'What are you doing here?'

Disappointment at his off-hand tone made her face

stiffen, and she struggled to find an answer. 'I've brought Tommy and Rhodri to see Dan,' she said uncomfortably. 'Where is he?'

'Out seeing coalfactors, hoping to increase our factorage,' he said too casually. 'Our sales have doubled these last few months.' He looked uncomfortable to see her there.

'Things are looking good, then?' Beth said conversationally, her smile tight. She felt a pain in her heart as he averted his gaze. Why wouldn't he look at her? Had he found someone else?

'Yes,' he said. 'I persuaded your father to buy two motor lorries to replace horse-drawn drays. Now we can look for customers as far away as Llanelli or Neath.'

'Neath? That's like taking coals to Newcastle, isn't it?'

He gave her a strained look. 'Why are you really here, Beth? It's been almost a year. Why come now?'

'I made a promise to Jarvis,' she said miserably. And I should never had made that promise, she told herself. I should have snatched at love while I had the chance.

'How is he?' Haydn's tone was flat, uninterested, just making conversation. There had once been so much ease and rapport between them. Now it was like two strangers meeting for the first time.

'Rhodri is helping him get over his loss,' Beth said, holding back a tremor from her voice.

'I don't have to ask how you are doing,' he went on. 'I hear Jarvis has given you a seat on the board of Prosser-Evans Provisioners. Your father's full of it. I suspect he's even proud of you in his way, and why wouldn't he be?'

'I doubt that,' Beth said sceptically. 'I'll never mean anything to him.'

Haydn's lips twisted. 'Oh, I don't know. You're the first female board member. There's a feather in your cap,

Beth, isn't it?' There was a suggestion of bitterness in his tone.

She gave him a keen look. 'You sound as if you don't approve, Haydn. You even sound resentful.'

His mouth tightened. 'Well, what with your directorship and Windsor Lodge doing so well, the money must be rolling in. And that puts you way out of my league, out of my reach, doesn't it?'

'That's absurd!' She didn't understand what he was getting at. Her tone was sharp and Rhodri began to grizzle in her arms. She hugged him tighter to soothe him.

'You don't have to pretend, Beth,' Haydn said harshly. 'I knew it was too good to be true. It never was real, was it? All that talk of loving me, of a life together.'

'What?'

'Almost a whole year!' he exploded. 'If you really cared for me as you swore, Beth, you would have come to see me, sent word, anything! Despite any promises to Jarvis.'

'Haydn! Don't talk like this!'

'Well, what do you expect?' he snapped. 'You used me, Beth, to amuse yourself and later to outwit your father and Jarvis. Then I was conveniently forgotten. Well, no man likes being used.'

'Nothing could be further from the truth,' she flared.

'You are manipulative, just like your father.'

She stared at him, blinking back tears, unable to speak for a moment. There was hurt in his eyes and unhappiness. Had she done that to him?

'Perhaps I deserve that,' she said miserably after a moment. 'Perhaps you are right about me. I only wanted to sort things out, for everybody's sake. But obviously Haydn, you have no real faith in me.'

'Faith! You mean I should be grateful for this position in someone else's business?'

'You are putting words into my mouth,' she exclaimed in distress. 'And then twisting them.'

'Beth!' Tommy piped up, sliding off his chair and scampering to her side to pull at her skirt. 'I want to go home! I want to go now.'

'Hush, Tommy! Grown-ups are talking.'

'Perhaps you should go,' Haydn said tersely.

'Why don't *you* try being honest, Haydn?' Beth caught her breath for a moment, not wanting to say the words. 'If you no longer love me or want to marry me, for God's sake, say so!'

He didn't answer but stared down at his hands on the counter. So it was true. His love for her had not stood the test of separation and time. His life had moved on, while hers had stood still.

'If I've hurt you, Haydn, I'm sorry,' she went on in a dull tone, her heart heavy as a boulder in her breast. She turned to take Tommy's hand again, ready to leave, eager to be gone. 'I should never have come here today,' she said. 'Taking you for granted, taking your love for granted. I should have realised a lot can happen in a year.'

She turned quickly towards the open door, pulling Tommy along with her.

'Wait, Beth!' Haydn stepped around the counter and came towards her, his face flushed. 'You make me feel ashamed.'

'What've you to be ashamed of?' she asked dully. 'We've been apart. You've met other people. These things happen.' She paused and stared up at him, struggling not to let her tears show. 'It's just that I always believed true love was forever, but I know now that's just silly dream.'

'No! No, it's not,' Haydn exclaimed. 'I am the one who sorry. My feelings haven't changed, but I believed yours had. I heard nothing from you and thought the worst. You're right.' He shook his head. 'I had no faith. Can you forgive me?'

She moved closer to him, and put her free hand on his shoulder. 'My heart is still true, Haydn, my darling. I've thought of no one but you every day, wanting you desperately. I always will.'

'The same with me,' he said simply, leaning forward to kiss her tenderly.

Rhodri took the opportunity to grab his tie. With a laugh Haydn gently disentangled it from the determined little clenched fist.

'You'll be taking on a ready-made family, Haydn,' Beth said, looking up anxiously into his face. 'Am I worth it?'

'You're worth any sacrifice, any struggle. I'd give my life for you, Beth, my darling,' he said earnestly. 'Don' ever stop loving me.'